Hablot Knight Browne, William Harrison Ainsworth

The Spendthrift

A Tale

Hablot Knight Browne, William Harrison Ainsworth

The Spendthrift
A Tale

ISBN/EAN: 9783337089313

Printed in Europe, USA, Canada, Australia, Japan

Cover: Foto ©Andreas Hilbeck / pixelio.de

More available books at **www.hansebooks.com**

THE

SPENDTHRIFT

A Tale

BY

WILLIAM HARRISON AINSWORTH

No care, no stop! so senseless of expense,
That he will neither know how to maintain it,
Nor cease his flow of riot: Takes no account
How things go from him, nor resumes no care
Of what is to continue: Never mind
Was to be so unwise, to be so kind

SHAKSPEARE: *Timon of Athens*

WITH ILLUSTRATIONS BY HABLOT K. BROWNE

LONDON
GEORGE ROUTLEDGE AND SONS, LIMITED
BROADWAY, LUDGATE HILL

CONTENTS.

CONTENTS.

CONTENTS.

ILLUSTRATIONS.

THE SPENDTHRIFT.

I.

WARD AND GUARDIAN.

HEIR to twenty thousand a year at twenty-one. This was the case with Gage de Monthermer. An enviable fellow. Let us see how he came by his fine property.

Warwick de Monthermer—Gage's sire—had a fine old family mansion in Suffolk—Monthermer Castle—noted for its beautiful situation, and the picturesque ruins in the immediate vicinity; a large park, well stocked with deer, and boasting some of the most magnificent timber in England—oaks, coeval with the Druids, towering elms, and wide-spreading beeches; a gallery of choice pictures, including portraits of his once-ennobled race, the first of whom, Radulphus de Monthermer, married Joane Plantagenet, daughter of King Edward I., and the last (the last of these haughty barons, we mean) lost his head and his honours in 1471; a house in perfect repair; fertile lands; farms well tenanted and well cultivated; property well managed; cellars well stocked with wine; a famous pack of hounds; a numerous stud of horses: everything, in short, that a country gentleman could desire.

Warwick de Monthermer lived altogether at Monthermer Castle, where he exercised unbounded hospitality. The house was always full of company. He was fond of hunting, shooting, fishing, and all manly sports; and equally fond of good cheer, so that the robust exercises he constantly indulged in were indispensably necessary to the preservation of his health. Warwick was a widower of long standing. Wedded to the Hon. Henrietta Gage, the beautiful and accomplished daughter of Lord Hengrave, he had the misfortune to lose her in the second year of their union. She left him an only son,

Gage—named after his mother—upon whom the whole of Warwick's affections were fixed. As may be anticipated, the child was
too much indulged by his doting father, who gratified his every
whim, and allowed him to do just as he pleased. Yet in spite of
such injudicious treatment, Gage was not utterly spoiled. His chief
faults were indolence, and proneness to self-indulgence. As a boy,
he was free from vice, and had a generous disposition, and a frank, un-
suspicious nature. When he grew up, his features developed a striking
resemblance to those of his beautiful mother, and this circumstance
endeared him yet more strongly to his father. At eighteen, Gage
was sent to college, and he had been at Oxford little more than a year
when he sustained the heaviest affliction that could have befallen
him in the death of his father, who broke his neck while hunting.

This sad event occurred in 1728.

During his minority, the care of Gage and of his large estates de-
volved upon Mr. Felix Fairlie, who had been appointed his guardian
by his father's will. Of this person, it will now be necessary to give
some account. Long and honourably (as it was supposed) had Mr.
Fairlie filled the post of steward to Warwick de Montherner. His
birth was obscure enough, but what of that, if the man himself were
respectable, and had sufficient ability to push himself forward in the
world! The son of an old servant at the Castle, brought up by the
family, and early displaying great quickness of parts, great method,
and great aptitude for business, Felix Fairlie had mounted step by
step, till he attained the chief place in his master's establishment.
"Master," indeed, Warwick could scarcely be termed. For some
time before his death, the Squire had begun to treat Mr. Fairlie as
an equal and a friend, consulting him upon all occasions, and en-
trusting him with the entire management of his affairs. Having
the most perfect reliance upon Fairlie's integrity and good judgment, he confided his property to him while he lived, and in contemplation of his demise, constituted him his sole executor, and
committed his beloved son to his charge.

How Mr. Fairlie fulfilled his trusts will be seen by-and-by.

A most respectable-looking man was Mr. Fairlie; very smooth-
spoken, bland and courteous in manner. Even those who dif-
fered with him in opinion acknowledged his excessive complai-
sance. From his gentlemanlike exterior, his politeness, and perfect

good breeding, it was difficult to conceive he could ever have filed
a menial capacity ; yet such, as we have shown, had been the case.
When his patron died, Mr. Fairlie was between fifty and sixty.
Tall and thin, with an aquiline nose, and dark eyes, overshadowed
by jetty brows, he had a very handsome and imposing exterior.
In attire he was unostentatious, but scrupulously neat; always wearing clothes of a sober hue, and a plain peruke.

In estimating the character of this highly respectable man, it is but
fair to state, that the favourable opinion entertained of him by his
patron was not altogether shared in by that patron's friends ; some
of whom fancied they perceived defects in him, which Monthermer
failed to discover. They did not think him so perfectly trustworthy
as he was deemed by the Squire, and felt sure Mr. Fairlie was
feathering his own nest at his employer's expense. Two or three of
the more courageous among them resolved to open Monthermer's
eyes to his danger ; but before this could be done, the worthy
gentleman's eyes were closed for ever.

Mr. Fairlie's position was then perfectly secure. For two years
he would be uncontrolled master of the Monthermer estates; while
the early destinies of the young heir were wholly in his hands.

Nothing therefore was left the friends but to fold their arms,
and look on.

As much attached to his guardian as his father had been, Gage
had equal confidence in him. Impossible to shake it. But no one
undertook the ungracious task, and things were allowed to pursue
their course.

On the next term after his father's decease, Gage returned to
Oxford. Heretofore, he had not read very hard, but he now left
off reading altogether. With a certainty of twenty thousand a year,
any great devotion to scholastic labour or mental discipline could
scarcely be expected of him. He had plenty of idle, extravagant
acquaintances, and he soon acquired a taste for their habits. Such
a well-plumed pigeon was sure to be plucked by all the kites and
rooks of the University. Mr. Fairlie occasionally remonstrated with
him for his heedlessness and extravagance—but so very gently and
cautiously as to give no offence—and then he always honoured his
ward's drafts upon him ; earnestly cautioning him against borrowing
money from any one but himself, and taking every means to pre-

vent him from doing so. The worthy man had no other object except a wish to keep the thoughtless young scapegrace out of bad hands.

At length, Gage's proceedings occasioned so much scandal, that the heads of houses would no longer tolerate his riotous conduct, and with two others—Nat Mist and Jack Brassey—he was expelled from the University. This gave him little concern, as he had never intended to graduate. But his guardian was much distressed by the occurrence—or affected to be so—and represented to him how much concern his indiscretions would have given his excellent father, if he had been alive. Some feelings of compunction were aroused in Gage's breast by these remarks, but his remorse was of short duration; and Mr. Fairlie had no intention of alienating the affections of his ward by over-severity. On the contrary, he desired to have him constantly near him—as the best means, he asserted, of keeping him out of harm's way. The poor young gentleman was so easily led into mischief.

Mr. Fairlie, however, had another motive besides the one he assigned for desiring to keep his ward constantly near him. Like his late patron, the somewhile steward was a widower—and like him he had an only child—a daughter, whom he would have gladly seen Lady of Monthermer. There was thus much in favour of Mr. Fairlie's scheme; in that his daughter Clare, who, at the time of Gage's removal from the University, was just eighteen, was a remarkably beautiful girl—tall, dark-haired, dark-eyed, exquisitely proportioned, graceful, gentle. Candour sat upon her open countenance; and truth looked out from the depths of her tender black eyes. Fashioned of finer clay than her father, she had none of the flaws to be met with in his coarser composition. She had been very carefully brought up by an excellent and exemplary mother, whose death was a loss, in every way, to Fairlie. Clare, therefore, might well be an object of attraction to Gage, and if the young man should become sufficiently enamoured to choose her as his bride, her father had no doubt she would be found fully equal to the elevated position. And therein he was right.

But if Mr. Fairlie expected any co-operation in his scheme from his daughter, he was greatly in error. Clare had no idea whatever of ensnaring the young man, and the accounts she had heard of his proceedings at Oxford had strongly prejudiced her against him. She therefore shunned him as much as possible; but in spite of all her efforts to avoid a meeting, they were frequently brought together. As young Monthermer's guardian, Mr. Fairlie had now his own set of apartments at the Castle, and, indeed, was more completely master of the house than the young gentleman himself. Most of the old servants had been discharged, and only such were retained as suited the new ruler of the establishment. Clare, of course, was looked upon in the light of a mistress by all the household; and, indeed, by her father's express injunctions she superintended everything. Necessarily, then, she must often be brought into contact with the young lord of the mansion. But though urged to do so by her father, she resolutely refused to preside at Monthermer's table, or even to appear at all when he had company.

Things turned out just as the steward had foreseen. It was impossible that a youth so inflammable as Gage could daily behold a charming girl like Clare and not fall in love with her. His marked attentions to her soon left no doubt as to the state of his feelings. Her father was secretly delighted; but he judged it most prudent not to interfere. He did not believe Clare could be indifferent to the handsome youth, yet the coldness of her manner towards him looked like it. As Gage became more ardent, she grew more reserved, until at length she declined altogether to meet him. The young man was too much in love to be offended, but he sought an explanation of her father, who professed to be taken by surprise by the communication made to him, good-naturedly chided his ward, but at length undertook to confer with his daughter on the subject. He *did* confer with her; and on finding she was determined to reject Gage, provided he offered her his hand, he poured forth a torrent of reproaches and invectives against her. But upbraidings and menaces were of no avail. All Clare could be brought to consent to was to grant a final interview to Gage on the morrow.

The interview took place. Gage offered her his hand. In declining it, she said she was fully sensible of the honour intended her, and grateful for it ; she frankly owned she was not indifferent to Mr. Monthermer; but the disparity between them was such, as to render a union impossible Neither was he of an age to know who would make him a suitable partner for life. On his knees, with protestations and tears, Gage combated these arguments as well as he could, and strove to move her. In vain. At last, by way of putting an end to a scene which, in spite of her firmness, greatly agitated and distressed her, Clare said: "A year hence you will be twenty-one, and will then have a right to act as you please· At that time, if you have not changed your mind, and think fit to address me, I may, perhaps, listen to your suit. I do not absolutely promise this—but it may be so. Meantime, we must not meet again—and if I might give you a counsel it would be to forget me."

It is useless to detail what passed between Mr. Fairlie and his daughter, when he learnt her decision from her own lips. It will be easily imagined how he stormed. But all to no purpose. Clare was not to be moved either by entreaties or rage.

Gage did not remain much longer at Monthermer Castle. He went abroad for a year; made the grand tour; launched into all the dissipations of the gayest cities in Europe; got fleeced by many a foreign sharper; tried to forget Clare (as she had recommended him to do, though not in a way she would have approved), by worshipping many a dark-eyed Italian beauty, and many a lively dame of France; scattered money about, wherever he went, with reckless profusion—for he had an unlimited supply from Fairlie—and returned to England, as he conceived, a finished gentleman—or as some censorious folk declared, a finished fop and rake—to take possession of his ancestral house and his broad domains on his twenty-first birthday.

Absence and pleasurable distraction had not obliterated Clare's image from the young man's breast. He had written to her several times, and though she returned no answer to his missives, their receipt was duly acknowledged by Mr. Fairlie, who said more than he had any warrant to do for his daughter, and took good care not to extinguish her lover's hopes. Gage's surprise and disappointment may therefore be imagined when his offers were a second time rejected, and more peremptorily than on the first occasion—for no further time of probation was allowed him. He was of age, and could judge for himself. Clare's reasons for her decision were these. In addition to disparity of position, their characters were wholly unsuitable.

She could not be happy with a man addicted merely to pursuits of pleasure. After a brief time he was sure to neglect her, and such treatment would break her heart. On these accounts, she must adhere to her original resolution. She could not cease to love him, but she would never marry him: in fact, she would never marry at all.

Again, Gage knelt, entreated, protested. She—and she alone, had been the cause of his wildness and folly. He had striven to forget her, but had failed. He now deplored his reckless conduct, and severely blamed himself. But he would reform—he wished to reform—he intended to reform. A wife would entirely change his character—would make another man of him. Clare should see how steady he would become. He was tired of town life, and would reside altogether at Monthermer Castle. She might shake her head, but it was quite true. It was nonsense to recommend some one else to him. No other woman, but she, should be his bride. Would she drive him to desperation by persisting in a refusal?

Refuse him, however, Clare did; gently, kindly, but firmly.

If Gage was irritated and keenly wounded in his self-love by Clare's decision, her father was mortified and hurt in a much greater degree. To the last he had indulged the hope that all would come right. His daughter's unqualified rejection of Gage came like a clap of thunder upon him—and for awhile took away his power of utterance. When he recovered his speech, he poured the vials of his wrath upon her head. She did not seem frightened, and when he had done, merely observed: "Were no other reasons wanting, father, you yourself would be an insuperable obstacle to the match." "How so?" Fairlie demanded, fiercely; but receiving no answer, he added, "If you have any regard for this young man you will marry him. It is the only chance of saving him. Recollect what I tell you." And he left her.

Great rejoicings had taken place at Monthermer Castle when the young lord came of age, and the tenantry hailed his return with delight, hoping he would remain among them. Mr. Fairlie had already become obnoxious from his exactions, and the loss of good Squire Warwick was universally deplored. The young Squire they hoped would rectify all abuses; reduce their rents, which had been suddenly raised; and restore the good old times. They were quite sure Squire Gage must be too like his worthy father, who would listen to any man, and help him if he deserved it, to turn a deaf ear to their just complaints.

But they found it difficult—indeed, impossible, to obtain a hearing from Gage. Mr. Fairlie took care that those, who would not hold their tongues, should never approach him. Gage hated business of all kinds, and could scarcely be got to look at an account. It bored him dreadfully, and he could not endure to be bored. Fully aware of his carelessness, Mr. Fairlie did not fail to profit by it. Placing piles of bills, documents, and vouchers before the young Squire, he opened ponderous green-backed account-books with large brass clasps for his inspection—quite certain he would examine none of them. And so it happened. Gage just glanced at the bills, and tossed them aside, closing the big green-backed books with a shudder.

His guardianship having expired, Mr. Fairlie offered to resign the managerial post he had hitherto filled to whomsoever the young gentleman might appoint. As he expected, he was urgently solicited to retain the office—and he reluctantly consented.

Next came a point the consideration of which could no longer be postponed; namely, the adjustment of accounts between guardian and ward. The latter, it appeared, had advanced to the former, during the two years of his minority, no less a sum than fifty-two thousand pounds; thus leaving Gage only a beggarly eight thousand for the first year of his coming into possession. Mr. Fairlie showed the astounded young man how extensively he had been pigeoned at college, what sums he had squandered at Paris upon Mademoiselle Colombe Mirepoix of the Grand Opera—how he had been plundered at the gaming-tables of the Palais Royal—how egregiously he had been duped at Naples by Signora Fulgioso, an adventuress whom he had taken for a duchess—how lavishly he had satisfied the demands of Señora Catalina Hermoso, prima ballerina at Seville—how he had been fleeced by Count Schaffiroff, lieutenant-colonel of the Semenowsky Guards at St. Petersburg—how he had paid the debts, twice over, of the charming Baroness Von Frolichlieben at Vienna—and how, in short, in one way or other, he had contrived to get through upwards of fifty thousand pounds.

Aghast at this recapitulation of his extravagance, Gage vowed he was not aware he had spent half so much, and endeavoured to hide his confusion by feigning to examine the accounts which Mr. Fairlie again pressed upon him. But he was soon tired of the task, and hastily signed a document, which was neither more nor less than his crafty guardian's full and complete release and discharge, by way of getting rid of a disagreeable matter.

"So I have only a paltry eight thousand for the present year, eh, Fairlie?" he remarked. "How the deuce am I to live upon it, eh?"

"Oh, you can have any money you please, of course, sir," the other replied; "but you'll excuse me for saying, that eight thousand pounds ought to go a long way—a very long way."

"It won't go a long way with me, Fairlie, I can tell you. I'll begin to economise, next year," Gage rejoined, walking away.

"Next year." the steward muttered, looking after him with a meaning smile.—"He economise—very likely."

II.

VISITORS TO THE CASTLE.—A GAME AT GLEEK.

WHILE Gage was yet smarting from his wound, half a dozen visitors arrived at the Castle; and as they were precisely the kind of persons calculated to cheer him, he hailed their appearance with unfeigned delight. All six were choice spirits—at least, Gage thought them so—various shades and grades of the fop, the rake, and the gambler. One he had met abroad—another in town—while the rest were old college chums, two of whom had participated in his pastimes at the University, and shared his disgrace.

With two exceptions, they were all very young men; indeed, the oldest of them was not more than thirty-five, and in right of his seniority, this person shall be first described. How stars of the first brilliancy in the fashionable hemisphere pale, and are for ever extinguished! From 1720 to —30, who did not know Beau Freke? Who knew him ten years later? Who recollects him now? Renowned for his daring gallantry—his success at play—his address at arms—(he had fought four duels, and each time killed his adversary)—his magnificent exterior, and his consummate taste in dress, Beau Freke was an arbiter in all matters of elegance and fashion. He was fond of taking young men in hand, and launching them into the world—though they generally paid rather dearly for their tuition—and with this view he had attached himself to Monthermer. Gage looked upon him as a model, worthy of imitation; and hoped some day to be like him.

In point of rank, the most important of the visitors was Lord Melton, a young nobleman, who was a good deal upon the turf; who consorted chiefly with blacklegs and jockeys, and looked like a blackleg and a jockey himself, betted heavily, and ran horses at

Newmarket, Doncaster, York, Lincoln, and every other race-course in England.

Next in consequence to the sporting lord, but incomparably his superior in manner and personal appearance, was Sir Randal de Meschines, the representative of a very ancient Cheshire family—a young man, reputed to be very rich, and known to be very profligate. Sir Randal had been one of Beau Freke's pupils, and did full credit to his instructor. Nat Mist and Jack Brassey were only varieties of the same genus. As we have mentioned, they had been expelled from Oxford at the same time as Gage.

The last on the list, and noticeable in some respects from the others, was Brice Bunbury. An odd fellow was Brice,—and very popular with a certain set of men about town. He was much patronised by Beau Freke, who found him very useful, and employed him upon some secret services not particularly creditable to Brice's notions of propriety and morality. But Brice was not strict. Strange how he got on. He had nothing—that was notorious. Yet he dressed well, dined well, lodged well — but always at other people's expense. Sometimes one person paid for him, sometimes another. Always borrowing a trifle, he never repaid the loan. On the other hand, it must be admitted that Brice Bunbury was worth a whole host of ordinary led captains and parasites. He was very droll and diverting, picked up all sorts of information about pretty actresses, and pretty women generally, and could convey a message or a billet-doux, if required, with unequalled dexterity or effrontery. Brice had already dipped a little into Gage's purse; and he was so delighted with the accommodating disposition of the young man, that he resolved to devote himself exclusively to him : that is, so long as the young man's purse should be well supplied, and continue accessible.

Mr. Fairlie was perfectly aware of the character of the visitors, and if his scheme had been successful, and his daughter had been engaged to young Monthermer, he would have done his best to prevent them from entering the house. As it was, he was not displeased to make the acquaintance of persons whom he felt sure would be useful to him in his ulterior designs. Beau Freke and Sir Randal came together in the travelling carriage of the latter, and Brice Bunbury was accommodated with a seat in the rear of the

conveyance, which he was compelled to share with Mr. Tibbits and
Mr. Trickett, the two fine gentlemen's very fine gentlemen.   Brice
was fain to confess that the valets were good company.   There
was no vast difference between them and their masters, and before
they reached their destination he had contrived to get a good deal
out of them.   Trickett boasted so much of the money he had won at
the servants' faro-table, that Brice thought of borrowing a trifle from
him.   But he abstained, and was so well pleased with his new ally—
for such he esteemed him—that he slipped a guinea into his hand on
parting—an unheard-of piece of generosity on his part.   Lord Melton
came attended by a couple of grooms and a couple of race-
horses, Comus and Gaylass—he was going on to the Spring
Meeting at Newmarket—and Nat Mist and Jack Brassey brought
each a servant with him.   There were several other guests in
the house—mostly country gentlemen—who had stayed on after
the great rejoicings, to which half the county had been invited, so
that the place was pretty full; and a large party was assembled daily
in the servants' hall, at which Messrs. Tibbits and Trickett cut a
conspicuous figure, and discoursed of town life and town pleasures,
Vauxhall, Ranelagh, and Marylebone Gardens, masquerades, routs,
and ridottos, to the delight and bewilderment of the cook and the
upper housemaids, who longed to participate in such amusements.
To be sure they had heard something of the kind from Mr. Bellairs,
young master's valet, but never such piquant details as were now
given, which made them blush and giggle at the same time;—
and then Mr. Bellairs was too consequential, and kept himself too
much to himself; and they couldn't very well understand the foreign
lingo of Monsieur Silvain Chassemouche, the French valet, whom
young master had picked up in Paris—a smart gentleman enough,
with a powdered peruke, and a prodigiously long plaited *queue*,
reaching down to the middle of his back, but not much accustomed to English ways.   Mr. Pudsey, the butler, was mightily
pleased with the new comers, and invited them to spend the
evening with him in his room, where they sat down, five of
'em, including Bellairs and Chassemouche, to a few bottles of old
Squire Warwick's best Burgundy, pronounced exquisite by Silvain.   After that, the table was cleared for a game at piquet,
from which Mr. Trickett, as usual, came off a winner.   At social

and friendly meetings like these, their masters' characters were freely discussed, and Mr. Bellairs did not hesitate to give his opinion that the young Squire would run through his property pretty quickly—an opinion which was backed by Pudsey and Chassemouche, the latter of whom said that the young gentleman had been joliment fourbé at Paris—and was sure to be diablement trompé à Londres. Mr. Tibbits and Mr. Trickett both entirely concurred in this view of the case, and affirmed that their masters were not the men to let such an easy dupe slip through their fingers. " Brice Bunbury has his eye upon him, I can see," Mr. Trickett added. " I shall have an eye upon master, too, gentlemen," Mr. Pudsey said—" and shall take care of myself as far as I can; but between you and me, for I shouldn't like it to go no further, I'll tell you who'll make most out of him."

" Mr. Fairlie you mean," Mr. Bellairs remarked. " I know he will. He has made a good deal already."

" Nothing to what he *will* make," the butler rejoined. " You'll see what he'll do. And yet, as you say, Bellairs, he has done pretty well in two years. What do you think he has pocketed, Mr. Trickett?"

" I can't say, sir, I'm sure—a thousand, perhaps."

" Nearer twelve thousand, Mr. Trickett—nearer twelve. I know it for a fact, sir,—and could prove it if I chose. Remember, we're speaking within four walls—nothing goes out of this room. Why he wanted to marry his daughter to the young Squire."

" Unheard of impudence!" Mr. Trickett exclaimed. " How the deuce did he hope to persuade your young gentleman to such folly?"

" Our young gentleman required no persuasion," Mr. Pudsey rejoined. " He was quite ready to put his head into the noose—that is, if there had been a noose; but the young lady declined to execute him."

" 'Slife! you don't mean to say she refused him?"

" Yes, Mr. Trickett—that's exactly what I mean, sir."

" Egad! she must be a girl of spirit," Mr. Tibbits remarked—" another attachment most likely?"

" I don't think she has, sir," Mr. Bellairs observed. " Her maid Letty Roughain tells me she's dying of love for the young Squire."

" Then why not cure herself if that be the case?" Mr. Trickett inquired, facetiously.

" Sapristi ! the remedy is in her own hands," Silvain said, with a laugh.

" True," Mr. Bellairs rejoined. " Letty declared she cried the whole night after she had refused him, but though the good-natured lass tried to reason with her, she wasn't to be brought to change her mind. And what do you suppose was the reason she gave Letty for refusing our young master ?"

" Faith, I can't say," Mr. Tibbits replied. " A woman's reasons always pass my comprehension."

" She said he was too much of a rake—he was sure to neglect her —ha ! ha !"

" A strange reason, egad !" quoth Tibbits. " Women generally like rakes—eh, Mounseer Shassy ?"

" Ma foi ! oui—en France surtout," Silvain replied. " They prafare always the roué to the man bien réglé."

" Well, I must say it for her, Clare Fairlie is very different from her father," Mr. Pudsey observed.

" And very different from most other young women, I should think," Mr. Trickett said. " O' my conscience ! she has lost a good chance. And that reminds me that I must give you a chance of winning back your money, Mr. Pudsey. Shall we have a game at Gleek ? You don't understand it—eh ? I'll soon teach you. Only three persons can play, so you and I and Mr. Bellairs will sit down. Cut the pack, and I'll deal. Four cards each at first. Now mark. In this game, an ace is called Tib, a knave Tom, and the four of trumps Tiddy. Tib counts for fifteen in hand and eighteen in play —Tom is nine—and Tiddy four. You understand. If you win nothing but the cards dealt you, you lose ten. If you have neither Tib, Tom, Tiddy, Queen, Mournival, nor Gleek—as is my case just now—you lose; but if you have Tib, Tom, King, and Queen of Trumps in your hand, as I see you have, you have thirty by honours, besides the cards you are likely to win by them at play. But I'll explain it more fully as we go on. You'll soon understand it. 'Tis Sir Randal's favourite game."

While they were playing, the others looked on and hazarded a bet now and then, and by-and-by the company was increased by the entrance of Lord Melton's two jockeys with Nat Mist's and ack Brassey's servants. Mr Trickett could deal exactly what cards he pleased, but he chose to let Mr. Pudsey win on this occasion, and the butler was delighted with his proficiency at Gleek. The evening concluded with a round game, to which all the party sat down.

The next morning, the butler was summoned to Mr. Fairlie's room. He saw in an instant that something was wrong.

"You are tired of your place, I presume, Mr. Pudsey?" Mr Fairlie said, drily. "I judge so from your indiscreet remarks last night, the whole of which have been reported to me. I am content to overlook the offence this once, but any repetition of it—you know to what I allude, sir—will be followed by your immediate dismissal."

"I thought Mr. Monthermer was master here now," the butler stammered, trying to brave it out.

"You will find I am still master here, Mr. Pudsey," the other rejoined, quietly. "I have cautioned you. Now you may go."

"Plague take it, who can have told him?" the butler muttered, as he left the room in confusion. "It must be that double-faced Bellairs. But I'll be even with him."

On being taxed with his treachery, the chief valet indignantly denied the accusation. He betray a fellow-servant! He scorned the imputation! So far from it, he himself had received a similar caution from Mr. Fairlie. Who could it be? Their suspicions fell upon Chassemouche, and they determined to be revenged upon him.

III.

On the day after their arrival, Gage conducted his guests over the Castle, and was rather disappointed that some of them did not admire the place as much as he expected. Beau Freke and Sir Randal thought it much too gloomy and antiquated, and recommended him to pull it down, and build another mansion on its site in the Palladian style, with stone porticos and an octagonal hall with a gallery round it. Gage admitted this might be much handsomer, but he was pretty well satisfied with the house as it stood, and as he didn't think he should spend a great deal of time in it, it might perhaps do—at all events, for the present.

"Do!—I think it will do very well," Brice Bunbury exclaimed. "I only wish I owned it. By Jove! it's splendid—magnificent. I'm sorry to differ with a gentleman of such consummate taste as Mr. Freke, but I really must say I don't find it gloomy at all. On the contrary, I think it remarkably cheerful and comfortable; and I never saw a finer staircase, nor a better dining-room. And as to this long gallery, surely you must admit it to be grand—surprisingly grand, Sir Randal?"

"The pictures are very good, no doubt," Meschines replied; "but they might be better placed; and I detest old oak furniture, and deeply-embayed windows, with small panes of stained glass. Give me light modern French casements—pictures by Watteau—painted ceilings—Sèvres china—gilt clocks—large mirrors—satin couches—and all the et ceteras of an apartment in the style of his Majesty Louis Quinze. I have an old hall in Cheshire, full of black antediluvian furniture, high-backed chairs on which it is impossible to sit, great oak tables so heavy no one can move them, mirrors so dim they make you appear like a ghost, and portraits of my ancestors, one of whom was Earl of Chester, so fierce and forbidding, that they freeze one's blood to look at them. I shall do what I recommend Monthermer to do with his castle—pull that old hall down, burn its old furniture and pictures, and build myself a handsome modern mansion, when I can afford it."

"You can afford to build just as well as I can, Sir Randal," Gage observed, laughing. "I've no money to throw away on bricks and mortar. Have I, Fairlie?" he appealed to the steward, who was accompanying them over the house.

"I certainly think your money might be better employed than in building, or even improvements at present, sir," the other returned. "Better sell the Castle than pull it down, I think."

"Sell the Castle!" Monthermer exclaimed. "I'd as soon sell myself to Old Harry. What! part with the seat of my ancestors! I should expect them all to issue from their vaults to reproach me. I'm surprised you should propose such a thing, Fairlie."

"You mistake me, sir. I did not mean to propose it; but I am glad my observation has elicited such sentiments from you. My advice to you is not to alter the place at all, till you have fairly tried it. As to selling it, that was merely a jest. Were it mine, I would never part with it."

"Egad, I would sell every acre I have, if it had belonged to my family since the Conquest, if I wanted to raise the wind," Beau Freke said. "Keep the house as it is, if you will—but if you love me, pull down those unsightly old ruins."

"What! pull down the remains of the old Castle, erected by Radulphus de Monthermer—I forget in whose reign," Gage cried. "It would be absolute sacrilege!"

"Pull them down, and build a summer-house in their place," Meschines said.

"Or stables, and a kennel for hounds," Lord Melton suggested.

"Or level the mound, and lay out the spot as a bowling-green," Jack Brassey remarked.

"I shall do nothing of the kind, gentlemen," Gage rejoined. "I love those memorials of bygone days, and shall do my best to preserve them."

"A very praiseworthy resolution, Mr. Monthermer," Brice Bunbury remarked; "and for my part I think the ruins exceedingly picturesque, and a great ornament to the grounds."

"They are generally considered so," Mr. Fairlie said.

"All this is matter of taste," Beau Freke observed ; "and if Monthermer prefers antiquity to beauty, I have nothing more to say. I should no more think of preserving those mouldering walls, than I should of keeping an ugly old woman about my premises. But you say you can't afford to build, Monthermer? With twenty thousand a year a man may do anything."

"But I haven't twenty thousand this year. Ask Mr. Fairlie, my late guardian, and he'll tell you I haven't half the amount."

"Since you force me to speak, sir," Mr. Fairlie replied, upon whom all eyes were directed, "I must explain to your friends— though I fancy the information will occasion them no great surprise —that you have anticipated your income by a few thousand pounds ; but I needn't add, you can command any money you please."

"That hint shan't be lost on me," the Beau muttered.

"Nor on me," Meschines said, in the same tone.

"Mr. Fairlie seems very obliging," Brice mused. "I dare say he would lend one a trifle. When an opportunity occurs, I'll try him."

Having sufficiently examined the house, the party adjourned to the stables, where Lord Melton began to depreciate the stud, just as much as Beau Freke had cried down the habitation. There was not a horse worth mounting, he declared ; and his two jockeys, who were standing by, confirmed his opinion. Distrusting his own judgment, and thinking his noble friend must be right, Gage ended by buying Comus and Gaylass. These matchless animals were to do wonders at Newmarket, and enable Gage, as their owner, to make a brilliant entry on the turf. As may be supposed, the young gentleman paid a good price for them ; but not so much as he would have done, if he had not thrown a couple of hunters, selected by Lord Melton from his stud, into the scale. Beau Freke and Sir Randal smiled at this transaction, as they well knew the young man was bitten—and so indeed, did all the others—but there seemed to be a tacit under-standing among them that no one was to interfere with hi neighbour's game. Even Mr. Fairlie did not offer the slightes

THE BEACON HILL.

opposition to the arrangement, but congratulated Gage on his bargain, and by this means completely established himself in Lord Melton's good graces.

Gage next proposed a ride, and steeds being provided for the whole party, they set off into the park. It was a lovely spring day, and the woods, either bursting into leaf, or covered with foliage of the tenderest green, were vocal with the melodies of the birds. The long glades were chequered with glancing shadows —the rooks were busy with their nests amid the tall elm-trees—the heron was winging her flight to the marshes—nothing could be more delightful than a gallop over the elastic sod of the park on such a morning—but Gage had an object in taking his friends beyond its limits, and accordingly, after crossing it in a westerly direction, he passed through a lodge-gate, and entering a lane, led the way along it for about a couple of miles, when they arrived at the foot of a considerable eminence, covered with furze and occasional brushwood. A narrow bridle-road led towards its summit, and tracking this they soon reached a bare piece of ground, with nothing upon it but a small circular stone structure, whence an extensive view was obtained. On one side lay the noble park, which they had just quitted, with its ancient mansion, and still more ancient ruins, distinguishable through the trees. On the other, a fair and fertile country, with a river winding through it on its way to the sea —numerous scattered farm-houses—and here and there a village, with a grey old church, contiguous to it. A range of hills, about six miles off, bounded the inland prospect, and other high land, about equidistant in the opposite direction, cut off a view of the sea, which would otherwise have been visible. The hill, on which the party were standing, seemed to rise up in the midst of a large vale of some twenty miles in circumference, and indeed there was no corresponding eminence near it except that part of the park on which the mansion and the old castle were situated.

"This is called Beacon Hill, gentlemen," Gage said. " What think you of the view?"

"By Jove! I think it remarkably fine," Brice replied. "I never saw anything to equal it—never, upon my veracity."

"I have brought you here," Gage continued, with a smile of pride, " because all you behold from this point is my property

"By Jove! you don't say so?" Brice exclaimed. "What! all those villages—stop! let's count—one, two, three, four—and innumerable cottages—all those yours, Monthermer, eh?"

"Every house—every cottage—every tree is mine," Gage answered. "I confess I feel some pride in surveying my possessions. My father used often to bring me here to look at them, and the very last time we were together on this spot, he said to me, 'All below us will one day be yours, my boy, and when you are master of the property, take care of it.'"

"Deuced good advice on the old gentleman's part," Brice said. At which remark there was a general laugh.

"I do not wish to check your merriment, gentlemen," Gage observed, "but I cannot join in it; and you will understand why I cannot, when I tell you it was at the foot of this very hill that my poor father met his death."

"Near yonder pollard willow, by the brook," Mr. Fairlie said. "His horse fell with him while jumping the hedge. I will show you the exact spot, if you please."

Hereupon, the party slowly and silently descended the hill, and they were approaching the scene of the catastrophe, when a tall, powerfully-made man, of middle age, and in the garb of a farmer, suddenly appeared from behind a haystack, and made his way towards Gage. As he neared the young Squire the man took off his hat, evidently meaning to address him. Mr. Fairlie, however, angrily motioned him with his hunting-whip to stand back.

"The Squire can't speak to you now, Mark Rougham," he cried. "Don't you see he's engaged? Another time."

"I must speak when I can," Rougham rejoined; "and if there be one spot in the whole country where I ought to be listened to by t' Squire, it be this—seeing it were here I lifted up his father when he fell, and tended him till assistance were brought. The worthy gentleman thanked me wi' his eyes, though he could not thank me wi' his lips."

"Indeed, I was never told of this till now, Rougham," Gage said. "Speak out, my good man. What can I do for you?"

"You had better not trouble the Squire, I tell you, Rougham," Mr. Fairlie interposed. "Come up to the Castle to-morrow morning."

" No, I'll speak now, since his honour be willing to listen to me," Mark said, stoutly. " Be I to quit Cowbridge Farm, sir, which I've held for twenty years myself, and which my father and his father held for nigh a century before me?"

" Quit your farm, Rougham! Certainly not."

" I knew your honour wouldn't do it," Mark cried, in a broken voice. " I told Mr. Fairlie so, sir."

" I'll explain all to you afterwards, sir," Fairlie said. " This man has to blame himself for being ejected."

" Good gracious! Mr. Fairlie—you don't mean to say you have ejected him from the house in which he was born and bred? He must have it again—together with the farm, and at a lower rent."

" I only want it at the old rent, sir," Rougham interposed.

" What! has his rent been raised?" Gage exclaimed. " Oh! Mr Fairlie."

" You dog, I'll make you pay for this," the steward muttered between his ground teeth; but he said aloud, " Very well, sir. The man shall be reinstated in Cowbridge Farm, and his rent lowered, as you desire."

" Heaven's blessings on your head, sir!" Mark ejaculated fervently, regarding Gage gratefully with eyes to which tears had sprung. " You ha' done a good deed, and one I be certain your worthy father would have approved of."

Gage made no reply, for his breast was too full, and he rode off attended by the others. As Mr. Fairlie followed them somewhat more slowly, he cast a vindictive glance towards Rougham, and shook his whip at him.

" Ah! you'd lay it across my shoulders, I make no doubt, sir, if you dared," Mark ejaculated. " Poor young gentleman, how kind-hearted he be! He be in bad hands, I misdoubt. Lucky for me I caught sight of him on the Beacon Hill. There be an old saying that one of the Monthermers should lose his fortune by this hill, and another win it. One part of the prophecy seems to have been fulfilled in the case of Squire Warwick. How it may be as to t'other we shall see."

A momentary impression was produced upon Gage by the foregoing occurrence, but it was speedily effaced. He had a vague notion that others of his tenants might have been treated in the same way as Mark Rougham, and he internally resolved to inquire into the matter on the first opportunity. But the opportunity never came. With a really kind heart and good disposition, he was so engrossed by pleasure, and so averse to trouble of any kind, that he was sure to let things take their course, even though aware that it was in a wrong direction. Besides, he stood in great awe of Mr. Fairlie, and it was only very rarely that he ventured to differ with him in opinion, for though seemingly easy and complying, the steward made it evident by his manner that he did not like interference. In regard to Mark Rougham, Mr. Fairlie volunteered an explanation to Gage as they rode home, which appeared to satisfy the young gentleman. For his own part, the steward declared, he was glad Mr. Monthermer had reinstated Mark, for though a thick-headed dolt, and as obstinate as one of his own hogs, he believed him to be a well-meaning fellow in the main. He could well afford to pay an increased rent for Cowbridge Farm, but did not choose to do so. He had been often latterly in arrear. Other people were ready and willing to take the farm at higher rent. In fulfilment of his duty to Mr. Monthermer, he (Mr. Fairlie) did not conceive he had any option but to act as he had done towards Rougham, and turn him out; though the proceeding might appear harsh, and was decidedly against his own inclinations.

"It won't do to listen to the complaints of these people, I assure you, sir," he concluded. "They will impose upon your good-nature if they can. The less you see of them the better—till you understand how to deal with them."

"I will never be a hard landlord, Fairlie," Gage said.

"No fear of that, sir," the other rejoined with a smile, "or you are not your father's son. But you must not err on the other side, and be too yielding, or there will be no end to their demands. Leave them to me."

This was all that passed on the subject

IV.

HOW SIR RANDAL DE MESCHINES PROPOSED TO CURE GAGE OF HIS PASSION.

Mr. FAIRLIE got on very well with the visitors, and the visitors got on very well with Mr. Fairlie. They met each other half-way. At first, the new comers, not knowing their man, regarded the steward with dislike, as a probable bar to their projects, but they soon found out that he was anything but unfavourably disposed towards them. A race in the park, between Comus and Gaylass, proposed by Lord Melton, was warmly supported by Mr. Fairlie —and he only laughed when Gage, who backed the mare, lost a heavy bet upon her to the noble lord. He might well laugh, for he had gone halves with the titled blackleg. Brice Bunbury borrowed a trifle from him, and was told by Fairlie, who acted as paymaster, he might make free with the liberal young gentleman's purse. Fairlie, we may be sure, didn't mean to supply him in this way for nothing. Nat Mist and Jack Brassey were more easily won over, being accessible on the side of good living The most sumptuous repasts were daily prepared, and the cellar was ransacked for its choicest wines. Some port as old as Charles the Second's time was produced, and much admired, especially by Nat Mist; so Mr. Fairlie took care a bottle of it should ever after be set before him. Jack Brassey was a great gourmand, and his tastes in this particular were carefully studied. The cook achieved wonders, and Jack did ample justice to her performances. Cards and dice were introduced each evening, without the slightest opposition from Mr. Fairlie, though he could not be unaware of the full extent of Gage's losings, since he was chancellor of the exchequer. It seemed a positive pleasure to him to hand over a hundred or two of a morning to Beau Freke or Sir Randal. Thus encouraged, the two latter gentlemen began to meditate a bolder

stroke, and though they hardly breathed a word of their intentions to each other, it would almost seem that their secret thoughts
were divined by Mr. Fairlie, for, one day, while discharging Gage's
debts of honour as usual, he remarked to them, with a significance
not to be misunderstood, "You are so lucky, gentlemen, that out
of consideration for my young friend, I ought to check his ten-
dency to play, or bid him select less skilful opponents. However,
he must buy his experience—I am quite aware of that. I only
wish I could go shares with you, for then, if you happened to
make a hit—a good hit, mind—I might chance to come in for a
thousand myself."

"Foregad! Mr. Fairlie," Beau Freke cried, "you would seem
to insinuate that we ought to win three thousand pounds."

"I insinuate nothing, sir, but if you *do* win that amount——"

"You will expect a third of it," Sir Randal said, concluding
the sentence. "Agreed, Mr. Fairlie. Henceforth, you are asso-
ciated with us. Our winnings are your winnings.—A precious
rascal! But we must have him with us," he added to the Beau, as
they left the room, "or he'll spoil our play—that's certain."

It will not be supposed that a youth of Gage's confiding disposition would hesitate to disclose his secret griefs to his friends, especially to such of them as he fancied would sympathise with him;
but he chose an odd time for making the revelation, and did it in
an odd way. One morning, while under the hands of Chassemouche, and while Beau Freke and Sir Randal were sipping
their chocolate beside him, he suddenly started up, and breaking
away from the astonished coiffeur, who stood staring at him, open-
mouthed, with comb and curling-irons uplifted, and with his queue
almost erect with astonishment, uttered a few frantic and unin-
telligible ejaculations, and proceeded to describe himself as the un-
luckiest dog in the whole world.

"What's the matter?" the Beau inquired, tranquilly regarding him.

"I cannot chase her image from my breast," Gage pursued. "I'm
wretched—distracted."

"Whose image?" Sir Randal demanded. "I thought you had
long since forgotten Colombe Mirepoix?"

"I heard there was a little milliner in St. James's-street whom
you cast eyes on," Beau Freke said. "Is she the cause of your
affliction? If so, egad, we'll send Brice for her at once."

"'This is a vraie affaire de cœur, messieurs," Chassemouche said. "Mon maître est eperdûment amoureux—I tell him he shall console himself—but he will not believe me. He fret—pauvre monsieur, how he fret—he break his heart—and about what?—a prude."

'Peace, Chassemouche. Clare is not a prude."

"Soh! we have learnt her name, at all events," Sir Randal said.

"Messieurs, I appeal to you," Chassemouche cried. "Am I wrong to style that demoiselle a prude, who shall refuse un si bon parti comme mon maître—refuse him when he kneel at her feet, and offer her his hand?—and she not his equal, messieurs, who ought to feel flattée—honorée by his notice."

"Silence, I say, Chassemouche," Gage roared.

"Pardon, monsieur. My devotion make me speak. It is Mademoiselle Clare Fairlie of whom monsieur est si amoureux. Jugez, messieurs, if I am wrong in saying she ought to be fière of the admiration of such a one as my master."

"Once more I bid you hold your peace, Chassemouche."

"Is it possible you can have offered this girl marriage, Monthermer?" Beau Freke asked.

"Monsieur, you juge it impossible—but it is perfectly true, parole d'honneur!" Chassemouche replied.

"You do not contradict him, Monthermer, and I must therefore conclude Chassemouche is right. 'Sdeath! what could put such a thought into your head? You must be bewitched. Marry at your time of life—with your fortune—your position. Marry Fairlie's daughter! Bah!"

"Exactly what I say to monsieur," Chassemouche interposed.

"Ten—twenty years hence, it will be time enough to think of a wife," the Beau pursued. "It were madness now."

"Word for word what I tell him," Chassemouche said. "Monsieur doit prendre une femme quand il a jeté le premier feu de sa jeunesse. He will tire of Mademoiselle Clare in a month."

"Chassemouche, I'll strangle you, if you go on thus," Gage cried, furiously.

"Faith! you've had a narrow escape, Monthermer," Sir Randal said; "and I congratulate you upon it. It is not every woman who would have let you off so easily."

"I tell him that too," the loquacious valet remarked.

"But what can be her motive for refusing you?" the young baronet pursued.

"She say he is too much of a rake," Chassemouche replied, with a laugh.

"Poh! poh! an idle reason. She must have another. Of course, she's handsome, or you wouldn't be in love with her, Monthermer."

"She's a divinity," Gage cried, rapturously.

"And the goddess inhabits this paradise? Strange she has not dazzled us with her presence. Her father locks her up, I suppose?"

"Mais non, monsieur," Chassemouche replied. "Mr. Fairlie scold —no matter—she not leave her room."

"My curiosity is piqued," Meschines cried. "I must contrive to see her. She may listen to me, though she won't to you, Monthermer."

"Sir Randal, I will not permit this," Gage cried, sternly.

"Let him alone," Beau Freke said. "Cost what it will, you must be cured of this foolish passion."

"But, my good fellow, I shall die under the operation."

"Die! pshaw! You will live to laugh at your infatuation."

"After all, there is no risk. Her heart is as hard as marble. Try her, if you like, Meschines."

"I mean to do so," the young baronet replied.

"Zounds!" Gage cried, with a sudden pang, "I was wrong in giving you permission. I recal it."

"It is too late," Sir Randal replied, with a laugh. "Why fear, if you think she is proof against me?"

"Oui, n'ayez pas peur, monsieur," Chassemouche said, with a grin. "Asseyez-vous, je vous en prie, et laissez-moi finir de vous coiffer."

His master's toilette completed, Chassemouche quitted the room. On the landing-place he was met by Bellairs, who informed him Mr. Fairlie desired to speak with him.

"Corbleu! What about?" the Frenchman demanded.

"Can't say," the valet replied; "but he seems in a terrible fume."

And the trembling coiffeur bent his steps towards the steward's apartments.

V.

INTRODUCING ARTHUR POYNINGS OF REEDHAM AND HIS SISTER LUCY—A LETTER FROM CLARE FAIRLIE.

SIR HUGH POYNINGS of Reedham was one of Warwick de Monthermer's oldest and most valued friends; and if things had turned out as they ought (which they rarely do), the two worthy gentlemen would have been united by ties stronger than those of mere regard—namely, by a family alliance. Lucy Poynings was destined by her father for Gage, and showed no inclination to thwart the old gentleman's designs. Squire Warwick was equally desirous of the match; but his son could not be induced to become a consenting party to the plan.

Very pretty, very amiable and accomplished was Lucy, and calculated, it would seem, in all respects to make the young fellow happy—only he could not be brought to think so. He liked her well enough; but she did not interest him in the least. When a boy, he used to call her his "little wife," but he dropped the tender appellation as he advanced in years and began to understand its import. Lucy played charmingly on the harpsichord, and sang some of Dr. Arne's and Dr. Pepuch's airs very sweetly; but he cared not to listen to her music or singing. Any one else pleased him just as well as Lucy as a partner in a minuet or a jig, though she was accounted a most graceful dancer. She had the softest blue eyes imaginable, and the fairest skin: unluckily, the eyes that did most execution with Gage were of the opposite hue, and the complexion he chiefly admired was that of a brunette. So Lucy, not being wanting in discernment, nor destitute of proper spirit, declared to her father (though her tearful eyes contradicted the assertion) that she could never think of Gage as a husband. Sir Hugh laughed at her, and said she didn't know her own mind, and would change it before she was a year older—she must leave him to judge what was best for her—he should dispose of her as he saw fit, and so forth. But he came round to her opinion in the end. Squire Warwick, also, perceiving it would be useless to argue the matter with his son, though surprised and vexed at the lad's insensibility to so fine a girl as Lucy, gave up the cherished idea of Gage's marriage with the daughter of his old friend —not without considerable regret.

Lucy Poynings had a brother, Arthur, about two years older than herself, who had been Gage's constant playmate during boyhood; and at this pleasant period of life the two lads were never happy apart, and little dreamed that their friendship could be interrupted. But as their respective characters began to be developed, and very opposite qualities and tastes in each to be displayed, the warmth of their feelings rapidly cooled down, and from being inseparable, they were rarely together.

A fine high-spirited youth was Arthur Poynings—handsome withal, well-made, well-grown, fair-haired, and with light blue eyes like those of his sister. But he had nothing of the fop about him. He excelled in all manly exercises, and even as a lad was considered the most straightforward rider in Suffolk. He thought Gage too much of a coxcomb and a Sybarite; while Gage thought him rustic, ill-dressed, ill-bred, and only one degree better than a clown. A sort of rivalry sprang up between the lads in the hunting-field, and they had frequent disputes as to which was the best horseman; till these were settled by young Poynings, who performed an extraordinary feat, which Gage dared not undertake. Our two youths were next at Oxford together, but little intimacy was kept up between them there; especially after Squire Warwick's death, when Gage launched out into such extravagance and folly. Arthur did not read very hard it is true; but neither did he drink, game, or riot, and he was therefore styled a milksop, a hypocrite, and a sneak, by Gage's associates, though you may be sure none of these opprobrious epithets could be justly applied to him. Jack Brassey even went so far as to molest him, but he had reason to repent his rashness; and the severe chastisement he received operated as a wholesome lesson to the others. Arthur was not annoyed afterwards.

Sir Hugh and Lady Poynings with their family had been bidden to the festivities at Monthermer Castle, when its young lord attained his majority, but they coldly declined the invitation; for, in fact, the old baronet disapproved so much of Gage's scandalous proceedings, and was so incensed against him for his folly and the little respect he displayed for his father's memory, that he could scarcely bear to hear his name mentioned. Sir Hugh declared he would not countenance such goings on by his presence; nor should any one belonging to him enter the young rake's disorderly house, much less Lady Poynings, or Lucy. The latter alone attempted to defend the young man, for whom she still nourished a strong affection. He was very young, she said, and might reform—nay, he was sure to reform, and make a shining character in time. Sir Hugh angrily bade her hold her tongue—she knew nothing about rakes—they never reformed till ruined in health and estate—she had had a lucky escape. It was well Squire Warwick was in his grave—or his son's misconduct would have hurried him there. Poor Lucy heaved a sigh, and thought she would take Gage with all his faults. Young women are more lenient towards our indiscretions, and more hopeful of our amendment, than flinty-hearted seniors, who judge of us by themselves.

However, there was another circumstance connected with Monthermer Castle and its inmates of which Sir Hugh was ignorant; but if he had been aware of it, it would have been sufficient in itself to deter him from going there—or allowing his son to go there. The old baronet was one of those who had early seen through Felix Fairlie, and he had determined to expose him to the master he was sure he was wronging; but, unluckily, he postponed his intention until too late. He thought the steward a consummate rascal and hypocrite; and all Fairlie's subsequent actions convinced him of the correctness of his opinion. Judge, then, what would have been his rage and mortification, if he had known that his son — his only son—the heir to his title—should have dreamed of uniting himself to Fairlie's daughter. Yet such was the case, as we shall see presently. Sir Hugh was exceedingly proud, and if Fairlie had been an honest man, he would have deemed the connexion a misalliance: as it was, he would have held it to be utterly disgraceful and dishonouring to his son, and never to be forgiven on his own part.

Arthur Poynings did not think of this when he fell in love with Clare Fairlie; or rather, he was over head and ears in love with her before he thought of his father's opinion at all. When fairly in the scrape, he began to consider how to get out of it. Sir Hugh, he felt, would be very angry at first, but he was sure to relent in time; and Clare was so sweet a creature she could not fail to win him over. Thus he argued, as lovers always argue, when similarly circumstanced. Luckily, Sir Hugh was not tried.

And now for the history of Arthur's passion.

Lucy Poynings had been long acquainted with Clare Fairlie, and thinking her the most beautiful creature she had ever seen, as well as the most amiable, she spoke of her in such rapturous terms to Arthur, that she naturally roused his curiosity to behold the marvel. The desire was not long ungratified, and the young man owned that his sister had good reason for her commendation. In brief, he fell in love with Clare—violently in love—and made Lucy the confidante of his passion. The heedless girl did not discourage him, for she thought as little of the consequences as he did himself, and never stopped to reflect whether Sir Hugh and Lady Poynings might like the match or not. She only considered how delightful it would be to have such a charming sister-in-law as Clare ; and when matters, as she conceived, had made sufficient progress—for Arthur and the steward's daughter frequently met, and the young man fancied his attentions were not disagreeable to the object of his affections— she willingly consented to speak to Clare on his behalf, and to plead his cause with her, if it required pleading, which she did not anticipate.

Imagine her distress on finding Arthur's suit hopeless, and Clare her own rival.

Though the flame of jealousy was kindled in her bosom on making the discovery, it was quickly extinguished when she learnt Clare's determination in regard to Gage. Lucy was too much in love herself not to know the cost of the sacrifice which the other was prepared to make; nor could she refuse her her profoundest sympathies. They mingled their tears together for a brief space, those two unhappy maidens, unable to afford each other any solace; and then separated, with sentiments of increased mutual regard.

The intelligence conveyed to him by his sister filled Arthur with bitter disappointment, and drove him almost to despair. Till then, ne had not known how deeply he loved. He became moody and unsociable, neglected the exercises of which he had been hitherto so fond, and execrated Gage as the cause of his misery. So changed was he in manner and appearance, that Sir Hugh could not help noticing the alteration, and wondering what could be the matter with him—half suspecting, as he told Lady Poynings, that the lad must be in love, and have met with some disappointment. Yet who could refuse *his* son—the future Sir Arthur Poynings? So handsome too,—the girls were all dying for him. Could it be that proud little minx, Lady Alicia Manvers?—Lady Poynings did not choose to enlighten him, though she was in the secret.

But a still harder trial was reserved for Arthur, as we shall proceed to show. A few days after Beau Freke and the others had arrived at Monthermer Castle, a letter was secretly delivered to Lucy. It was from Clare Fairlie, and ran as follows:

" We must preserve him from ruin—yes, from ruin, Lucy. The danger is imminent He is surrounded by a set of gamblers, who are daily winning large sums of money from him, and who, it is quite evident, will never leave him so long as he has anything to lose.

" You will wonder at his infatuation, and, indeed, it is inconceivable, for he can scarcely be blind to their designs. Yet such is the singular irresolution—what shall I call it?—weakness of his character, that, once caught in toils like these, he will not make an effort to escape from them; though the silken meshes might be burst in a moment.

" He must be freed, Lucy, or he is lost. But how ?

" I cannot help him—and I will tell you why—though the avowal is made with pain and shame, and is only wrung from me by circumstances. He I am bound to love, revere, and obey, is, I fear, in some way a party to the schemes of these wicked persons. I judge so from many reasons; but chiefly, because he stands by, an apparently calm spectator, while his former ward, whom he ought to counsel and protect, is shamefully plundered in the way I have described. He is sharp-sighted enough, and must know these men are little better than sharpers —yet not a word of remonstrance from him. He seems to like them, and willingly enters into all their plans. Cards and dice are introduced every evening, and the company remain at play till a late hour—with invariably the same results, so far as Gage is concerned. *He* never wins. But in spite of his constant ill-luck, he perseveres, and, as I am told, doubles his stakes. You will perceive how this must end.

"I have told my father what I think ; and I never knew him so greatly offended with me as upon this occasion. He spoke so harshly, that I really dare not mention the subject to him again. He asked me how I ventured to meddle with matters in which I had no concern ! What business was it of mine it Mr. Monthermer played ! Mr. Monthermer was his own master ; could do as he pleased ; and would naturally resent any improper control over his actions—and such he should never attempt—and he would advise no one else to attempt it. If I had been his wife—(O, Lucy, he knew how those words would wound me, but he did not heed my anguish)—I might have had a right to interfere —but now, having thrown away my chance, I had none. He had already affirmed that Gage's destiny for good or evil rested with me ; and if I chose to cast him off, and the young man fell into bad courses, I must bear the blame, and not repine. (O, Lucy, I felt there might be truth in this—but I could not—could not— marry him !) As to the apprehensions I appeared to entertain of Gage's ruin, they were idle. He would take care he did not go too far. But he must be taught prudence, at any cost. Experience was a dear schoolmistress, but the only one in his case. (This sounded well, but I felt little confidence in the sincerity of the observation.)

"My father then went on to say that the gentlemen who were staying in the house, and whom I had chosen to designate as sharpers, were, most of them, young men of the first rank and fashion, of high honour, and incapable of resorting to any tricks at play such as I had hinted at. If he had suspected any such malpractices, he would have been the first to denounce them ; but I might rest assured I was mistaken. (But no,—I am *not* mistaken, Lucy.)

" My information must have been derived from my maid, Lettice
my father continued), and he was surprised I should listen to silly
tittle-tattle from the servants'-hall. Servants always calumniate
their masters, and attribute the worst motives to their actions. According to this class of persons, there is no respectability of character
out of livery. Servants never cheat at cards, nor use false dice—
not they !—but their masters invariably do. If Beau Freke and
Sir Randal Meschines are sharpers, and their valets know it, why
do they stay with them? There had been much mischievous talk
of late below stairs (my father added), and he had found it necessary
to give some of the offending parties a caution; and he fancied they
would be more on their guard in future. He hoped he should
not have to give Lettice a similar lesson; for retailers of falsehood
and scandal were just as bad as the originators. And so our conversation ended.

" And here I must remark, Lucy, that my maid was *not* my sole
informant, though I can depend upon her, for Lettice, though a little
giddy, is a good girl, and much attached to me. She is daughter
of Mark Rougham, whom you must know. My opinion of the
' gentlemen' remained unshaken, notwithstanding all my father's
assertions; and I have since had personal reason to complain
of one of them—Sir Randal Meschines. On two or three occasions, latterly, this coxcomb has contrived to throw himself
in my way, though I have done my best to avoid meeting any
of Mr. Monthermer's guests; and he has greatly annoyed me
with his impertinence and adulation, and his professions of a
violent passion for me, which I am certain he cannot feel. He is
so daring in his manner that he quite terrifies me. I kept my
room yesterday to avoid him, but he managed to send me, by
Gage's French valet, Chassemouche, a note, full of flaming nonsense, which I returned immediately by the bearer. I could laugh at
what this silly fop says, but I am in no mood for mirth just now;
and, sooth to say, his attentions alarm me. He is not like Gage.
or your brother Arthur—but has a bold, insolent tone, which is
quite intolerable. He says he will kill himself, if I do not take pity
on him, and I almost wish he would put his threat into execution.

" But I must check myself, Lucy. I meant only to send you a
few lines, praying you to help one dear to us both, and I find

myself writing about my own troubles. My lengthy narrative will, at all events, serve to let you know how I am circumstanced, and how impossible it is for me to aid Gage in what I believe to be a most critical position. I apply to you, Lucy, because, with all his faults, I know you still love him ; and I would fain hope, if he can be rescued from the perils and temptations now environing him, that he may one day requite your devotion.

"He is in need of a true friend, Lucy. Will your brother be that friend ?   "CLARE."

Of course, there was a postscript. No young lady's letter, however voluminous, would be complete without one. It was to this effect :

"I have just heard that some new scheme is on foot, and that the planners of it expect to win a larger sum than usual from Gage. Will Arthur come over this evening? Pray of him to do so, Lucy. I must see him first, and will meet him at nine o'clock at the Ivy Tower adjoining the ruins of the old Castle. He may recollect the spot, for he once spoke to me there. Do not think this proposal wrong, Lucy. I shall have Letty Rougham with me. You will persuade Arthur to come, will you not, Lucy? Another note has just been brought to me from that impertinent coxcomb Sir Randal. I have burnt it unread.   "C."

"And she would have me save the man I hate?" Arthur cried, in a fury, when this letter was shown to him by his sister. "He may go to perdition for aught I care. What is it to me if he is surrounded by sharpers and rakes? What matter if they ruin him? What matter if Fairlie lends them a helping hand? The idiot must pay the penalty of his folly and vice. I can't help him, and I wouldn't if I could."

"Yes, you can and will—for my sake, Arthur," Lucy said, imploringly. "At all events, go and see Clare, that's a dear, kind, good fellow, and hear what she has to say."

"No, I daren't trust myself with her. She would make a fool of me."

"Nonsense. Only think, if you should be the means of rescuing Gage from the snares that beset him, how grateful he would be."

"And as a matter of course throw himself at your feet, Lucy, and offer you his hand as a recompense. By my faith, he would do us great honour."

"If he did, and I accepted him, would not that remove a difficulty from your way, sir? Would not Clare then be quite free—and might not all be happily arranged? I'm sure if you only prove yourself his friend, as Clare says, all will come right."

"But don't you see, Lucy, that she is not thinking of me at all in the matter, but only of him. I am only a secondary consideration with her—scarcely considered at all. You yourself are just as selfish, and display as little regard for me. You care only for Gage. He is in a scrape, from which he cannot disentangle himself. 'Save him—or he is lost,' you both of you cry out. What is it to me, if he *is* lost? A gain rather than otherwise. If I felt that Clare despised him as I despise him—if she expressed a quarter of the affection for me that she expresses in every line of that letter for *him*, I would obey her slightest behest, and deliver him at the hazard of my life. But it is too much to expect me to aid a successful rival."

"Nothing is too much to expect from a generous nature like yours, Arthur. Even as revenge, your interposition at this juncture would be noble: but do not view it in that light. Rather look back to the days of your affectionate intercourse with Gage—when you were boys together—shared everything in common, and would have defended each other against any attack—when no rivalry existed in your breasts. Look back to that time, Arthur, and for the sake of your early regard, render him an important service, which no one is able to perform but yourself. For consider, he has no true friend. All those calling themselves such, and supposed such by him, are his worst enemies. I do not believe Gage to be so bad—so depraved as he is represented. There is much good in him, I believe, though it is sadly overclouded; and the very tastes and qualities which now lead him into such extravagances and follies—such excesses if you will—might, if properly directed and controlled, render him an ornament to society. Such, through your friendly agency, he may become. And what a reflection this will be to you hereafter, Arthur!—what a consolation!"

"I am scarcely convinced by your reasoning, Lucy," her brother replied, sadly; "but I will act as you desire, and I trust good may

come of it. As a boy, I always liked Gage—better, indeed, than
any one else ; and one cannot quite forget early friendship. Latterly, I have hated him."

" O, do not say so, Arthur !"

" I have hated him, I repeat, Lucy, and with good cause. A
man cannot love as I love, and not detest his rival. Nevertheless, I
will serve him, for the sake of old times, and for your sake, Lucy.
I despair of success—but the effort shall be made."

" Have no misgivings, Arthur. Your cause is good, and Heaven
will prosper it."

Accordingly, an answer was sent back to Clare by her messenger that Arthur would keep the appointment she had made.

On that evening, the young man rode, unattended, towards Monthermer Castle, and when within a mile or so of his destination, began
to consider where he should leave his horse, as he did not intend to
announce himself to Gage until after his interview with Clare—
resolving to be governed in what he did by her advice; and while
debating this point with himself, he overtook a farmer slowly
jogging along, and mounted on a good specimen of that sturdy
description of animal known as a Suffolk Punch. As he happened
to be acquainted with the man, who was no other than Mark
Rougham, he slackened speed to have a few moments' talk with
him.· He had heard that Mark had been ejected from his farm by
Fairlie, but was not aware of his reinstatement, and his first inquiries were, as to how he was going on?

" Why, pretty well, thank your honour," Mark replied. " I be
got back to t' owld house, thanks to t' young Squire ; but how long
I'm to remain there t' Lord above only knows; for Muster Fairlie,
I reckon, has more power in his hands than t' young Squire, and
will do what he likes, and set all crooked again when t'other's
back be turned. He ha' given me to understand as much already,
deuce take him ! That man be like t' Unjust Steward we read
on i' Scripture. As to t' young Squire, I've nought to say against
him, but much to say in his favour. His heart be i' th' right
place, I be sure; and he'll do nothin' wrong if let alone—but it be
a pity, Muster Arthur,—a great pity,—he do let others do wrong
in his name, and abuse his authority—and a greater pity still, if
it be true as I hear tell, that he ha' gotten a set o' gambling folk

stayin' wi' him at the Castle, who be preyin' upon him as I've seen a swarm o' wasps feast upon a ripe pear. Ah! sir, the poor young gentleman is sadly in need of good advice, and wants some one like yourself, or Sir Hugh, to talk to him."

"It is for that very purpose I am now proceeding to the Castle," Arthur rejoined. "I am glad to have met you, Mark, for what you say about Mr. Monthermer gives me better hopes of success than I previously entertained. I hope I may be able to chase away those greedy insects."

"Take care you don't get stung yourself while doin' it, sir." Mark observed. "They'll fight for the prize, you may rely on it. Ah, sir, if you could only free him from Muster Fairlie, you would render him a service indeed!"

"That, I fear, is beyond my power, Mark. Besides——" And he hesitated.

"I fear I've said what I ought not, Muster Arthur, and I ask pardon for my boldness, sir, but it's the custom wi' us Suffolk yeomen to speak out, as you well know, for you ha' lived among us; and so hopin' to gi' no offence, for I mean none, I may as well tell the truth, and confess that I know your honour has been a little bit smitten wi' Mistress Clare—more than a little bit, mayhap. My daughter Letty be her maid, and she ha' dropped a word ·or two to her mother concernin' it, and the good dame of course couldn't keep the secret, but must needs blab it to me. Havin' confessed this, I must add—always without offence—that a tidier lass, or a sweeter or prettier lass, or, what is more, a better lass—though she do ca' owld Felix her father—is not to be found in the whole county, than Mistress Clare; and though some folk might turn up their noses, and say you were demeanin' of yourself by such a marriage, Muster Arthur—always without offence, sir—I think you'd do well: for a virtuous woman, as we're told by them as knew what they said, is a jewel above price, and such a one I believe Mistress Clare Fairlie to be. You be not offended wi' my freedom, I hope, sir?"

"Not in the least, my good fellow," Arthur replied; "and to prove I am not, I will take you into my confidence, and tell you I am about to meet Clare privately in the garden near the Ivy Tower, to concert measures with her for——"

"For runnin' away wi' her fro' t' owd chap," Mark interrupted, delightedly. "The best thing you can do, sir. I'll help you wi' all my heart. Only tell me what to do."

"Much obliged to you, Mark, but I'm not exactly bent upon the enterprise you suppose. Indeed, to tell you the truth, I don't think the young lady *would* run away with me. My sole object is to consult with her as to the best means of freeing Mr. Monthermer from the harpies who are draining his life-blood from him."

"And be she the best person to consult wi' on such a matter, do you think, sir?—However, it's no business of mine, and I begs pardon for my freedom. If I were you, I'd go at 'em at once. Show 'em up in their true colours. I'll back you up, if you want any one to stand by you."

"Again I thank you, Mark, but I trust I am equal to the disagreeable task I have imposed upon myself. However, since you volunteer your services, I will take advantage of the offer to this extent. I am to meet Clare at nine o'clock, as I have told you. You shall go with me, and remain within call."

"That I will, sir, wi' pleasure. And I shall be quite ready, in case you should follow out my notion—supposin' the young lady should be agreeable to it."

"No fear of that, Mark. But perhaps I may have to send a message by you to my sister. That is why I want you to accompany me."

"I'll do whatever you tell me, Muster Arthur; and I only hope I may have somethin' better to do than take a message—unless it be a message to say you're off wi' Mistress Clare—no offence, sir. But as there be a good hour and a half betwixt this and nine o'clock, perhaps you'll ride on wi' me to Cowbridge Farm, and put up your horse there. We can then start for the Castle a-foot when you think proper."

Arthur agreed to this proposal, and accordingly they proceeded to the farm, where they dismounted, and on entering the dwelling, which looked a snug tenement—though it was scarcely got into thorough order after its recent disarrangement—the young gentleman was heartily welcomed by the honest yeoman's buxom spouse. Three or four children crowded round Mark's leather-cased legs, and struggled for a caress, but he took a crowing infant from the arms of his wife, and holding it towards Arthur, exclaimed: "Here's wishin' you well married, sir, and as fine a babby as this to bless you—meanin' no offence, sir"—and then suddenly changing his tone, and patting the curly heads of his other children, he added, "Muster Fairlie thought little of these poor things when he turned us all out of doors. However, I won't speak of it. Come, bestir thyself, dame, and get us somethin' to eat and drink. We must be off soon. Young Squire Poynings and I have some business to do up at the Castle. We may chance to bring a young lady back wi' us. Don't stare, dame, but draw a jug o' beer. Sit ye down, Muster Arthur—do sit ye down, sir. Get away childer, and make less din."

Half an hour after this, Arthur and his companion set out on their expedition. Leaping the park palings, they took their way silently and at a quick pace over the elastic sod.

Every inch of these broad and beautiful domains was known to Mark, so no better guide could have been found than he. It was a bright starlight night, and by the time they reached the ruins the moon would have risen, Mark said, though he didn't know whether Muster Arthur would be pleased or not at the circumstance.

At length, on emerging from out a dense grove of trees into which they had plunged, they beheld a vast, black, jagged mass before them. It was the ruined Castle, and as they drew near the venerable structure, one tall tower, partially overgrown with ivy, and tipped by the crescent moon, began to detach itself from the rest of the hoary pile.

Presently they came to an iron railing, surrounding the garden, and leaving Mark near a tree, Arthur sprang over this slight fence, and approached the place of rendezvous alone.

VI.

IN WHICH LETTICE ROUGHAM DISPLAYS A READY WIT.

CLARE FAIRLIE had the highest opinion of Arthur Poynings. She did not love him, but she esteemed him for his many excellent qualities, and could not help admiring his manly appearance. What her feelings might have been towards him, if she had known him earlier, when her affections were disengaged, we need not inquire. Perhaps, she herself might regret not having a heart to bestow upon a youth so deserving. Be this as it may, he was the first person she turned to in her trouble. It was rather hard to put his generosity to so severe a test as to call upon him to aid a rival; but Gage's danger (it appeared to her) did not admit of hesitation. Scarcely, however, was the letter to Lucy gone, than Clare repented her boldness, and would have recalled it. What would Arthur think of her? He might be angry, but he would come. She knew the influence she had over him—but had she any right to exert it?—Yes, yes, she was bound to do everything she could to save Gage. So easily do we find excuses for our actions when love is the prompter.

At last, Clare's suspense was relieved by Lucy's reply, which was brought her by Lettice Rougham. O, how cheered she was by the dear girl's expressions of sympathy! Lucy was quite as anxious as herself about Gage — just as eager to serve him. Arthur, too, would obey her summons. O, how kind, how generous in him to come! But she knew he would.

Little Lettice Rougham, who had been watching her as she read the letter, and saw it contained some satisfactory intelligence, now threw in a word. But before we attend to her, let us see what Lettice was like. This then is her picture. Small in stature, plump as a partridge, rosy-cheeked, bright-eyed, rising nineteen,

—she was altogether a very merry, coquettish, engaging little creature. The exuberance of her person was carefully restrained by tightly-fitting bodice, crossed outside with pink ribbons ; her fair hair was taken back from her smooth forehead, and rolled under a very becoming little cap; and her scarlet grogram petticoat, with the chintz dress looped up above it, was luckily not long enough to hide the smallest feet and the neatest ankles to be seen at Monthermer Castle.

Little Lettice had just been adding an inch or two to her height, by standing on tiptoe, and trying to peep at the letter over her young lady's shoulder ; but finding she could discover nothing in this way, and that she was not likely to gain much information by remaining silent, she began the discourse by inquiring whether Clare had any orders for her?

" No, Lettice," the other replied; but after a moment's hesitation, she added, blushing slightly as she spoke, " I shall want you to accompany me to the Ivy Tower at nine o'clock this evening."

" What, to see the moon rise, miss—or hear the nightingales sing? I don't think they've begun yet. Won't it be very cold ? I declare it makes me quite shiver at the idea of a solitary walk at such an hour. And then somebody may be hidden in the ruins—and may rush out upon us, and frighten us—and we should be so far away from the house, that our screams couldn't be heard."

" Don't be afraid, Lettice. No harm will befal us."

" I don't know that, miss. Strange things have been seen in those old ruins. I'm not very fond of going there alone, even in the daytime ; and at night the owls make such a noise in the towers, and puff and whoop so angrily, and the jars scream so, as if they didn't desire one's company, and the bats wheel about so awsomely overhead, that they quite scare me; and—and—with your leave, miss, I should prefer supper in the servants'-hall. An evening stroll may be very well, if it's to meet somebody."

" Well, Lettice, to satisfy you that I do not mean to go out merely to see the moon rise, or hear the nightingales sing ; and to prove that we shall have some company among the ruins besides the owls and bats, I will tell you that I *do* expect to meet somebody there—a young gentleman."

"Law, miss, you don t say so ! You so very particular, meet a young gentleman in the ruins ! Everybody calls me a silly girl, and if I were to do such a thing, it wouldn't be surprising—but you !—I should never have expected it."

"I don't wonder you disapprove of the step, Lettice ; and, indeed, I can scarcely reconcile it to my own notions of propriety. But it is necessary I should see Mr. Arthur Poynings alone, and unobserved, before he enters the house."

"Is Mr. Arthur the gentleman you expect to meet, miss ? If I'd known that, I wouldn't have said a word against it—not I ! I'm quite ready to go. Never mind the moon, or the owls, or the bats. I don't care, if it should be as dark as pitch. Bless me ! how things do come round, to be sure. They say it's not easy to whistle a lost lover back again, but you seem to have found out the way, miss ; and very glad I am of it. You'll excuse me—I'm free-spoken, like my father—and I may say now, that I always thought you very cruel to Mr. Arthur. I couldn't have been so hard-hearted to so nice a young gentleman."

"You would have acted precisely as I have done, if your affections had been engaged, Lettice. But I must set you right as to the cause of Mr. Arthur's visit. He comes here at my request, it is true, but his errand does not relate to me at all, as you will learn, for you will be present at our interview."

"O, don't be afraid of me, miss ! I shall shut my eyes, and stop my ears, all the time you're together, I can promise you."

"I beg you will do no such thing, Lettice. I have nothing to conceal from you, and I dare say your assistance will be required in my project, should it be carried out. You're dying to know what it is I perceive, but your curiosity cannot be indulged till the proper time. And now, Lettice, a word of advice, in return for your disapproval of my behaviour to Mr. Arthur Poynings. As you well know, I love another, and therefore I could not encourage Mr. Arthur's suit. But are you not similarly circumstanced, let me ask, Lettice? Is not the son of an honest yeoman in love with you? Have you not plighted your troth to Joyce Wilford?"

Lettice made no reply, but hung down her head.

"You do not contradict me, and therefore admit that I am

right. Then how can you allow other young men to pay you attention? Such levity is highly improper, and very unfair to Joyce; and if he hears of it, he is certain to resent it. If you lose him you will be very sorry; but no one will be sorry for you, Lettice, for they will say you were rightly served."

"I don't care what folks say of me, miss," Lettice replied, pouting; "and if Joyce chooses to turn his back on me, he is quite welcome. I shan't break my heart about him, I can tell him. I don't like to be rude to young men, and if they're polite to me, I'm civil to them—that's my way."

"And a very silly way it is, and extremely reprehensible. You are sadly too fond of flattery and admiration, Lettice."

"Why, if men will pay one compliments, miss, what is one to do? Looking cross won't check 'em; besides, I *can't* look cross for the life of me, if anybody compliments me, and says I'm good-looking."

"But you can help trying to attract attention, you giddy creature!"

"I don't try to attract it, miss; it comes naturally. Men show me attention whether I like it or not. There's Mr. Bellairs, he's always teasing me with his nonsense, though I do my best to keep him at a distance,—and that grinning Frenchman, Mounseer Shassymouse, who tells me I'm so jolly and so bell,—I'm sure I don't encourage *him*, for I can't abide him. Then there's the two fine gentlemen from Lunnon—the two valets, I mean—Mr. Tibbits and Mr. Trickett,—I must say they're the forrardest of all, though I can't but allow they're the best-looking and genteelest, and I shouldn't object to their company, if they weren't quite so familiar. Would you believe it, miss, it was only yesterday that Mr. Trickett squeezed my hand, and the night before Mr. Tibbits tried to kiss me!—he did indeed, miss. These two impudent fellows are just as troublesome to me as Sir Randal is to you. I told 'em I was engaged to an honest young man, and couldn't listen to any one else; and would you believe it, they burst out laughing, and said that didn't signify in the least, they'd soon get rid of young Clodpole—though I don't think they'd find it such easy work as they fancy, for Joyce is a broad-shouldered fellow, and knows how to use his fists—and as to me, I might have whichever of 'em I pleased for a husband, and when I got to Lunnon I should ride in a gilt coach like a grand lady."

"Don't let your head be turned by any such nonsense, Lettice. These two valets are rakes and gamblers like their masters, and equally dangerous and designing. You cannot be too careful with them."

"I'm sure of it, miss. I didn't believe what they said at the time, and it proved to be all stuff, for Mr. Tibbits whispered in my ear that Mr. Trickett was married already, and soon afterwards Mr. Trickett told me the same thing of Mr. Tibbits; so as you say, miss, they're a couple of arrant deceivers."

The conversation was here interrupted by a tap at the door. Without waiting for permission to enter, the person who knocked opened it, and came in. It was Chassemouche. Advancing a few paces towards Clare, and making an obsequious congee at each step, the French valet held out with the points of his fingers a little note, enclosed in an envelope of satin paper, with a broad silver border, and highly perfumed.

"Encore un billet pour mademoiselle," he said, throwing himself into a pose like a dancing-master, "de la part de Sir Randal de Meschines."

"This is intolerable," Clare exclaimed, her cheek flushing with indignation, and her eyes lighting up. "How dare you present yourself again to me, sirrah? I have already told you I will receive no communication whatever from Sir Randal. If he is a gentleman he will desist from annoying me in this way. Take back the note to him. I will not touch it."

"I have convey your pleasure to Sir Randal, mademoiselle— once, twice, tree time—but he no mind. He love you, mademoiselle—si furieusement—he not listen to reason. Il est ensorcelé jusqu'à la folie. Ma foi! he draw his sword just now, and placing its point at my poitrine, he swear a grand juron to run me through de gizzard, unless I take dis billet to you, and bring him back une réponse favorable."

"Say to him I have none," Clare cried. "If I am further annoyed in this way, I shall appeal for protection to Mr. Monthermer."

But Chassemouche grinned, and stood his ground.

"Pardon me, mademoiselle, si je suis plus éclaire que vous sur les desseins de mon maître. He has resign his pretensions to you in favour of his particular friend Sir Randal."

"What does he say, miss?" Lettice inquired. "Does the wicked wretch mean to insinuate that Squire Gage has given you up?"

"Exactly what you say, coquine," Chassemouche replied, grinning. "Mon maître retire from de field, and leave it open to Sir Randal."

"Don't believe the vile monster, miss," Lettice said. "It's false! Squire Gage couldn't be capable of such conduct."

"If mademoiselle will condescend to peruse dis billet she will have proof dat I assert de naked truth," Chassemouche rejoined.

Clare looked for a moment irresolute, but quickly overcoming the feeling of curiosity, she said—"No, I will not be tempted. Take back the letter. I do not desire to know its contents."

"Eh bien!" the French valet exclaimed, shrugging his shoulders, "I must perforce return, and leave my mission inachevé. If Sir Randal fulfil his threat, and kill me, I claim one tear of pity for my sad fate from les beaux yeux de mademoiselle. You laugh, friponne," he added, shaking his hand at Lettice, "but you know not what a man will do when under de influence of de grande passion. You almost drive me mad, yourself, wid your bewitching caprices Adieu, mademoiselle!" with a profound obeisance to Clare; "I depose my respectful homage at your foot. If you hear of my sudden decease, you will know at whose door to lay it."

"O gemini, miss!" Lettice interposed, "if you think Sir Randal really will kill him, you had better not let him go. I don't care a pin for Mounseer Shassymouse, but I shouldn't wish him to be spitted like a calf. Wouldn't you like just to look at the letter, and see what it says about Squire Gage? There may be something in it to set your mind at rest. You can tear it up, you know, when you've read it, as you did the first note."

Chassemouche, thinking his chance not quite over, still lingered, and now interposed a remark.

"Perhaps mademoiselle will permit me to recite de contents of de billet. I know dem by heart—since I hear it read to my master."

"Impossible!" Clare indignantly exclaimed. "If aware of the

purport of that letter, Mr. Monthermer would never sanction its delivery to me. You are asserting more than you have any warrant for, sirrah; and when your master learns—as he *shall* learn—how you have dared to traduce him to me, you will have reason to regret your impertinence."

"I have no fears on that score, mademoiselle," the Frenchman replied, apparently unmoved by the threat. "Mon maître et le Sieur Freke hear de billet read, and dey both approve it—and Mr. Monthermer bid me give it into your own hands. I hesitate to obey—when Sir Randal menace my life, as I before narrate. Sapristi! how de two oder gentlemen laugh. Dey tink it a bonne plaisanterie—but I find it no joke."

"More shame for 'em for laughing," Lettice cried. "Do let him tell us what's inside the note, miss."

Clare was too much agitated to speak at the moment, and Chassemouche did not wait for her permission, but went on.

"Sir Randal profess de most violent regard for you, mademoiselle," he said. "Dat you comprehend; but you not comprehend l'excessif ardeur de sa devotion—unless you read his letter. Mais, n'en parlons plus. He implore you to grant him an interview dis evening."

"Bless me, miss, how strange!" Lettice exclaimed.

"Sir Randal next take leave to fix de hour and de place of rendezvous, mademoiselle."

"Well, tell us what he says without more ado?" the impatient handmaiden cried.

"Doucement, coquine. If you will accompany your jeune maîtresse, I will be dere too. De place, mademoiselle, is de petit jardin near de ruins of de old château—de Ivy Tower, mon maître tell Sir Randal to call it—de hour is nine o'clock precise. You not forget dat, pretty Mistress Lettice, and come wid your young lady. You shall find me, and I will tell you something you like to hear."

"My stars, miss! was there ever anything so strange?" Lettice almost screamed. "What shall we do?"

Clare imposed silence by a look.

"I tell Sir Randal you come, mademoiselle," Chassemouche said, bowing and backing hastily towards the door. "Au revoir, pretty Mistress Lettice! I expect you."

" O no!—you're not to expect either of us. Stop a minute !"

But before she could prevent him, the Frenchman was gone.

" Mercy on us, miss!" Lettice exclaimed, running back to her young lady, as Chassemouche disappeared. " Here's a pretty business ! Only think this troublesome Sir Randal should fix the exact spot and the exact hour that you have appointed with Mr. Arthur."

" It cannot be accidental," Clare remarked. " He must have learnt my intention, in some way or other—but how?"

" Yes, miss, that's just it. How can he have discovered what you meant to do ? Even *I* didn't know it."

" Nor any one else that I am aware of, except Mr. Arthur and his sister. Can my letter to Lucy, or hers to me, have been tampered with? I thought the messenger trusty."

" Ned Clinch! he's trusty enough for a groom, but I'm afraid a guinea might tempt him. Most likely the letters have been opened."

" But if such should unluckily be the case, my object would be defeated," Clare cried.

" We can't be quite sure, miss, but it's better to be prepared for the worst and think so. I'd try and get it out of Ned, but he'd be cunning enough to keep his own counsel. What do you propose to do? Mr. Arthur, I suppose, is sure to come ?"

" Quite sure, Lettice. And I see no means of informing him of the difficulty in which I am placed."

" It's very perplexing indeed. I wish I could think of a plan —but I'm quite at my wits' end. Stay, miss—I have it—shall I go in your place?"

" But are you not afraid to do so, Lettice?" Clare observed, evidently much relieved by the suggestion.

" Not a bit, miss. You can tell me what to say to Mr. Arthur, and I shan't mind Sir Randal in the least. It'll be good fun to laugh at him. He won't find out who it is just at first in the dark. You must lend me your mantean and hat, and though I'm not quite so tall as you, I dare say if I walk on the points of my feet in this way, Sir Randal won't notice the difference."

" If you can only warn Mr. Arthur of Sir Randal's proximity before the latter can surprise him, it will be sufficient, Lettice, and

E

may prevent a quarrel between the two gentlemen. I shall never forgive myself if Arthur should suffer on my account. But you must not go alone. I will be within call."

"Why can't you put on my red camlet cloak, miss, and draw the hood over your face, and then you may pass very well for me, and may find an opportunity of speaking to Mr. Arthur, while I engage the other's attention."

"You are very adroit I must say, Lettice, and seem to have quite a talent for an affair of this kind. But you must now leave me. I will try to collect my scattered thoughts, and consider what is best to be done under the circumstances. I think I shall adopt your plan, though it is not altogether to my taste. Come to me by-and-by."

"Don't hesitate, miss. It will be turning the tables nicely on Sir Randal. For my part, I'm so eager for the frolic that I wish it only wanted a quarter to nine, and we were on our way to the Ivy Tower—you in my camlet cloak, and I in your silk manteau."

And she quitted the room, leaving Clare to her meditations.

VII.

INSTEAD of at once returning, as might naturally have been expected, to the young baronet, whose emissary he professed to be, Monsieur Chassemouche, on quitting Clare's presence, betook himself to a room on the ground-floor which Mr. Fairlie claimed as his own, and in which he usually transacted business. Tapping against the door, the Frenchman, in this instance, *did* pause, and it was not until he had knocked twice that he was admitted. It then appeared that the steward was just dismissing Ned Clinch, the groom. The latter was grinning and thrusting a coin into his waistcoat-pocket, which the quick eyes of the Frenchman detected as a piece of gold; and as Ned passed out he bestowed a knowing wink upon his fellow-servant, and probable accomplice.

As soon as they were alone, Mr. Fairlie, who was seated at table with writing materials before him, and with one of those big account-books, which were Gage's especial aversion, close at hand, proceeded to set Chassemouche's tongue at liberty, and having done so, speedily learnt all that the Frenchman had to impart concerning his recent interview with Clare. Mr. Fairlie seemed vexed that his daughter could not be prevailed upon to open the billet, which Chassemouche laid upon the table beside him, and which he presently took up and placed in a drawer; but he complimented the Frenchman upon his address in contriving to make her aware of its contents, which he said would do just as well as if she had read the letter. This recital over, Mr. Fairlie seemed to be occupied a few minutes in reflection, during which he kept turning the key in the lock of the drawer, heedless that his movements were keenly watched by Chassemouche. At last, as with an effort, he took out a guinea from a small wooden bowl, half full of such glittering coin, carefully locked the drawer, and gave the money to the Frenchman, who received it with his usual obsequious bow.

"Secret service costs one a good deal, Chassemouche," he remarked. "This is the third guinea I've parted with on that account to-day. I've just paid Ned Clinch for bringing me the letter he received from Miss Poynings, in answer to my daughter's communication, which he laid before me in like manner previously to setting out on his errand. Two letters, two guineas, Chassemouche. The fellow will get rich, if he goes on at this rate. It will be your own fault, if you don't get rich in the same way. I'm always ready to pay for intelligence—in proportion to its value, Chassemouche. I like to know what is going on in every part of the house—what is said, as well as done, by the servants, where they go, and whom they see. There are fine doings just now in the butler's pantry. Pudsey and Bellairs, I hear, have lost a great deal of money at gleek and other games to Sir Randal's valet, Trickett. Mr. Freke's servant, Tibbits, is also, I'm told, a considerable winner. You play a little yourself, I know—nay, no excuses, I'm not going to take you to task—I wish to put you on your guard against that rascal Trickett,—a regular sharper, who will never rest till he has fleeced Pudsey and Bellairs of every farthing they possess."

"Ma foi, monsieur," Chassemouche replied, with a grin, "dat is done already. Deir pockets were quite cleaned out last night. Corbleu! dey both owe money to Trickett, and dey give him deir paroles d'honneur to pay him dis evening. Poor Pussey lose a great deal—more den I like to mention, monsieur,—and it puzzle me to tink how he shall get out of de scrape—ha! ha! Bellairs want to borrow money from me—but I not lend him one sou. He may go hang—le maudit chien—for vat I care—he! he!"

"Just as I could wish," Fairlie muttered—"then they are sure to apply to me. Now go to Sir Randal, and tell him you have succeeded this time."

"Mais, monsieur—I fear he not credit me."

"Yes—yes—he will. The coxcomb will believe anything that flatters his vanity. Do as I bid you. Tell him the young lady received his note, and though she didn't say so, she looked consent.

That will be sufficient for him. Such good tidings ought to be worth another guinea to you."

"Assez, monsieur—I shall swear to him she will come."

"About it at once, then," Fairlie cried.

The Frenchman had not been gone many minutes when his place was supplied by Mr. Bellairs. The usually smirking valet wore rather a hang-dog look. Mr. Fairlie perfectly understood the cause of his trouble, but choosing to feign ignorance, he inquired whether anything was amiss?

"Why yes, sir," Mr. Bellairs replied—"I am a little inconvenienced, that's the truth of it. I've a debt of honour, which must be paid to-day, and I don't know how to meet it, unless you will be so very obleeging as to advance me a quarter's wages."

"Why, you've been gambling, rascal!"

"I've only followed my master's example, sir. The gentlemen are always at play up-stairs, and there's something so enticing in the rattling of a dice-box, or the dealing of a pack of cards, that I'm sure to sit down to a game if there's a place at table."

"And equally sure to lose when you have sat down, I fancy, Bellairs,—especially if Mr. Trickett should happen to be your adversary. However, that's your own affair. I'm not going to point out to you the folly of your conduct. I'm not a moralist, Bellairs."

"I should think not," the valet mentally ejaculated.

"By-the-way, Bellairs," Mr. Fairlie pursued, "you are a great deal about your master, and very much in his confidence. He may sometimes make remarks about me which it is desirable I should know."

"O yes, sir," the valet replied, at once taking the hint. "He often converses with me about you."

"Well, what does he say, Bellairs?—what does he say?"

"Excuse me—but I've a very bad memory, sir."

"You want it refreshing—eh?"

"Why yes, sir; I should like to know whether I am to have the quarter's wages?"

"You shall have them provided I am sure you will earn them. Hark ye, Bellairs—there's no use in beating about the bush when we can come to the point. You may be useful to me in bringing

me early intelligence about your master—as to his plans and movements—what he says and what he does——"

"In a word, to betray him, sir. I can't do it," Bellairs said,
placing his hand upon his heart—"I can't, upon my honour."

"Pshaw, fellow! this affectation won't pass with me. You want
to be bought. Well, make yourself useful, and you shall have no
reason to complain. You can play the spy as well as another,
I suppose?"

"I should hope I can, sir, but I object to the appellation. It's
a low term, and not in use now-a-days amongst gentlemen."

"I perceive we understand each other, Bellairs, and so you
shall have the sum you require. Forty pounds a year—that's ten
pounds the quarter," Fairlie said. taking money from the drawer,
and opening a small book in which he entered the amount,
he handed it to the valet, bidding him write a receipt.

This done, and while pocketing the money, Bellairs observed:

"I hope you don't trust that Frenchman, sir—a double-dealing
scoundrel who will be certain to betray you."

"I've no great opinion of him, Bellairs, and if I catch him
tripping, I shall pack him off. Keep an eye upon him. I rely
on your discretion."

Just at this moment another tap was heard at the door, and Mr.
Pudsey came in. The butler stared at the valet, and the valet
stared at the butler, but neither spoke. At a sign from Mr.
Fairlie, Bellairs withdrew, but he remained outside, with his ear
to the keyhole.

"Soh, Pudsey, you are come on the same errand as Bellairs—
eh?" Mr. Fairlie began. "You have been gaming like him, and
lost your money, eh? I read an answer in your face. How
much do you want?"

"Really, sir, I didn't expect you to oblige me so readily——"

"I haven't said I would oblige you, Pudsey. I make no promises. But I again ask how much you require?"

"Why, sir, since it must out, I should be glad of fifty pounds."

"I dare say you would, Pudsey; but you won't get it from me.
I admire your assurance in preferring the request. It does you
infinite credit—ha! ha! Why, Bellairs was content with ten."

"That may be, sir, but my losses have been greater than his.

Besides, I stand on wholly different ground from Bellairs, an I am able to make better terms. You pay him for intelligence—you must pay me to be silent."

"Pay you to be silent! What do you mean?" Fairlie demanded, knitting his brows.

" I mean this, sir—that I want money, and must have it. You will make a better bargain with me than you would have done, it I hadn't been in this strait, and may therefore congratulate yourself upon the smallness of my demand. It was my intention to ask —ay, and to *have*—as many hundreds, as I now require pounds."

"Having explained why you so modestly limit your demand, Pudsey, you will next, perhaps, have the goodness to inform mo how it is you venture to make any demand at all?"

" Readily, sir. A pocket-book was dropped in the dining-room yesterday. I picked it up, and on inspection discovered it to belong to Sir Randal de Meschines, as his name is stamped upon it. It contains nothing of importance—nothing valuable, I mean— except certain entries of sums of money won at play from my master. These sums are divided among three parties: one share being allotted to the young baronet himself—another to Mr. Freke —and the third to you."

"Zounds!" ejaculated Fairlie, unable to repress his anger.

"That these memoranda refer to you," Pudsey pursued, "is confirmed by two notes from Mr. Freke, enclosed in the pocketbook, in which your name is alluded to, in no very complimentary terms, as their partner."

"I believe you are lying, Pudsey. I dare you to produce that pocket-book."

"Nothing more easy, sir; and depend upon it, if we cannot come to a right understanding, which for your own sake is most desirable, it shall be laid before my master."

" And you want to borrow fifty pounds from me?"

" No, sir, I require that sum; but I have no intention of returning it."

" It must be a loan on my part, unless you deliver up the pocketbook. I will lend you the money, and you shall sign a memorandum, which I will give up to you when you bring me the book and the letters."

"I am quite content with that arrangement, sir. You may trust to my honour to deliver them to you."

"Rather a poor security, I fear, Pudsey. Nevertheless, I will trust you."

"Because you can't help yourself," the cunning butler thought, as the other drew up the memorandum.

It did not take Mr. Fairlie long to write it out, after which Pudsey signed the paper without troubling himself to read it, and then received the money, which he took care to count.

"All right, sir," he observed, after going through this agreeable ceremonial; "you may depend upon it I'll deal with you on the square. To-morrow your mind shall be made easy as to the pocket-book and its contents."

"Before then, I trust," Mr. Fairlie cried, as the butler took his departure. "An hour shall not elapse before I have them in my possession. By Heaven! I should like to hang the villain. I'll have his boxes instantly searched."

While he was considering how he should set about this business, Mr. Bellairs suddenly stood before him.

"Behold the man you want!" the valet said, with his customary confidence.

Fairlie regarded him inquiringly.

"I have overheard what has just passed between you and Pudsey, sir," Bellairs continued, "and I can assist you. I know where he has hidden this pocket-book, and will bring it to you."

"Do so, and you shall not find me ungrateful."

"Better reduce your gratitude to figures, sir. You must give me as much as you have just given Pudsey."

"Agreed."

"In ten minutes you shall have what you require. I watched Pudsey go down stairs—the rogue was laughing to himself—I'll steal up to his room at once."

"Take care to bring both the letters."

"Never fear, sir; I'll leave nothing behind. I wish I'd asked a hundred. He would have given it just as readily as fifty," the valet muttered as he left the room.

"How excessively incautious in Sir Randal to make those entries, and to preserve Mr Freke's letters!" Fairlie cried as he was left alone. " I shall lose a hundred pounds, but I shall get rid of these damnatory proofs, and Pudsey will then be fifty pounds in my debt, and consequently in my power."

Mr. Fairlie was not long left to his ruminations, whatever they might be. Voices and loud laughter resounding in the passage informed him that some persons were approaching his retreat, and presently afterwards the door opened, and Gage entered, accompanied by Beau Freke, Sir Randal, Lord Melton, and Brice Bunbury. The whole party seemed in high spirits, and did not cease laughing as they took possession of the room, throwing themselves into lounging attitudes, wherever they could find a seat—some on chairs, and the others on the edge of the steward's table. Amongst the latter were Gage and the young baronet

" Well, Fairlie," Sir Randal began, patting his shapely leg, encased in a silken stocking to the finest web, embroidered with golden clocks, " I have come to tell you I shall win my wager. You betted me a hundred pounds, and Monthermer did the same, that your daughter never would consent to meet me."

" We betted that she would not meet you at the Ivy Tower at nine o'clock this evening. Pray be particular, Sir Randal."

" Yes, that was our bet, and I think it pretty safe, Fairlie, eh?" Gage remarked, laughing. " It was made at your suggestion, for I should never have thought of such a strange proposal, which I look upon as an affront to the young lady. However, if it is so, you are bound to resent it, not I, Fairlie."

" I look upon the affair as a mere jest—a jest at my own expense, perhaps—but still I can afford to laugh at it; and, therefore, I see nothing to resent," Fairlie replied. " Sir Randal offered to lay me a hundred pounds that my daughter would meet him, leaving it to me to fix the time and the place of rendezvous. I took the bet—naming the most unlikely spot, and the most unlikely hour—and I shall win his money."

" And so shall I," Gage cried. " Notwithstanding what he affirms, I would make it a thousand she don't come."

" Done !" Sir Randal exclaimed. " A thousand be it. I only wish you would say ten. Are you disposed to increase your bet to the same amount, Fairlie ?"

" I should feel perfect security in doing so, Sir Randal," the other replied, " but I do not wish to gain so large a sum of money in such a way.   I will rest content with the hundred."

" We must all be present.   We must see fair play," Beau Freke cried

" You must keep out of sight, then," Sir Randal rejoined. " I will allow no interference."

" I won't answer for myself if she *does* come !" Gage exclaimed ; " but that is wholly impossible."

" Not quite so impossible as you fancy," the young baronet rejoined.   " When you are satisfied that it *is* the young lady—as you shall be—I call upon you as men of honour to withdraw."

" O yes, we'll retire," all the young men replied, laughing, except Gage.

" And we'll take Monthermer along with us," Beau Freke said. " Your interview shan't be interrupted."

" 'Sdeath ! if I thought there *would* be an interview I'd spoil it," Gage cried.

" Poh ! poh ! let things take their course," Beau Freke whispered.   " If she meets him, it will cure your silly passion for her.   If not, you will win a thousand pounds.   Either way you are benefited."

Gage was not quite convinced by this reasoning, but he suffered himself to be tranquillised by it.

Just then the door suddenly burst open, and Bellairs rushed in with a small packet in his hand, exclaiming—" I've got it ! here it is, sir !"

Aghast at the sight of the assemblage, he let the packet fall, and would have beaten a hasty retreat, had not Gage commanded him to stay.

" What have you dropped there, sirrah ?" the young gentleman demanded.   " Give it to me."

" I beg pardon, sir," the valet replied, tremblingly handing him the packet.   " I didn't know Mr. Fairlie was engaged, or I wouldn't have intruded in this way."

" Your master will excuse you, I am persuaded, when he learns that you have come on urgent business," Mr. Fairlie remarked, not at all disconcerted.   " Here, take this money," he added, giving him a bank-note, " to the person who is waiting for it, and bring me a receipt." And as the valet joyfully retired, he observed with admirable self-possession to Monthermer—" I don't think you need open that packet, sir. It won't interest you much. It consists merely of a heap of old bills which have been accidentally mislaid."

"Why didn't you tell me so at first, Fairlie, and then I would never have touched it?" Gage cried, tossing the packet to him in supreme disgust. "Bills! faugh! nothing disgusts me so much as a bill."

"I'm quite of your opinion, Monthermer," Brice Bunbury exclaimed. "Nothing is so intolerably annoying as a bill. By Jove! I can't bear the sight of one."

"Then you shan't be further troubled by these," Fairlie observed, locking up the packet.

"Hark! the dinner-bell, gentlemen," Gage exclaimed; "I hope your appetites will not fail you."

"Most assuredly mine will not, for I never felt in better cue," Brice replied. "I shall do justice to all the good things, and not flinch from the burgundy. By Jove! that clos-de-vougeot is magnificent, Monthermer."

"Enchanted you like it. Allons, messieurs," Gage said, leading the way.

Beau Freke and Sir Randal lingered for a moment behind the others.

"We've had a narrow escape. What do you think that packet contained, Sir Randal?" Fairlie remarked.

" I guess—my lost pocket-book. I at once suspected the truth, and was terribly afraid lest Monthermer should open it. Burn it, Fairlie. I shall be more careful in future what I put down—and what letters I keep."

"Ay, you were highly imprudent, as I told you, to keep mine, and I'm very angry with you for doing so," Beau Freke observed. "However, we've no time to talk now. The grand coup will be made this evening, Fairlie. We shall ply him with wine as much as we can."

"He wants little persuasion to drink," the steward replied; "and I have told the butler to put out some of his favourite claret. It will fire his veins."

"We shall have no difficu   then," Sir Randal remarked.
"Egad! Fairlie, I must say this is a clever contrivance of yours to
get rid of young Poynings, who, if he had obtained admittance to
the house, might have given us trouble. We shall now be able
to fasten a quarrel upon him before he has an opportunity of
explanation."

"An admirable device, o' my conscience," Beau Freke said;
"but all Fairlie's schemes are admirable. But we must go. Do
you not dine with us, Fairlie?"

"No; these late dinners do not suit me," the steward replied.
"I must keep a clear head. I will join you before you begin
to play."

Hereupon the two gentlemen withdrew, and the steward
once more left alone.

VIII.

HOW GAGE LOST A FEW THOUSANDS AT BASSET.

A BETTER dinner could not be than that to which Gage and his friends sat down. Just the sort of easy unceremonious entertainment that the hard-drinking bloods of the last century delighted in; and that might have found favour even with some of the fast young men of the present generation. Restraint was banished from that festive board. No need for the host to bid his guests make themselves at home. A week's experience of his princely hospitality had taught them they might do so; and this was just what they liked.

But though there was no restraint, it must not be imagined there was no display. On the contrary, the dinner was magnificently served, entirely on plate of silver, and the sideboard was gorgeously arrayed. A crowd of lacqueys in rich liveries were in attendance, marshalled by Pudsey and Bellairs. Delicacies the most refined, wines the most exquisite, furnished forth the banquet. The seasons were anticipated; and though it was still early spring, the richest fruits of summer regaled the guests.

Habitual self-indulgence had made Gage an epicure, and a simple diet would have been as distasteful to him as it would have been to Lucullus. He enjoyed eatables for their costliness and rarity as much as for any other quality; a new dish was a new pleasure to him; and he cared not what expense he incurred in gratifying his palate. On this occasion some highly-seasoned Spanish ragoûts, described by Beau Freke, made their first appearance, and were much admired,—especially by the young Amphitryon—only they made him thirsty, and induced him to drink an unusual quantity of claret: thus probably accomplishing the main object of their introduction.

If there was not a great deal of wit among the company, there was infinite merriment; and Gage, at all events, thought his friends exceedingly pleasant fellows. Their jests, it must be owned, were a little free, and they talked overmuch of their gallantries; but they one and all agreed that Monthermer was the best fellow breathing, and confidently predicted that he would attain the highest pinnacle of fashionable distinction, and become the theme of general admiration; that pleasures and successes of every kind awaited him on his return to town; and that his conquests amongst the fair sex would be numberless. All this adulation was swallowed by Gage as readily as the claret, and it produced much the same inebriating effect upon him. He really believed himself the irresistible hero described, little dreaming how his guests were laughing at him in their sleeve, and what schemes they were contriving against him.

Taking advantage of his excitement, Lord Melton so dazzled him with the notion of the vast sums to be won at Newmarket and elsewhere by racing, that he commissioned the noble blackleg to buy him half a dozen more horses, and to engage him a couple of jockeys; and his accommodating lordship, we may be sure, consented to help in these respects, with all the pleasure in life.

Meanwhile, the glasses were constantly replenished by the ever-attentive Pudsey. Jack Brassey and Nat Mist, confirmed topers both, took their wine kindly. Brice Bunbury found the clos-de-vougeot delicious—magnificent, by Jove!—and stuck to it. What a head Brice must have had! His veins were boiling with Burgundy, yet he looked quite steady. Beau Freke and Sir Randal, as we know, had work to do, and therefore fought shy of the claret, though it was of a renowned vintage, and in perfect order.

But it had now become quite evident that Gage had had enough for their purpose. If he drank more, he would be too far gone. An immediate move must be made, and the Beau accordingly rose, and proposed an adjournment to the drawing-room.

Some of the others would have willingly tarried a little longer, 1 t Gage was completely under Mr. Freke's control, and always ready to obey his behests. So the whole party went up-stairs—three or four of them with rather uncertain steps.

The drawing-rooms were brilliantly lighted up, as if for a much larger assemblage than the present, and card-tables were set out. Coffee served, after a brief chat they sat down to basset; Sir Randal acting as tailleur, and Brice Bunbury as croupier. Unluckily, Brice had no money, so Gage threw him his purse; but the twenty guineas it contained, being laid upon the tapis, were almost instantly afterwards swept off by Beau Freke. Gage's usual ill-luck attended him, and being heated with wine, he played recklessly, constantly doubling his stakes. Mr. Fairlie, who had joined the party in the drawing-room, and who, as the young man's cashier, made a note of his losses in his tablettes, warned him to desist—but this only inflamed him the more. He would go on. What was the loss of a few thousands to him? And, strange to say, from that moment the capricious goddess of chance deigned to cast a few smiles upon him. In an astonishingly short time he won back his losses, and exulted in the superiority of his own judgment over that of Fairlie. It had been well for him if he had stopped at this point. But he was now clearly in the vein, and must win. And so he did. He staked two hundred and fifty pounds and gained it. Bending the corner of his card, he went on, cried "A paroli,—sept, et le va!" and the winning card coming up again, made his gains seven hundred. Quinze-et-le-va followed, and gave him 1500*l.* Now he glanced triumphantly at Fairlie, but the latter merely shrugged his shoulders.

Everybody seemed excited by the progress of the game—everybody, except Sir Randal and Beau Freke, the former of whom held the bank. Gage turned down the third corner of his card. "A paroli,—trente, et le va." He was a winner of 3000*l.*

"Ha! ha! ha! who was in the right, you or I, Fairlie?" he cried, in tipsy tones. "Shall I go on, eh?"

"Just as you please, sir," the steward replied, evasively. "You had better not appeal to me. You don't heed what I say."

"Then, by heaven, I won't hesitate!" the young man exclaimed, bending the fourth corner of his card. "A paroli, soixante, et le va!"

This was the highest stake that could be made according to the rules of the game.

All looked at Sir Randal as he dealt the cards—quietly, gracefully, as if nothing at all depended on the turn of his fingers. Most of them knew what would occur, but still they liked to see it done, and Brice Bunbury, who was up to a trick or two, fancied he could see the cards shifted in the skilful dealer's hands. Gage appeared quite confident, and was preparing to deride Fairlie again, when suddenly his countenance fell.

Luck had deserted him. A knave came up. He had lost 6000*l.*

Without displaying the slightest excitement, Sir Randal stated the amount to Fairlie, who jotted it down in his book, and then, turning to Monthermer, the young baronet asked him if he wished to go on.

"No, I have had enough of this," Gage cried. "Confound it! the cards are always against me."

"You had better have been content with your first losses, sir," Mr. Fairlie drily remarked.

"Sir Randal ought to give you your revenge, Monthermer," Beau Freke interposed. "If you are tired of basset, we will try lansquenet or Spanish whist."

"No, no—let us play piquet," Gage rejoined. "I am luckier at that game than at any other."

"I am for Pope Joan," Brice Bunbury cried. "If Mr. Fairlie will lend me ten guineas, I will pay him out of my first winnings."

"Bad security, Mr. Bunbury. Shall I let him have the money, sir?" the steward inquired of Gage.

"Oh! of course," the good-natured young man returned.

And Brice became the possessor of a second purse.

"I'm for bankafalet, or grand trick-track," Lord Melton said. "Sit down De Meschines."

"Ay, sit down, Sir Randal," Gage cried. "You shan't desert us. We'll play at piquet, bankafalet, or what you please."

"I'm sorry to baulk your humour, Monthermer," Sir Randal replied, glancing at his watch. "But remember, I have to meet a young lady. It only wants a few minutes to the appointed hour."

"You may as well stay where you are," Gage rejoined, with a derisive laugh. "She won't come.'

"You will alter your opinion, if you choose to accompany me. Though you failed, there is no reason why another should not be successful."

"Especially a person of such irresistible attraction as Sir Randal de Meschines," Gage rejoined, somewhat piqued.

"Pshaw! don't quarrel about a woman," Beau Freke interposed. "We are all going with you, Sir Randal."

"To assist at my triumph," the young baronet said.

"Rather to witness your disappointment," Gage returned.

"Before you go, let me make one observation, gentlemen," Mr. Fairlie said. "I have changed my opinion. I have reason to think my daughter will go to the Ivy Tower."

"To be sure she will!" Sir Randal exclaimed, triumphantly, "I told you I should win my wager."

"You are mistaken, Sir Randal," Fairlie said. "You will *not* win it. Her object is not to meet you."

"'Sdeath! sir—what do you mean? Has any one dared to interfere with my appointment?"

"You will allow the young lady to choose for herself, I presume, Sir Randal," Gage remarked. "If she prefers some one else to you, it cannot be helped—ha! ha!"

"May I ask who is the favoured individual?" Beau Freke inquired.

"If I am rightly informed, and I believe my intelligence to be correct, it is Mr. Arthur Poynings," Fairlie answered.

The mention of this name produced an instantaneous effect upon Gage, rousing him to sudden anger.

"Arthur Poynings!" he exclaimed. "Does he presume to come hither? But the thing appears incredible. How should an appointment have been made with him?"

"Clare, I regret to say, has written to his sister Lucy, expressing a wish to have an interview with Arthur this evening, at the very spot and hour appointed by Sir Randal. I have seen the messenger who brought back an answer from Miss Poynings stating that her brother would come."

F

" If this be true, he shall have reason to regret the visit," Gage exclaimed.

" Let us go, or I shall be late," Sir Randal said. " I must not keep a lady waiting. This is my affair, Monthermer."

" No, it is mine," the other rejoined. " I will yield my right of quarrel to no man. The affront is to me, if this puppy presumes to come here uninvited, and he shall render me an account of his conduct."

" The real affront is to me, sir," Fairlie remarked ; " and I trust you will allow me to settle the affair in my own way."

" By ordering him off the premises, eh ? Very business-like and proper, no doubt, Fairlie, but scarcely consistent with my notions as a gentleman. No, no; I shall pursue a different course. Either Arthur Poynings shall apologise for his intrusion, or we cross swords. No interference, De Meschines. I am master here. Allons, messieurs. To the Ivy Tower !"

On this, the whole party hurried down the great staircase, and snatching up their hats, canes, and swords in the hall, issued forth into the open air, pursuing their way in silence over lawns as soft as velvet, in the direction of the ruins of the old Castle.

IX.

THE IVY TOWER.

THE Ivy Tower, towards which the several personages connected with this history appear to be tending, had been the keep of the ancient Castle, standing at the south-east angle of the vast pentagonal structure; but the intervening walls having long since disappeared, it was now left alone. Circular in form, loftier, and of greater dimensions than the other square towers flanking the sides of the Castle, it presented an exceedingly picturesque appearance, with its embattled and machiolated summit, its narrow slits of windows, its hoary masonry relieved by the bright green of the ivy, whose folds encircled it like the coils of a gigantic boa-constrictor, and the brushwood allowed to grow near its base. Some of its chambers were in tolerable preservation, and had been occasionally used for festive purposes by the late lord of the mansion; and beneath it, hewn out of the solid rock, were profound and gloomy vaults, kept constantly closed, and connected with which were many dismal legends of captivity and torture in the olden time. Common rumour, indeed, affirmed the tower to be haunted; and if old wives' stories were to be credited, many terrible crimes had been committed in its subterranean chambers; so no wonder apparitions were seen there. Wiser folk, however, knew that these spirits had a good deal to do with the sea-coast, and certain Dutch luggers which landed kegs of brandy and hollands, or other contraband articles, on dark nights. Squire Warwick laughed at the ghost-stories, and gave little heed to them; but Gage, when a boy, shared in the popular belief, and never could be prevailed upon to visit the ruins after nightfall. Terrace-walks, commanding lovely views of the park and the surrounding country,

had been laid down on the crest of the scarps on either side of the
ancient keep, while these steep slopes, rugged in places with project-
ing rocks, were mostly covered with hazels, alders, and briars.   The
level space, planed by the builder of the castle to form an inner
court, had been long since converted into a garden, compassed on
two sides by grey and mouldering walls, with here and there a
tree springing from out them, and still flanked at each angle by
an old square ruinous tower.   The principal approach to this
garden was by means of a flight of stone steps, mounting by easy
gradations from the lower grounds; but there were other and
readier, though steeper, paths for those who chose to avail themselves of them.   At the foot of the eminence, on which the
ancient Castle was situated, the park spread out in all the beauty
and the pomp of lengthening avenues, sweeping glades, and venerable and majestic groves.

It was by a side-path, cut through the brushwood and dwarf
timber covering the most precipitous part of the slopes, that Arthur
Poynings, after quitting Mark Rougham, and entering the lower
garden, as already described, ascended, with an agile step, to the
terrace-walk leading to the Ivy Tower.   He looked around, but
no one was visible.   How beautiful was the scene before him!—
how soothing, how calm!   How solemn seemed the brown woods
below, with the grey park beyond them, the more distant objects
lost in obscurity and mist, but all hushed in deep repose!   How
reverend appeared the ruins close at hand!   Yet he involuntarily
turned from the contemplation of this tranquillising scene towards the adjoining mansion, the sight of which at once changed
the current of his thoughts, and troubled them anew.   Its windows were brilliantly illuminated, showing that its young lord was
holding his customary revels within.   Folly and vice there held
court, and unless they could be banished, the ruin of the reckless
youth was certain.   That proud structure, with its rich domains,
held by his family for centuries, would pass away from him.
But what was he to Arthur, that Arthur should put forth his
hand and save him?—A friend—no!   A rival,—ay!   Let him
perish.   He deserved his fate.   But again Lucy's gentle intercessions
came to mind, and the young man's better feelings prevailed.

Just then, nine o'clock was struck by a clock in a building at the left of the mansion, and presently afterwards two female figures could be descried at the head of the steps communicating with the terrace. Arthur instantly flew towards them, but as he drew near he was puzzled by their appearance, and hardly knew which of the two was Clare, until her well-known accents dispelled his doubts.

"You do not recognise me, I perceive," she said, with a slight laugh, and removing the hood which concealed her features; "the truth is, I have disguised myself in Lettice Rougham's cloak, and have given her my manteau and hat to wear."

"And very well they become me, I'm sure, miss," Lettice interposed; "and I declare you never looked better than you do in my village-cloak. Joyce Wilford used to call me little Red Riding-Hood, when I first put it on. You recollect Joyce, Mr. Arthur?"

"What is the meaning of this masquerading?" Arthur inquired, without noticing Lettice's question.

"You shall learn in a moment," Clare replied; "but tell me! —have you seen any one here?"

"Did you expect some one besides myself?" Arthur rejoined, in surprise. "Explain yourself, quickly, I beseech you, Clare."

"You are very impatient; but indeed I must give you an explanation, and I am glad to be able to do so without interruption. In my letter to Lucy I mentioned the annoyance I have experienced from an impertinent coxcomb, Sir Randal de Meschines. He has had the audacity to make an appointment with me here this evening."

"Here! You amaze me!"

"And at this very hour, Mr. Arthur," Lettice remarked. "Isn't it odd? We were afraid you two gentlemen might meet, and a quarrel ensue, and then we should have enough to do to separate you."

"How can Sir Randal have dared to make such an appointment with you, Clare,—unless—— ?"

"I forgive you the unjust suspicion, Arthur, because you do not know Sir Randal."

"Yes, you don't know Sir Randal at all, Mr. Arthur," Lettice interposed, "or you wouldn't wonder at his assurance. Mr. Trickett is nothing to him."

"Don't stay here, Arthur," Clare said, "or we may be observed Let us go on to the tower. Lettice will keep watch. Don't be disquieted, but come along"

"You quite perplex me, Clare," the young man replied, following her as she tripped along, ever and anon casting a glance over her shoulders. Just as they gained the screen of the dwarf trees heretofore described as growing at the base of the tower, the slender and graceful figure of Sir Randal could be distinguished at the head of the steps.

"Answer me, Clare," Arthur cried, not altogether satisfied— "are you interested in this young man?"

"In Sir Randal—not in the least. My desire is to effect his expulsion from this house, and I trust I may never behold him again."

"Then remain where you are, and let me have a few words with him."

"Not unless you promise me not to provoke him, or to treat what he may say with the contempt and indifference it deserves."

"You now ask more of me than I can fulfil, Clare. An opportunity unexpectedly offers of getting rid of one of the most dangerous of these schemers, and I must not let it slip. Let me go, I pray of you."

"This is what I dreaded. Arthur, I beseech you not to expose yourself. I shall be wretched if anything happens to you."

"Why you have brought me here for this express purpose, Clare, and now you would have me turn aside at the first show of risk. What is there in this coxcomb so formidable that I should fear him? Let me confront him."

"Not yet—not yet! till I have spoken," she cried, laying her hand upon his arm to detain him.

But before proceeding further, let us see how little Lettice Rougham played her part. On drawing near, Sir Randal commenced in a very impassioned strain, but could not elicit a word from her in reply, for though she longed to talk, she feared to betray herself. At last, however, the impulse was too strong, and she hazarded a whisper. There was little in it, but the little there was gave the young rake encouragement, and he became more ardent than ever. His feigned passion was not without effect on the poor girl's susceptible bosom, and she secretly confessed that the tenderness of his accents would melt a heart of stone. When he took her hand, she did not attempt to withdraw it. Her face was averted from him, but she felt a great inclination to look round.

"Am I to interpret your silence as favourable to my hopes?" Sir Randal said. "Unless I have a distinct disavowal from your own lips, I shall believe you share the passion you have inspired."

"H..> very pretty," Lettice thought—"Joyce couldn't talk so. Heigho!"

"Your sighs confess it. Speak! speak, my charmer, and make me the happiest of mortals.'

"What must I say?" Lettice murmured, in very subdued tones.

"Say you love me—say you love no one else."

"But I can't say that," Lettice rejoined, still in a whisper, "because it wouldn't be true."

"What do I hear? Surely you cannot nourish any regard for that clownish Arthur Poynings?"

"Hush! not so loud. You may be overheard."

"Overheard! Are there eavesdroppers near us?—Ah! I comprehend. The impudent puppy is at hand—concealed near yonder tower. Come with me, and you shall see how I will treat him."

"Oh! no—not there—don't take me there. I won't go. You mustn't fight. Indeed, you mustn't," Lettice cried, vainly attempting to hold back, as he dragged her along.

Just then, a loud burst of laughter was heard, and several persons were seen emerging from the covert on the side of the lopes. This merry crew had evidently gained the terrace by the same path as Arthur.

"Mercy on us!" Lettice exclaimed, "that's Mr. Monthermer's voice. I wouldn't for the universe he found me here. Do let me go, sir, I beg of you."

"Excuse me if I detain you a moment longer, my angel," Sir Randal replied, still keeping fast hold of her. "I happen to have a wager dependent upon our meeting, and Mr. Monthermer and the other gentlemen must be satisfied that you have really been condescending enough to grant me an interview."

"And what was the wager, may I ask?" Lettice said.

"Oh! a mere trifle. But I felt so certain you would not dis-appoint me, that I would have hazarded thousands upon the issue," Sir Randal replied. "I betted that you, Miss Fairlie, would meet me here, according to my appointment—and I have won."

"Ha! ha! ha!" Lettice broke out, unable to refrain from laughter

"You appear diverted by what I have told you," Sir Randal remarked.

"I am indeed—excessively diverted," Lettice rejoined, laughing more heartily than ever. "How very droll it is, to be sure—ha! ha! ha!"

"I see nothing so very droll in it," Sir Randal observed; "but I am glad you are amused."

"There must be some mistake here," Gage cried, hastening to-wards them. "I can never believe Clare Fairlie would conduct herself with so much levity. Ah! 'tis as I suspected. You are duped, Sir Randal—duped!"

"Duped!—impossible!—Nay, madam, I must insist upon be-holding your face."

"Well, if I must, it can't be helped," Lettice rejoined, taking off her hat, and fully disclosing her pretty features; "I never told you I was Miss Fairlie, sir."

"No, but you led me to believe as much," Sir Randal rejoined "As I live, a very pretty girl. I don't know that I haven't gained by the exchange. Who the deuce is she?"

"Miss Fairlie's lady's maid, Lettice, sir, at your service," the little soubrette replied, with a curtsey.

This announcement occasioned shouts of laughter at the young baronet's expense. The merriment was rather increased than dimi-nished as a stalwart personage, who had drawn near the group unperceived, now stepped forward, and claiming the damsel as his daughter, demanded rather gruffly what she was doing there? On seeing him, Lettice looked a good deal surprised, but nowise dis-concerted, and in reply to his inquiry, said rather saucily,

"What are *you* doing here, father?"

"You shall learn that presently, mistress," Mark replied "Meanwhile, please to come wi' me. You ha' stayed ower long i' this disorderly house."

" No such hurry, father! I'm quite as good a judge as you what's right and what s wrong. I shall please myself about accompanying you, and I've no such intention at present, 1 can promise you."

" Egad! the lass has a rare spirit!" Sir Randal cried, approvingly. " You perceive, my good friend, that your presence is altogether unnecessary, and I would recommend your immediate retirement."

" Not without my daughter," Mark rejoined, in a determined tone. " It is from such roarin' lions as you I desire to guard her. And if any one attempts to detain her after this notice, let him look to hisself," he added, striking the ground with his knotty buckthorn stick.

" Your challenge is accepted, friend," Sir Randal replied. " Your daughter is a charming creature, and shall stay with me as long as she thinks proper."

" Now then, Lettice, be ye comin', wench ?" Mark cried.

" A moment, father, and I *will* come," said the damsel, in a tone calculated to appease the angry yeoman; adding in a whisper, " that is, if you hold to your mind about taking me with you. What are you thinking about to go on so ? You seem to have taken leave of your senses, you silly man. Can't *you* trust me if Miss Clare trusts me ?"

" Oh! she put ye up to this work, eh?" Mark said, rather confused.

" To be sure! and you'll spoil all, if you don't take care. Why, if there isn't Mr. Fairlie coming up to have a word with you."

" Nay, if he be here, I'd better make myself scarce. that's sartin," Mark rejoined.

But it was too late. The steward was upon him before he could move off.

" Good even to you, Rougham. Be pleased to let us know what business has brought you here?" the steward said.

" I will explain my business to the Squire, Muster Fairlie, but not to you," the yeoman rejoined.

" O, dear father, don't answer him so," Lettice whispered " Moderate your speech."

" Tut, lass, I'm not afeard on him

"The Squire will see how his kindness to you has been abused, when he finds you have come here with Mr. Arthur Poynings," Fairlie remarked.

"If this is true, Mark, I shall indeed be deeply offended with you," Gage said.

"Offended or not, your honour, I cannot deny it," Mark replied. "I did come wi' him."

"He avows it, you see, sir," Fairlie cried, turning to Gage; "he glories in his ill conduct."

"I'm right glad to ha' come here to-night, if you mean that, Muster Fairlie, becos it gies me an opportunity o' tellin' his honour that he hasn't a better friend, nor one as 'll stand by him more stoutly through thick and thin, than Muster Arthur."

"And where may my good friend be?" Gage demanded. "I look for him in vain."

"I dunnot doubt but he'll show hisself at the proper time," Mark replied; "and when he does, I trust your honour wunnot turn a deaf ear to him. You may be quite sure he has your true welfare at 'eart."

"Oh! I'm quite sure of it," Gage rejoined, ironically. "I'm infinitely obliged to him for the trouble he has taken on my account, and shall not fail to thank him."

"If you would like to speak to him, sir," Lettice said, taking his words literally, "you'll find him near the tower, with my young lady. I'm quite certain they're only talking about you, sir—only about you."

"They do me great honour, I must say, and I shall be sorry to interrupt their pleasant discourse, be it about whom or what it may; but as I wish to have a few words with Mr. Arthur Poynings, I must crave your pardon for a few moments' absence, gentlemen."

"Will you not allow me to go with you, Monthermer?" Sir Randal said.

"Or me?" Beau Freke added.

"Neither, I thank you," Gage rejoined, in a tone that did not admit of dispute.

But, in spite of his expressed wishes to the contrary, Fairlie made a movement to accompany him, but the young man impatiently waved him back, and proceeded towards the tower alone.

X.

As Gage approached the tower, Arthur, who was standing near the entrance with Clare, came forward, and greeting him courteously, put forth his hand; but Gage refused to take it, and haughtily returning the other's salutation, drew himself up, and said:

"I am sorry to interrupt this tête-à-tête, but having accidentally heard that Mr. Arthur Poynings was here, I wished to satisfy myself of the correctness of the information. I scarcely believed it, for I did not think it possible that a gentleman would voluntarily intrude himself upon the privacy of another, when no intimacy subsisted between them to warrant the liberty. I have not forgotten the answer I received from Sir Hugh Poynings when I did myself the honour to invite him and his family to visit me on my return home; and after the insulting message then sent, and which nothing but Sir Hugh's age caused me to overlook, I little expected that the first time I should see his son would be in the character of a nocturnal intruder upon my domains."

"I excuse your rudeness, Gage," Arthur replied, "and I trust you will permit me to explain the motive for my apparent intrusion."

"If an apology is necessary, it is due from me," Clare interposed, "since it was by my invitation that Arthur came hither."

"Enough," Gage rejoined, bowing stiffly. "You exercise full control here, Miss Fairlie; and consequently, your friend is quite welcome to remain as long as his company may be agreeable to you. I have only to express my regrets at disturbing you, but you may rely upon it you shall experience no further annoyance."

"Stay, Gage," Clare cried; "you must not go till you have heard what we have to say. You are under an entire misapprehension as to the object of this meeting between Arthur and myself. No change whatever has taken place in my sentiments towards him; but, as an honourable gentleman and a true friend, he consented, at my instance, to come here for the purpose of aiding me with his counsel."

"Had I not heard this from her own lips, I should not have thought it possible Miss Fairlie could need advice," Gage rejoined. sarcastically; "but as she affirms it, doubtless it is so; and if a counsellor must be chosen, none could be better qualified by age and experience for the office than Mr. Arthur Poynings."

"None could be better qualified than he by old friendship for the person I desire to serve," Clare said. "He has known him and loved him from infancy—loves him still, though their friendship has been overclouded. Arthur and he were brought up together, Gage, and were once like brothers—nay, I have heard that, in years gone by—happy, innocent years—they sported together, in gamesome childhood, on these very terraces, and chased each other amongst yonder ruins. It may be you remember such days, Gage. If you have forgotten them, Arthur has not. He sees the boy he loved become a man—unhappily estranged from him, but not less dear. He sees him surrounded by false friends—by masked enemies, by sharpers, parasites—all such creatures as make rich men, who submit to their practices, their prey. He sees his friend in danger, and heedless of their present coldness, thinking only of the past, flies, at the first summons, to his assistance."

"This is true, Gage," Arthur said. "Every word Clare has uttered reflects a sentiment of mine. You are the friend I have come to serve."

"Upon my word, I ought to feel greatly obliged by the exhibition of so much zeal—so totally unmerited on my part," Gage rejoined; "but my satisfaction is somewhat tempered by the reflection that no such officious interference was necessary in my behalf; and I am therefore inclined to think it unwarrantable. I am not in the habit of meddling with other people's concerns, and I therefore conceive myself entitled to the privilege of being let alone."

"You view the matter in a wrong light, Gage," Clare said, "and do not give Arthur and myself credit for the motives that actuate us. Having spoken for him, let me speak now for myself. You have never had reason to doubt my sincerity, and on this occasion, more than any other, ought not to question it. My desire to serve you makes me bold—and has induced me to transgress certain limits of decorum which I ought not to have passed. Otherwise this meeting between Arthur and myself would not have taken place. But it was appointed by me to devise some scheme for your deliverance!"

"My deliverance!" Gage exclaimed, with a bitter laugh. "One would think I was a wild beast caught in the hunter's toils. On my soul, I was not aware I was so entrapped."

"It is the very unconsciousness that increases the danger by which you are menaced," Clare rejoined. "If your eyes can be opened to it, there will be nothing to apprehend. By all the affection you have professed for me—by any feelings you may still entertain for me—I beseech you to pause in your headlong career, which, if pursued, can only lead to destruction. Be worthy of him from whom you sprung, and of your ancient race, and do not be the first Monthermer to dishonour the name."

A pause ensued, during which it was evident the young man was struggling with his feelings. At last, he broke out with fresh impatience: "I will not be tutored thus by man or woman. I will not give up my friends at the bidding of any one. You have an answer, Clare. As to Mr. Arthur Poynings, I have nothing more to say to him."

"O, Gage, I had hoped better of you," Clare cried, reproachfully. "Reflect! this may be the turning-point of your career."

"Listen to your good angel," Arthur said.

"I will listen to no one, so enjoined," Gage retorted. "If I am a degenerate Monthermer, at least no one shall command me here."

"Gage! Gage! for the last time I implore you to listen to me," Clare cried.

"Change the subject of your discourse, and I will listen to you with pleasure; but you keep too much upon one theme to be altogether agreeable."

"Clare, I can be of no further use to you," Arthur cried. "This besotted young man does not deserve the interest you take in him. If there had been any good in him, it must have been roused by your zealous kindness. Leave him to his worthless associates, and to the ruin and disgrace they will infallibly bring upon him."

"You talk of concealed enemies, sir," Gage said; "I am glad you yourself have at last thrown off the mask, and displayed your features in their true light. I like you better as a foe than friend, and though I leave you now, it will not be long, I hope, ere another meeting shall be arranged between us."

"When and where you please, sir," Arthur rejoined.

The tone of defiance in which these words were spoken could not be misunderstood; and Clare saw that a duel between the two young men was imminent. She almost despaired of preventing it, but an effort must be made.

"Arthur, for my sake, do not let this quarrel proceed," she cried. "Gage, I entreat of you to be reconciled to your old friend. If I fail in all else, let me accomplish thus much."

"My friends await me, madam," Monthermer rejoined, coldly. "I have already trespassed too much upon their patience."

"Do not detain him longer, I beg of you, Clare," Arthur said. "It were a pity not to give his 'friends' the opportunity they desire of fleecing him. On my faith, I never saw so willing a victim '

"Then spare him," Clare cried—" spare him these bitter taunts, which wound me more than they do him

"Harkye, Mr. Arthur Poynings," Gage said; "you talk fiercely and freely enough in the presence of a lady. Will it please you to accompany me, and repeat some of the choice epithets you have so liberally bestowed upon my friends in their hearing?"

"Willingly," the young man replied.

"You shall not stir, Arthur," Clare cried.

"He need not give himself the trouble," Gage said, "for here they come. They are tired of waiting for me, I suppose.—Just in time, gentlemen," he added, as the others drew near.

"Just in time for what?" Sir Randal demanded, who was a little in advance of his companions.

"To hear your praises sung by this young gentleman," Gage replied.

" I will endeavour not to disappoint your expectations, gentlemen," Arthur said ; " but before any further remarks are made,
I must request Mr. Fairlie, whom I see amongst you, to take
charge of his daughter, and remove her from a scene which must
be distressing to her."

" O, Arthur, forgive me for bringing you into this great peril,"
Clare tremblingly murmured.

" Have no fears for me," the young man rejoined. " Take her
hence, and quickly, sir," he said, consigning her to Fairlie, who
led her away.

On seeing her mistress depart in this way, Lettice instantly
quitted her father, and followed Clare towards the house. If
truth must be told, Mark was by no means sorry to be rid of her,
as in spite of his anger and frowns, she had been coquetting with
some of the gentlemen near her, and her absence enabled the
honest yeoman to take up a post beside Arthur.

XI.

ALL altercations were suspended till Clare was out of hearing.
When this was understood to be the case, Sir Randal remarked
to Arthur, who was standing at a little distance from them, con-
versing in a low tone with Mark Rougham:

"Now, sir, you promised to treat us to something amusing.
We await it with impatience."

"I shall come to the point at once," Arthur rejoined. "I denounce you all as a pack of gamblers and sharpers. Mr. Monthermer best knows what his losses have been; but he does not
know that he has been unfairly dealt with—plundered, in fact,
by a set of rooks."

Great was the tumult that ensued on this address. Oaths and
denunciations of vengeance against the speaker exploded on all
sides. Canes were flourished, and many a blow must have fallen
upon him if he had not been shielded by the stout arm and buckthorn stick of Mark Rougham, who kept the assailants at bay.
Arthur, however, did not flinch for a moment, but manfully kept
his ground, till Gage took upon him to quell the disturbance.

"One at a time, gentlemen, if you mean to attack him, or I
shall be compelled to take his part," he cried; "he must have
fair play."

"You do not believe this foul-mouthed slanderer's assertions,
Gage?" Sir Randal exclaimed. "For my own part, I hurl them
back in his teeth—and give him the lie direct."

"And so do I," Beau Freke added. "If he has courage

enough to stand by his word, he will have enough to do before
morning. This affair must not cool on our hands."

"I am glad to hear it, gentlemen," Arthur rejoined. "I am
ready for one or all of you."

"Ay, let 'em come on," Mark roared, making his stick whistle
round his head; "we'll show 'em sport, I'll warrant 'em. They're
three to one; but three such puny creaters as them ben't equal
to one man, so the odds be in our favour—and besides that, we've
right o' our side. Take that, you dotterel," he added, striking
Brice's sword out of his grasp, and dealing him a rap on the
sconce which made him reel backwards, "and see how you like
the taste of a stout Suffolk cudgel."

"If I have any authority here," Gage cried, "I command an
instant cessation of hostilities on both sides. My words ought at
least to have weight with you, Mark, and I order you to be quiet.
You have broken poor Mr. Bunbury's head."

"Nay, your honour," the yeoman replied, with a laugh, "I
think it be too thick to be so easily broken; and if he loses a little
blood, it'll save the expense of calling in a barber-surgeon."

"A truce to your ill-timed jests. Mr. Arthur Poynings, you
have brought most serious charges against my friends."

"Do you still style them 'friends' after what I have stated?"
Arthur rejoined.

"You have heard me, and will therefore understand the importance I attach to your slander."

"I am indeed amazed," Arthur said. "I could not have believed in such blind infatuation without this proof of it."

"It be enough to make his father rise from the grave," Mark
groaned. "I be out o' a' patience wi' him."

"You are a noble fellow, Monthermer," Beau Freke said, pressing his hand, while the others were equally warm in their expressions of regard, "and only do us justice. Our characters as gentlemen, methinks, should have saved us from such imputations as
have been thrown out against us by this meddlesome and crazy
fellow—for crazy he must be to act in such a way. Nevertheless,
his folly and insolence must be punished."

"It must and shall be," Sir Randal cried. "I claim the right to
chastise him. His malice seemed chiefly directed against me."

G

"You do well to appropriate the sting of my remarks, sir," Arthur remarked. "If I made any distinction among you, it was that you, Sir Randal, had attained greater proficiency in your nefarious practices than your companions, and are therefore entitled to rank as leader."

"Look to yourself, sir," Sir Randal cried, foaming with rage, and drawing his sword. "Stand aside, fellow."

"Not a step nearer, sir, as you value a whole skin," Mark said; "you saw how neatly I sarved your friend just now, and I can disable you, as you'll find, before you can touch me; so stand back, or I be down upon you like a hammer."

"Sir Randal, you must give place to me in this affair," Gage said; "your turn may come by-and-by. I demand an apology from Mr. Arthur Poynings for his intrusion, and a retractation of the calumnies he has uttered against my friends."

"You shall have neither one nor the other, sir," Arthur rejoined. "I came here to serve you; and as to what I have said of your friends, so far from withdrawing the charges, I reiterate them with greater force than before."

"Well done!" Mark exclaimed—"that be plain speakin', at all events."

"No more words need be wasted," Gage cried. "Our present appeal must be made to our swords."

"To it, then," Sir Randal cried; "I am impatient to be at him. I would give a hundred pounds for your chance."

"You should not have it for two hundred," Gage replied, with a laugh. "But we must proceed like men of honour. Lord Melton, will you do me the favour to act as second to Mr. Arthur Poynings?"

"Willingly," his lordship replied, "on the understanding that if no one else manages to slit his weasand, I may have that pleasure myself."

Upon this he moved round to Arthur, and bowing to the young man, who ceremoniously returned the salutation, proffered his services as second, which were of course accepted. With some difficulty, Mark Rougham was induced to stand aside, and as he quitted his post he said to Gage,—"He wished his honour and Master Arthur could shake hands, and agree, and leave him to fight it out wi' the rest of 'em."

In a few moments more the combatants had made the requi site preparations, and having taken up a position, made their appeals, saluted each other, and stood on guard. The crescent moon rode high in the cloudless sky, affording light enough for their purpose. Gage was a very skilful swordsman, but being heated with the wine he had drunk, he did not observe proper measure and distance, and therefore more than once exposed himself, if Arthur had desired to take advantage of his indiscretion. But it was obviously the young man's wish to disarm him, and he contented himself for some time with parrying all Gage's feints and thrusts without making a reply. At length, he succeeded in his design; and battering Gage's point as the latter recovered with a stretched guard, flung down his sword.

"I own myself defeated," Monthermer cried. "You are a gallant enemy, Arthur, and I wish the quarrel might terminate here."

"Impossible!" Sir Randal exclaimed, "unless Mr. Poynings will admit he has spoken falsely and calumniously of us."

"That I will never do," Arthur rejoined; "and I am as anxious as yourself, Sir Randal, that the affair should proceed."

"Be it so," the young baronet said.

The same forms were gone through as in the first encounter; but, before saluting, Sir Randal measured with his eye his adversary's height and the length of his sword, and took up a distance accordingly. When the conflict began, he tried Arthur with appeals, beatings, disengages, and extensions, in order to judge of the thrusts he might deliver; but his designs were baffled by the dexterity with which all his feints were parried. Never for a moment did Arthur quit his adversary's blade — never for a moment did his prudence or firmness desert him—nor did he suffer a glance or a movement to betray his own designs. The combatants were so well matched, and both so wary, that it seemed impossible to foresee the issue of the strife. Cunning at length decided it. Sir Randal laid a snare for his opponent, pressing upon his blade, and turning his hand, as if about to parry the half circle, while Arthur sought to seize his blade inside. He then suddenly disengaged, and lounged over the arm. The

G 2

point of his weapon entered Arthur's breast, glancing along his
side, and the latter, feeling himself wounded and unable to continue the conflict, lowered the point of his sword.

" You are hurt, Arthur," Gage cried, rushing up, and catching
him ere he fell.

" Not much," the young man replied, in a faint voice, and trying to stanch the blood which was flowing from his side. " Give
me your arm, Mark Rougham; I can manage to reach your farm-
house."

" You mustn't think of it, Arthur," Gage replied. " You shall
be conveyed to the Castle, where instant assistance shall be procured, and every care taken of you. Lean on me."

" No arm but Mark's shall support me," the young man cried,
" and I will not be removed to your polluted dwelling. I would
rather die on the road."

The words were scarcely uttered, when a mortal faintness seized
him, and he sank to the ground insensible.

" Bear him to the Castle," Gage cried.

" Not so, your honour," Mark rejoined. " I am bound to see
his wishes fulfilled, and he shall not be taken there."

" Then do what you will with him, you obstinate fool,"
Monthermer rejoined. " Stay," he added; " I cannot suffer him
to perish thus. Take him into the tower, and attend to him there
till assistance is procured, and some means of transporting him to
Reedham can be obtained."

To this compromise Mark saw no objection, and accordingly,
with the help of Pudsey and Bellairs, who by this time had
approached the scene of action, the wounded young man, still in
the same inanimate condition, was borne to the interior of the
tower and carefully laid upon an old couch, which, with a few oak
chairs, formed the sole furniture of the chamber.

This done, Gage and his friends returned to the Castle.

XII.

NEWMARKET.

A FEW days after the occurrences last narrated, the party assembled at Monthermer Castle broke up; and Beau Freke and Sir Randal, perfectly satisfied with the result of their expedition into Suffolk, returned to their customary haunts in Saint James's, —richer by some thousands than when they left town a fortnight before. Though they had plucked the pigeon pretty handsomely, they had not done with him. Gage was to join them in London very shortly, when they counted on fleecing him far more extensively. Meanwhile, they committed him to the tutelage of Lord Melton, under whose auspices he was to make his entrance on the turf.

We have already said that the honourable personages, whom we have described as combining together for the purpose of plundering our thoughtless young hero, made it a rule not to interfere with each other's projects; not from friendship, but from a wholesome dread of retaliation and exposure. Thus the two principal schemers were forced to relinquish their prey for awhile, because it was a comrade's turn to deal with him; and the noble blackleg was allowed to carry off his prize to Newmarket without hindrance; while the rest—with the exception of Brice Bunbury— quitted the scene of action.

The arrangement met with no opposition from Mr. Fairlie, and for an especial good reason—all Lord Melton's secret gains, it was understood were to be shared with him.

No beneficial effect was produced upon Gage by Arthur Poyn-

ing's futile attempt to serve him.   The infatuated young man felt
incensed rather than obliged.   While admitting that Arthur had
displayed great courage, and somewhat reproaching himself for his
conduct towards one who professed so much zeal for him, and for
whom he himself had formerly entertained strong sentiments of
regard, he still could not forgive the liberty taken with him.
Neither did he attach the slightest credit to Arthur's statements.
We must, however, do him the justice to say that his mind was
much relieved when he learnt from the surgeon, who was hastily
summoned to attend the young man, that the sufferer's wound,
though severe, was not dangerous, and that in all probability he
would be perfectly recovered within a month.

As to Arthur, during the whole of the night succeeding his
duel with Sir Randal, he remained within the chamber of the Ivy
Tower; and after his hurt had been dressed, a further balm to his
anguish was afforded by the soothing attentions of Clare, whose
solicitude led her to visit him.   In company with Mark Rougham
and Lettice, she continued to watch by him till morning.   She
knew that her conduct might be misconstrued, but her feelings
of humanity overcame all scruples.   Besides, she could not
conceal from herself that she had been the cause of Arthur's disaster.
Ought she not, therefore, to tend him like a sister?   Ought she
not to make any sacrifice for one who had jeopardised his life for
her sake?

The next morning a litter was provided, and the wounded man
was safely transported to Reedam, where we must leave him for
the present.

Nowise discouraged by what had taken place, and ever confident
in his own powers of pleasing, Sir Randal persisted to the last in
pressing his attentions upon Clare, and after many unsuccessful
attempts to obtain another interview with her, succeeded upon one
occasion in momentarily barring her way as she traversed a corridor.
But she repelled him with so much loftiness and scorn that even he
felt abashed, and was forced to retire, amid the derisive laughter of
those who witnessed the scene.

Gage saw nothing more of her; and left the Castle without even
bidding her adieu.   His good angel had deserted him—just at a
time when her presence was most needed.

A new temptation awaited him: the same which assailed Saint Anthony, and which that devout personage himself had scarcely power to resist.

Owner of four race-horses, for each of which he had given a long price, master of two jockeys, reputed the cleverest of their class, and attended by a whole retinue of servants, our young hero arrived at Newmarket, eager to play a new part on the stage of life. He was accompanied by Lord Melton and Brice Bunbury, the latter of whom stuck to him like a leech. Gage's *début* on the turf was as brilliant as could be desired. It was the policy of the sporting peer to lure his dupe on by slight successes, till he was too far "in" to retreat. Gage liked the excitement of racing, and the reckless society he met amused him. He thought the members of the Jockey Club, who gladly admitted him amongst them, amazingly fine fellows. They drank hard; betted deeply; and swore lustily, whether they lost or won; and Gage followed the fashion, drinking, betting, and swearing like the rest.

In those days the habitual frequenters of horse-races were pretty much what they are at present—unprincipled, and unscrupulous enough; but generally, much more roguery was practised then than now. The jockeys were notoriously to be bought, and the trainers up to all sorts of tricks. Indeed, unless report belies them, these gentry are not yet entirely free from suspicion. But let this pass. Our business is with a time when the regulations of the turf was not so strict as at present, and though no doubt even then there were honourable exceptions, the majority of sporting men were sharpers and cheats. By this pack of scoundrels the appearance of Gage was hailed like a wealthy galleon by pirates on the Spanish Main. All were anxious to board him, and ease him of his treasure. But they were kept off for a time by Lord Melton, who had no idea of parting with even a modicum of his booty.

It was the first Spring Meeting, and Newmarket was exceedingly full—for though there were then no express trains, and scarcely any stage-coaches, people over whom the sporting mania was strong, rode almost incredible distances to witness a race. The two coffee-rooms in the town, where betters resorted, were daily crowded, and a tumultuous throng on horseback gathered outside the doors and open windows, vociferating to each other, or offering odds, in stentorian tones, to those inside.

Whenever Gage showed himself in these places he was eagerly beset by a swarm of these locusts, and tempted by all sorts of offers, but as Lord Melton kept constantly at his elbow, he managed to brush them off. The betting crew, as may be supposed, were indignant at such treatment, but they did not dare to resent it—hoping to make their game at some more favourable opportunity, when Lord Melton should have other fish to fry, and be less vigilant.

Everybody is aware there is no race-course like Newmarket, no turf so fine, or so favourable to all purposes of horsemanship, whether as regards the steed and his rider, or the spectators of the contest. It is a jockey's own fault, if he is fairly mounted, and does not ride well upon that wonderful heath, while the looker-on can scarcely place himself in such a position as not to command what is going on. Racing *is* racing at Newmarket. It is the business of the place. The people who flock thither are all sporting characters. Young or old, they belong to the same class. You almost trace a resemblance in feature amongst them—certainly a similarity of manner and deportment, while a particular expression of countenance is common to all. The freshman from Cambridge, the greenhorn from Bury St. Edmund's, the smart young buck from Ely, on his bit of blood, all look alike. So it was at the time of which we write—so it is now. Epsom and Ascot, with their vast assemblages, have a hundred different attractions, and to half the concourse even the Derby or the Cup may be a secondary consideration. But at Newmarket the race is *the* thing people come to see—and nothing else.

Hurrah then for Newmarket, and its incomparable course.

On a fresh spring morning, full of confidence and spirit, and rejoicing in the prospect of a capital day's sport, Gage rode forth from the town. He was splendidly mounted, and cut a gallant figure in his feathered hat and light green riding-dress laced with silver. His handsome features looked unusually animated. This was his third day at Newmarket, and he had already won a plate, a sweepstakes, and a cup—so he had not done amiss, and might well look satisfied. Hundreds of horsemen, on all sorts of animals, from the stout roadster to the thorough-bred hunter, from the rough heavy cart-horse to the sturdy punch, were moving in the same direction as himself. Almost all of them were talking loudly, and Gage could hear his own name coupled with that of his horse, Comus, frequently mentioned in terms that seemed to imply he was likely to be a winner.

To explain this, we must mention that Gage had matched Comus against Captain Dashwood's Lightfoot, for a thousand pounds, and the race was about to come off on that day. The match had been made at Lord Melton's suggestion, so of course Gage felt quite safe, and, consequently, had backed his own horse to a large amount. Lord Melton backed him too—at least he so affirmed, and displayed his book in proof of the assertion. Comus was to be ridden by that trump of a jockey Nat Sharp—and Nat had assured his master with an oath that he would win the race for him, wishing " he might break his neck if he didn't do it."

Gage was accompanied by Lord Melton and the everlasting Brice, and a few minutes placed the trio upon the heath, which spread out before them in every direction for miles.

The young man, we have said, was in unwonted spirits, laughing and jesting with Brice, who, exhilarated like his patron by the scene, and the fresh air, was equally gleeful—but Lord Melton, who smiled rarely, maintained his customary character for taciturnity. His lordship's hard dry features had little mobility about them—and nothing showed what was passing within but an occasional glance from his keen, quick, grey eye.

Just as Gage was about to indulge his impatient steed with a gallop across the heath, he was checked by a light gay laugh behind him, and turning at the sound was greeted by the sight of the most lovely creature he had ever beheld.

Turn away, young man, and gaze not upon her, for this is the temptress you ought to shun. See! she spreads her wiles for you, and you will not heed the warning, but are already ensnared by her devices.

The temptress appeared in the guise of a young and exquisitely-beautiful woman, with eyes of tenderest summer blue, fair hair, a complexion of transparent clearness slightly tinged with delicate bloom, ripe lips, and teeth of dazzling whiteness. A certain voluptuous character pervaded her countenance, and as she cast a soft enticing glance at Gage, he felt it penetrate to his heart's core.

She was richly and becomingly attired, and what could be seen of her figure left little doubt that it corresponded with the extreme beauty of her countenance. She was seated in an open carriage, and was accompanied by an elderly woman in a dark dress, who looked not unlike a duenna, as represented in Spanish comedy.

Close beside the carriage, and engaged in animated discourse with this bewitching syren, rode a handsome young man in a military dress. It was Gage's adversary in the coming race. The sight of Captain Dashwood, who nodded to him as he passed, at once apprised our hero that the lady could be no other than a beautiful actress, by whose matchless charms the gallant gentleman was known to be enthralled.

"It must be Peg Jenyns!" Gage exclaimed, as soon as the bright vision was gone. "No other woman could be so beautiful. What a happy fellow Dashwood must be."

"He has bought his happiness pretty dearly, as we all of us must, where pretty actresses are concerned," Brice Bunbury replied. "Peg has got leave of absence from Goodman's Fields, and arrived last night at Newmarket—just in time to see Dashwood lose his match."

"Or win it," Gage observed, with a laugh.

"Little chance of that," Lord Melton observed, drily.

"The thousand won't be Dashwood's only loss," Brice went on. "Peg Jenyns is a great gambler, and is sure to back Lightfoot, and the simpleton of course must find money for her bets."

"I should like to have a bet with her," Gage cried, eagerly.

"Nothing more easy," Brice rejoined. "She'll be delighted to make your acquaintance, I'm sure. She's an old friend of mine. I knew her when she acted at Tom Cibber's Booth at Bartholomew Fair and Southwark, and before her beauty set the town on fire, and drove poor Dashwood and twenty others wild. On second thoughts, I had better not introduce you to such a dangerous syren."

"Poh! nonsense. Let us ride after the carriage. I must have a little talk with her before the race begins."

XIII.

THE RACE.

A FAVOURABLE opportunity for Gage's introduction to the beautiful actress soon occurred. Her carriage almost immediately came to a halt, and approaching it, Brice Bunbury begged permission of its fair occupant to make known to her his friend, Mr. Monthermer. A gracious assent being accorded, our hero was presented in due form. Captain Dashwood did not look so well pleased as the lady, but just at this juncture receiving a sign from Lord Melton, who had followed hard upon the others, he was obliged to ride off with his noble friend towards the enclosure where the grooms were exercising the horses. A proficient in the art of love making, our hero exerted all his skill on this occasion. He did not attempt to conceal his admiration, but his eyes spoke far more eloquently than his lips. Mrs. Jenyns must have been inexperienced indeed, if she could not read his feelings in his glances. Poor Dashwood could not help casting a wistful look now and then in the direction of the carriage, and was evidently ill at ease.

Finding her new admirer showed no disposition to quit his post, Mrs. Jenyns, though by no means anxious to dismiss him, at length archly inquired, "If he did not mean to see his jockey mount?"

"No," Gage replied; "I leave all to Melton. I would rather spend five minutes with you than win the race."

"Vastly polite indeed. I appreciate the compliment. But no doubt you feel certain of success."

" Tolerably so. I'm in rather better luck than usual just now. Ten minutes ago, when I came upon the course, my mind was entirely fixed on the issue of the match. Now I am wholly indifferent to it."

" Well, if you are indifferent, I am not; and I should like to have a stronger interest in it than I feel at present."

" Shall we have a bet?"

" With all my heart. You back your own horse of course. What odds will you give me?"

" Nay, it must be an even bet, for the horses are well matched. A hundred to a hundred, if you please."

" Pshaw!—a mere bagatelle. Such a trifle would afford me no excitement."

" Make it any sum you please," Gage rejoined, laughing. " I won't refuse your challenge; and to say truth," he added, in a lower and tenderer tone, " I would rather lose than win."

" I don't believe you," she replied smiling. " The match is for a thousand. Our bet must be for the same amount."

" Agreed."

" I'll enter the bet in my book," Brice said. " Hark! the bell rings. By Jove! the horses are saddled—the jockeys are about to mount. Come along, Monthermer. Lord Melton is beckoning to you."

" Well, go and see what he wants," Gage replied—" I'm too agreeably occupied just now to attend to him."

" Any message to Nat?" Brice asked, preparing to start.

" Tell him to win. I've now another thousand dependent upon the race."

" No, tell him to lose, Mr. Bunbury. Say Peg Jenyns has betted against him—that will be enough."

" I'll deliver your message, madam," Brice replied, laughing, and galloping off.

" I almost wish Nat may take your hint," Gage said. " Were I in his place, I certainly should."

To this gallant remark the lady made no reply; but her heightened colour showed it was not lost upon her.

By this time the two jockeys had come out of the enclosure, and were cantering their horses along the course preparatory to the start. Nat wore a green jacket and white cap, while blue was the colour of Lightfoot's rider. As the two horses went past them, their glossy coats glistening in the sunshine, Comus displayed so many good points, and looked altogether so well, that Mrs. Jenyns could not help remarking—"Upon my word, Mr. Monthermer, your horse is magnificent. I begin to quake for my money."

Gage laughed, and a glance which he caught at the same moment from Nat's keen eye, made him think her apprehensions were not altogether unfounded. The horses now turned, and prepared to start. All was anxious expectation amidst the crowd near the ropes, and amongst the persons in the various equipages around.

In another moment the horses were off.

Off! and at a good pace, Comus leading, with Lightfoot close behind. Great was the hubbub; loud the clamour of the betters. Mrs. Jenyns was highly excited. Her cheek was flushed; her eyes were dilated like those of the thorough-bred steeds engaged in the contest. In her eagerness to obtain a good view, she sprang upon the seat of the carriage, and Gage had now an opportunity of noticing the admirable symmetry of her figure. He gave her his hand to support her in the somewhat dangerous position she had assumed — and her ardent pulsations quivered through his frame.

No advantage had as yet been gained by either horse. The speed increased, but they were still close together—close—close.

The crowd shouted, trying to stimulate the jockeys, who, obedient to the calls, flogged and spurred. They were now near at hand, and in another instant flew past the carriage as on the wings of the wind—so swiftly that the beholders could scarcely distinguish their colours.

But Mrs. Jenyns perceiving that Lightfoot did not gain upon his adversary, and could not repress her agitation. She trembled, and turned pale. Even to please her Gage could not now arrest Nat's headlong course.

The horses dashed on. Another moment would decide it. They were within a bow-shot of the winning-post—and tremendous shouts arose. "Comus wins!—Comus!—Comus!" Thinking

all lost, Mrs. Jenyns uttered an exclamation of despair, and dropped
the broidered kerchief she had been waving to Lightfoot. She
almost sank back into Gage's arms.

A new cry suddenly aroused her—and she was all spirit and
vivacity again. It was now "Lightfoot wins—Lightfoot!—Lightfoot!" And this continued till the struggle was decided.

Dashwood was proclaimed the victor,—his horse having gained
the race by a neck. Could Nat have held back, and have given
his opponent the chance? All the losers thought so, and hooted
and upbraided him, while the backers of Lightfoot cheered lustily,
and declared nothing could be fairer than the race. Huzza!
huzza!

And Mrs. Jenyns, too, cried "Huzza," as she sank exhausted
upon the seat.

How did Gage feel? Disappointed, no doubt; but he put a
very good face on the matter, and with a smile, which, under the
circumstances, did him credit, told Mrs. Jenyns he should be
quite compensated for losing the race, by the pleasure of paying his
bet. She did not affect to disbelieve him, but rewarded him with
a look which completed her conquest.

How much may a look convey!

O silly young man, to be so easily ensnared! Think of Clare,
or Lucy, either of whom is worthy of your love, and resist the
allurements of this syren.

"Who is the person eyeing us so attentively?" Mrs. Jenyns
asked, as she glanced around.

Gage looked in the direction indicated, and to his surprise
beheld Fairlie.

"It is my late guardian," he replied. "I didn't expect to
see him here. Pray come forward, Mr. Fairlie," he added to the
steward, "and let me make you known to Mrs. Jenyns. I have
lost some money to her, and you must act as my paymaster."

"I shall have great pleasure in doing so," the steward rejoined,
in his blandest tones. "May I ask the amount?"

"Only a thousand pounds," Gage said.

"Only a thousand, eh!—It's very well I came tolerably provided. I thought I might have some drafts upon me. I suppose
I shall likewise have an account to settle with Captain Dashwood?"

" Exactly--another thousand," Gage rejoined. And as Fairlie bowed and retired, he bent towards Mrs. Jenyns, and in a low impassioned tone said—" Do you really love Dashwood?"

" What a question, Mr. Monthermer?"

" The answer is easy—and your reply will influence my future career."

" I will tell you this evening. Come and sup with me at the Greyhound. You must go now. Bring Mr. Fairlie with you o supper. I will invite Lord Melton. Au revoir :"

XIV.

HOW MRS. JENYNS AND MR. FAIRLIE CAME TO AN UNDERSTANDING.

THE supper at the Greyhound was excellent, with all sorts of delicacies, and plenty of well-iced champagne, of which the guests with one exception, drank freely. The exception was Mr. Fairlie, who was abstemious as usual. Lord Melton and Brice Bunbury were likewise of the party and the duenna-like dame in black, who it appeared was a superannuated actress, Mrs. Clive by name—a beauty and a toast in her day—countenanced it with her presence. Intoxicated by his passion, as with the wine, Gage became each moment more enamoured of the fair actress, and paid her the most devoted attentions. On parting, he proposed a drive to Bury St. Edmund's on the morrow, and Mrs. Jenyns assented at once, without deigning to consult Captain Dashwood as to the arrangement.

As soon as the guests were gone, and they were alone together —for he seemed to consider poor Mrs. Clive as nobody—Dashwood said:

"I wish you joy of your new bargain, my dear. He is a deuced fine fellow, and enormously rich."

"Why yes, as you say, Harry, Mr. Monthermer is remarkably handsome—nearly as handsome as you, my pet—and what is still better, he is immensely rich. What a pity it is, Harry, you are so poor!"

"Who has made me poor, Peg?" he asked bitterly. "I was rich enough before I knew you."

"Well, well, never mind," she replied, with a gay laugh: "you were fated to be ruined by our sex, and I was the instrument appointed. I couldn't help it, and I executed my commission in the pleasantest manner possible. Let me see, we have just been nine months together—nine months!—almost an existence, Harry."

" You may pass double the time with Monthermer."

" No, I shan't. I shall tire of him in less than a year. I feel I shall. He's handsome, well-bred, good-natured, but somehow not entirely to my taste. I wonder whether I shall ever *really* love any man."

" Then you own you never did love me? Nay, you may deal frankly with me now."

" Well then, frankly, I never did; but don't distress yourself. I loved you as much as I shall ever love Monthermer."

" At all events, we part good friends?"

" I shall always be delighted to see you."

So saying, she gracefully extended her hand to him. Dashwood pressed it to his lips, and departed without another word.

Next morning, while Mrs. Jenyns was sitting in an elegant dishabille, sipping her chocolate, Mr. Fairlie was announced. After a few preliminary remarks the steward begged to have a few words in private with her, and Mrs. Clive, at a sign from Peg, withdrew.

" First of all, madam, let me give you the thousand pound which Mr. Monthermer lost to you yesterday," Mr. Fairlie said, producing a rouleau of notes.

" Your pardon, sir," the pretty actress said, with a captivating smile, which, if the steward's breast had not been adamant, must have melted it—" you only owe me half that sum."

" Only half, madam !—Surely Mr. Monthermer betted a thousand pounds with you?"

" Very true, Mr. Fairlie, and depend on it, I am not going to let him off. But between you and me the case is different. You have only to pay me five hundred."

" I don't exactly understand you, madam."

" Then you are duller than I fancy, Mr. Fairlie. Come, sir— there must be a proper understanding between us. I know you manage Mr. Monthermer's affairs——"

" You are right, madam. He commits them entirely to my direction."

" You can therefore control his expenses, if you please?"

" Very likely, madam—if I see occasion."

" You no doubt comprehend what my relations with Mr. Monthermer are likely to be?"

" I have some idea, madam."

" And you have no objection?"

" Hum!"

" You will have none—you can have none, when you have heard me out. Mr. Monthermer is violently in love with me."

" So it appears, madam."

" He will gratify all my caprices. He will ruin himself for my sake."

" It must be my care to prevent that consummation, madam——"

" I don't think you could prevent it, sir. At all events you won't."

" Won't, madam?"

" No; because it will be your interest to act in concert with me. You hold the strings of the young gentleman's purse, and when you open it for me, you can help yourself. In other words, you shall go shares with me."

" Upon my word, madam, you arrange matters in a most extraordinary way, I must own."

" Don't I?" she cried, laughing. " O, Mr. Fairlie, I see we shall be great friends. I understand your character perfectly. To tell you the truth, I came down to Newmarket—not to see poor Dashwood—but to meet Monthermer. I had heard all about him from Sir Randal de Meschines, who has just returned to town—and about you, too, my good sir. Sir Randal said he would introduce his friend when he came to town, but I resolved to be beforehand with him. And so I set off at once to Newmarket."

" Admirably managed, on my faith. But you woman have far more cleverness than we can ever pretend to."

" Yes, you will find me an efficient ally. Now tell me candidly, Mr. Fairlie. If I had taken the thousand pounds you offered me just now—and had not made my present proposition—would you not have done your best to defeat my object, and prevent this young man from attaching himself to me?"

" You deal in such a straightforward manner, madam, that I should be treating you most unworthily if I did not give a candid answer. I *would* have prevented the liaison. Nay, I will confess still more. Gage would have been with you before this, but I stopped him till I had had an interview with you, by the result of which I meant to be governed."

" And are you quite satisfied with me now?"

" Quite, madam."

" Then send Gage to me. I want to see him. Stay! you have not given me the five hundred pounds."

" Here are the notes, madam. Mr. Monthermer shall be with you presently. I have the honour to kiss your hand."

As soon as the door was closed by the steward, Peg threw herself back in her chair, and burst into an immoderate fit of laughter.

" Was there ever so consummate a rascal! Sir Randal described him exactly. But clever and unscrupulous as he is, it shall go hard if I don't outwit him. And now for my poor despairing swain. I must make myself look as captivating as I can."

With this she summoned Mrs. Clive, and with her aid had just disposed her fair tresses in the most becoming manner, and rearranged her costume, when the door was thrown open, and Gage was at her feet.

The Temptress had prevailed.

XV.

WHEREIN SEVERAL PERSONAGES CONNECTED WITH THIS HISTORY FIND THEIR WAY TO THE ANGEL AT BURY ST. EDMUND'S.

SIR HUGH POYNINGS was one of the proudest men in Suffolk, and his feelings may, therefore, be imagined when he learnt that his son had been secretly attached to Felix Fairlie's daughter, and had even offered her his hand. That Clare was beautiful, accomplished, irreproachable—all that could be desired in woman, except that she was not well-born—weighed nothing with him. The connexion was degrading—dishonouring—and he would sooner Arthur had fallen by the sword of De Meschines, than have seen him so mated. At least, in the first transports of his rage, he affirmed as much to Lady Poynings, who, when their son was brought home wounded, could conceal nothing from her husband. Remonstrances, at first, appeared unavailing with the indignant old gentleman. All that could be urged in Arthur's behalf by his mother, in her affectionate anxiety to exculpate him, served only to inflame Sir Hugh still more.

" What! you attempt to defend him, Lady Poynings!" he exclaimed. " Zounds! madam, you will drive me distracted. You are as bad as he. Do you suppose for a moment, if you had been in the same sphere of life as this girl, and had owned a knavish steward for sire, instead of a gentleman of a lineage as ancient as my own—if you had been a Fairlie instead of a Bourchier—do you think, under such circumstances, I should ever have married *you?* I know better what is due to my ancestors. They shall never be disgraced by me. Until now I always thought Arthur shared my sentiments. Undoubtedly, I have sometimes regretted an over-familiarity in his manner towards those beneath him, a want of sufficient self-respect,—a want of a little of my dignity, in short; but I attributed these faults to his excessive good-nature, and never anticipated any ill consequences from his too great condescension. I now see my error. My excuse is, that I could not believe a son of mine—a Poynings—a proud Poynings, as we have been styled for centuries, though we shall probably lose the designation now—I could not believe, I say, that a son of mine could be capable of such folly."

"You must recollect that the affections are not always under our control, Sir Hugh."

"Nonsense, madam; my affections were always under proper control, and why should not Arthur's be so? But even if he were in love with this girl, there is no reason why he should marry her. And to crown the absurdity—to heighten the disgrace— you tell me she has rejected him. A pretty story, forsooth! Why we shall be the laughing-stock of the whole county. I shall go mad with shame and vexation."

Lady Poynings thought it best to let her husband's passion evaporate, and as he grew somewhat calmer, she again ventured to refer to Arthur's hurt.

"Is he severely wounded?" Sir Hugh inquired, with an expression of anxiety which, notwithstanding his efforts, he failed to hide.

"Not dangerously, I trust; but he suffers much pain, though he bears it with great fortitude. Peyton is now dressing his wound. You will hear the report presently." And perceiving that the old baronet's heart was rapidly softening, she went on: "I do not say you have not just grounds of anger, my dear, but the turn that affairs have taken, unlucky in some respects, though fortunate in others—at least in your view of the case—may induce you to overlook the past, and extend forgiveness to our poor boy. His love for Clare Fairlie, and his rejection by her, need not surprise you so much. Gage Monthermer was just as much enamoured of her, and equally unsuccessful in his suit."

"Indeed! you surprise me, madam. But Gage Monthermer is no rule for our son. Because he is a prodigal and a rake, is it desirable that Arthur should resemble him?"

"Certainly not, my dear. But entertaining the poor opinion you do of Clare Fairlie, it is due to her to state that her motives for rejecting Gage were disparity of position and unsuitableness of character, while her rejection of Arthur was occasioned by her attachment to Gage."

"On my soul! a noble-spirited girl. Her rascally father must have laid a trap for his silly ward. I see it all now. Her conduct is most praiseworthy, and I admit I have wronged her. She cannot have a spice of Fairlie in her composition. I fear Lucy would not have shown so much discretion and self-denial. She would have taken Gage with all his faults, or I am much mistaken."

"Well, my dear, Lucy might hope to reform him."

"Pshaw! Gage will never reform," Sir Hugh exclaimed. "What a pair of madcaps are our children! What is to be done with them?"

"That must be for after-consideration, Sir Hugh. Our first business is to get Arthur well again, and to ensure this he must have your forgiveness. The certainty that you are not offended will do him more good than the surgeon."

"Well—well—tell him I am very angry——"

"Nay, I will say you are not angry at all, but much distressed——"

"But, zounds! madam, I am angry—I am furious. I will rate him soundly when I see him."

"You will do nothing of the sort, my dear. I know you better. When you see how much our son suffers, you will use every endeavour to alleviate his anguish."

"Well, I can't hold out against your entreaties. I will go to him at once. Pray Heaven his wound be not dangerous. If anything happens to him, I'll cut the throat of that sharper—that bravo, De Meschines, myself. Come along, madam."

It is needless to say, after this, that Arthur was forgiven, and that his father was constant in his attendance upon him. As to Lucy,—reproaching herself as she did with being the cause of her brother's mischance, she could not sufficiently manifest her devotion to him.

Young Poynings was blessed with a vigorous constitution, and his wound speedily healed. In less than a month the surgeon pronounced him cured. Meanwhile, Lucy had been seized with an ardent desire to visit London, and set to work to coax her good-natured papa into compliance with her wishes. Sir Hugh, not perhaps comprehending the real motive that influenced the request, was not unwilling to gratify her, and her brother, though he did nothing to aid the project, would not interfere with it. Accordingly, a visit of the family to town for a couple of months was resolved on, and preparations made for it. All was in readiness; and as Arthur had now perfectly recovered, it was not necessary to delay the journey on his account.

On a fine morning in the middle of May, Sir Hugh's cumbrous travelling carriage, with four horses attached to it, and laden like a waggon, with boxes, portmanteaus, and all kinds of luggage, wheeled round in front of the hall. In those days a journey to town was an event to most country gentlemen, and to Sir Hugh Poynings it was an extraordinary event, for he had not been to London for ten years and upwards. He sighed as he took leave of his large and comfortable mansion, and wondered how he could ever have made up his mind to quit it—but there was no help now. The carriage was at the door, and go he must. Lady Poynings, Lucy, and Parson Chedworth, the chaplain, were already deposited in the lumbering vehicle, and Sir Hugh, still groaning dismally, seated himself beside them. Mrs. Pinchbeck, Lucy's maid, and three other women servants found accommodation behind, and two lacqueys were seated with the fat coachman on the box. Arthur preferred travelling on horseback, and did not start quite so early as the others, but promised to overtake them long before they reached Bury St. Edmund's, which it was fixed should be the limit of the first day's progress.

Just at starting some little display was made by the coachman, who trotted his horses merrily through the park, two miles of which he had to traverse before he gained the road, and he again urged them on as he approached the village of Reedham—all the inhabitants of which came forth to salute Sir Hugh, my lady, and Miss Lucy, and wish them a pleasant journey and speedy return—but the first pretence of a hill brought the smoking team to a walk, and after that they went on leisurely enough—never exceeding four miles an hour. Indeed, it must be owned that the state of the roads was so abominably bad that rapid travelling was out of the question. More than once the carriage stuck fast in a rut, and great exertions on the part of the two footmen were required to get it out. In this way much time was necessarily lost; but to such delays people at that period were accustomed, and took them as matters of course. Sir Hugh grumbled, but sat still; while Lucy, tired of talking to the prosy chaplain, looked out of the window for Arthur, but could discern nothing of him.

On setting out, instead of taking the road to Bury St. Edmund's, young Poynings rode in the opposite direction, shaping his course towards Monthermer Castle. Did he intend to bid farewell to Clare? No: for though she was uppermost in his thoughts, and though he would have given much to catch even a glimpse of her, his purpose was not a stolen visit, which he felt would be a betrayal of his father's renewed confidence. His destination was Cowbridge Farm. Having heard nothing of Mark Rougham since the worthy yeoman had helped to transport him to Reedham, he wanted to thank him for his services on that occasion. As he rode tolerably fast, and took the shortest road, he was not long in reaching Mark's dwelling, but on entering the yard, he was surprised to perceive a stranger at the door, brought thither by the sound of the horse's footsteps.

To his inquiries from this personage, whom he recognised as a farmer named Abel Skinner, he was informed that poor Rougham had again been forcibly ejected by Fairlie, and this time, no doubt, with the young Squire's consent. So at least Skinner affirmed, and he declared he had seen the order signed by Gage. Mark had gone away with his family, no one knew whither.

"Why did he not come to me?" Arthur exclaimed. "I would have given him and his wife a home."

"I can't say, your honour," Skinner replied; "but Mark be self-willed and proud, and most like he ha' gotten some scheme o' his own to carry out—leastways I thinks so."

"But where is he? Can he not be found?"

"I dare say he can, your honour, if search be made for him," Skinner rejoined. "If I should light on him, shan I send him over to Reedham?"

"Yes—yes—but stay! I forget myself. I am going to London, and shall be absent for more than a month. Hark'ee, Skinner, you must find out Mark for me. I will make it worth your while. Bid him go with his family to Reedham, and take up his abode there till I return, or give further directions respecting him. Here is a guinea, and I will add a couple more hereafter, if you do my bidding expeditiously and well."

"I'll do my best, your honour may rest assured," Skinner replied; "and at the same time your honour will be pleased to understand that it be no fawt o' mine that poor Mark ha' lost his farm. I be reet sorry for him; an' I'd turn out to-morrow if he could come back. But that's impossible, as yo' may weel suppose."

"Ay, ay, I know that. But do not fail to execute my orders.'

"Your honour may depend on me."

In less than an hour after this, Arthur had gained the high road to Bury, and come in sight of the carriage slowly toiling up a hill.

But he contented himself with keeping it in view. If he had been less preoccupied, the ride through this lovely part of Suffolk would have been enchanting. Even as it was, he was not quite insensible to the beauties of the surrounding scenery, but now and then paused for a brief space to look about him. At one of these halts the fair town of Bury St. Edmund's met his eye, crowning a hill, some three miles off, and he was gazing at it admiringly, when he perceived Lucy wave her handkerchief to him.

Thus summoned, he could no longer tarry behind, and had just ridden up to receive the scolding he so richly merited, when the noise of wheels was heard rapidly approaching.

In another moment a superb coach, gilded and of the newest mode, dashed by them, drawn by a pair of blood horses of great swiftness. Two persons were inside it: one of these, who sat on the left, and nearest to Lucy, was a lady—young, and of extraordinary beauty, but with a certain boldness of expression, noticeable even in a passing glance. She was evidently laughing at the antiquated travelling carriage, and regarding Lucy with an insolent stare, called her companion's attention to her.

The other turned round, and as his features became revealed to Lucy, and their eyes met for a moment, she uttered an exclamation, and fell back in the carriage.

"What's the matter, my dear Lady Poynings cried, anxiously.

"Nothing—nothing," Lucy gasped.

"Why, as I live, it was Gage who passed us!" Sir Hugh exclaimed. And the truth flashing upon him, he said no more. Arthur, who was riding on the further side of the carriage, stole a glance at his sister, and saw in her mantling cheeks and confusion how much she was affected.

After awhile conversation revived, and Lucy in some measure recovered her composure; but no allusion was made to the incident that had just occurred, or to Gage. Ere long they entered Bury; mounted the steep street leading to the central part of the town; and crossing a wide open space, drew up in front of the Angel.

Down the steps of this renowned hotel came the portly landlord, Mr. Briscoe, as fast as his gout would permit him—while servants of all kinds rushed forth to welcome the new comers.

Sir Hugh thought there was something odd and constrained in the landlord's manner when he announced his intention of putting up at the house for the night, and inquired what he could have for dinner. Mr. Briscoe hemmed and ha'd, bowed and scraped, but gave no direct answer as he ushered the old baronet, the chaplain, and the two ladies into a large room, commanding from its windows a full view of the venerable abbey-gate on the opposite side of the square, and the grey walls and monastic ruins beyond it.

And now let us see how Gage chanced to be at Bury.

Thus it was. Instead of returning to town after the meeting at Newmarket, as she originally intended, Mrs. Jenyns decided upon spending a week or two in the country—with what motive we shall explain presently; and proceeding to Bury, she took up her quarters at the Angel. Of course Gage accompanied her. The manager of the theatre in Goodman's-fields wrote to the pretty actress in despair, imploring, nay commanding her immediate return, and threatening her with a heavy fine in case of refusal. She laughed at his entreaties and menaces, and replied that she needed repose. She was amusing herself very much at the prettiest and most salubrious town in England—had charming rides and drives every day—and though she was sorry to disappoint her numerous admirers, her health must be cared for. She might return in a fortnight—or in a month—or not at all. He might inflict any fine he pleased. Mr. Monthermer would pay it.

With all her cupidity, Mrs. Jenyns had not managed to enrich herself. Excessively extravagant, and vying in her equipages and establishment with a lady of the first quality, she was ever in debt. That she remained on the stage was owing to love of excitement and admiration; and besides, the robe of the actress served to turn off the darts of scandal. Her chief failing was love of play. A confirmed gambler, she was almost always unlucky. When a woman games she seldom stops half-way,—and so it was with Peg Jenyns. She came to the gaming-table with hundreds in her pocket, and covered with costly trinkets, and left without a guinea or a ring. In this way she had been frequently reduced to the greatest straits, but somehow or other had always contrived to right herself.

Amongst those who had won large sums from her was Sir Randal de Meschines; but then he often lent her money when in difficulties, and there seemed now to be an understanding between them, as he employed her in some of his schemes. By his instigation she undertook the journey to Newmarket, and having succeeded almost beyond her expectations, she was unwilling to concede a share of the spoil. Indeed, as she had to divide with Mr. Fairlie, according to her bargain with the steward, her gains would be terribly diminished by a like process with Sir Randal. She therefore feigned a sudden inclination to stay at Bury, professing to be enchanted with the town and its beautiful environs, and Gage willingly assented to the arrangement. The poor dupe was infatuated by her witcheries, and squandered large sums upon her. Fresh amusements were constantly devised for her, so time passed on pleasantly enough. Everything Mrs. Jenyns fancied must be procured—no matter at what cost.

Shortly after his arrival Gage took possession of the whole hotel, and sent for all his servants from the Castle, so the house was just like his own, and he gave large dinners and other entertainments daily. But great as were his general expenses, the chief inroads upon Gage's purse were made by play. Though Mrs. Jenyns lost to everybody else, she won from him; and as cards were introduced each evening — merely to pass the time — her gains in the course of a week were considerable. Fairlie could have told how much exactly, for he kept an accurate account.

But she was not allowed to carry on this game undisturbed. Sir Randal had received a hint as to what was going on—pro-

bably from his ally, Brice Bunbury, who had never quitted Gage—
and felt the necessity of immediate interference.   Beau Freke quite
concurred with him in opinion.   If left to herself, Peg Jenyns
might outwit them.   She had cleverness enough for anything.
No time must be lost if they intended to thwart her plans.   Brice
Bunbury could not be trusted—besides, he was a poor hand, and
drank too much.   So the confederates set out for Bury at once.

Gage was surprised to see them, and not over well pleased,
though he put a good face on the matter.   Mrs. Jenyns quite
understood the cause of their coming, and waited to see what
move they would make.

Thus affairs stood, when the number of guests at the Angel
was increased by the unexpected arrival of the party from Reedham.

XVI.

A PRINCE of the blood might have been quartered at the Angel. The inn-yard was crowded with equipages of various kinds, and the stables were full of horses. On this side were trainers from Newmarket and jockeys discussing the respective merits of half a dozen splendid racers which had just been brought home after exercise by the grooms; on that, cock-masters and breeders were taking their valiant birds out of deep straw baskets or bags, and shielding their spurs with stuffed rolls of leather, in order that they might not hurt themselves while sparring for practice on the straw. Round the latter individuals were collected a host of lacqueys all habited in the richly-laced orange-coloured livery of Monthermer, examining the cocks, and betting with each other as to their prowess in the coming trial of skill;—this backing a grey, that a ginger, another a red with black breast, and a fourth a pied-pile. Again there were two or three huntsmen in scarlet coats, and as many gamekeepers in dark green jackets— though what these gentry could be doing there it was difficult to conceive, unless they had been summoned from the Castle, to swell out their lord's already too numerous train.

At the side door of the inn stood another party, consisting of our old acquaintances, Pudsey, Bellairs, and Chassemouche, with their sparkish friends, Tibbits and Trickett. The two latter coxcombs had just returned from a stroll through the town, and were regaling Bellairs and the French valet with an account of the conquests they had achieved among the pretty girls of Bury. Tibbits, it appeared, by his own showing, had been eminently

successful. The whole party agreed, however, that Bury was un-
commonly dull, and if they had not some amusement in scouring
the streets at night with their masters, breaking the lamps, beating
the watch, and wrenching off knockers, they should not know
how to spend their time.

The arrival of Sir Hugh Poynings and his family was a source
of infinite satisfaction to these amiable personages, because they
foresaw that some disturbance must ensue ; and even if the prin-
cipals failed to quarrel, which seemed next to impossible, they
could get up a little brawl on their own account with the servants
from Reedham. With this design, they scarcely made way for
Arthur Poynings as he passed them, after dismounting and consigning his steed to the ostler, and Mr. Tibbits received a cuff
on the ear for his especial insolence ; an indignity he would
have resented if he had dared. But he was too much daunted by
Arthur's fierce looks to retaliate, and when the young gentleman
shook his whip menacingly at him, he retreated behind his companions, who offered him no support. Arthur, however, had no
sooner disappeared, than with one accord they began to abuse him,
and Mr. Tibbits swore a great oath that he would be revenged
upon him before the morrow.

Just then Sir Hugh's coachman, Beccles, came into the yard with
his horses, and the whole pack instantly set upon him, jeering him,
his cattle, and his master, and telling him he should not have a stall
in the stable unless he fought for it. Now Beccles was a sturdy
fellow, and did not budge an inch. Letting go the bridle of the
horse he was leading, he put himself into an attitude of defence, and shouted to his fellow-servants, who at once answered
the summons, and arranged themselves beside him. As there
seemed to be every prospect of a fight, the whole yard was instantly
on the alert. The liveried menials deserted the game-cocks in
the hope of witnessing a more exciting contest. Trainers, jockeys,
cockers, grooms, stable-boys, and ostlers rushed forward, and a
ring was speedily formed ; but before a blow could be struck a
scream was heard, and with loud cries a female forced her way
through the crowd to the combatants. It was Mrs. Pinchbeck.
At sight of her Tibbits turned pale, and made an effort to slink
off. But he was kept in his place by those around, till a pair of
arms, flung round his neck, effectually secured him.

From what could be collected in the midst of Mrs. Pinchbeck's sobs and hysterical ejaculations, it appeared that the gay and gallant Tibbits had married her some five years ago, at which time she was the young widow—and the very pretty widow too, though she said it, that shouldn't—of an old haberdasher in Cheapside, yclept Duckweed, to whom the insinuating Tibbits had been apprenticed. Having spent all her money, and ruined her business by his gross neglect, the wretch absconded—basely deserted her—inhuman monster that he was!—whereupon, having no other resource, she who had once lived in affluence, and had been doted upon by her departed Duckweed—a duck he was, if ever there was one on earth!—she, who had never even waited upon herself in her dear Ducky's time, was forced to go into service. (Here a flood of tears drowned her utterance for a moment.) Friends she had in Bungay,—relatives of her dear Ducky,—and *they* didn't turn their backs on her, notwithstanding her misfortunes, but procured her a situation as lady's maid to Lady Poynings—a situation she didn't blush to say—though Tibbits might blush to hear it—that she had filled to her ladyship's entire contentment. Her ladyship and Miss Poynings knew she had once moved in genteel circles, and treated her accordingly. " Pinchbeck, you are not a common domestic," my lady said; " you must have your own room, and your own table." " Pinchbeck, you must come and sit with me," Miss Lucy would often say, " for I like your society better than that of the noisy fox-hunters down stairs." Pinchbeck, she added in explanation, was her maiden name, and she resumed it, when she was abandoned by Tibbits. Never, since the day he left her, till that moment, had she set eyes on her worthless spouse—never heard a word of him— and she never should have done, she felt quite sure, if she had not accidentally popped upon him ! But she would show him what an injured wife's rights were, unless he arranged matters to her satisfaction—that she would !

Leaving the tender couple to adjust their differences as best they could, we may mention that their meeting caused a cessation of hostilities between the adherents of the houses of Monthermer and Poynings. Instead of fighting, the stalwart lads of Reedham shook hands heartily with their lace-bedizened, silken-hosed, powdered antagonists of the Castle; and sundry tankards of strong ale, called for by the chiefs on both sides, completed the amicable understanding.

If Arthur had looked up at all, when he rode into the inn-yard, instead of occupying himself with matters of infinitely less concern, he must have seen, at an open window on the first floor—just above the great gilded sign of the Angel—a very pretty face, the owner of which was anxiously, but vainly, striving to attract his attention by slightly coughing, and waving a handkerchief. But as he looked everywhere but in the right direction, the pretty face lost its smile, the red lips pouted, and she who owned them leaned so far out of the casement as almost to endanger her personal safety. How could Mr. Arthur be so stupid? What could he be dreaming about, to keep his eyes constantly fixed on the ground? Perhaps he didn't wish to see her? No, she would never believe that. Come what would, she was determined to have a word with him, so down stairs she darted, and reached the passage leading to the yard-door just as the young gentleman entered by it. No mistake now as to his being glad to see her. He uttered an exclamation of surprise and delight, and almost caught her in his arms, as she sprang towards him.

" So, then, you can see me at last, sir," Lettice Rougham cried. " I thought you wished to avoid me, but I was resolved you shouldn't. Horses and grooms seem to interest you now more than our sex. But don't you know that if you would learn your fortune you should consult the stars. Had you done so just now, you would have beheld——"

" A little angel," Arthur supplied, gallantly.

" Yes,—painted on a signboard," Lettice laughed. " But you have lost your memory as well as your sight, sir. Why don't you inquire about my mistress?"

" You don't give me time, Lettice. Is she here?"

" Yes, sir, she *is* here, or you wouldn't see me. We're staying in the house—but we're confined to our own room, and never stir out of it—that is, very seldom. My mistress wouldn't remain here a minute, if she'd any choice, but her cruel tyrant of a father drags her about like a slave. Of course, I share her captivity. I hope you're come to release us, sir."

" I don't see how I can help you, Lettice."

" You don't! Then you're not the brave knight I took you for.

Perhaps you don't like to run the risk of another wound. And that reminds me that I ought to ask about the hurt you got when you last visited us at the Castle. How are you getting on? You look tolerably well. Of course, you've heard of the gay doings we're to have here to-night?"

" I've heard nothing as yet, Lettice. I've only this moment arrived. What gay doings do you refer to?"

" Mr. Monthermer's grand masked ball. It takes place in this house to-night, and as everybody's talking about it, I thought somebody might have mentioned it to you. All the fine folks of Bury are invited, and most of 'em are coming. O, it'll be a splendid ball! no expense spared, as you may suppose, since Mr. Monthermer gives the entertainment. The long room is adorned with mirrors, and festooned with flowers—the floors are chalked—and there's to be a band of musicians from London in the orchestra When the company are tired of dancing, they are to sit down to such a supper, sir."

" Very tempting, no doubt. But I presume your mistress does not mean to attend this ball, Lettice?"

" Entirely against her own inclination, sir—entirely. But Mr. Fairlie insists upon it,—and she daren't refuse, poor soul! You'd better go too, to take care of her. Put on a domino and mask, and no one will find you out. I see you'll do it."

" You are always ready to promote mischief, Lettice, and a worse plan than yours might be devised. But I cannot consent to it, for many reasons."

" I'll dispose of the reasons at once if you'll state them," Lettice said.

" Well then, first and foremost, I'm not alone here. Sir Hugh and Lady Poynings are with me—and my sister."

" Pooh! that's easily settled. The old people will retire to rest before the ball begins, and need never be aware of your presence at it. And why not bring Miss Lucy with you? I'm sure she would like it. I'll find her a dress—a perfect disguise.'

" You arrange matters very readily, Lettice; but there are difficulties you cannot get over."

" I see none whatever, sir, unless you create them yourself. Miss Lucy, I'm certain, will be enchanted with the scheme—so will my mistress—so will you—and so shall I—for I must have a share in ıt. But I mustn't stand talking here, or I shall be noticed. I shall tell my mistress she may expect to meet you."

"On no account, Lettice."

"But I shall—and I shall deliver a great many messages which you ought to have sent her. If you want me, mount to the second floor—the second, mind—walk down the corridor and tap against the last door on the right."

So saying, she tripped away.

And just in time, for scarcely was she gone, than Sir Hugh Poynings, whose angry tones had for some moments before been resounding in the hall, now strode down the passage, and met his son. The old baronet was in a towering passion.

"What's the matter, sir?" Arthur inquired.

"Why, sir, starvation is the matter—no dinner is the matter— no wine is the matter. We can't have a joint or a roast fowl, or a bottle of claret, unless it pleases Mr. Gage Monthermer. We can't have a bed except in the garret. Mr. Monthermer has taken the whole house—bedrooms, parlours, kitchen, larder, cellars, and stables. It's no longer the Angel, it's the Monthermer Arms; and young Gage—and be hanged to him—is landlord, and not old Briscoe. 'Sdeath! sir, things are come to a pretty pass, when one can't call for what one likes at an inn, without being told that Mr. Monthermer must be consulted."

"You amaze me, sir."

"And well I may—but I shall amaze you still more before I've done. Old Briscoe has just been with me, to explain, with many apologies, how matters stand. He confesses he can scarcely call the house his own. He will do his best to make me com-fortable under the circumstances, and if he fails, he hopes I will ex-cuse him. He was never so perplexed before. His honoured guest and patron, as he styles Gage, pays like a prince—throws about his money, right and left, as if it were of no value—never looks at a bill, but tosses it over to Fairlie—but then he expects to have all his own way, and won't bear the slightest interference. Everything and everybody must bow to him. What he wills is law. No person of inferior quality to himself must enter the house—unless invited. Not a bad rule that, i' faith, if properly carried out. Then, if a guest's looks don't please him, he must go, or the house will be made too hot to hold him. He served Dick Jernigan of Somerly

so yesterday. Dick was obliged to decamp. And the night before
last, two maltsters from Woodbridge, with their wives, decent folk
enough, had been smuggled into the house without Gage's leave
—but the dog heard of 'em, and though they had gone to roost
more than an hour, he had 'em out of bed, ay, and into the
street, too. Oons! I can't help laughing when I think on't."

" Surely you are jesting, sir, in saying that we can't dine here
without Gage's permission?"

" Egad! it's no jesting matter with me, Arthur. I'm as hungry
as a hunter after my journey. But I tell ye, sir, old Briscoe
daren't serve a dinner in private for the life of him."

" Well, sir, we must dine in public then—that's all. There's
an ordinary in this house—the best in Bury—to which all the
young gallants in the town resort. We must put up with their
company for the sake of the meal. It's about the hour of dinner."

" Ay, but the ordinary is no longer an ordinary. One person
pays all charges instead of each paying for himself. The young
gallants you speak of dine here daily—but only as Gage's guests.
Unless we choose to be considered in the same light we can have
no place at the table. Zounds and the devil!—I beg your pardon,,
boy—but it's enough to make a parson swear."

"Have a little patience, sir."

" That's what the chaplain says. As well preach patience to the
winds as to an empty stomach. I'm in no humour for it. If I
could only stay my appetite with a cold pasty or a chine of pork, I
might be patient. But it serves me right," he groaned, " for leaving my own comfortable mansion, where I had only to ask and
have. I won't remain in this inhospitable hole another minute.
The horses shall be put to again at once, and we'll be off to Long
Melford, or Sudbury."

" Your pardon, sir,—that will never do. We mustn't let Gage
and his friends accuse us of poltronery. Remember your own saying, which you learnt from your father, and he from his father:—
'No Poynings ever retreated.' "

" True, i' faith! and as you say, Arthur, our sudden departure
might be misconstrued. Poltronery!—zounds!—that's a word must
never be applied to a Poynings. No one shall charge us with
want of mettle. Udzooks! boy, we'll stand our ground in spite of
em. But we are likely to have as little sleep as food. This riotous

young prodigal gives a masked ball and supper to-night—in this
house, sir. He has hired musicians from London—and the devil
knows what besides!"

"I have heard as much, sir; but as it is not probable he will
honour us with an invitation to the ball, we need not concern ourselves about it."

"I wish I could shut my ears to all the sounds of catgut-
scraping, and caper-cutting, certain to assail 'em," Sir Hugh
groaned. "It'll be the death of your poor mother, who is troubled
with nerves. Then there's Lucy!—why, zounds! Arthur, when
she heard of this masked ball, she said she should like nothing so
much as to be present at it! I cut the silly jade's longing short,
pretty quickly, I can promise you."

"Girls have strange fancies, sir; and no wonder Lucy, who has
seen nothing of the kind, and may have been dazzled by descriptions she has heard of such assemblages, should be seized with a
transient desire to be present at the ball. But it will pass off, since
you have pointed out its impropriety."

"I trust so; but at any rate, I'm sure she'll not be sorry at my
change of plans. She looked plaguily downcast when I expressed
my determination of leaving Bury at once. Oddslife! she may
dance with Pinchbeck to the sound of the fiddles in her own
chamber—ha! ha!"

Arthur joined in his father's lusty laughter, and they repaired
to the large room in front of the hotel, to which the old baronet
had been conducted on his arrival. Here they found the two
ladies and the chaplain, in a state of uncertainty as to their movements; and Sir Hugh having communicated his intention of remaining where he was, the announcement was favourably received
by all, especially by Lucy, who could not restrain her delight.

"I couldn't bear the thought of quitting Bury so soon!" she
cried. "Never mind dinner—or supper—I don't feel hungry in
the least—and as to a bed, it doesn't matter—I can sleep very well
in the carriage."

"And see all the folks go to the masked-ball, eh?" Sir Hugh
cried. "No—no, Loo, you shall be locked up in your room; and
your mother shall keep the key.—Not a bad notion that of the
carriage, though," he mentally ejaculated. "I've a good mind to
take possession of it myself. I should be out of hearing of the

confounded fiddles. Wrapped up in a blanket, with a nightcap over my ears and a pillow to rest on, I should be just as comfortable as in my own bed. By Heavens! I'll do it. But as to dinner and supper, I can dispense with neither. If that silly girl has no appetite, others have—and deuced keen ones, too!"

Shortly afterwards, and while his father was engaged with the chaplain in planning an assault on the larder, Arthur drew his sister into the recess of a window, and detailed to her his conversation with Lettice.

"Oh! how fortunate that papa has altered his mind!" Lucy exclaimed. "If I had missed seeing Clare Fairlie I should have gone distracted. And you, Arthur! are not you delighted at the prospect of meeting her again? Nay, don't sigh, and put on such a long face—see her you will before the night's spent. We *must* go to the masked ball."

"But you are to be locked up in your own chamber, as you have just heard."

"Pshaw!—Papa was only joking."

"Oh, no, he's in earnest, rely upon it."

"Well then, Pinchbeck shall steal the key, and let me out. Go to the ball I will."

"You take it for granted I shall accompany you."

"Of course. You'd never allow me to go alone,—as I should, if you refused. But I know you won't stay away since Clare Fairlie is to be there."

"Her presence at it offers a great temptation to me I must admit. But I don't like you to witness such a scene, Loo."

"If Clare witnesses it, I may. No one will recognise me—for I shan't unmask. And I shall have you, *mon preux chevalier*, as a protector, in case of need."

"I can't get rid of my scruples. I ought not to yield to a giddy girl like you."

"Giddy as I am I can take care of myself. So you consent,—yes!—yes!—I'll have no denial."

"But suppose my consent obtained,—what are we to do for masks and dominoes?—Again, we have no tickets."

"Don't raise any more objections, Arthur, for I won't listen to them. Lettice Rougham will provide everything requisite. I

must see her at once. I shall find her, you say, in the first room
on the left—second staircase?"

"No; the last room on the right. Stay! Don't you perceive
who is approaching? You'll meet him in the hall to a certainty,
if you go out now."

As Arthur spoke, a sight met Lucy's gaze that riveted her to
the spot. Two running-footmen, in the Monthermer livery, dashed
up to the door of the inn, and one of them loudly rang the bell,
summoning forth Mr. Briscoe, several waiters, and a long train of
lacqueys. The landlord had just reached the bottom of the steps
as a splendid carriage drove up. It was such an equipage as had
never before been seen in Bury—of the newest town make—
richly gilded—sumptuously appointed—and having its panels emblazoned with the proud armorial bearings of Monthermer. In
an instant the broad space in front of the hotel was half filled
with a curious crowd who had followed the carriage, vociferating
with delight at its splendour, and the unwonted spectacle of the
running-footmen. Many of these pressed forward to see Gage
alight, and the lacqueys had to draw up in lines, to prevent intrusion, and keep a passage clear for their master and Mrs. Jenyns.

" Come away!" Arthur cried to his sister; but she was unable
to obey the mandate;—apparently fascinated by what she beheld.

Oh, how handsome Gage looked, she thought, as he placed his
small, well-gloved hand on Briscoe's arm while descending—how
graceful was his deportment—how modish his manner! And how
well his rich attire became him. If the young coxcomb had
sought an opportunity of displaying his fine person to advantage,
he could not have found one better than the present. Many
admiring eyes besides Lucy's were fixed on him, and he seemed
fully aware of the circumstance—for he kept Briscoe for a few
minutes in idle discourse, after alighting from the carriage. During
this interval he went through all the most approved forms of
foppery; setting his laced cravat; placing his feathered hat over
his flowing peruke; flourishing his clouded cane; taking snuff
from a jewelled snuff-box, with a grace and air peculiar to himself; smiling listlessly; and throwing himself—so his fair observers
deemed—into the most becoming posture imaginable. Thus he
rested until he had allowed them ample time to examine his

splendid attire; to criticise (if they could) his azure velvet coat, with its wide, deep cuffs embroidered with silver; his white satin waistcoat with its luxuriant pockets laced like the coat; his silken hose with silver clocks and the finely turned limbs they encased; and his red-heeled shoes, secured by magnificent diamond buckles.

All at once Gage raised his eyes, and discovering Lucy at the window, made her a gracious congee, which caused her instantly to retire and hide her blushes.

XVII.

WHAT happened after Lucy's retreat from the window she knew not, but she had scarcely recovered from the confusion into which she was thrown by Gage's salutation, when Mr. Briscoe made his appearance, with a silver salver in his hand, having several cards of invitation upon it, and a smile on his rosy countenance. He was charged, he said, by his honoured guest and patron, Mr. Monthermer, to bear these cards to Lady Poynings and her party, and entreat the favour of their company at the masked-ball to-night.

"Hang the masked-ball," Sir Hugh exclaimed. "Will Mr. Monthermer let us have dinner, Briscoe,—that's the question?"

"I am happy to be able to answer it most satisfactorily, Sir Hugh. My honoured guest and patron bade me say he should be delighted if you and Mr. Arthur would dine with him at the ordinary. The ladies," he added, "must be served in their own room."

"I dine with him!" the old baronet bounced out. "'Sdeath! sir, I'd rather starve."

"At your worship's pleasure. But——"

"But what, sir?"

"I was going to observe that my honoured guest does not make your attendance at the ordinary compulsory."

"I should hope not, Briscoe. Zounds! I should like to see him drag me to the table. He'd have a tough job, I promise him."

"My honoured guest has no such intention, Sir Hugh. Far from it. His injunctions to me are to treat your worship with every deference. 'I have the utmost respect for Sir Hugh, Briscoe,' his honour says; 'and though we have the misfortune to differ in opinion on some points, I can never forget what is due

to my father's oldest and best friend, as well as to one of the st
men in the county.'"

"The young gentleman has a very proper appreciation of your
merits, Sir Hugh," the chaplain remarked.

"He displays better feeling than I expected,' the old baronet
rejoined, considerably mollified; "but I'm sorry I can't dine with
him."

"My honoured guest begs you will entirely consult your own
inclinations, Sir Hugh—dine with him, or in your own room, at
your option."

"But not at his expense, Briscoe. That must not be.'

"Pardon me, Sir Hugh, that is the only point on which he is
peremptory."

"I think, Sir Hugh, you had better accept Mr. Monthermer's hospitality," the chaplain observed—the poor fellow was
suffering extremities of hunger like the old baronet. "He means
it civilly."

"Yes, yes, I'm quite sure he does," Lucy subjoined.

"Well, well, I can't stand out against you all. Be it as you
will, Briscoe. Only let us have something to eat quickly. I'm
famishing."

"And so am I," the chaplain muttered.

"Dinner shall be served directly, Sir Hugh," the landlord rejoined; "and I'll engage you shall complain neither of the dishes
nor the wine. Allow me to offer these cards to your ladyship."

"Zounds!—no—take 'em away, Briscoe," Sir Hugh roared.

"I think, my dear, they had better be left," Lady Poynings
observed. "We should not offer Gage an affront in return for
his civility."

"But you don't mean to go to the ball, madam?" the old
baronet cried, staring at her.

"Of course not," she rejoined, taking the tickets and placing
them on the mantelpiece. "There they will remain undisturbed
till to-morrow morning."

"Not undisturbed, mamma," Lucy said to herself, with a furtive
glance at Arthur.

"Make our compliments to Mr. Monthermer, Briscoe," Lady
Poynings added, "and say we are infinitely obliged to him."

"I will, my lady," the landlord replied, bowing profoundly.
"So far so good," he muttered, as he left the room.

XVIII.

PIPES AND PUNCH.

CONTRARY to his expectations, Sir Hugh fared sumptuously that day. A copious dinner was followed by a magnum of admirable claret, and the claret was succeeded by a bowl of delicious punch. The ladies disappeared early, and Arthur soon afterwards followed their example, leaving the old baronet and the chaplain alone together. Parson Chedworth had entirely allayed the pangs of hunger, had drunk his share—and Arthur's too—of the claret, and now felt in a state of perfect beatitude. Not absolutely perfect: he yearned for a pipe, and at length ventured to give audible expression to his desires. The old baronet acquiesced in fact, he was a great smoker himself. So pipes were called for and when the host appeared with them, the attentive fellow took the opportunity of inquiring, in his customary deferential manner, whether his worship approved of the punch; and being answered in the affirmative, begged permission to prepare another bowl.

" My honoured guest and patron," he said, with a low bow, " has again enjoined me to leave nothing undone to satisfy your worship. I told him you had ordered a bowl of punch, and he bade me brew it strong and good. ' Plenty of rack and sugar, Briscoe, quoth he; ' Sir Hugh must have of the best.' "

" Your honoured guest has a design upon our heads, methinks," the old baronet rejoined, as he proceeded to light his pipe. " However, I must needs own your punch is excellent, Briscoe."

" I have a character to lose, Sir Hugh, seeing I am accounted the best brewer of punch in Bury. Give me leave to taste the liquor, gentlemen. A leetle more of the old rum might improv it."

"Oddslife! no," Sir Hugh exclaimed; "you will blow out our brainpans, Briscoe. Not a drop more rum an you love me!"

"Ha! ha! ha! Your honour is pleased to be facetious."

"Ay, his honour is always jocular over his cups, Mr. Briscoe," the chaplain cried, his fat cheeks quivering with laughter. "Brew as you list, sir—brew as you list. You are the best judge of the right proportions of the mixture—though it's a rare compound, as it is," he added, filling his glass to the brim, and smacking his lips over its contents—"no fault can be found with it."

"I shall try and mend it, nevertheless, with the next brewage, your reverence," the landlord rejoined, shuffling off.

"I defy you to do it, Mr. Briscoe,—I defy you," Parson Chedworth shouted after him, with a mellow laugh.

The second bowl of punch proved more potential than the first, though neither of the two joyous souls complained of it; but when the landlord proposed a third, Sir Hugh raised no objection, but insisted upon more lime-juice.

"Your honour will spoil the drink," Briscoe said, in a deprecatory tone. "Consider, Sir Hugh, my reputation is at stake."

"Ay, you are bound to maintain it at all hazards," the chaplain roared. "Too much lime-juice would be a mortal heresy. Away with you, sir," he added, winking at the host, who took the hint and departed.

"Egad! parson," Sir Hugh exclaimed, as soon as they were alone, "since we are forced to dine at Gage's expense, we'll make him suffer exorbitantly—ha! ha! Help yourself."

While the twain were thus convivially employed, time wore away insensibly. Evening approached and found them still engaged with their pipes and glasses. At length, Lady Poynings, thinking they must have had enough—perhaps too much—sent Arthur to try and break up the sitting; but as he failed, she went herself with Lucy, though with no better success. Sir Hugh was not in a mood to be disturbed in the midst of his enjoyments. He meant to make a night of it, he said, with the parson. They had never drunk such delicious punch before. Its only fault was too much lime-juice—too little he meant. Wouldn't her ladyship taste it? A glass would do Loo no harm. Her ladyship had better retire to rest before the silly folk came to the masked-ball;—but she must be sure to lock Loo up in her chamber, first. What was the little gipsy about that she didn't buss him? There, they had better go now; and her ladyship need give herself no further concern about him. He and the chaplain should take a quiet snooze in the carriage. He had arranged it all with Briscoe. He wished her and Loo a good night:

Lady Poynings did not approve of her lord's arrangement, but aware that, under the circumstances, opposition would be idle, she reluctantly retired with her daughter.

Lucy, we must not omit to state, had taken advantage of her short stay in the room to approach the chimney-piece unperceived, and possess herself of the tickets for the ball.

An hour after this, and before the first guest had arrived at the ball, the two topers were fast asleep in their chairs.

Briscoe peeped in, and seeing how matters stood, withdrew with a chuckle. The last bowl of punch had done the business.

XIX.

A PEEP AT THE MASKED BALL.

GREAT was the uproar outside the Angel, as soon after nine o'clock those invited to the masked-ball began to arrive. The spacious area in front of the hotel was thronged by dense masses, through which carriages and sedan-chairs with difficulty forced their way. Footmen and link boys kept up a continual clamour; the former laying about them, right and left, with tall canes, and the latter thrusting oil-dripping flambeaux in the faces of such of the spectators as pressed too forward. But notwithstanding a few squabbles with the chairmen and coachmen and their satellites, the bulk of the crowd was in high good humour, and vastly amused by the various habits of the masqueraders. Droll and fantastic characters pleased them most, and figures in motley, scaramouches, pierrots, polchinellos, harlequins, and other buffoons were received with shouts of laughter. Some of these jested with the lookers-on, especially the gentler portion of them, as they passed along, and many a smart repartee was exchanged; the damsels being always ready with a rejoinder, and giving as good as they received. Bury has always been renowned for the beauty and liveliness of its fair inhabitants, and on this occasion its reputation for both qualities was fully maintained. Never were a collection of prettier girls brought together in the same space— most of them boasting the charming blond locks for which, as well as for other personal attractions, the female denizens of our English Montpellier have, time out of mind, been celebrated.

But we must now leave this merry concourse, with its squeezing, its trampling, its pushing forward and pushing back, its laughing faces lighted up by the flashing torches, its jokes, its fun, and its pretty girls — though we regret to part with *them;* we must leave it, we say, and follow the guests inside. Most of them, indeed, have arrived, for they have kept pouring in in uninterrupted succession for nearly an hour. Large as it is, the ball-room must be nearly full, the crowd think, and they are right. How many turbaned Turks, high-heeled mandarins, cavaliers in the costume of the Merry Monarch, Dutchmen in enormous trunk-hose, stately Spaniards and grave Venetians in velvet mantles, silken doublets, and hose—how many comical personages with huge paunches and bolster-like legs, some with two faces, at front and back, so ingeniously disposed that you could not tell which was the right one—how many black dominoes and pink dominoes —how many burly friars, quack doctors and pilgrims—how many sultanas and shepherdesses, Grecian nymphs and Indian princesses, double-faced women, fit partners for the doubled-faced men, antiquated village dames in steeple-crowned hats, supporting themselves with crutch-handled sticks, and attended by lightsome and trimly-attired peasant girls—how many such characters and how many others entered the wide-opened portals of the Angel that night we pause not to inquire—suffice it, that when they had all been ushered into the ball-room by Mr. Briscoe and his attendants, too much space was not left for the dancers.

As may be supposed, nothing had been neglected to give splendour and attraction to the ball. The room was magnificently decorated, and scores of perfumed tapers shed lustre on the motley groups. Borees and courantos—those lively dances of the day— were performed to enchanting strains from a powerful orchestra. Each musician was an artist of renown. Bouquets of the choicest flowers were offered to all the ladies. Cooling drinks of every kind and delicious hot-house fruits were served at a buffet, to refresh the dancers after their fatigues, and sustain them till supper came, at midnight, the marvels of which were discussed beforehand, though the reality far exceeded any anticipation formed of it. It was a repast worthy of a Roman Sybarite, abounding in tempting viands and exquisite wines, while plate and crystal glasses, brought for the occasion from Montherner Castle, decked the board.

But we are anticipating, and must go back to an earlier period of the evening. The majority of the guests had arrived, and dancing had already commenced, when a black domino, the upper part of whose features was covered by a mask without curtain, quitted a group of maskers of which he was the centre, and repaired to the ante-chamber. Several bright eyes followed him, for, despite his disguise, he was known to be the giver of the revel, and more than one fair challenger strove to arrest his progress. But he had matter on hand that claimed his immediate attention, and went on. On reaching the ante-chamber he found the person he expected, amidst a host of other attendants, male and female, and beckoned him to him. Briscoe—for it was he—instantly obeyed the summons.

"Are they come?" Gage demanded. "I have carefully scrutinised every mask on its entrance into the room, but have not been able to detect them."

"They are not yet arrived, your honour. I have marked their tickets, so they cannot pass in undiscovered. I will take particular notice of their dresses, and point them out to your honour."

"And you have disposed of Sir Hugh and the chaplain?"

"All has been done according to your honour's directions," the host replied, with a chuckle. And he was going to furnish some more information relative to the individuals in question, when a trio of masqueraders entered the room, and cut him short. "Here they are, as I live!" he cried, hurrying forward, as the new comers presented their tickets.

The two foremost masquers represented a Spanish hidalgo and his wife, or sister—she might be either, of course. Of the señora or señorita first, for she was eminently piquante and attractive. A basquiña of black silk, richly fringed with the finest lace, allowed, from its shortness, a view of feet and limbs that would have done credit to an Andalusian, and even a true daughter of Seville could not have moved more gracefully or more bewitchingly than did her present representative. A thick mantilla fastened at the back of her head, and descending over the shoulders, partially concealed her features, but what could be discerned of them through this veil gave evidence of extraordinary beauty. What with her fascinating deportment and grace of person, she seemed calculated to create a prodigious sensation amongst the assemblage she was about to join. Her costume would have been incomplete if she had wanted the Spanish dona's telegraph of love-messages,—a fan. She carried one in her hand, and understood its use too, for as she passed Gage its gentle rustle, plainly as whispered words, incited him to follow her.

Her companion, upon whose arm she leaned, was apparelled as a Spanish nobleman of the sixteenth century, and so well did he sustain the character by haughtiness of carriage, that he might have been taken for a veritable grandee. Of his countenance no judgment could be formed, since he was closely masked, but it was only fair to suppose it must correspond with his extremely handsome person.

Behind this striking pair came a very pretty page, clad in a white satin doublet and hose, with a sky-blue velvet mantle. He had a sword by his side, and his broad-leaved white hat had a drooping feather in it. A profusion of blond ringlets fell over his shoulders. He was closely masked like the others. Daintier limbs than this page owned were never seen ; but though his figure was slight almost to effeminacy, he bore himself gallantly, and had all the airs of a grown man. Mr. Briscoe and the ushers in the ante-chamber had a taste of his superciliousness and foppery, and he chucked some of the flower-girls under the chin, as they offered him bouquets.

Satisfied that these were the persons he expected, Gage stepped behind a screen and threw off his domino, almost instantly appearing again as the Earl of Rochester, in a splendid court dress of Charles II.'s time. Thus attired and putting on a curtained mask, he re-entered the ball-room.

XX.

THE TWO PAGES.

Mr. BRISCOE thought all the guests must have arrived, but he was mistaken. Soon after Gage's disappearance three fresh masquers presented themselves, cards in hand, at the outer door of the ante-chamber. At sight of them the landlord was quite startled, and the usher and other attendants were equally amazed. The cause of this general astonishment was the remarkable resemblance offered by the new comers to three personages who had recently preceded them, and had attracted particular attention on their entrance. Here were a second Spanish hidalgo and his dame followed by a dainty little page. Not only was hidalgo number two attired exactly like hidalgo number one—certain minutiæ of costume being carefully observed in both cases,—but he appeared to be just the same height, just as well-proportioned, and just as haughty of carriage as his predecessor. Like him, too, he wore a collar of gold with an order attached to it, and had the cross of Santiago embroidered on his mantle. The second doña looked quite as bewitching as the first, and was arrayed in the same style, with a black mantilla and basquiña—moving with equal grace, and managing her fan with equal coquetry. There was not a pin to choose between them. Then the page was the very double of the pretty little coxcomb who had gone before, and might have been his twin brother. Blond ringlets, white satin habiliments, limbs of almost feminine beauty, foppish and forward manners—all were the same. The flower-girls simpered as he approached them, and pressed their bouquets upon him, hoping he would treat them as the first young rogue had done, and they were not disappointed.

Mr. Briscoe was bewildered. Who were they? What could

K

it mean? Could they be the original hidalgo and his companions? Impossible! Nevertheless, in his perplexity, the landlord went to the open door of the ball-room, and satisfied himself
that the others were there, amidst the crowd.

But the mystery increased. The tickets were delivered, and
proved to be marked exactly in the same way the others had been.
After all, then, these might be the very persons his honoured
patron expected. Who could tell?

At the risk of appearing intrusive, Mr. Briscoe begged the
hidalgo would do him the favour to step behind the screen for a
moment, and take off his mask. But the don declined, and the
señora, tapping the host playfully with her fan, inquired if he was
master of the revel, that he presumed to question them. At the
same time the page, disengaging himself from the flower-girls, who
had crowded round him, came up, and with a wave of his hand
pushing Briscoe aside, all three passed on and entered the ball-
room.

Here they presently mingled with the crowd, and nothing was
left the host but to take an early opportunity of informing his
honoured patron of the trick that had been played with the
tickets.

Half the ball-room was in motion when Gage returned to it, and he
could only, now and then, catch a glimpse of the lovely figure of the
first señora as she flew past with her partner—the stately hidalgo
—in a gavot. However, he did not give himself much concern.
He had but to wait a few minutes, and the dance would be over.
She would then be disengaged, and he might, without impropriety, claim her hand for a rigadoon or a jig, and so obtain the
interview he sought.

While he was looking on, much amused by the efforts of a
cumbrously-clad Dutchman to keep pace with the brisk strains
from the orchestra, he felt his mantle gently plucked, and turning
beheld the page. The youth beckoned to him to withdraw a little
from the crowd, and when they were sufficiently removed to be
out of hearing, said archly: " So you are in pursuit of the fair
dame I serve? Nay, it will be useless to deny it. I know your
design, but am not going to betray it, either to her brother, or a
certain lady, who would be sure to thwart you, if she had the least
inkling of it. I can help you if you choose to confide in me."

" Upon my word I am greatly indebted to you, young sir,"
Gage replied. " But as mistakes are not uncommon at a masked-
ball, let me ask whom you take me for ?"

" I take you for one who may be better and happier than he is
now, if he does not throw away his present chance."

" You would have me reform and marry—eh ?" Gage rejoined,
with a laugh.

" I would; and if you will promise to turn over a new leaf,
I will engage to find you a charming wife."

" Egad, I thought so. But to tell you the truth, my young
Mentor, I have abandoned all idea of matrimony. It is not in the
least to my taste. Amusement is all I want, and in seeking an
interview with your captivating mistress I have no further thought
than to pass half an hour agreeably."

" I am out of all patience with you," the page cried, " and shall
caution my lady's brother not to let you approach her."

" Your lady will not thank you for your interference. Her chief
motive in coming to this ball, as you must know, was to meet
me, and if you throw any obstacles in the way you will cause her
infinite disappointment."

" You are a great coxcomb, and flatter yourself all women are
in love with you."

" I am vain enough to think some are not altogether indifferent
to my merits, and amongst the number I may count your adorable
mistress."

" If my mistress were of my mind and my spirit, she would die
rather than let you know how much she cares for you."

" Luckily your mistress does not resemble you in all respects.
And now, before we part, treat me to a glimpse of your face. It
ought to be pretty to match such a figure."

" Pretty or not, I don't intend you to behold it. And I beg
you will reserve all your fine compliments for those who heed them.
They are quite wasted upon me."

" Then you are not a woman, as I deemed you ?"

" You shall find I can draw a sword if you provoke me or insult
my mistress, so don't presume upon my belonging to the softer sex.
I am more dangerous than you think. I'll wager you what you
please that I make love to Mrs. Jenyns before the evening's
over;—ay, and that she listens to me."

" Pshaw! she will laugh at you."

" You are afraid to bet."

" To bet with a stripling like you would be ridiculous."

" You dare not point out Mrs. Jenyns to me."

" I would do so at once, but i' faith I know not the disguise she has assumed."

" A mere evasion. Never mind! I'll find her out without your assistance, and if she laughs at me, as you say she will, she won't laugh at my lady's brother. He shall put her to the proof."

" A saucy young coxcomb!" Gage exclaimed, as the other left him.

A general promenade now took place, but Monthermer did not care to quit his position, since it enabled him, without trouble, to scrutinise the various masks passing in review, as well as to converse with those he pleased; and he felt sure the circling stream would soon land the fair Spaniard at his feet. Ere many minutes, he perceived her slowly approaching, still leaning on the arm of the stately hidalgo, and he was preparing to step forward and address her, when Mr. Briscoe, whom he had noticed struggling through the motley crowd, succeeded in forcing his way up to him. The corpulent landlord had got terribly squeezed, and his gouty feet had been trodden upon, so that between pain and want of breath he could scarcely make himself understood.

" An' please your honour," he commenced,—" the tick—tick—tickets——Mercy on us! how my poor feet are crushed!"

" If you have anything to tell me, Briscoe—be quick!" Gage cried, impatiently.

" I beg your honour's pardon," the landlord gasped—" I was about to say——Oh! what an awful twinge!"

" Well,—well,—another time. I can't attend to you now. I've business on hand. Hobble back as fast as you can, and for your own sake keep out of the crowd."

" Your honour is very considerate. I would I had kept out of it—but the mischief's done. I shall be lame for a month. My duty required me to acquaint your honour that the tickets——"

" Deuce take the tickets! Stand aside, my good fellow, or I shall miss her. I must speak to that Spanish lady."

" But I entreat your honour to hear me first."

" Out of my way, sir!"

" Ay, out of the way, huge porpoise!" a youthful voice exclaimed behind him.

Glancing over his shoulder to see who spoke, the landlord beheld the page.

" Ah! are you there, little jackanapes?" he cried. " Beware of him, your honour. He is a cheat—an impostor."

" Mend your speech, sirrah host," the page retorted, " or I will clip off your ears."

" What!—here again, young saucebox!" Gage exclaimed. " Have you discovered her?"

" Discovered whom?" the page demanded.

" Why, Mrs. Jenyns, to be sure. Have you forgotten it already? You were to make love to her, you know—and so was your lady's brother—ha! ha!"

" Yes, so we were,—I recollect it now," the page replied, after a moment's hesitation. " I have a very treacherous memory."

" I should think so," Mr. Briscoe remarked. " Do you chance to remember where you got your ticket?"

" What means this impertinence?" the page exclaimed. " I received my card of invitation from Mr. Monthermer, of course."

" Marked, no doubt?" the landlord said.

" It might be marked for aught I know to the contrary; but what is this to the purpose?"

" A great deal—as his honour will comprehend."

" His honour comprehends that you are a very tiresome fellow, and wishes you far enough, with all his heart," the page rejoined. " Don't you perceive you are in the way, man?"

" Your honour——"

" Not a word more," Gage interrupted. " She will escape me."

" That for your pains, meddlesome fool," the page cried, snapping his fingers derisively in the landlord's face, and following Monthermer.

" And this is all the thanks I am likely to get," Briscoe groaned, as he hobbled back to the ante-chamber. " I won't interfere again, whatever happens."

XXI.

THE CARD-ROOM.

GAGE succeeded in his object. The señora graciously consented to dance with him, and contrary to what might have been expected, the jealous-looking hidalgo offered no opposition. Indeed, to judge from his courteous manner, he was rather pleased than otherwise. Our hero would fain have called for the kissing-dance; but his partner objected, as it would compel her to unmask, and this she declared she would not do at present. She preferred a country-dance—the liveliest that could be played—and her wishes were complied with.

As the orchestra struck up, all the couples who chose to join in the dance ranged themselves in two long lines, extending from top to bottom of the ball-room. Gage and his partner led off with great spirit. The latter appeared to be endowed with inexhaustible energy, considering the fatigue of the previous gavot. Gage complimented her upon her powers, but she only laughed, and bade him order the musicians to play faster. Faster and faster still! So light and nimble-footed was she that it required the utmost exertion on Monthermer's part to keep up with her.

Faster yet! the musicians as well as the dancers had a hard time of it, but they resolved not to be outdone, fiddling away furiously, and nearly cracking their lungs with blowing away at the wind instruments. Everybody had to be on the alert. If Gage contemplated a flirtation with his partner he must needs postpone it till the dance was over. Scarce a word could be uttered in the midst of such hurrying backward and forward—such rapid whirling round. Hands across—change partners—down the

middle—up again! Not an instant's pause. Long before he
reached the bottom Gage began to flag. He was not accustomed
to such violent exercise. But his indefatigable partner urged him
on,—and he would not be the first to give in. Luckily, but little
remained to do. Not more than a dozen couples were left, and he
was working his way as well as he could through them, when,
to his infinite surprise, a Spanish dame, exactly resembling his
partner, offered him her hand. As he took it, he experienced a
very perceptible pressure. At the same time he remarked that
the stately hidalgo was there—dancing with this second señora.
But no time was allowed for explanation. Seeing he lingered, and
guessing the reason, his partner stamped her little foot impatiently,
and hurried him on. After a few turns more, they reached the
bottom, when the panting dame confessed she was quite exhausted
and must sit down.

Every sofa was occupied, so they had to proceed to the card-
room where they found a seat.

In the centre of this *salle de jeu* stood an oval table, around
which a multitude of punters of both sexes was collected. Indeed,
we regret to say the female gamblers preponderated. Brice Ban-
bury officiated as tailleur at the faro-table, and Jack Brassey and
Nat Mist, who had arrived that very evening—quite unexpectedly,
of course—at the Angel, as croupiers. Every opportunity for play
was here afforded. Besides faro,—hazard, piquet, French ruff,
and gleek were going on at smaller tables placed in each corner.

So fearfully catching is the fever of gaming, that the fair Spaniard
could not escape it. She had not been long exposed to its baneful
influence before she expressed a strong desire to approach the faro-
table; and once within view of the *tapis vert* the impulse to try her
luck proved irresistible. She had never played in her life before, she
assured Gage in a low, earnest tone—never!—indeed, she scarcely
knew one card from another—but he should instruct her.

Our hero was not the person to baulk her inclinations. Applaud-
ing her resolve, he bade her select a card, and placed a heavy stake
upon it. She lost—and he renewed the stake. Again the señora
was unfortunate, and as Gage's purse was now emptied, he had to
apply for more money to Mr. Fairlie, who was standing in the

card-room, distinguishable from the rest of the assemblage from the circumstance of being in his ordinary attire. But Gage had no immediate occasion for the funds thus obtained. Before he could join the señora, the haughty hidalgo suddenly entered, and marching up to her with an angry gesture, took her away.

Unquestionably Gage would have interfered to prevent this uncourteous proceeding had he not been withheld by Fairlie.

" Let her go, sir—let her go," the steward said. " There is some mistake. Are you not aware that two Spaniards and two Spanish dames have gained admittance to the ball? Now I feel quite sure that the don who has just left us has got the wrong doña, and consequently there will be a diverting scene between them before long. I recommend you to follow and witness it."

" One word before I go, Fairlie. Have you any idea who this second couple of Spaniards are?

" Perhaps I have, sir—but it's mere conjecture—not worth mentioning. In fact, I'm scarcely at liberty to tell."

" Well, I won't press you. But I should like to know which of the two is Miss Poynings?"

" Not the lady you brought here, you may depend, sir," Fairlie rejoined.

" Egad! I thought not," Gage cried, reflecting how tenderly his hand had been squeezed by the second señora. " How could I be so stupid! But tell me, Fairlie, where is Mrs. Jenyns? I have not discovered her yet."

" She was here a few minutes ago, sir."

" What sort of dress does she wear? She declared I should dance with her without finding her out."

" Very likely you have done so already," the steward remarked, with a laugh.

" Why I have only danced with one person. Ha!" Gage exclaimed, a light suddenly breaking upon him—" I see it all. That Spanish dame was Mrs. Jenyns. I' faith I have been nicely tricked. But who is the hidalgo?"

" Since you have made so good a guess, sir, I must needs own that her companion is Sir Randal—and the page by whom they are attended is no other than Mrs. Jenyns's maid, Lucinda. Understanding that young Poynings and his sister were about to attend the ball, Mrs. Jenyns resolved to mystify you — and apparently she has succeeded."

" I'll have my revenge," Gage rejoined ; " but I must first lo '- after Lucy."

With this, he returned to the ball-room.

XXII.

MASQUERADE FROLICS.

By this time the real business of the evening had commenced, and the bulk of the masquers began to think it necessary to support the characters they had assumed—whether successfully or not mattered little, so that a laugh was raised.   Mountebanks and jugglers performed surprising feats.   Quack-doctors vaunted the wonderful merits of their nostrums.   One of them, an Italian charlatan, fantastically attired in a flame-coloured robe, and having an immense pair of spectacles over his aquiline nose, ran away with all the custom.   He had elixirs of long life, love-potions, and love-powders; a collyrium made of the eyes of a black cat, that enabled you to see in the dark ; an unguent that, rubbed over the lips, would compel a sleeper to answer all questions, and confess all secrets— especially useful to jealous husbands ; and, above all, a precious liquid, a few drops of which in a bath would make an old woman young again.   The love-potions were eagerly bought by many a sighing swain and ineffectually pressed on obdurate fair ones; but the efficacy of the elixir of youth was marvellously attested.

A phial was purchased by the antiquated dame in the tall conical hat, and she had no sooner swallowed its contents than her cloak and hat fell off as if by magic, and she appeared in the guise of a young and lightsome columbine.   Hereupon a roving harlequin, who had witnessed the transformation, bounded towards her, and bent the knee, placing his hand upon his heart, as if ravished by her new-born charms—then pointing his feet and rolling his head round rapidly, he danced off with her, hotly pursued by a couple of pierrots, screaming out that she belonged to them, and calling upon the crowd to stop her

These pierrots, by the way, together with the scaramouches and punchinellos, seemed perfectly ubiquitous, and played all sorts of mischievous pranks—interrupting many a tender *tête-à-tête*—tripping up the heels of old women and grave and reverend signors—launching quips and jests, so hardy that they often brought them a buffet in answer—making love to all the prettiest masks, and running off with several of them — appropriating cloaks, swords, and scarves, and then wrangling about them with the owners — and never to be checked in their practical joking except by sharp and sounding slaps from the harlequins' wands, which, it must be owned, were very freely administered.

In addition to all this buffoonery and fun, grotesque dances were executed, in which Jews, Turks, courtiers, shepherds and shepherdesses, gentlemen of the long robe, friars, and even pontiffs took part, producing a very droll effect. Perhaps the best of these was a clog-dance, by a couple of peasants, which elicited loud applause.

But it must not be supposed that all the company were engrossed by such gamesome performances, or cared for the boisterous frolics of the mimes. Many of the young gallants liked the uproar because it favoured their own designs, and consequently added to it, encouraging the scaramouches in their tricks; but they always contrived to come up in the nick of time to assist a distressed damsel, or ease a credulous duenna of her timid charge.

Introductions were unneeded. Everybody asked anybody he pleased to dance, and rarely met with a refusal. Hitherto, the harmony of the assemblage had been uninterrupted. If a quarrel seemed likely to ensue from some practical joke, it was instantly put down, and the brawlers were separated and laughed at.

Flirtations were frequent and desperate. Several couples who kept aloof from the crowd, or took possession of the sofas and settees, were evidently far gone in the tender passion ; while others plunged into the thickest of the motley throng, thinking they were securest there from observation.

Amid a scene of so much confusion, it was not easy to discover those you sought, and no wonder many careless husbands and chaperons, who had trusted their spouses and protégées out of sight, never found them again during the whole evening. Like difficulty might have been experienced by Monthermer in his search for

Lucy Poynings, if the page had not unexpectedly come to his aid
and volunteered to conduct him to his mistress.

"Is your mistress unattended?" Gage inquired, in surprise.

"She is in the ante-chamber," the page replied.

"Are you sure you are not an ignis-fatuus?" Monthermer said,
regarding the young coxcomb with some distrust.

"I don't know what that is," the page rejoined; "but I am not
a dupe, as some one is whom I could mention."

"Do you venture to apply that term to me, sirrah?" Gage
cried.

"No, you apply it to yourself, but it is not undeserved. Since
we met, I have ascertained that Mrs. Jenyns has assumed the same
dress as my lady, and my lady's brother has ascertained it too. I
told you Mrs. Jenyns would listen to him if he made love to her—
and I was right. Look there!"

"'Sdeath! what do I behold?" Monthermer exclaimed.

Glancing in the direction indicated by the page, he perceived
a couple reclining on a settee at the opposite side of the room,
evidently engaged in amorous converse. To all appearance they
were the señora and hidalgo who had recently quitted the card-
room. The lady's manner left no doubt on Gage's mind that she
was much interested by her companion, and the lively gestures and
the quick movements of her fan, with which she seemed almost to
converse, proclaimed what was passing between them.

"Well, do you now confess yoursel a dupe?" the page inquired,
in a tone of mockery.

"I must be satisfied that yon pair really are Mrs. Jenyns and
Arthur before I answer," Gage cried, angrily.

"And expose yoursel to the ridicule of the whole room by
making a disturbance," the page rejoined, arresting him. "What
good will that do? You are too much a man of the world to care
for so trifling a matter as the loss of a mistress, and ought to congratulate yourself rather than repine. You are well rid of her."

"On my soul, I think so!" Gage said, in accents that rather
belied his words. "Take me to Miss Poynings."

"This way," the page replied,—muttering as he plunged into
the crowd, followed by Monthermer. "If we can only keep him
in this humour for an hour, he is won."

XXIII.

WHAT HAPPENED DURING SUPPER.

Two ladies were seated in the ante-chamber when Monthermer entered it with the page. One of these was the charming Spanish señora he expected to find there : the other might be taken, from her dress, for a young Venetian dame of the sixteenth century. She was attired in a robe of rich dark velvet, and looked like a portrait by Tintoretto. Both were closely masked. As Monthermer approached, they rose, and courteously returned his salutation. Gage turned first to the señora.

"I have been thoroughly mystified this evening," he said, "and find that a masked ball has its inconveniences as well as its pleasures. Hitherto, ill-luck has attended me. You must have remarked that another lady has adopted a Spanish costume precisely similar to your own. I have been dancing with her for the last half hour, under the impression that my partner was Miss Poynings."

"Very flattering to Miss Poynings. But how do you know you are right now?" the señora replied.

"I can scarcely be deceived a second time," Gage said; "and though I cannot pretend to peer through a mask, something assures me that I am perfectly familiar with your features, as well as with those of your companion."

"Indeed. Whom do you suppose this lady to be?"

"An old friend."

"Nay, you must name her."

"Well then, I shall not be very far from the mark, I imagine if I call her Clare Fairlie."

Here the two ladies began to laugh, and the page joined heartily in their merriment.

"You display great discernment, I must say," the Venetian remarked, in a tone of slight pique. "I did not think you would find me out so soon."

"You are both so perfectly disguised that a conjuror might be puzzled to detect you," Gage replied. "Besides, you speak in so low a tone, that there is no judging by the voice."

"The curtain of the mask alters the sound,' the señora said.

"So much so that your accents seem to resemble those of Clare Fairlie," Gage observed.

"Mine!" the Venetian exclaimed.

"Egad! your voice is like Lucy's. Well, I suppose it must be mere imagination. But why should we remain here? Supper will be served shortly. Let me have the pleasure of conducting you to it." So saying, he offered an arm to each of the ladies, and led them into the ball-room.

But he was soon robbed of one of his charges. Scarcely had they joined the motley throng when the troublesome hidalgo came up, and whispering a few words to the señora, carried her off. No time was allowed for explanation, for at that moment the doors of the supper-room were thrown open, and the eager crowd rushed in to the long-expected repast. Every seat at the magnificently-furnished table, except a few at the upper end, reserved for the giver of the revel and his particular friends, was instantly filled, and a general assault made upon the tempting viands. Leading his partner to a reserved seat, Gage pressed her to take some refreshment—but she declined, alleging unwillingness to unmask. While glancing down either side of the board at the long array of his fancifully-attired guests, and speculating as to who they all were, Monthermer discovered, as he supposed, the hidalgo and the señora seated at the lower end of the table, and he would have sent to beg them to come up to him, but at this juncture, Mr. Fairlie made his appearance—evidently much disturbed. Almost rudely addressing Gage's partner, the steward desired her to unmask. The lady drew back, positively refusing compliance.

"Hold, Fairlie,—this must not be," Gage interposed.

"Your pardon, sir," the steward rejoined. "I wish to be satisfied that this is my daughter."

"Take my assurance that she is so," Gage said.

"I have reason to think you are mistaken," Fairlie cried. "I have just ascertained from the female attendants in the ante-chamber that the two ladies have changed dresses there."

On hearing this, the Venetian removed her mask.

"Miss Poynings!" Gage exclaimed. "I am doomed to be a dupe."

"But where is my daughter all this while?" Fairlie demanded.

"You will easily discern her if you will take the trouble to look down the table," Gage answered.

"That is not Clare," Fairlie said, glancing in the direction Gage pointed; and he added, with some significance, "that is the lady you danced with, and afterwards took to the card-room."

"Ah! indeed, and the hidalgo next her I presume is——"

"Not my brother Arthur, I hope?" Lucy cried.

"No, it is Sir Randal de Meschines. The other couple—that is, my daughter and Mr. Arthur Poynings—have disappeared."

"You don't say so, Fairlie," Gage exclaimed, unable to refrain from laughing. "Well, don't make yourself uneasy. I dare say they will turn up presently. Sit down to supper with us."

"Pray excuse me, sir. I must go in quest of Clare."

"Why, you don't surely suppose that Arthur has run away with her?" Monthermer cried, with renewed laughter. "That would be a jest indeed."

"I don't know what to think, sir. Perhaps Miss Poynings can give me some information on the subject?"

"If she can, depend upon it she won't, so you may spare yourself the trouble of questioning her," Gage returned.

"So I perceive, sir. Suffer me to retire, and pursue my inquiries elsewhere."

"As you will, Fairlie. But I advise you to take the matter easily. I have as much reason to be annoyed as you, and yet I do not disquiet myself." And as the steward departed, he turned to Lucy, and said, "To what am I to attribute the pleasure of your company this evening, Miss Poynings?—Mere curiosity to see a masked ball?"

"Not entirely," she replied. "I had mixed motives

coming. I shall be blamed by all—even by you—for the bold step
I have taken, but if I am able to serve you I shall not care."

"To serve me—in what way ?"

"By opening your eyes to your danger."

Gage regarded her with a smile.

"Clare Fairlie, I see, has been prompting you," he said. "A
propos of Clare—what has become of her ? Perhaps you will tell
me, though you would not inform her father."

"I have reason to believe she is gone," Lucy replied, with
some hesitation.

"Gone !" Gage cried, much startled. "How am I to understand you ?"

"Do not question me further. I have already told you more
than I ought to have done."

"If it be as I suspect, I shall be much grieved," Gage returned,
in a serious tone. "It is a rash step—and she will repent it."

"She is not happy with her father."

"Why not ? He is dotingly fond of her."

"That may be—but—I cannot explain now. Oh! Gage, how
can you place confidence in such a person as Fairlie ?"

"Because I have ever found him trustworthy. But let us
choose some more lively topic."

"This scene does not inspire me with lively thoughts, Gage.
On the contrary, it depresses me. Is it possible such an entertainment can afford you pleasure ? Look round the room—listen
to the sounds that assail our ears. Are these guests worthy of the
splendid banquet you have spread before them ? Few, if any of
them, have real friendship for you; while there are some amongst
them who seek your ruin—ay, and will accomplish it, if you continue blind to their arts."

"I am a bad listener to sermons, Lucy, and you have chosen a
strange season for yours."

"I have taken advantage of the only opportunity likely to occur
to me of offering you counsel, which I feel must prove distasteful,
but which friendship would not allow me to withhold.—I have
now done, and must beg you to take me to the ante-chamber,
where my brother will speedily join me, if he be not there already."

"Nay, I cannot part with you thus, Lucy. Remain with me a

APPEARANCE OF SIR HUGH POYNINGS AND HIS CHAPLAIN AT THE
MASKED BALL.

few minutes longer. I would rather be chided by you than praised by almost any one else. If you will but adopt the right means, you may bring about my reformation."

Lucy shook her head.

"How must I begin the good work?" Gage asked.

"Abandon this society altogether."

"Rather a difficult commencement. What next?"

"You must give up play."

"But how am I to exist without it? I have no other excitement. If I were to make the attempt I fear I should fail. You must aid me."

"I must first see some symptoms of amendment. But I can bear this riotous scene no longer. The noise stuns me. Pray conduct me to my brother."

By this time, the champagne and other wines, quaffed in flowing bumpers, had begun to do their duty, and set loose the tongues of the guests. Great was the clamour—loud the laughter that ensued. No wonder Lucy was anxious to escape from such a scene of uproar and confusion. But at the very moment she had prevailed upon Gage to lend her his escort to the ante-chamber, Beau Freke, who personated an Ottoman prince, and was very gorgeously arrayed, rose, and enjoining silence on the noisy revellers, proposed their host's health. It is needless to say how the toast was received—nor that it was drunk with frantic enthusiasm. After the tumultuous applause had subsided, Gage was about to return thanks for the honour done him, when the attention of the whole assemblage was turned to the door of the supper-room, where a struggle was taking place between the lacqueys there stationed and two persons who were bent upon obtaining forcible admission. After a while the strenuous efforts of the intruders prevailed, and Sir Hugh Poynings and Parson Chedworth burst into the room. Amid a storm of oaths and incoherent ejaculations, Sir Hugh made it understood that he was in search of his daughter. His appearance as well as that of the parson occasioned general merriment, and the shouts of derisive laughter with which both were greeted did not tend to allay the old baronet's displeasure. Sir Hugh was without coat, cravat, or wig, and had an exceedingly tall nightcap on his head. Mr. Briscoe followed close at his heels, vainly endeavouring to restrain him.

"Where are you, Loo?—where are you?" he roared. "Why don't you show your face, hussy?"

"Moderate yourself, Sir Hugh, I implore of you," the landlord cried. "You'll frighten all the ladies out of their senses."

"Find my daughter for me without delay, Briscoe—or by Heavens!——"

"There she sits, Sir Hugh," the host replied, pointing to the señora.

"What! in that black dress, all bedizened with lace? Are you sure, Briscoe? Don't deceive me, or I'll make minced-meat of you."

"I am quite sure, your worship."

Whereupon the old baronet seized the luckless señora's hand, and dragged her, notwithstanding her cries and resistance, out of her chair.

"Pretty doings!" he cried. "Come to your mother, Loo. How dared you attend this ball without leave? But you shall answer for your conduct by-and-by."

"Will nobody free me from this tipsy old fool, and turn him out of the room?" the señora cried. "You deserve horsewhipping for your rudeness, sir, and should be horsewhipped if I were a man. I thank my stars I am no daughter of yours."

"Let's see your face then, since you disown me," the old baronet rejoined.

And, as he spoke, he plucked off her mask, and disclosed the pretty features of Mrs. Jenyns.

"Whew!" he ejaculated; "a charming face, i' faith, but certainly not Loo's. Madam, I must apologise for my violence."

Meanwhile, as may be supposed, the real delinquent had watched her father's proceedings with no little dismay.

"How shall I escape without attracting his observation?" she said to Gage. "Oh! if I could only regain my own room."

"I'll manage it," the young man replied. "Come with me." And taking her under his arm he made his way towards the door, keeping on the further side of the table.

They might have got off without notice, if Mrs. Jenyns had not called the old baronet's attention to them.

"Look there," she said, maliciously.

"Ay, there she goes," Sir Hugh roared ; "that's my Loo—I'll swear to her. Stop! stop! I say."

But the more he shouted, the less the fugitives seemed inclined to attend to him. Quickening their steps, they presently gained the door, and disappeared long before Sir Hugh could reach it, his progress being barred by the servants, while Briscoe helped to pull back Parson Chedworth.

XXIV.

AND now, in order to afford some needful explanations, we must revert to that period of the evening when we left Sir Hugh Poynings and his chaplain fast asleep in their chairs, completely overcome by the potent punch brewed for them by the wily Mr. Briscoe.

As soon as the landlord perceived that his guests were in this helpless condition, feeling satisfied that the sleeping draught he had administered would last till morning, he caused them to be transported to the coach-house where Sir Hugh's travelling-carriage had been placed, and deposited at full length on the seats of the roomy vehicle. The removal was accomplished without the slightest difficulty, for the pair of topers were too far gone to offer any resistance; and their wigs, cravats, and upper vestments being removed, and nightcaps, pillows, and blankets provided, they were left to their repose. As the cunning landlord locked the coach-house door, and put the key in his pocket, he chuckled at the success of his scheme.

But his precautions were defeated, as we shall now proceed to relate. About midnight, a man wrapped in a cloak, beneath which he concealed a lighted horn lantern, made his way to the coach-house, unlocked the door, and went in. This personage was no other than Mr. Tibbits, who, having registered a vow of vengeance against Arthur Poynings, to be fulfilled before the morrow, took the present opportunity of executing his threat. The mischievous valet had passed part of the evening in the society of his newly-restored wife, and learnt from her that her young lady and Mr. Arthur were about to disobey Sir Hugh's orders, and clandestinely attend the ball. Mrs. Pinchbeck wouldn't for worlds the old gentleman should know it. He would never forgive Mr. Arthur or her young lady the deception practised upon him—never, she was convinced! This was just what Tibbits wanted. Revenge was now in his power, and he inwardly rejoiced. With affected indifference he asked what costumes the young folks meant to wear, and soon obtained from his communicative spouse all particulars likely to be serviceable to his design.

Later on, when the revel began, Tibbits hovered about the entrance-hall and passages until he had seen with his own eyes the Spanish hidalgo and his companions enter the ball-room. While he lingered for a few minutes, gazing at the motley assemblage inside, and envying the merriment he could not share, the second hidalgo and his companions arrived, filling him with astonishment at their exact resemblance to the previous party. Who could these be?—It would be vain to inquire. Nor did it much matter. Either the first Spaniard or the second must be Arthur. Both were in the ball-room. Of that he was assured; and though some confusion might arise, still young Poynings could not escape detection. He would now wake up Sir Hugh and communicate the pleasing intelligence to him.

A keen-witted fellow like Tibbits does not do business by halves. Thus we may be quite sure the knowing valet had made himself acquainted with the strange quarters in which the old baronet was lodged; and though Mr. Briscoe had secured the key of the coach-house, the clever rascal had found means of opening the lock. A crown piece bestowed on the ostler placed another key, as well as a lantern, at his disposal. But he was interrupted just as he was going forth on his errand. Mrs. Pinchbeck had been engaged for the last two hours in attiring her young lady for the ball, and being now at liberty, was on the look-out for him to take her to supper. Not to arouse her suspicions, Tibbits was forced to comply, and very reluctantly sat down with her in a back room appropriated to the servants, meaning to make a speedy escape. But he stayed longer than he expected, for Mrs. Pinchbeck excited his curiosity by repeating a conversation she had overheard between her young mistress and Clare Fairlie, from which it appeared that the latter had determined upon leaving her father that very night.

" And I'm sure I can't blame her," Mrs. Pinchbeck said, in conclusion, "if all I hear of Mr. Fairlie be true. Poor thing, she's dreadfully unhappy."

" I can't see any great cause for her affliction," Tibbits rejoined; " and as to Mr. Fairlie, he seems a very good kind of father, as fathers go. However, that's the young lady's affair, not mine. If she chooses to elope, I shan't hinder her. But I suppose she don't mean to go off alone. There's a lover in the case, I'll be sworn."

" No—no—she's half distracted, I tell you."

" She must be entirely so, to commit such folly," Tibbits rejoined, with a sneer. " I can't say I commiserate her. But I *am* rather concerned for old Fairlie, as I fancy he won't like it."

" Your compassion is thrown away upon such a rascal. I feel no pity for him whatever, and should like to see him hanged at Tyburn."

" Hush! not so loud, my dear," Tibbits cried, looking round in alarm. " It's very well nobody heard you. You musn't speak in such disrespectful terms of Mr. Fairlie. He's no worse than every other worthy gentleman's steward, whose master is foolish enough to trust him," he added, lowering his tone.

" Perhaps not," Mrs. Pinchbeck rejoined; " but that's no excuse for his knavery. Why, he is doing his best to ruin Mr. Monthermer."

" I must again impress upon you the necessity of caution, my love. This is not the place where private matters can be discussed. Luckily all the household are absent just now. Listen to me," he added, sinking his voice to a whisper: " Mr. Monthermer is born to be a dupe—some men are so. Old Fairlie will profit most by him no doubt—but there are others I could mention who will come in for a share of the spoil. My own master, Mr. Freke, and Sir Randal will be large gainers—to say nothing of Mrs. Jenyns."

" Don't mention that horrid creature to me, Tibbits," Mrs. Pinchbeck cried, with a look of virtuous indignation. " I'm perfectly scandalised at such proceedings. I don't wonder at Miss Fairlie's determination to fly. I should fly too, if I were so circumstanced. My young lady approves of her design, and so does Mr. Arthur."

" Oh! Mr. Arthur approves of it, does he ?" Mr. Tibbits cried.

"Soh!—soh! I begin to see more clearly into the matter. Perhaps he will assist in the flight—eh?"

Mrs. Pinchbeck gave a slight nod in token of assent.

"Now it's out. I knew there must be a lover in the case," Tibbits cried. "When are they to meet?—and where?"

"Oh! I know nothing more than I've told you. But how's this?—surely, you're not going to leave me?" she said, with a look of tender reproach as her husband rose to depart.

"I must tear myself away, sweetheart," he replied. "I am obliged to wait on my master during supper. As soon as he sets me at liberty I'll return."

"You know where to find me, Tibbits," she said.

The valet replied that he did, and hurried away, fearful of further detention.

On gaining the inn-yard, he stood still to reflect, and after a moment's consideration, decided upon seeing Mr. Fairlie in the first instance, and acquainting him with his daughter's intended flight. With this purpose he shaped his course towards the ball-room, and having stated to Mr. Briscoe that he had a message of pressing importance to deliver to Mr. Fairlie, the landlord directed him to proceed to the card-room, where he would find the object of his search. Mr. Fairlie chanced to be engaged, and some little time elapsed before the valet could obtain speech with him. Greatly astounded by the communication, Mr. Fairlie took Tibbits aside, and questioned him sharply as to how he had gained his information. At first the steward seemed incredulous, but ere long his uneasiness became manifest. Promising the valet a reward proportionate to the service he had rendered, he enjoined silence, and dismissed him. Fairlie then commenced his investigations, which speedily resulted in the discovery that his daughter had disappeared—at all events, he ascertained that a Spanish señora and don had recently quitted the ball-room with so much haste as to attract attention. Further inquiry showed him that two ladies, whom he could not doubt to be Clare and Lucy, had changed dresses behind one of the screens in the ante-chamber. We have already seen what occurred to him in the supper-room, and shall leave him for the present to follow Mr. Tibbits.

Having succeeded in alarming Mr. Fairlie, the valet next

betook himself to the coach-house, in order to go through a like process with Sir Hugh. On opening the door of the carriage he found its two occupants comfortably wrapped up in their blankets, and snoring away as if in emulation of each other. Holding the lantern to the old baronet's face, he gave him so vigorous a shake that he soon wakened him. Alarmed by the light, and not comprehending where he was, Sir Hugh roared out, "Thieves! thieves!" and at the same time endeavouring to spring from the seat and becoming entangled in the blanket, he fell upon the still slumbering chaplain, whose outcries were instantly added to his own. Half suffocated by the weight imposed upon him, and fancying he was about to be murdered, Parson Chedworth seized Sir Hugh by the ears, and buffeted him soundly. The old baronet replied in the same style, and the conflict might have been of some duration if the valet had not interposed, and by thrusting forward the lantern, enabled the combatants to distinguish each other's features. Great was the chaplain's surprise and dismay to find whom he had been cuffing so heartily; while Sir Hugh was no less amazed. However, the old baronet's wrath was speedily turned into another channel when he learnt from Tibbits that his son and daughter were actually present at the masked ball. The chaplain strove to pour oil on the troubled waters, but in vain. Sir Hugh got out of the coach, and without stopping to put on his coat, or remove his nightcap, went in search of some of his own servants, and proceeding to the inn-kitchen as the most likely place to hear of them, found his coachman there playing at cribbage with Tom Maddocks, the head ostler, and a couple of grooms. Beccles stared at seeing his master in such a strange guise, and thought he must have become suddenly demented; and he was confirmed in the notion when he received peremptory orders to bring out the carriage and put to the horses without a moment's delay.

"What! at this time of night, Sir Hugh?" he remonstrated.

"Do as I bid you, Beccles," Sir Hugh rejoined, in an authoritative tone. "Be ready to start in half an hour's time, or you lose your place."

"Well, I'll do my best," the coachman replied, getting up sulkily. And followed by Tom Maddocks and the grooms, he repaired to the stables.

XXV.

UNDER WHAT CIRCUMSTANCES SIR HUGH POYNINGS'S TRAVELLING-CARRIAGE WAS DRIVEN OFF.

SHORTLY afterwards another extraordinary incident occurred, which led Beccles to conclude that his old master was not the only one of the family touched in the upper story.

Scarcely had the coachman and his assistants got out the carriage, and cleared it of the blankets and other things left inside it by its late occupants, when a tall Spaniard, with a lady under his arm of a noble presence, but rather singularly dressed as it appeared to Beccles, and whose features were concealed by a mask, came quickly up to him, and ordered him to open the door of the vehicle without an instant's delay. Greatly amazed, but recognising Arthur's voice, though the young gentleman's masquerade attire had puzzled him at first, Beccles complied, and the lady instantly sprang into the carriage, and retired to its furthest corner, as if anxious for concealment. Arthur bent forward for a moment, addressed a few words to her in an under tone, and then closing the door, took Beccles out of hearing of the ostler and the grooms, and told him to keep careful watch over the young lady, and see that she was not molested in any way.

"I have promised her protection, Beccles, and I put her under your charge, as I know I can rely on you. Search may possibly be made for her, but let no one look into the carriage—above all, Mr. Fairlie. Take your own way of inducing those fellows to hold their tongues," he added, pointing to Tom Maddocks and the grooms.

"But Sir Hugh has ordered me to put to the horses directly, Muster Arthur," Beccles remarked. "Must I do it?"

"Of course. Get ready for starting as quickly as you can, but on no account allow Sir Hugh to enter the carriage till you see me."

"Oons, Muster Arthur, that's easily said. But suppose he *will* get in, how am I to hinder him?"

"Oh! you'll find out a way of doing it. Make any excuse to gain time."

"Lord lovee, Muster Arthur, I'd go through fire and water to serve you, but I daren't offend Sir Hugh. It's as much as my place be worth."

"Rest quite easy, Beccles. I'll hold you harmless, and reward you handsomely into the bargain. Attend to my orders."

"Very well, Muster Arthur, I suppose you must have your way. But it be sorely against my inclination to disobey Sir Hugh."

"I'll make it all right, I tell you," Arthur rejoined, walking quickly away.

"Dang me if I can understand what he'd be at!" Beccles thought. "It's my opinion both father and son be cracked. Well, I suppose I must side wi' young master."

With this self-communion he returned to the ostler and the grooms, and in pursuance of his intructions bound them over to secrecy in regard to the lady inside the carriage; and while the horses were put to, debated with himself what had best be done under the circumstances; the result of his cogitations being an order to Tom Maddocks to mount the box, and hold himself in readiness to drive off, when he, Beccles, should give him the hint. Maddocks had just got up, and taken the whip in hand, when Mr. Fairlie, accompanied by Bellairs, Chassemouche, and a link-boy, bearing a flambeau, suddenly burst into the inn-yard. The unusual spectacle at such an hour of a travelling-carriage, with horses attached to it, naturally attracted the steward's attention, and, addressing Beccles, he asked what was the meaning of his master's sudden departure. Receiving no very satisfactory answer to the inquiry, he ordered the coachman to open the carriage door.

"What for, sir?" Beccles demanded, sulkily.

"Because I suspect some one is concealed within. That's enough for you."

"No, it isn't. I'm sure Sir Hugh would never allow you to set foot in his carriage, and while I can raise a hand to prevent it you never shall."

"Ah, ma foi! dere is a lady in the coche—I see her quite plain," Chassemouche exclaimed. He had snatched the flambeau from the link-boy and run to the other side of the carriage.

"It's only Mrs. Pinchbeck," Beccles shouted. "I won't have her disturbed."

"Be off, you meddling hound," Maddocks cried, cutting at the Frenchman with his whip.

"Ah! sacrebleu! do you dare strike me!" Chassemouche cried. And he hurled the flambeau at the ostler, who luckily avoided the dangerous missile, and retaliated with a further application of the whip to the Frenchman's shoulders. The torch fell into a little pool, and became extinguished, leaving all in darkness as before.

"Come, sirrah!" Fairlie cried, "I will be trifled with no longer. I am sure my daughter is in the carriage. You had better be reasonable. I have the means of enforcing obedience to my orders, and rely upon it I will use them."

"Once more I tell you, Muster Fairlie, you shall never set foot in my master's carriage—and now you're answered, sir."

At this juncture, a slight diversion was occasioned by the appearance of two other actors on the scene, the foremost of whom was Sir Hugh Poynings. The old baronet suddenly issued from the side-door of the hotel, and was followed by his chaplain.

"What's all this?" exclaimed Sir Hugh. "Oddslife! are you going to take my carriage by storm?"

"It may put an end to this unseemly altercation, Sir Hugh," Mr. Fairlie said, "if I inform you that I am in search of my daughter."

"Precisely my own case, sir—I am in search of mine. I saw her quit the ball just now with that young prodigal—Gage Monthermer, and I've lost all traces of her."

"I shall be happy to aid you in your quest, Sir Hugh, if you will first oblige me by a sight of the lady inside your carriage."

"I didn't know there was a lady inside it," the old baronet rejoined. "Who is she, Beccles?"

"I've already told Muster Fairlie it be Mrs. Pinchbeck, but he won't believe me, and wants to get in and satisfy himself. I know your honour won't permit it."

"Well, I don't know what to say," Sir Hugh rejoined. "If it be Mrs. Pinchbeck, there can be no harm in her getting out."

" Oons, your honour," Beccles exclaimed, " I didn't expect you
to knock under to the like of Muster Fairlie."

" Knock under! rascal—I'd have you to know that a Poynings
never yet knocked under."

" So I've always heard say, Sir Hugh; but this looks woundy
like it."

" Really, Sir Hugh, the impertinence of this fellow is past all
endurance, and I wonder you can tolerate it," Mr. Fairlie remarked,
in a bland tone. " I am sorry to put you to any trouble, but I
am sure you will excuse me under the circumstances. If you will
get into the carriage, and assure me from your own observation
that the person inside is not my daughter, I shall be perfectly
satisfied. I think I may venture to ask thus much of your politeness."

" Well, I see no objection to that, sir," the old baronet replied.

And he approached the carriage, but Beccles planted himself
sturdily before the door.

" Your honour don't do it," he said, doggedly.

" Don't do what, rascal? Zounds! will you dare oppose me?"

" Your honour shan't demean yourself by obeying Muster
Fairlie. I'm too trusty a servant to let my master be cajoled by
his flummery. Let him and me settle it."

" You must be drunk, fellow, to act in this way," the old
baron   roared.

" ' ur pardon, Sir Hugh," Fairlie interposed—" the man is
sobe   nough, but is evidently bent on thwarting me, and takes
this   .nning means of doing so. But it shall not succeed. I am
no'   atisfied that my suspicions are correct. Allow me to deal
with him? Will you listen to reason, sirrah?" he demanded, in
a stern tone, of Beccles. " I ask you for the last time."

" My answer's the same as before," the coachman rejoined.
" Now, Tom," he roared to Maddocks, " drive on."

The whip resounded, and in another instant the lumbering
vehicle was in motion. As Mr. Fairlie saw it move off he uttered
an exclamation of rage, and felt inclined to knock down his
audacious opponent, but some fears of the consequences perhaps
restrained him. As to Sir Hugh, in spite of his anger he could
not help laughing at this unexpected termination of the dispute.
No one doubted that the carriage would be speedily stopped, and

most of the party followed it as it rolled out of the inn-yard.

By this time, a large portion of the assemblage which we have described as congregated in front of the Angel had dispersed. Still, there was a considerable crowd near the door of the hotel, while numerous carriages were drawn up on the opposite side of the square. Besides these, there were sedan-chairs in abundance, and around the latter were collected groups of footmen, chairmen, and link-boys, smoking, drinking, and otherwise amusing themselves. As Sir Hugh's enormous travelling-carriage came rumbling into the square it astonished all beholders. No one could conceive what had brought it out at that time of night. The shouts raised by Mr. Fairlie and the others of " Stop it!—stop it!" were echoed by a hundred voices, and even if Maddocks had intended going further, he could not have got beyond the portal of the hotel.

Just as he pulled up, half a dozen lacqueys, in the gorgeous Monthermer livery, rushed down the steps, and posted themselves on either side of the door of the vehicle. Mr. Briscoe followed them almost immediately, and ordered Maddocks to descend from the box. While Mr. Fairlie was struggling with the crowd, trying to get up to the carriage, and wondering what was about to happen, to his infinite astonishment he beheld Gage issue forth from the hotel, with a lady under his arm, masked and enveloped in a black domino. Behind them came a smart little page, whose white satin habiliments were partially concealed by a cloak. Unlike the other two, Monthermer wore no vizard, and his features were therefore fully distinguishable by the torchlight. A large roquelaure was thrown over his shoulders.

As Gage hastily descended the steps with his fair companion, the coach door was opened by the lacquey nearest it, and in another moment the lady and her page were inside, and the door closed upon them. All this was the work of a few seconds, but brief as was the space, it sufficed to show Fairlie that the coach was tenanted by another lady—most likely, his daughter. He redoubled his efforts to press through the throng, but in vain. As a last resource, he shouted to Gage, but the young gentleman took no notice of him, being otherwise occupied.

Mounting with unwonted activity to the seat lately vacated by Maddocks, Gage snatched up the reins and applied the whip to the horses with such good will, that they instantly started off at gallop. Free course was now made for the rattling vehicle by the assemblage, who were greatly entertained, and amidst general laughter and cheering, it speedily disappeared. Sir Hugh came up just as the coach had started, and laughed as heartily as the rest of the bystanders, till Fairlie made him alter his tone.

" Are you aware that your daughter is gone, Sir Hugh? " Fairlie said. " She is inside the carriage—and so is mine."

" My daughter! What! has he dared to carry her off? 'Sblood! I must give chase instantly. A coach!—a coach!" But though there were plenty of vehicles at hand, not one stirred at the call.

"It's my fault that this has happened, sir," Arthur cried, coming up. " But I'll repair the error. As soon as my horse is saddled I'll follow them."

" You shan't go alone," Mr. Fairlie said. " A horse instantly, Briscoe."

" And another for me," Sir Hugh roared. " We'll all start in pursuit. But zounds! I must put on my coat, and get myself a little in order for the chase. If Gage should break his neck in going down that infernal hill without a drag, it would serve him right—but then what would become of poor Lucy ?"

XXVI.

THE DEBT OF HONOUR, AND HOW IT WAS PAID.

THREE MONTHS have elapsed. A long term in the life of our last-going hero. In three months he could squander away as much money, and commit as many follies, as other and slower folk could contrive to do in as many years. In three months, by a lucky hit, some people *have* made a fortune: in the same space of time Gage found it equally easy to spend one.

Three months then have gone by: three months of unheard-of extravagance and waste—of riot, profligacy, exhaustion.

These three months have been passed in town, in the society of rakes, gamblers, and other ministers to so-called pleasure. They have been passed in an eternal round of dissipation. No pause— no restraint—ever onwards at the same headlong pace.

Each day has brought some fresh amusement—some new excitement. Each day has been marked by some act of folly or profusion—by some mad frolic, unbridled excess, or piece of scarcely-conceivable prodigality.

Each night has been spent in debasing orgies—in the gambling ordinaries, in scouring the streets, in conflicts with the watch.

The cup of pleasure has been drained to the very dregs. The supposed inexhaustible purse of Fortunatus is almost emptied. The race is nearly run.

At first view, it seems scarcely credible that any person in his senses should be guilty of the outrageous follies and vicious excesses we have imputed to our hero: the more so, as we have always affirmed that he was not destitute of good qualities. But the good in him was now overmastered by evil. Yielding to temptations of all kinds, he had fallen. His wealth, which, properly used, would have given him a proud position, and enabled him to perform a thousand beneficent and worthy actions, had proved a bane instead of a blessing. It served to enervate his nature and corrupt his principles; rendering him a mark for the parasite, the sharper, and their harpy train. Indolent, luxurious, profuse, he was content at first to purchase pleasures; but as these palled, from repetition and over-indulgence, he sought excitement in play, and what in the commencement had been mere distraction, became in the end an all-engrossing passion. He could not exist without cards and dice—and though his immense losses at the gaming-table might have operated as a check, they incited him to go on. He was not without moments of compunction—indeed of remorse—but he banished these feelings as quickly as they arose. Of late, he had begun to drink deeply, and when inflamed with wine, he committed frantic excesses. By such a course of conduct, if he accomplished nothing else, he fully achieved the grand point of his ambition, which was to be accounted the greatest rake of the day. His unbounded extravagances had long been the talk of the town; and his wild freaks gained him an unenviable notoriety. Still, though his speedy downfal was predicted on all hands, he maintained his position, for his debts of honour were duly discharged. Whether his less honourable debts were paid with equal punctuality was of small concern—except to his creditors.

With the fair syren, whose charms had enslaved him, and whose extravagance had contributed in no slight degree to his ruin, Gage continued wildly infatuated as ever; more so, perhaps, for since he had been unable to gratify her caprices to the same extent as formerly, she made it evident that she cared little for him, and her manifest indifference, so far from diminishing his passion, increased it almost to frenzy. He became furiously jealous of her, and as she frequently, from the mere pleasure of tormenting him, encouraged the attentions of some presumptuous coxcomb, more than one duel resulted from her heartless conduct. Little recked Mrs. Jenyns that her lover thus jeopardised his life on her account. She laughed when told of the hostile meetings in which he had been engaged, and vowed they gave her éclat. Gage now made the discovery—but too late to profit by it—that the beautiful actress was totally without heart. Not only did she not love him now, but she had never loved him. This he understood; yet his insane passion remained incurable. The Circe had thoroughly bewitched him. Once, and once only, since he had been first entangled, had an opportunity occurred to him of breaking the fetters of the enchantress. This was immediately after the memorable masked ball at Bury Saint Edmund's, when for a few days he regained his freedom, and yielding to better influences, shunned her baneful society. But ere a week had gone by, he was again at her feet; and though the fair conqueror was willing to forgive, she took care that her clemency should not be too easily obtained, and exacted pledges for future obedience. It is possible that Gage might at this time have succeeded in wholly estranging himself from her, if she had not had a secret and powerful ally in Fairlie. It was chiefly owing to his instrumentality that the ill-starred reconciliation was effected. Thenceforward the syren maintained her sway.

Hitherto, Mr. Fairlie had answered all his reckless employer's pecuniary demands upon him—not without feigned remonstrances, certainly—nor without cent. per cent. interest for the loans, and sufficient security for repayment; but he had already begun to debate with himself how soon matters ought to be brought to an end. The mine was ready to explode, and the train had but to be fired. The steward waited for the fitting moment to apply the match, and meanwhile, like a skilful engineer, took every precaution to ensure himself from damage.

By this time the position of the two had become reversed. Fairlie was master; Monthermer dependent. Gage's estates in Suffolk were all mortgaged—mortgaged, it would seem, past redemption—and the real owner of Monthermer Castle, though he had not as yet asserted his claim to it, was Felix Fairlie More than this, all Monthermer's sumptuous furniture, magnificent plate, pictures, equipages, stud of horses, everything, in short, of value, once belonging to him, had been pledged to Fairlie, and could be seized by the rapacious steward whenever he chose.

Still Gage went on recklessly as ever, and kept up the same gay and gallant exterior. His horses and equipages were still the admiration of all who beheld them in Piccadilly or the Park; and not one of the fops to be met on the Mall or in Saint James's-street was distinguished by greater richness or taste of apparel. His entertainments at his mansion in Dover-street were still mag-

.ilicent, and of his numerous retinue of attendants not one had
oeen discharged. Most of these, seeing how matters were going
on, had taken good care of themselves. It is true that some of
the tradesmen whom our prodigal hero honoured with his custom,
having received private information as to the state of his affairs,
had become rather clamorous for payment, but Mr. Fairlie had
hitherto taken care that Gage should not be personally annoyed
by duns.

Having thus shown how the last three months had been spent by
our hero, we shall proceed with his history.

One morning, towards the end of July, a party of young men,
most of them richly attired, but of very dissolute appearance, were
breakfasting at a rather late hour in the large room of White's
Chocolate House, in Saint James's-street. Some few, while sipping
their chocolate, glanced at the journals of the day, not for the
purpose of ascertaining what was going on in the political world
—for they cared little about such information—but in order
to pick up a scandalous anecdote or story with which they
might subsequently divert their acquaintance. Others, and these
were the noisiest of the company, were recounting their adven-
tures overnight in the streets and gambling-houses—telling how
they had scoured High Holborn and Chancery-lane, and broken
the windows of those old rogues the lawyers abiding in or near
that thoroughfare; how they had bravely battled with the watch,
what tremendous blows they had given and received—in proof of
which latter assertion the plaisters on their pates were exhibited;
how they had been captured, and rescued as they were being
haled by the constables and their myrmidons to the round-house;
and how in the end they had come off victoriously, with a vast
quantity of trophies in the shape of smashed lanterns, disabled
rattles, and splintered constables' staves.

The person to whom these roystering blades owed their deliverance from the minions of the law was no other than Gage
Monthermer, who came up most opportunely with another band
of scourers from Long-acre and Drury-lane, and speedily put the
watchmen to rout. Gage, it appeared, had been drinking deeply
and "roaring handsomely"—in other words, he had been creating
terrible disturbances in the quarters which he and his inebriate
companions had visited.

And here we may as well explain, for the benefit of the uninitiated, that the young bloods of the time, after a hard drinking-bout, were wont to amuse themselves and cool their heated brains by scouring the streets, and insulting and maltreating every decent person they encountered. Occasionally, with frantic yells, which they termed "roaring," they would burst into the taverns, clear them of their guests, and then proceed to trounce and kick the waiters. Daubing over signs, wrenching off knockers, breaking windows, extinguishing street-lamps, and tripping up chairmen, were among the mildest frolics of these jovial gentlemen. Long ere this, Gage had earned so much distinction amongst the scourers, or Mohocks, as they delighted to be called, that by common consent he had been elected their chief. Gage was proud of the title, and naturally enough attributed his election to his eminent merits as a scourer; but there was another reason, though this was not put forward, which had influenced the Mohocks in their choice of a leader. Such pranks as they played were not to be committed altogether with impunity. Some one must pay the piper, and who so able to do it as Gage? Our hero soon discovered, that if it was a fine thing (as surely it was) to be chief of the scourers, it was rather expensive work to maintain the position; and that to mend all the windows broken by his followers, re-gild and re-paint the signs they had disfigured, and find new knockers for the doors they had injured—to say nothing of fees to watchmen and others, as well as plaisters for broken heads—he soon discovered, we say, that these things, when of constant recurrence, and coming upon himself alone, cost a trifle.

Many of Gage's nocturnal exploits were recounted with infinite zest by the young bloods we have described, and great admiration was expressed at his courage and skill; all agreeing that he well deserved to be their leader, and only regretting that he could not hold the post much longer.

Seated at a table, somewhat removed from the rest of the company, were four personages whom we first met at Monthermer Castle, and who at that time professed the strongest regard for its wealthy owner. To listen to their discourse, it would seem that the warmth of their friendship must have considerably abated. As to assisting Gage in his hour of need, such an idea never for a moment entered their heads: if it had, they would have scouted it at once, as errant folly. From the time when we first encountered them up to the present moment, these ingrates had never lost sight of their dupe. It was not their fault that, towards the end of his career, Gage had fallen into the hands of a lower grade of cheats. They had warned him, but he would not take counsel. When he could lose his money like a gentleman—lose it *to* gentlemen—why should he play with common rooks at a gaming-ordinary—knaves who used false dice and cramped boxes? Was there ever such a bubble!

These four personages, it will be guessed, were Sir Randal de Meschines, Beau Freke, Lord Melton, and Brice Bunbury. Hark to their discourse.

"Then you think it is all up with our friend, eh, Sir Randal?" Brice Bunbury remarked.

"I am quite sure of it," the young baronet replied. "He lost five hundred pounds to me, two nights ago, at hazard, and when I applied to Fairlie for the money yesterday, it was refused."

"Humph! that looks suspicious indeed!" Brice exclaimed. "Hitherto all his debts of honour have been paid."

"He paid me a thousand pounds last week," Beau Freke observed, with a smile. "I have not played with him since. Old Fairlie gave me a hint when he handed over the money, and I have acted upon it."

"Fairlie cautioned me at the same time," Sir Randal said.

"Then you must put up with the loss with patience," Brice remarked. "You should not have played under such circumstances."

"I don't mean to lose the money. He *must* pay me."

"How the deuce is he to manage it, if Fairlie has stopped the supplies?" Lord Melton said. "He owes me a small bet of a few hundreds, but I consider it gone."

"Your lordship will act as you think proper," Sir Randal rejoined; "but I mean to be paid."

"Again, I ask—how?" Lord Melton said.

"You will see, if you remain here till two o'clock," Sir Randal returned, with a laugh. Then taking out his watch, he added, 'You won't have to wait long. It only wants a quarter of an hour of the time."

As these words were uttered, a young gentleman at an adjoining table, who up to this moment had been apparently occupied with a newspaper, looked up, and glanced at the speaker. He did not, however, attract Sir Randal's notice.

"I will tell you what I have done, and you will then judge what is likely to occur," pursued the young baronet, coldly. "I have despatched a note to Gage acquainting him with the failure of my application to Fairlie—and reminding him that the debt is a debt of honour. I have told him I shall be here at the hour I have just named, and expect to receive the money."

"He will send an excuse," Brice said.

"No, he will not," Sir Randal rejoined. "He knows I will take no excuses. Were he to fail me, I would publicly proclaim him a defaulter, and then his reputation as a man of honour would be for ever blasted."

"Scoundrel !" ejaculated the listener, under his breath.

"My opinion therefore is, that the money will be forthcoming." Sir Randal continued. "Notwithstanding old Fairlie's protestations to the contrary, I am sure this small sum may be screwed out of him."

"Egad, I don't consider five hundred pounds a small sum," Brice remarked. "I wish to goodness I possessed as much. But I hope you won't proceed to extremities with Gage. Recollect how much you have got out of him—and how often you have feasted with him."

"I don't care," the young baronet rejoined. "I must be paid. Let me see," he added, again consulting his watch—"ten minutes to two."

"By Jove! I begin to feel quite uneasy," Brice observed, rising. "I shall be off."

"Sit down," Sir Randal cried, authoritatively. "I want you to be present at the interview."

"Interview!" Brice exclaimed, reluctantly complying with the injunction. "Do you think he will come in person?"

"Not a doubt of it."

"The best thing Gage can do to repair his fallen fortunes will be to marry a rich heiress," Beau Freke remarked.

"Where is he to find her?" Lord Melton laughed.

"Fairlie's daughter, if she would have him, would be the thing just now."

"Poh! poh! old Fairlie would not now consent to the match—much as he once desired it," Brice said.

"A truce to jesting on this subject, gentlemen, if you please," Sir Randal interposed. "Fairlie has promised me his daughter in marriage."

"You!" the beau ejaculated. "Why, he has given me a like promise."

"With the view of sowing discord between you," Brice said; "but don't let him succeed in his purpose. For my part, I wish Gage could win her. It would set him on his legs again."

"I tell you he has no chance," Sir Randal cried, impatiently. "Fairlie knows too well what he is about to wed her to such an irreclaimable spendthrift."

"Well, then, there is Lucy Poynings," Brice suggested—"a charming girl—far prettier, to my fancy, than Clare Fairlie. If he will promise to reform, and retire to the country, he may persuade her to accept him."

"Pshaw, she has been long cured of her silly attachment to him," Sir Randal replied. "Gage and myself have often met her at Ranelagh, Marylebone Gardens, and other places, and she would not even look at him."

"Apropos of Clare and Lucy, do you remember how he drove off with them both in Sir Hugh Poynings's travelling carriage, after the masquerade at Bury?" Beau Freke observed.

"Ha! ha! ha!" Brice roared, "what a laugh we had at that droll adventure! It might have been no laughing matter, though, to Gage. Ten to one he had broken his neck when he upset the coach in galloping down that steep hill. It was lucky the poor girls inside were uninjured. But they must have been confoundedly frightened, as well as terribly shaken. Do you recollect the woeful appearance they all presented when they were brought back to the Angel? The only lively one amongst them was little Lettice Rougham, and she had lost none of her spirit. Odd, that her father should come up just in time to rescue them all from their peril, and get Gage from under the horses' feet, or most assuredly he would have had his brains dashed out."

"Supposing him to have any, which may admit of a doubt," laughed Sir Randal.

"Well, I fancied that night's adventure had wrought a great change in his character," Brice continued. "For a few days, on his return to town, he seemed disposed to turn over a new leaf, and not to be over fond of *our* society. Things, however, soon came round, and he resumed his old habits."

"For that we have chiefly to thank Mr. Fairlie," Lord Melton remarked.

"Yes—because we were necessary to him," Beau Freke rejoined. "I shall never forget his alarm when, for a brief space, he *really* believed that Gage was about to reform. He thought his prize would be snatched from him. Mrs. Jenyns, who had been cast off, had to be reinstated without delay."

"That was to counteract a purer influence which had begun to tell upon the dupe," Brice said. "If Gage had been left alone for another week he would have married Lucy Poynings—that is, if she would have had him—and then he would have bidden adieu for ever to Mr. Fairlie, and to some other of his obliging friends."

"Not so loud," Beau Freke said; "I fancy the person at that table, who appears to be a stranger here, is listening to us."

"Well, unless he is a friend of Monthermer's he can have heard nothing to interest him," Lord Melton laughed. "We have been talking of no one else."

More than once, the young man referred to had cast an indignant glance at the speakers, and seemed about to interrupt their discourse. But he now took up the newspaper again, and seemed occupied with it.

"It is two o'clock!" Sir Randal exclaimed. "He won't come."

"You are wrong,—he is here," Brice Bunbury cried. "I wish I could vanish," he added to himself.

As the exclamations were uttered, Gage entered the room, and after returning the salutations of such of the company as greeted him, he passed on towards Sir Randal. His habiliments, though rich, were slightly disordered, and he looked more rakish than heretofore. His laced cravat was carelessly arranged, his peruke dishevelled, and his features haggard and worn by debauchery; while, despite his efforts to conceal it, there was a visible embarrassment in his manner. As he approached the table at which his quondam friends were seated, Brice sprang forward to meet him, and pressed his hand with affected warmth. Beau

Freke and Lord Melton were cordial enough in manner—but Sir Randal made no advance, and merely bowed stiffly.

"I knew you would be punctual, Monthermer," he said. "I told our friends so."

"I must beg you to accept my apology, Sir Randal," Gage replied. "I am extremely sorry to disappoint you, but Fairlie will not make the required advance. Such a paltry sum can be of no consequence to you I— will pay you in a few days."

"You will pardon me, Mr. Monthermer," Sir Randal replied, "if I remind you of what I intimated in my letter, that this is a debt of honour, and must be repaid on pain of forfeiture of your character as a gentleman."

"Oh! yes,—that is quite understood. I will pay it—I mean to pay it—only give me a few days. I am a good deal harassed at this moment."

"Your perplexities are not likely to decrease, sir, and I cannot therefore grant you further delay."

"But 'sdeath! what am I to do, Sir Randal?" Gage cried. "How am I to raise the money?"

"Ay, that's just it—that's precisely what Lord Melton said," Brice interposed. "What the deuce is he to do to raise the money?"

"You should have thought of this before," Sir Randal said.

"Will you lend me the amount for a few days, Freke?" Gage said to the beau, who, however, shook his head, and expressed his regrets at being compelled to decline. "Will you oblige me, my lord?" Monthermer added, appealing with equal ill-success to the sporting nobleman. "I suppose it is in vain to ask you?" he concluded, addressing Brice Bunbury.

"You shouldn't need to ask twice, if I had the money, Monthermer," Brice replied. "I'd lend it you with all the pleasure in life."

"Then I must positively throw myself upon your good nature to hold me excused for a few days longer, Sir Randal," Gage said to the young baronet. "You must take my word, as a gentleman, for the payment of the money."

"I will *not* take it," Sir Randal rejoined, insolently.

"How!" Gage exclaimed, starting, and involuntarily laying his hand upon his sword. "This is the first time I have been doubted. I must have satisfaction for this affront."

THE DEBT OF HONOUR.

" Pay me the money, and I will give you satisfaction, Mr. Monthermer. But do not imagine I will cross swords with any man of tarnished honour—and such you will be held when once I proclaim you a defaulter."

" Tarnished honour !" Gage cried, in a voice of anguish. " Can such an opprobrious term be applied to me ? Have I no friend left ?"

" Apparently not," said the young man described as seated at an adjoining table, and who, as he came forward, proved to be Arthur Poynings. " I will lend you the money you require," he added, placing a pocket-book in Gage's hands. " Pay this *honourable* gentleman," he cried, with scornful emphasis, and regarding Sir Randal with supreme contempt.

" I will not take the money thus offered," Sir Randal exclaimed.

" By Heaven ! you *shall* take it," Gage cried, opening the pocket-book, and forcing the bank-notes it contained upon the young baronet. " Count them, sir—count them in the presence of these gentlemen, for I will not trust your word. Huzza ! my honour is saved. Arthur, I am for ever beholden to you."

" Gratitude is all your friend is likely to get, Monthermer, so it is well to be lavish of it," Sir Randal said. " Mr. Arthur Poynings, you will have an account to settle with me. It is not the first time we have met—but if you will afford me another opportunity, I promise you it shall be the last."

" I refuse your challenge, Sir Randal," Arthur said.

" Refuse it, sir !"

" Ay, utterly refuse it—on the ground that you are a sharper— and as such I will everywhere denounce you."

Scarcely were these words out of Arthur's mouth, than Sir Randal's sword sprang from its sheath, and he would have attacked young Poynings if Gage had not seized him by the throat, and hurled him forcibly backwards.

In an instant the whole room was in confusion. All the rest of the company arose, and rushed to the scene of strife. Sir Randal was so furiously exasperated, that, fearful of mischief ensuing, Beau Freke and Lord Melton judged it prudent to get him away, and with difficulty succeeded in removing him. When order was at last restored, Gage looked about for Arthur, to renew his thanks to him for his opportune assistance, but the young man had disappeared.

XXVII.

MR. FAIRLIE was alone in a spacious apartment in Monthermer's magnificent mansion in Dover-street. We call the house Monthermer's—but only by courtesy—for in reality it belonged to the present occupant of the chamber. The room we propose to inspect lay at the back, on the ground-floor, and opened upon a garden, in which there were some fine trees, now of course in full foliage, since it was summer season. Between the lofty windows and the table at which the steward was seated stood a screen, so that he could not be overlooked from without. The trees intercepted the sunshine, and the tall screen further darkened the chamber, and gave it a gloomy air. The furniture, too, was dingy, and the walls—where not occupied with bookcases—were hung with choice pictures, chiefly of the Dutch school. It was, in fact, the library, or study, and had been the favourite retreat of the Honourable Sackville Spencer, the former possessor of the house, who used to pass many hours of each day within it in the society of his beloved authors. All the rest of the mansion had been newly and splendidly furnished by Gage at the time of its purchase, but this room was allowed to remain in its original state to please Fairlie, who made choice of it for his own occupation. Here he passed as many hours daily as the lettered Sackville Spencer had been wont to pass, but in very different studies. Our steward, it will be readily conceived, made but slight acquaintance with the poets, philosophers, and divines, by whom he was surrounded. He had no greater taste for art than for literature. He might sometimes condescend to look at the pictures; but he rarely, if ever, noticed the marble busts on the pedestals, whose cold gaze seemed to regard him as an intruder on their sanctuary. The only books that engrossed him were account-books, while the sole object on the walls that he deemed worthy of attention was a plan of Monthermer's Suffolk property. Whenever he had a few minutes to spare, or sought relaxation from his self-imposed toils, he would plant himself before this map, and tracing out with his finger the boundaries of some particular plot of land, would consider whether any change, beneficial to himself (for he now regarded himself as owner of the estates), could be effected. In fact, he was always making what he considered improvements in the property, without the slightest regard to the wishes or convenience of the tenants; offering in this respect, as in all others, a notable contrast to old Squire Warwick. There was little else worth remarking in the room; but we may just mention, that on the left of the fireplace was a deep closet, the door of which now stood partially open; while beyond the closet, and nearer the garden, was a side door, communicating by a short passage with an adjoining apartment, and forming a private entrance to the library: a means of access never used, except by Fairlie himself, or with his permission. Within reach of the steward, at the moment we have chosen for intruding on his privacy, was a large strong-box, provided with double locks, and secured by broad bands of iron. This mysterious-looking chest was ordinarily deposited for better security in the closet, but had been brought out on that morning, in order to facilitate the examination of certain documents which it contained.

Mr. Fairlie had been occupied with his accounts for more than five hours, verifying entries by reference to vouchers and memorandum-books, and casting up long columns of figures. He had just brought his labours to an end,—apparently to his entire satisfaction, for as he closed the ponderous ledger and fastened its brazen clasps, a triumphant smile played upon his countenance. He then turned round in his chair, unlocked the strong-box, and was in the act of placing a bundle of papers within it, when the side door we have alluded to suddenly opened, and admitted Mrs. Jenyns.

The smile on the steward's countenance instantly faded away, and gave place to a very different expression. He did not like to be disturbed, and showed his displeasure.

—

" What business have you to come in by that door, madam?"
he exclaimed, sharply. "You know it's against orders. I must
beg you to withdraw. I am particularly engaged at this moment."

The pretty actress, however, paid no attention to what he said,
but springing forward, arrested him before he could shut down the
lid of the chest.

" I've often longed to see the contents of that strong-box,"
she cried, "and now I can gratify my curiosity. What's here?"
she added, snatching at some parchments, and carrying them off
towards the window. " As I live, a mortgage from Gage de Monthermer of certain lands and farms in the county of Suffolk to
Felix Fairlie for forty thousand pounds! Why, bless me, Fairlie,
you don't mean to say you have lent Gage forty thousand pounds?"

" Never mind what I've lent him. Give me back the deed."

" Not till I've examined it," she continued. "What does this
memorandum mean, Fairlie?"

" It means that the mortgage-money not being paid when due,
the power of redemption has been cut off. In plain terms, the
lands are forfeited to me."

" Very sharp practice on your part, in sooth, Mr. Fairlie. The
estates, I conclude, must be worth at least double the sum lent upon
them?"

" Possibly so," the steward replied, drily.

" Thrice as much, I dare say, would be nearer the mark. Now
I'll be bound, Fairlie, you have gained nearly a hundred thousand
pounds by this transaction?"

" Nonsense! madam. How absurdly you talk."

" Not so absurdly, sir. But I've not done yet. Lud ha' mercy!
here's another mortgage on other lands in Suffolk,—including the
park and castle!"

" And here again I've been compelled to foreclose, madam—to
foreclose—d'ye understand?"

" To act the Jew I suppose you mean. You say you were
compelled to take this rigorous course; but I fancy very little com-
pulsion was required. In one way or other, you appear to have
got hold of all poor Monthermer's property."

" Poor Monthermer!" the steward echoed, with a sneer. "How
long is it since you began to feel compassion for him? You had
no scruple in helping to pluck the pigeon. I can count your

MRS. JENKYNS TAKING A PEEP INTO FAIRLIE'S STRONG BOX.

gains exactly if I choose—but in round numbers I may say that
you have lightened Monthermer's purse to the tune of some twenty
thousand pounds."

"Well, that's a mere trifle compared with your gains, Fairlie.
Besides, I've lost all my profits at play."

"Whose fault is that, pray? I manage to keep my winnings;
and since you desire to know what they are, I'll tell you." So
saying, he took her hand, and directed her attention to the plan
hanging against the wall.

"Look there, madam. All you behold upon that map is mine
—those domains—that castle—those villages—those farms—those
moorlands—those hills—that broad tract stretching from fifteen
miles inland to the very verge of the German Ocean—all belong
to me!"

"What a large landed proprietor you have contrived to make
yourself, Fairlie! But let me ask you, my good sir—and, since
nobody is by to hear you except myself, you may answer with sincerity—do you think all this property has been acquired honestly?"

"Just as honestly as if it had been bought in the ordinary
way. I have done no more than any one else would have done
under like circumstances."

"Oh, fie! you abominable hypocrite! Why, if you had not
played the extortioner with Gage, he would still be as well off
as any gentleman in Suffolk. For every thousand pounds lent
him you have exacted three. You are a terrible usurer, Fairlie—
a perfect Sir Giles Overreach. Pray, are you in funds now?"

"If you mean to inquire whether I hold any stock of money
belonging to Gage, I answer 'No.'"

"Then I'm almost afraid it is useless to ask you to cash me
this order from him—a mere trifle—a few hundreds?"

"Quite useless. I have closed accounts with Mr. Monthermer,
and will make no more advances. I am already on the wrong side.
Henceforth, he must raise money where he can, and how he can.
He gets no more from me—of that you may rest assured. He
must pay his debts,—or go to gaol."

"Go to gaol! You hard-hearted old wretch!"

"I must speak plainly, madam, or you will affect to misunderstand me. Your rich adorer is ruined—absolutely ruined. I recommend you, as a friend, to find another lover—equally wealthy

if you can—and equally lavish. Let me relieve you from these parchments."

And, as he spoke, he took the deeds from her, and placed them carefully within the box. While he was thus employed, Mrs. Jenyns came stealthily behind him, and peeped over his shoulder at the contents of the chest—showing by her gestures that she had made some discovery which she fancied of import-ance. Satisfied with the information she had acquired, she drew back quietly.

When Fairlie had locked up the chest, he turned to her, and said hastily, "I wait your further commands, madam? Pray be brief. I have told you I am busy."

"Oh! I've not the least desire to prolong the interview. All I want is cash for this order."

"I have already explained to you, most fully, as I conceived, that I cannot pay it. Mr. Monthermer ought not to have given it you. He cannot plead ignorance of his position. For the last few days I have been obliged to discontinue all payments on his account. You may have heard that I yesterday refused him five hundred pounds to pay a debt of honour to Sir Randal de Mes-chines."

"A very mean trick of you, Fairlie. I hope you heard how nobly Arthur Poynings behaved to him. But come, sir. I must have the money. I won't stir without it."

"You won't, eh?"

"Positively not. Hitherto I have been your accomplice—now I mean to act on my own account. I am sure you don't wish to make me an enemy, Fairlie."

"If I should be so unfortunate—owing to my refusal to comply with your demands—I shall regret it ; but it cannot be helped."

"Indeed you *will* regret it, Fairlie—and with good reason. I can do you a mischief—and I will."

"Poh! poh! I laugh at such silly threats, madam."

"You may laugh now, sir, but you won't laugh when I give Gage some information which I have derived from a peep into your strong-box."

"'Sdeath! what d'ye mean?—what do you fancy you have dis-covered?"

"Quite enough to make it worth your while to pay me a thousand pounds to hold my tongue.

"Accursed jade! what can she have seen?" Fairlie muttered. "She must have detected something, or she would not assume so bold a front.—Well, madam, we have always been good friends, and I have no desire to break with you. You shall have this thousand pounds. But mind! not in payment of Gage's order."

"As you please about that. Provided I get the money I am content. I thought you would prove reasonable," she added, with a mocking laugh.

Fairlie made no reply, but sat down to write out a memorandum. While the actress signed it, he unlocked a drawer, and taking from it a pile of bank-notes, handed them to her.

"You mustn't trouble me again," he said.

"I make no promises," she replied.

"Mrs. Jenyns," Fairlie remarked, rising, "before we part, let me give you a piece of advice. Believe me, nothing more is to be got from Gage. For your own sake I advise you to leave him at once. Indeed, I am surprised you should stay so long."

"I have no intention of abandoning him at present, Mr. Fairlie. I do not think so badly of his case as you would have me do. He may yet come round."

"Never! His case is hopeless, I tell you," the steward exclaimed, almost fiercely. "If you were inclined to listen to me— but I see you are not," he added, checking himself. "Good day, madam. Do as you please."

"I think I ought to tell you how I intend to employ the money you have given me so obligingly, Mr. Fairlie."

"I care not how you employ it—in some folly—at the gaming-table, no doubt."

"Five hundred pounds will be devoted to the repayment of Mr. Arthur Poynings."

"Zounds! madam. Are you mad?"

"The other five hundred will be used in an experiment which I hope may help to retrieve Gage's fortunes."

"Retrieve them!—pay Arthur Poynings! Give me back the money. You have obtained it under false pretences. You have robbed me."

But with a loud derisive laugh the actress broke from·him, and made a rapid exit by the same way she had entered the room.

XXVIII.

FROM WHICH IT WOULD APPEAR THAT MR. FAIRLIE SOMETIMES PROMISED MORE
THAN HE INTENDED TO PERFORM,

MR. FAIRLIE was highly incensed. He paced to and fro for some time, and had scarcely recovered his equanimity, when the door at the lower end of the room was opened, and Pudsey entered to announce Sir Randal de Meschines. The baronet was close at hand and could not be refused. So, though he would willingly have declined to see him, Fairlie put on a gracious aspect, and saluting his unwelcome visitor, offered him a seat.

" Of course you have heard what took place at White's yesterday, Fairlie?" Sir Randal observed, as soon as they were alone. " Since then, I have sent a friend to young Poynings, but he refuses me satisfaction for the insult offered."

" But you won't let him escape?" Fairlie cried.

" Make yourself easy on that score. I will force him into a duel, and then——"

" Run him through the lungs—eh? Quite right—quite right! I hate the fellow as much as you do, Sir Randal. By-the-by, you will be surprised to hear that Mrs. Jenyns is about to repay him the money he lent Gage yesterday."

" Mrs. Jenyns repay him!" the baronet exclaimed, with unaffected astonishment. " I should as soon have expected Gage to pay his debts. What's in the wind now? Has she conceived a sudden caprice for young Poynings? If so, I'll nip the amour in the bud. Plague take her! Peg is like all the rest of her fickle sex." Then suddenly changing his manner, he added, " When is this bubble to burst? Everybody is talking of the occurrence at

White's yesterday, and as it is now generally known that Gage cannot pay even a debt of honour, all his acquaintance will fight shy of him. You appear not to know what's going on outside the house, Fairlie. The doors are beset by importunate creditors. This state of things cannot endure much longer."

"I don't intend it should. If you will take the trouble to call here to-morrow, Sir Randal, and inquire for Mr. Monthermer, you will find he has suddenly left town—on urgent business."

"Oh! you mean to speed him off into the country—to Monthermer Castle, eh?"

"He shall never set foot inside the Castle again with my consent; and I don't think his journey is likely to be a long one. His first halt will be at the Fleet, where he will probably remain for a few months."

"Ha! ha! ha!" cried the baronet, laughing at the jest.

"I have planned it all," Fairlie pursued; "his arrest will take place this very day. Of course, I shan't appear in the matter, but the acting creditor, Mr. Nibbs, is merely my instrument. As to the clamorous fellows whom you saw outside the house, not one of them will get a farthing. My claims are paramount. They can touch nothing."

"Egad, you are a devilish clever fellow, Fairlie. I have an infinite respect for you. And now, since you are fully in a position to carry out our arrangement respecting your daughter, it is time to bring it before you."

"Nay, Sir Randal, it is premature to touch upon it now. Whatever I may be in reality, I am not yet ostensibly master of the property. Once in possession, I shall be willing to listen to your proposals."

"My proposals! 'Sdeath! sir, I have gone beyond proposals. The affair is settled. I require fulfilment of our compact."

"Fulfilled it shall be in due time, Sir Randal. Why should you doubt me?"

"Because—but no matter—I won't be left in any uncertainty. I must be satisfied your daughter will accept me."

"You will only defeat your object by precipitancy, Sir Randal. I must have time to prepare her. She has been very ill of late —very ill indeed—and I have been so much engaged in winding

N

up Monthermer's affairs that I have had no time to think of any thing else—but I will attend to this business immediately."

At this juncture, a seasonable interruption was offered by Pudsey. The butler came to say that Mr. Freke was without, and desired to have a word with Mr. Fairlie.

" Say Mr. Fairlie is engaged, Pudsey," Sir Randal cried.

" Hold, Pudsey!" the steward interposed; " I must see Mr. Freke."

The butler bowed, and retired.

"'Sdeath! this is provoking," Sir Randal cried. " I don't want to meet Freke. I'll leave by the private door, as I've often done before."

" Pray do so, Sir Randal," the steward cried, delighted to get rid of him.

" Have a care how you attempt to play me false, Fairlie!" the baronet cried, proceeding towards the side door as if with the intention of passing out. But perceiving that the steward's back was turned, he opened the door quickly, and as quickly closed it; contriving to slip, unobserved, behind the screen. The next moment Beau Freke was ushered in by Pudsey.

" I dare say you guess my errand, Fairlie?" Beau Freke remarked, as soon as the butler had withdrawn.

" You give me credit for greater penetration than I possess, sir," the steward replied, bowing. " I am not aware to what circumstances I am indebted for the pleasure of seeing you this morning."

" Really—you surprise me. I fancied you would expect me to complete the terms of our arrangement."

" In my turn, I must express surprise, Mr. Freke. I thought all our arrangements were concluded."

" You affect an astonishment which I am sure you do not feel, Fairlie. But there is no need of circumlocution. I will come to the point at once. My errand refers to your daughter."

" You have heard, then, of her illness, and are come to inquire about her?"

" Her illness! no. I hope it is nothing serious."

" I hope not, also, sir; but I have been very uneasy about her ---very uneasy, I assure you."

" She has always appeared charming whenever I have had the happiness of beholding her," Beau Freke replied, looking as if he did not place implicit credence in the steward's assertions. After coughing slightly, he added, "I cannot believe you design to behave unhandsomely to me, Fairlie, though my confidence in you has been somewhat shaken by finding you have promised your daughter to Sir Randal."

"May I ask from whom you derived your information, sir?"

"From the best authority—Sir Randal himself."

"Sir Randal is the very worst authority you could have, my dear Mr. Freke. He has a motive for deceiving you."

"Then you deny having given him such a promise?"

"Flatly deny it. He has often spoken to me about my daughter, and, being desirous to continue on good terms with him, I have not altogether discouraged him. He has construed some slight expressions of assent on my part into an absolute promise— that is all."

"This alters my view of the matter unquestionably, Fairlie. I can quite understand why you should not wish to quarrel with Sir Randal ; and I can also readily understand how his vanity may have led him to believe he would be irresistible with the young lady—but he would never do for her husband."

"Never, my dear Mr. Freke—never. Sir Randal is the very last person I should desire for a son-in-law, while you are the first I should select. I assure you I should esteem it a high honour to be connected with a gentleman of your character."

Of course not a syllable of these remarks was lost upon Sir Randal as he stood behind the screen, and he had some difficulty in controlling his rage.

"I am much flattered by your good opinion, Fairlie," Beau Freke said; "and I have now no hesitation in asking you to ratify our agreement by at once affiancing me to your daughter."

"I must crave the delay of a few days, my dear Mr. Freke. As soon as Monthermer's affairs are entirely settled I will attend to the matter; but just at this moment I have more on my hands than I can easily manage; neither do I think the present a favourable opportunity so far as my daughter is concerned. She is far too unwell to be troubled just now."

"I don't believe a word about her illness," Beau Freke thought. "The rascal means to throw me over. But I'll tie him down.—

No occasion in the world to trouble Miss Fairlie," he added, aloud. "Reduce your promise to writing, and I shall be perfectly content."

"A written promise, Mr. Freke! Won't my word suffice?"

"In such cases it is best to have some evidence of the intentions of the parties. I must have a written undertaking, with a penalty —a heavy penalty—in case of non-performance. You have taught me caution, Fairlie."

Thus driven into a corner, Fairlie scarcely knew what to do, and Sir Randal was considering whether he should step forward and put an end to the scene, when, to the steward's inexpressible relief, Mr. Pudsey again made his appearance, and said that Miss Fairlie had just arrived, and wished to be admitted to her father's presence without delay.

The steward replied that he would see her in a moment, and as Pudsey withdrew, he added, "We will settle this matter some other time, my dear Mr. Freke. You must not meet my daughter. Pass through the private door, sir—there!—you know the way. Quick, sir, quick!—she'll be here before you are gone."

Fairlie fancied he had got rid of his troublesome visitor. But he was mistaken. Beau Freke practised the same manœuvre as Sir Randal, and with equal dexterity and success. But, instead of gliding behind the screen, he slipped into the closet, the door of which, we have said, stood conveniently open. He had scarcely ensconced himself in this hiding-place, when Clare Fairlie entered the room.

XXIX.

HOW CLARE FAIRLIE ENDEAVOURED TO PREVAIL UPON HER FATHER TO PAY GAGE'S DEBTS.

FAIRLIE had not exceeded the truth in declaring that his daughter was unwell; but she was far worse than he supposed. In appearance she was greatly altered since we first beheld her. Her beauty was unimpaired; but it now inspired uneasiness, rather than excited admiration. To look at her, you could not help apprehending that the insidious disease which seeks its victims amongst the fairest and most delicate had begun its work upon her already fragile frame. Her complexion was transparently clear, and tinged with a hectic flush, which heightened the lustre of her large dark eyes. A settled melancholy sat upon her marble brow, and there was an air of lassitude about her that proclaimed extreme debility.

Since their arrival in town, now more than three months ago, Fairlie had seen little of his daughter. He had provided apartments for her in Jermyn-street, at the house of an elderly lady, Mrs. Lacy, with whom he was acquainted, and she had resided there, during the whole of the time, with only one attendant, Lettice Rougham. Fairlie was so much occupied with Monthermer's affairs—so bent upon bringing his machinations to a successful issue—that he had little leisure for the performance of domestic duties. Clare never came near him, and a week would sometimes elapse between his visits to her. Ever since the occurrence at Bury St. Edmund's, when Clare had meditated flight, and accident only had brought her back, an estrangement had taken place between father and daughter. Fairlie could not altogether forgive her disobedience, and she only consented to remain

with him, on condition that she was no longer to be compelled
to reside under Monthermer's roof.

Poor Clare's existence was blighted. She had ceased to take
interest in almost all that yielded pleasure to persons of her own
age; neither mixing in society nor going to any public places of
amusement; and avoiding in her walks, as much as possible, all
spots to which gay crowds resorted. One friend was constant to
her. Lucy Poynings strove to dispel her gloom, and beheld
with great anxiety the inroads that secret sorrow was making
upon her health. But even Lucy's well-meant efforts failed. In
vain did the lively girl essay to tempt the poor sufferer with glowing descriptions of fêtes and reviews, of operas and theatres, of
ridottos at Marylebone Gardens, and masquerades at Ranelagh—
Clare was not to be moved. She could not even be prevailed to
go into the Parks or to the Mall, except at such hours as she knew
no one was likely to be there—much to Lettice Rougham's discon-
tent. But we must not do Lettice an injustice. The little damsel,
though volatile, had a really good heart, and felt the sincerest
sympathy for her young mistress. She often shed tears on her
account, and declared her belief to Lucy that Miss Clare was
dying of a broken heart. And Lucy began to share her apprehensions.

The person who was last to notice the altered state of Clare's health
was the very first who ought to have discerned it; and he might
have continued still longer unconscious of the change—for Clare
made no complaint to him—if Mrs. Lacy had not thought it her
duty to communicate her misgivings to him. To do him justice,
Fairlie was greatly shocked. He enjoined that every attention
should be paid his daughter, and that she should have the
best advice. Mrs. Lacy shook her head despondingly, as if she
thought this would be of no avail; but she promised compliance.
For several days after this, Fairlie was extremely solicitous
about Clare, and paid her frequent visits, but by degrees he became less uneasy, and in the end succeeded in persuading himself
that his fears were groundless. Clare was ill, no doubt—but not
dangerously so. And he was confirmed in this opinion, because,
notwithstanding Mrs. Lacy's entreaties, she declined all medical
advice. Fairlie's heart was so hardened by covetousness, that it
was scarcely susceptible of any tender emotion, and in his blind
pursuit of gain he cared not if he sacrificed all that should have

been dear to him. Compared with the vast stake for which he was playing, all other matters appeared of minor interest; but when the object he aimed at was obtained, he promised himself to watch over his daughter carefully. Meantime (so he thought), she could take little harm.

From what has been premised, it will be easily imagined that Clare's unexpected visit occasioned her father great surprise, and some little misgiving. Both were silent for a few minutes, during which Fairlie regarded her with natural anxiety. She had evidently collected all her energies for the interview—and the flush on her cheek deceived him. He thought her looking better; and told her so.

"I know not if I am better or worse," she replied, in feeble accents; "but I did not come to speak about my ailments. What I have to say relates to yourself and Gage."

Fairlie's brow darkened, and he appeared disposed to check her

"Father, I beseech you to listen to me," she pursued. "You have wronged this young man, who was entrusted to your care, and over whose interests it was your duty to watch, grievously wronged him—but it is not too late to remedy the injustice."

The steward shook his head, but made no other reply.

"For the sake of his father, who was your patron, and to whom you owe everything—for the poor misguided young man's own sake, whom you once professed to regard—for my sake, if you have any love left for me—I implore you to save him.."

Still Fairlie maintained an obstinate silence.

"Do not turn a deaf ear to all my entreaties. Speak to me, I beg of you."

"What can I say? I can do nothing for him."

"Father," Clare said, with a solemn earnestness, "this is the last request I have to make of you. Discharge Gage's debts. Set him free."

"What monstrous absurdity you talk, girl!" Fairlie cried, angrily. "I pay this prodigal's debts. Stuff and nonsense! What good would it do him if I did? He would be exactly in the same position two months hence. I am sorry you have troubled yourself to come to me, Clare, if this is your sole business. Believe me, Gage deserves no consideration."

"He deserves every consideration on your part, father. I

am told he is in danger of arrest. Is this true? You do not deny it. Father, will you stand by quietly and allow the son of your benefactor to be dragged to gaol? Oh! shame! shame!"

And she burst into a paroxysm of tears.

"The law must take its course. I cannot prevent it," Fairlie said, in an inexorable voice.

"Do you tell me this?" Clare cried, raising her head, and regarding him scornfully.

"Well then, I *won't* prevent it—if you will have the truth."

Clare made an effort, and arose.

"Farewell, father!" she said; "we meet no more in this world."

"Sit down, girl—sit down," Fairlie cried. "I entreat—I command you. It is for you, and you alone, that I have laboured to acquire a fortune. I have no other child—no other object of affection. All will be yours one day. Why should my gains be wasted on a prodigal?"

"Give him back his own. I will have none of it."

"Clare, you drive me mad. Let things take their course. He must have a severe lesson. It may do him good, and perhaps some plan may be devised for aiding him hereafter."

"And meanwhile he is to be thrown into prison by your privity— by your contrivance."

"By my privity—by my contrivance, Clare?"

"Yes, you make yourself a party to the wrong by not preventing it. But I have said my say. Farewell!"

"No, no, girl—we must not part thus."

"I will only remain on your consenting to discharge Gage's debts."

"Well, if I agree to do as you would have me—though against my own inclination—against every dictate of common sense—will you show yourself more tractable in future?"

"In all reasonable matters."

"Ay, but you may consider what I require unreasonable."

"Let me know it, then."

"Will you marry as I would have you do?"

"I have far other thoughts than those of marriage, father. —Have you made choice of a husband for me?"

"Two gentlemen aspire to that happiness—Sir Randal de Meschines and Mr. Freke."

" I would rather be led to the grave than wed either of them."

" Nay, I but said this to try you," Fairlie cried, alarmed by her increasing paleness. " Be assured I will never sacrifice you to a gambler or a rake, and both these persons are such. I have other designs in regard to you."

" Trouble yourself no more about me. Let me go."

And she tottered towards the door, but ere she could reach it her strength utterly failed her, and she sank upon a chair.

" What ails you?" her father cried, springing towards her.

" A sudden faintness," she replied. " It will pass off soon."

Just then there was a noise of hasty footsteps without, and in another instant the door flew open, and Lettice Rougham rushed into the room.

" Oh, Miss Clare!" Lettice screamed, " it has happened just as we expected. They've arrested him."

" Peace! hold your tongue, hussy!" Fairlie cried. " Don't you see your mistress is ill. Bring something to revive her."

" Here, miss, smell at this bottle. Oh dear! dear! what will become of him ? I won't be silent," she said to Fairlie. " Poor Mr. Monthermer is arrested, miss. They're going to take him away."

" Arrested!" Clare cried, looking at her father.

" Yes, miss; and the servants say it's Mr. Fairlie's doing. They all cry shame upon him—and well they may. I cry 'shame,' too. Nay, you may look as angry at me as you please, sir. I ain't a bit afraid."

Clare seemed to regain her strength as suddenly as she had lost it.

" Give me your arm, Lettice," she cried, " and help me forth. I will set him free."

" You! how will you do it ?" Fairlie exclaimed.

" Come with me, and you shall see !" she rejoined.

" I cannot face him," Fairlie said, shrinking back.

" But you must—you shall!" Lettice cried, laying hold of his hand, and dragging him along. " Your presence is necessary."

Fairlie would have resisted, but his daughter's looks compelled him to accompany her.

As soon as the coast was clear, the two eavesdroppers issued from their respective hiding-places, and met face to face. They stared at each other in silence for a few moments; and then both burst into a roar of laughter.

"What! were you there?" Beau Freke asked, pointing towards the back of the screen.

"And were you there?" Sir Randal rejoined, pointing to the closet. "I thought you were gone; but I find you have as much curiosity as myself. Well, we have had listeners' luck. We have heard ourselves called gamblers and rakes; but at the same time we have learnt something it was expedient to know. Fairlie has duped us, and means to cast us off. So far as I am concerned, he shall find this no easy task."

"If he thinks to get rid of me, he'll find himself deucedly mistaken," Beau Freke said. "I'll stick to him like a leech."

"Marriage with his daughter is of course out of the question, after what we have heard. But we will find other means of bringing him to book. If he proposes to enjoy his ill-gotten gains in quiet, he must pay us a heavy per-centage as hush-money."

"Exactly," Beau Freke replied, laughing. "He shan't easily get out of our toils, that I promise him. But let us see what they are about. A hundred to one he don't pay Gage's debts." .

"I take you," Sir Randal replied, as they left the room together.

XXX.

A RASH PROMISE.

RUIN now stared our reckless hero in the face. Yet, surprising to relate, considering the dire extremities to which he was reduced, his spirit remained unbroken. Beset by a host of duns, who would take no more excuses; every present means of supply exhausted; without a hope for the future; deserted by his friends, and with the Fleet Prison only in prospect; it was certainly wonderful that he could preserve even a show of cheerfulness. His gaiety might be assumed, but at any rate it imposed upon his attendants, and excited their admiration. On the morning of the last day it seemed likely he would spend in his own house, he arose late, and made his toilet with his customary deliberation and care—chatting all the while gaily with Chassemouche and Bellairs, as they assisted him to dress, and brought him his chocolate. Both valets were so captivated by his pleasantry and good-humour, that they deferred to the last moment a disagreeable communication which they had to make to him. At length, however, their avocations ended, Bellairs felt compelled to broach the subject, which he did with considerable hesitation.

"I really am concerned, sir," he said, "to disturb your gaiety by any unpleasant observations, but it is only right you should be informed—ahem!—— You know what I want to say, Chassemouche,—help me out with the sentence."

"Parbleu! I am almost too much embarrassed to speak," the French valet said; "but I trust monsieur will forgive me. He has been the best of masters, and I shall be quite *désolé* to lose him."

"Exactly my sentiments, sir," Bellairs subjoined. "I am

grieved beyond measure that I can no longer have the honour of serving you."

"Why should you leave me?" Gage demanded, regarding them with well-feigned astonishment. "You both give me entire satisfaction."

"If I were to consult my own feelings, sir, I should never leave you," Bellairs replied; "but——"

"I see how it is," Gage cried, with a laugh. "You want your wages increased. Well, speak to Fairlie."

"You are very good, sir, and both Chassemouche and myself appreciate your generous intentions. You have always behaved to us like a gentleman——"

"Like a prince I should say," the Frenchman interposed.

"Exactly,—like a prince. We have never had the slightest cause of complaint—have we, Chassemouche?"

"Not the slightest," the French valet responded. "Our new master is very different."

"Your new master!" Gage cried. "'Sdeath! have you engaged yourselves without giving me notice?"

"We would not do anything unhandsome to you for the world, sir," said Bellairs; "but Mr. Fairlie made it a point that his arrangement with us should remain secret till he gave us permission to disclose it."

"So Mr. Fairlie takes you off my hands, eh?" Gage said.

"Not us alone, sir," Bellairs replied; "he has engaged the whole household."

"What! without saying a word to me?" Gage exclaimed.

"He did not appear to think that necessary, sir," Bellairs replied. "Pardon my freedom, sir—but, devoted as we are to you, we could not have remained so long in your service if Mr. Fairlie had not undertaken to pay our wages."

"Apparently, then, you had no confidence in my ability to pay you?"

"We had every confidence in your desire to do so; but we feared a day might arrive when you would lack the means. Forgive me for adding that that evil day *has* come."

A brief pause ensued, during which Gage, who was evidently much put out by what he had just heard, strove to regain his composure. At length Chassemouche ventured to offer an observation

"If monsieur will condescend to take my advice," he said, "he will get out of the house as quietly and as speedily as possible, and keep out of the way of his creditors."

"What! fly, Chassemouche. No, I will stand my ground to the last. Fairlie will never allow me to be molested."

"Upon my faith, sir, I don't like to say it, but I almost believe he has planned your arrest," Mr. Bellairs observed.

"Oh! you calumniate him," Gage cried. "He is incapable of such treachery."

"Well, time will show, sir," the valet rejoined; "and I only hope you may prove correct in your estimate of our new master. But if you should be tempted to take an airing in the Park this morning, let me recommend you to go out by the back-door. You will find it the safest means of exit. Your creditors are abroad by hundreds, sir. The street is full of them — tailors, coach-builders, wig-makers, shoe-makers, jewellers, hosiers, glovers, linendrapers, silk-mercers, lace-embroiderers, pastrycooks, poulterers, butchers, saddlers, watchmakers, wine-merchants—all your tradesmen are on the look-out for you."

"The devil! have none of them been paid?"

"Nobody has been paid, sir — since your arrival in town," Bellairs replied. "You have lived entirely on credit."

"'Sdeath! this is scandalous," Gage exclaimed. "How has my money gone? Fairlie would tell me at the gaming-table ; but though I have lost large sums, all cannot have disappeared in this manner. I have been cheated most abominably—but by whom ? —It is too late now to inquire—fool! fool that I have been." And loading himself with reproaches, which we can scarcely consider unmerited, he sank into a chair, while the two valets, thinking their presence no longer desirable, slipped out of the room.

Gage continued lost in deep and painful reflection, until aroused by a slight touch on the shoulder, when, looking up, he beheld Mrs. Jenyns standing beside him.

"You seem greatly disturbed," she said.

"And well I may be disturbed, Peg," he replied. "I have not a guinea left in the world—nor do I know which way to turn to obtain one. You smile as if you didn't believe me—but I swear to you it is the truth. House, servants, equipages, pictures, plate —all my possessions are gone. Fairlie has taken everything, or will take everything; and I am only waiting the moment when he will turn me out of doors, and consign me to the 'tender mercies' of the pack of creditors who are lurking without to seize me. But I may balk them all yet. At least they shall not have an opportunity of deriding me in my misfortunes."

"I divine your desperate purpose," Mrs. Jenyns rejoined. "But you need not have recourse to pistol, sword, or poison for the present. Your case is not quite so hopeless as you imagine."

"You give me new life, Peg. Is there chance of escape from this frightful dilemma?"

"Tranquillise yourself, or I won't open my lips. I have just seen Fairlie. He appeared inexorable at first, but I found a way to move him. I managed to frighten him out of a thousand pounds."

"And you have got the money with you? It may save me from perdition."

"You shall have it, provided you promise to use it as I direct. Half the sum must be devoted to the repayment of Arthur Poynings's loan."

"It could not be better applied. And the other five hundred, what is to be done with it?"

"You must try your luck with the dice. I am sure you will be successful. I dreamed last night that you won back all your fortune at hazard."

"May the dream be realised! I will play as if my life were on the stake. And so it will be, for if I lose——"

"Pshaw! you mustn't think of losing. You must resolve to win."

"I *will* win!" Gage exclaimed.

"Stop! half your gains are to be mine, whatever the amount. Is this a bargain?"

"It is."

"Then here's the money. Place the amount of your debt to Arthur Poynings within an envelope, and I will take care that the packet is safely delivered to him."

"I shall not readily forget the obligation you have conferred on me, Peg," Gage replied, as he wrote a brief note to Arthur, and folded the bank-notes within it. "You have taken a great weight from my breast in enabling me to make this payment," he added, giving the letter to her.

"The debt is only transferred," she replied. "And now, adieu, for a short time. Do not attempt to quit your room till I return. And then you must hasten to the Groom-Porter's! Your luck will have a turn. Mind! half your gains are to be mine."

"My hand upon it," he rejoined. "If I should be lucky enough to win a hundred thousand—as I hope I may be—fifty thousand will be yours!"

"And you will allow no one to dissuade you from playing?"

"No one is likely to make the attempt—but if made, it will fail."

"Enough," Mrs. Jenyns replied. "Au plaisir!" And with a smile of triumph she withdrew.

The interview with the pretty actress dissipated all Gage's gloomy fancies, and aroused an entirely different train of thought Giving the reins to his imagination, he beheld himself seated at the gaming-table, with piles of gold and rolls of bank-notes before him, the result of successful play.

XXXI.

THE ARREST.

WHILE Gage was indulging in these delusive dreams, Mr. Bellairs hurriedly entered, showing by his countenance that something alarming had occurred.

"Come with me, sir—quick!—quick!—not a moment is to be lost," the valet cried. "The bailiffs are in the house, and are making their way up-stairs. You must hide in some out-of-the-way corner till the danger be past. Ha! it is too late. They are at hand."

"Fasten the door, Bellairs. Don't let them in!" Gage shouted.

The valet endeavoured to obey the injunction, but before he could accomplish it, two sturdy, harsh-featured men, armed with bludgeons, burst into the room.

"Ha! ha! we're a little too quick for you, my friend," the foremost of the twain vociferated. "Here we have him, Martin," he added, with a coarse laugh, to his brother bailiff.

"Ay, ay, Ned Craggs," the other rejoined—"that be the gem'-man, sure enough." And with these words he rushed up to Gage with his companion, and exhibiting a writ, cried, "You are our prisoner, Mr. Monthermer. We arrest you at the suit of Mr. Isaac Nibbs, of Billiter-lane, scrivener."

"Keep off, rascals, if you value your lives!" Gage exclaimed, springing back, and drawing his sword. "I know nothing whatever of Mr. Nibbs, and never had any dealings with him."

"There you are in error, sir," cried a civil-spoken little man, appearing at the door. This personage was plainly attired in a suit of rusty black, and wore a long cravat, grey stockings, and square-cut shoes. "You are in error, sir, I repeat," he continued,

THE ARREST.

in very mild accents. "You borrowed five thousand pounds from me, for which you gave me your bond."

"I recollect nothing about it," Gage replied.

"Possibly so slight a circumstance may have escaped your recollection, sir," Isaac Nibbs replied. "But I happen to have the instrument by me. Here it is," he added, producing a parchment. "The money was paid on your behalf to Mr. Fairlie. You will not, I presume, attempt to deny your own signature?"

"I deny that I ever received the five thousand pounds. I have been cheated!" Gage cried.

"I shall not argue the point with you, sir," Mr. Nibbs rejoined, with undisturbed politeness. "It is sufficient for me that I have your bond. Officers, do your duty."

But Gage stood on his defence, and with his sword kept the bailiffs at bay.

"Come, come, sir," Craggs cried, "it's of no use. You must not resist the law."

At this moment the door was suddenly thrown open, and two more personages stepped into the room. These were Sir Hugh Poynings and his son Arthur. Gage was greatly disconcerted by their appearance, and taking advantage of his confusion, the bailiffs rushed upon him, and disarmed him.

"I am sorry to see you in this position, Gage," Sir Hugh said, advancing. "I heard you were in difficulties, and came to see if I could be of any use."

"Spare me your commiseration, Sir Hugh," the young man replied, proudly; "I do not desire it."

"Nay, you utterly mistake me, Gage," the old baronet replied, kindly. "Far be it from me to insult you in your distress. I would aid you if I can. What is the sum for which you are arrested?"

"Five thousand pounds," one of the bailiffs replied.

"'Sdeath! that's not a trifle," Sir Hugh ejaculated—"and more than I like to throw away. Cannot this matter be arranged?"

"Only by payment of the debt, Sir Hugh," Mr. Nibbs rejoined.

"I would not interfere with your generous purpose, sir, if it could profit Gage," Arthur observed; "but this is merely a small part of his liabilities. As you have seen, the house is full of his

o   •

creditors, and if he is liberated from this person, he will be seized by the others."

"That's true, Arthur," Gage replied. "I cannot accept Sir Hugh's assistance. And let me tell you that the money you so handsomely advanced me the other day at White's chocolate-house will be repaid you by a friend."

"Do not concern yourself about it," Arthur replied.

"We are losing time here," Mr. Nibbs said to the bailiffs. "Bring your prisoner along. Place him in a coach, and convey him to the spunging-house in Chancery-lane."

"And is it come to this!" Sir Hugh groaned. "Oh! Gage, it grieves me to the soul to see your father's son in such a disgraceful predicament. I would help you if I could—but, as Arthur rightly says, it is impossible."

"If another day had been allowed me, this would not have happened, Sir Hugh," the young man replied, as he quitted the room in custody of the bailiffs.

By this time, the rest of the creditors had obtained admittance to the house, and the large entrance-hall was crowded by them. On seeing Gage, as he descended the staircase, with a bailiff on either side, and closely followed by Nibbs, the whole party set up a furious cry, and held up their bills to him, demanding instant payment. It was no very pleasant thing, it must be owned, to run the gauntlet of a pack of infuriated and disappointed creditors, and Gage vainly endeavoured to mollify them by expressions of regret. His explanations and apologies were treated with derision. The tumult was at its highest, when all at once a diversion was made by the entrance of Clare Fairlie and her father into the hall, and the clamour partially ceased.

To meet Clare under circumstances so degrading to himself aggravated Gage's distress almost beyond endurance. He was covered with shame and confusion. His proud heart swelled almost to bursting, and averting his gaze from her, he besought the bailiffs to move on, and pass through the crowd as quickly as possible. "Take me wherever you please," he cried. "Only don't—for Heaven's sake—detain me here." But though the officers were willing enough to comply with the request, it could not be accomplished, owing to the pressure from the crowd, who derived too much amusement from their victim's distress to let him easily escape. Driven to desperation, Gage then tried to shake off Craggs's grasp, and might have succeeded in getting free from one bailiff, if the other had not lent his powerful aid to restrain him. Pinioned by these two sturdy fellows, he was compelled to remain quiet

At the head of the staircase stood Sir Hugh Poynings and his son, by no means uninterested spectators of the scene. It was long since Arthur had beheld Clare; for though, as we have already stated, his sister frequently visited her friend, he had never accompanied her. Lucy's description of the delicate state of Clare's health had prepared him for a great change in the appearance of the latter, but he was inexpressibly shocked on beholding her. The flush which had risen to her cheeks during her painful interview with her father had now given way to a deathlike paleness. She leaned on Lettice for support, and had evidently taxed her failing strength to the uttermost. Still her dark lustrous eye blazed with resolution, and as its glance fell for a moment upon Arthur, he thought he understood the motive that had brought her there. As to Fairlie, he seemed to be in a great state of perturbation, and, next to Gage, was perhaps the most uneasy person in the whole assemblage.

"Lead me on, Lettice," Clare said, in a low tone, "or I shall not be able to go through with it." And advancing a few steps with the aid of her attendant, she asked, "Who is the creditor by whom the arrest has been made?"

"I am the person," Mr. Isaac Nibbs replied.

"Then I must demand Mr. Monthermer's immediate release," Clare said.

"I shall have great pleasure in complying with your request, provided my debt be discharged in full," the scrivener returned. "Unless I am mistaken, I have the honour of addressing Miss Fairlie, and if it be so, your respected father will explain to you that I am obliged to act with a harshness repugnant to my feelings. But I really cannot afford to lose so large a sum of money as five thousand pounds."

"Neither can we," chorussed the other creditors—"we can none of us afford to lose our money. Hundreds are as much to some of us as thousands to a wealthy man like Mr. Nibbs."

" You will be satisfied, I presume," Clare continued, addressing the scrivener, " if you have my father's assurance that your deb shall be paid ? "

" Oh! yes, I shall be perfectly satisfied with Mr. Fairlie's promise to that effect," Nibbs replied, in a tone and with a look that implied considerable doubt as to the likelihood of receiving any such assurance. " How am I to act, sir ? " he added, appealing to the steward. " Must I set Mr. Monthermer free ? "

Fairlie was so agitated by conflicting emotions that he was utterly unable to answer. Mr. Nibbs regarded him with surprise. He expected a decided negative.

" My father will take care that your debt is paid—you may rely upon it," Clare said.

" I cannot for a moment doubt your word, Miss Fairlie— especially as your respected father offers no contradiction—still I should like to have his consent."

Clare then turned to her father.

" Remember what has just passed between us," she whispered. " I claim this act of justice from you."

" Mr. Nibbs, the debt shall be paid, I promise it," Fairlie said, with a great effort.

" Enough, sir. I am perfectly content," the scrivener replied. And he signed to the bailiffs to release the prisoner.

Every one seemed taken by surprise, and for a moment there was silence amongst the other creditors, but as soon as they recovered from their astonishment they turned with one accord upon Fairlie, calling out that exceptions ought not to be made, that favour must not to be shown to any one in particular, and that, in common justice, all their debts ought likewise to be paid.

" All who have just claims upon Mr. Monthermer shall be paid in full," Clare said.

" Do you know what you are promising, girl ? " Fairlie exclaimed, half distracted. " Why, twenty thousand pounds will not satisfy all these people."

" Were twice that sum required," Clare rejoined, with an air of authority which overwhelmed him, " it must be forthcoming."

" But these are debts incurred for the veriest follies——"

" It cannot be helped. Mr. Monthermer must be set clear."

" Do not urge me to it—my fortune will be swept away. For your own sake, be advised."

"I care not—I want nothing," she rejoined, in a low tone. "Do as I would have you, if you would make my last moments easy."

At this juncture Gage forced his way to her through the crowd.

"I cannot consent that your father should suffer from my folly, Clare," he said. "I must bear the consequences of my own imprudence."

"You need have no scruple in accepting aid from my father, Mr. Monthermer," Clare replied. "He is only discharging a long debt of gratitude to one whom he owed his prosperity—I mean your father. Besides, I am certain that when he makes up his accounts with you, he will be no loser."

"Most undoubtedly he shall be no loser by me," Gage cried. "Under these circumstances, Fairlie, I suppose I may assure Messieurs my creditors that all their bills will be paid by you without delay."

"Let us hear what Mr. Fairlie has to say to this proposition?" observed a coach-builder, who acted as spokesman for the others.

"Bring in your bills to-morrow, and rid us of your presence now," Fairlie cried furiously.

"Come along, friends," said the coach-builder; "we will no longer intrude upon Mr. Monthermer, or the rest of the company. We are infinitely indebted to Miss Fairlie, and rejoice that a business which promised to be unpleasant, should have terminated so satisfactorily."

And bowing respectfully to Clare, he took his departure, followed by the rest of the creditors; Mr. Isaac Nibbs and the bailiffs bringing up the rear.

As soon as the entrance-hall was free from them, Gage turned to Clare, and said,

"What can I do to prove my gratitude for the service you have rendered me? My life is at your disposal."

"Abjure play. That is all I ask."

"Promise like a man, Gage," Sir Hugh cried, coming up with his son. "Register a vow before Heaven to leave off cards and dice, and there will be hopes of you."

"He may make the vow, but he will not keep it," Fairlie remarked, scornfully.

"I will not think so badly of him," Clare said. "Give me

your word, Gage, as a man of honour, that you will henceforth abandon play, and never again enter a gaming-house."

"As a man of honour I give you my word," Gage repeated. And a secret tremor passed through his frame as he spoke, for he remembered his rash promise to Mrs. Jenyns.

"We are witnesses to the pledge," said Sir Hugh Poynings and Arthur.

"And so are we," subjoined Beau Freke, who stood with Sir Randal at the outlet of the passage opening into the hall. "We shall see whether he will keep his word."

"Trust me, I will find some means of luring him to the gaming-table, despite all his vows to the contrary," Sir Randal replied. "Qui a joué jouera, is an infallible axiom."

"I have something more to say to you, Gage," Clare cried. "For my sake, I implore you to——"

The young man looked anxiously at her. But the entreaty could not be preferred. A sudden faintness seized her, and she fell senseless into his arms.

XXXII.

THE EVIL GENIUS?

THE period we have now reached is fraught with shame and dishonour to our infatuated hero. Willingly would we pass it by,—willingly would we cast a veil over his errors. But it must not be; it is necessary to show to what depths of degradation a victim to the ruinous passion of play may be reduced.

Hitherto, the proud name Gage received from his ancestors has been untarnished. Follies and excesses innumerable, and almost unparalleled, have marked his career; but he has done no act unbecoming a gentleman. His word has been ever sacred; his honour without stain. But of what value are a gamester's oaths? Of what account are his professions of amendment? Is he to be moved from his fatal purpose by the tears and anguish of those who love him and are dependent upon him? Can their clinging arms withhold him from the accursed tables where ruin awaits him? The drunkard may become temperate—the rake may reform—but the gamester, never!

So was it with Gage. Notwithstanding the services rendered him by the noble-hearted girl who had stepped between him and destruction; though at her earnest solicitation he had abjured cards and dice; though he knew that the violation of his oath would inflict the keenest wound upon her, to whom he was so deeply indebted; though he felt all the infamy of his conduct, and feared, and justly feared, that henceforth his name would be a by-word of scorn—with all this before him, little more than a week had elapsed after the occurrences described in the foregoing chapter, ere his promises to Clare were forgotten, his oath broken, and he was once more seated at the gaming-table, surrounded by the false

friends and profligate companions who had despoiled him of his
fortune, and basely deserted him in his hour of need.

By what agency this was accomplished we shall proceed to
narrate.

Freed from all liabilities and embarrassments by the discharge of
his debts—for Fairlie, it must be mentioned, had strictly fulfilled
his promise to his daughter, and paid the whole of Gage's creditors
—the young man had now an opportunity of commencing a new
and wholly different career. But the reckless life he had led had
completely unfitted him for active pursuits. He had never possessed any habits of business, and had now become so enervated
by pleasurable indulgence and dissipation, that he shrank with
alarm and disgust from the very idea of laborious employment.
No profession but the army seemed to suit him; but how could
he enter the service in his present miserable plight? What sort
of figure should he cut without ample pecuniary resources?—and
he had none! His pockets were empty; his credit gone; and
he could not devise any scheme by which money could be raised.
No one would make him advances; and he had no security to
offer for a loan. Possibly, the difficulties he experienced in this
respect might have been removed by the instrumentality of Clare,
who scarcely would have left her good work unfinished; but
she was unable to assist him. Ever since her efforts in his behalf,
and the trying scene she had previously undergone with her
father, she had been utterly prostrated, and incapable of mental or
bodily exertion. Thus Gage was deprived of his only chance of
succour, for pride prevented him from applying to Sir Hugh
Poynings.

As yet he continued an inmate of the mansion in Dover-street,
having received permission from Fairlie to remain there for a few
days. But of necessity this state of things could not endure.
Something must be done. Money must be had—but how? He
sat in his own chamber from morning to night, racking his brain
in search of expedients; but none occurred to him, except that
which was interdicted.

As to the five hundred pounds given him by Mrs. Jenyns, to be
employed at the gaming-table, he had returned it with a letter
explaining the impossibility of compliance with her wishes. To
this letter the actress did not deign to reply, and from that time,
for nearly a week, he saw nothing of her—and heard nothing.

Confinement to the house became at length so insupportably irk-some—for very shame at his total want of money prevented Gage from visiting his customary haunts, or even stirring forth at all—that he mustered courage to write to Fairlie, entreating the loan of a few hundreds ; but with very slender hopes, it must be owned, of a favourable response to the application. Fairlie's rejoinder was as follows : " You shall have the sum you require, if you will engage to leave the country at once ; but on no other condition. Let me have your decision to-morrow morning."

While Gage was pondering over this proposition, feeling more than half inclined to accept it, he received an unexpected visit from Mrs. Jenyns.

" Ah ! Peg," he said, rising to greet her, " I am very glad you are come. I might not otherwise have seen you again. I am about to leave England for ever."

" Leave England !—of your own free will ?" she inquired.

" I have no great choice in the matter, certainly."

" I thought not. Then why go ? Why abandon society which you have found so agreeable ? Nobody used to have such keen relish for town life as you ! I have heard you declare a hundred times that nowhere else could you find so much amusement as in London, and you had tried every capital in Europe. ' Give me London,' you said, ' with its charming theatres, its nocturnal revels, its gay and exciting masquerades, its operas, its ridottos, its coffee-houses, its gaming-houses !' Yes, once upon a time there was nothing like a night at the Groom Porter's in your estimation, Gage."

" Those times are gone by," the young man replied, sigh-ing. " My purse is empty and must be replenished. I have no means of living here. Fairlie wishes me to go abroad."

" He wants to get rid of you. Now I recommend you to stay and plague him."

" I should plague myself much more by so doing," Gage rejoined. " How am I to participate in the amusements you have mentioned ? My tastes are unchanged, but I am wholly unable to gratify them. The theatres and masquerades are just as at-tractive to me as ever, but I am obliged to shun them. I cannot enter a coffee-house because I dare not call for a bottle of wine, not having wherewithal to pay for it. I, who once gave the

most magnificent entertainments in town ; who have spent hundreds—ay, thousands—in every coffee-house in Saint James's and
Covent Garden ; who have given gold by the handful to any
woman who pleased my fancy for the moment ; who have rioted
in pleasures like an Eastern monarch; who have bought enjoyment at any price ; who have laughed at my losses at play,
though those losses were ruinous ;—I who three months ago was
master of this mansion and all in it, and could call twenty miles
of one of the finest counties in England my own—I am reduced
to this horrible extremity. Of all the wealth I have squandered,
not even a guinea is left, and I am obliged to hide my head
because I cannot brook the world's scorn. No! no! I must perforce accept Fairlie's offer. I shall go abroad, and enter some
foreign service. You will hear of me no more—or if you do, it
will be that I have fallen on some battle-field."

"This is mere folly, Gage. Take a rational view of your
situation. You have run through your fortune as many a man
has done before you. That is not surprising, considering your
character. You are without resources, and grasp at the first
offer of assistance, without reflecting *why* it is made. Beware
how you take another false step! Do you not detect Fairlie's
motive in wishing you to quit the country? Do you not comprehend that your presence is troublesome to him, and that he
would fain remove you altogether? But do not accede to his
treacherous proposal. Stay where you are. Place yourself under
my guidance, and I will engage to repair your fortunes. I have
a hold upon Fairlie, which he would gladly shake off, but which
your presence renders secure. I cannot explain myself more fully
now, but you may rest assured I am not talking idly. As a means
to the end I have in view, your exhausted coffers must be replenished, and this can only be done in one way. You understand
me."

"Too well," he replied, avoiding her dangerous regards. "I
understand you too well, Peg. But you tempt me in vain. I
cannot—dare not play. You know that I have vowed never to
touch cards and dice again."

"And what of that?" she, cried contemptuously. "Will you
allow a rash vow, uttered at a moment when your judgment was
blinded, to control you? Clare Fairlie had no right to extort the

oath. Her claims upon your gratitude are ridiculous, and ought to be discarded. She compelled her father to do a bare act of justice—that is all. But even admitting—which I do not—that she acted generously, and that her generosity bound you to her, no oath extorted by her can liberate you from your previous promise to me. I confided a certain sum to you to be employed in play—half your winnings to be mine. Was it not so? Did you not give me your word to this effect?"

"I cannot gainsay it—but I could not foresee how I should be circumstanced with Clare. Release me from the promise, I entreat of you."

"Never! I require its fulfilment this very day. Here are the five hundred pounds I entrusted to you. Use them as I have directed."

"For Clare's sake I implore you not to urge me thus."

"What is Clare to me—and why should she step between me and my designs? I am resolved you *shall* play. Settle your accounts anon with her. Mine must be disposed of first."

"Oh, if I could but repay Fairlie the sums he has disbursed on my account, I might feel exonerated from all obligation!"

"Why are you so scrupulous? I tell you Fairlie is a cheat —a knave, who has robbed you all along; but if it will ease your mind, repay him with your winnings at play what he has paid your creditors."

"An excellent notion!" Gage exclaimed, eagerly grasping at the suggestion. "Yes, it shall be as you recommend."

"I recommend no such folly. Were I in your place, Fairlie should never have another farthing from me; nor would I rest till I had made him disgorge the bulk of his plunder. But of this hereafter. You must begin by obtaining funds."

"You seem to make sure I shall win. Recollect how unlucky I have hitherto been."

"You will win now. I am quite sure of it. Come and sup with me to-night at my lodgings in the Haymarket, and we will go afterwards to the Groom-Porter's, where you can play as deeply as you please. Sir Randal and Mr. Freke are sure to be there."

"I won't play with them!" Gage exclaimed.

"Not play with them! Nonsense! Why, the best revenge you can enjoy will be to beat them at their own weapons, and win back the money you have lost. And you *shall* do it. I promise you a run of luck such as you never had before."

"You are very confident, Peg, but it is well to engage with a good heart in a trial which, come what will, shall be my last."

"Make no more resolutions against play, for you are sure to break them," Mrs. Jenyns cried, with a laugh. "And now take the money. At eight o'clock I shall expect you."

And she hastily quitted the room, leaving Gage like one in a dream.

A long struggle took place in his breast, which ended, as might have been foreseen, in his Evil Genius obtaining the mastery.

XXXIII.

A LETTER FROM CLARE.

EVENING had arrived. A sedan-chair was standing in the hall to convey Gage to the Haymarket, and he was about to step into it, when Lettice Rougham entered by the open door. Perceiving Monthermer, she ran towards him and gave him a note, earnestly entreating him to read it before he went forth.

"Is it from your mistress?" he inquired.

Lettice replied in the affirmative, adding: "Alas! sir, she is very ill; but she made an effort to write these few lines to you, hoping they might not be without effect. Do read the letter, I implore you, and then perhaps you won't go. It will break her heart if you do—indeed it will!" she cried, bursting into tears.

"Why, where do you suppose I am going?" Gage exclaimed, looking at her in surprise. "What is the meaning of these tears?"

"They aren't shed for you, sir, I promise you," Lettice rejoined, rather sharply. "You don't deserve that any one should grieve on your account—much less such a sweet, tender-hearted creature as my mistress. Oh dear! oh dear! what will happen to her if you go?"

"A truce to this nonsense, Lettice! What silly notions have you got into your head?"

"They're not silly notions, but plain truth. Just step this way a moment, sir, that I may speak to you in private." And as soon as they were out of hearing of the chairmen and servants, she said, lowering her voice, "You're bound on a wicked errand, and will repent it all the rest of your life. Don't attempt to deceive me, for you can't do it. I know perfectly well where you are going to sup, and with whom—and what you mean to do afterwards—and so does my dear mistress."

For a moment Gage was speechless, and, thinking she had obtained an advantage over him, Lettice determined to follow it up.

"I am glad you have some sense of shame left," she continued, "and I begin to have hopes of you. You may wonder how I know all about your proceedings, so I had better tell you. I was coming to your room this morning with a message, which it is too late to deliver now—but it was something very kind and considerate—something greatly to your benefit—on the part of my dear mistress—when I found the door ajar, and hearing a female voice, which I at once recognised, I stopped to listen. It was wrong in me to do so, perhaps—but I couldn't help it. I heard what passed between you and that bad, deceitful woman. I knew what she was trying to bring you to from the first word I heard her utter, and I shuddered when you didn't at once, like a man of honour, reject her base—her abominable proposals."

"Lettice, how dare you use such language to me?"

"I can't help my feelings, sir—and they make me speak out. You were to blame to listen to that woman at all, but much more so to consent to what she asked of you. You little thought what had brought me to your room."

"Why, what did bring you there, Lettice?"

"I can't tell you now. My mistress has forbidden me. 'He must never know what I meant to do for him, or he may put a wrong construction on my motive,' she said, as I went back to her with a sorrowful heart, and related what had happened. 'I will take no further interest in him,' she added; 'he is unworthy of regard.' 'Indeed, miss, I can't help agreeing with you,' I replied; and I won't attempt to conceal from you, sir, that such were, and still are, my sentiments. Poor soul, she cried for a long time as if her heart would break, and though I did my best to comfort her, I couldn't succeed. After a while she grew more composed, and remained quiet till evening drew on, when she asked for pen and paper, and I propped her up in bed while she wrote this letter to you. Slowly—very slowly was it written, and with great difficulty. Oh, if you could have seen her angelic countenance, her dank, drooping hair hanging over her shoulders, and her thin, thin fingers! it was a sight to melt a heart of stone—and I think it would have melted yours. When she had done, she sealed the letter, and bade me take it to you. 'Tell him it is the last time I will ever trouble him,' she said; 'but implore him to attend to my request.' And now, sir, having said my say, I will withdraw while you read the letter."

" There is no occasion to do so, Lettice," Gage replied, putting aside the note; " I cannot read it now."

" Not read it! You cannot be so cruel! I won't believe in such black ingratitude."

" I cannot stay. I am behind my time. I will write to your mistress to-morrow morning. If you really have the regard you profess for her, you ought not to have disclosed what you accidentally overheard this morning, as you must have been aware it was calculated to give her needless pain. But the best way to repair your error is to keep silence now. You mustn't betray me, Lettice. I rely on your discretion."

" Don't rely on me, sir—don't do it. I won't hide anything from my mistress."

" Well, as you please. But if any ill arises from your imprudence, the blame will rest with you."

This was too much for poor Lettice. She was quite bewildered.

" Oh, do be persuaded to open the letter before you go, sir!" she cried, making a last effort to detain him. " Open it, and I'm certain you won't persist in your wicked purpose."

Gage made no reply, but, breaking from her, hurried to the sedan-chair, and ordered the bearers to proceed with all possible despatch to the Haymarket.

Lettice did not tarry to listen to the jests of the footmen, or satisfy their curiosity as to the motive of her visit, but betook herself sadly, and with slow footsteps, to Jermyn-street, uncertain what course she ought to pursue in reference to her mistress, and almost inclined to think it might be best to follow Gage's recommendation and keep silence as to his delinquencies. As she was crossing Piccadilly she met Arthur Poynings and his sister returning from an evening walk in Hyde Park, and perceiving her distress, Lucy anxiously inquired the cause of it. Seeing no reason for disguise, Lettice told her all that had occurred, and both sister and brother— but especially the former were greatly troubled by the recital.

Arthur, indeed, was roused to positive fury against Gage; though, for Lucy's sake, he repressed his indignation. Advising his sister to pass some hours with Clare, and, if need be, to remain with her during the night, and recommending both her and Lettice to observe the utmost caution in what they said to her respecting Gage, he accompanied them to the door of Mrs. Lacy's house in Jermyn-street (where it will be recollected that poor Clare had sought refuge), and then left them, promising to call at a later hour. Lucy was not without misgiving as to his intentions, but she thought there was little chance of his meeting with Gage that night, and on the morrow he might be calmer.

She was wrong. Arthur had resolved that the morrow should not dawn before he had seen Gage, and told him his opinion of his conduct.

And now to return to Gage. While he was borne rapidly along towards the Haymarket, he took out Clare's letter, and broke the seal. There was still light enough to enable him to distinguish its characters, and he read as follows:

"I have been told that a confirmed gamester can never be reclaimed. I did not believe it, for I entertained a better opinion of our nature, than to suppose that any passion could be so overwhelming and irresistible as to subvert every good resolution and principle, and obliterate all sense of honour. I now perceive my error. I find one, on whose plighted word I had implicitly relied, again ensnared by the toils from which I trusted he was delivered —his oath broken—himself dishonoured.

"But be warned, Gage—be warned while there is yet time! Turn back from the very door of the Temptress! Repulse her when she would entice you in! Shut your ears to her soft persuasions and falsehoods. Burst the chains she has cast around you. Fly from her! If you enter you are lost—irretrievably lost!

I had indulged in dreams of your future happiness—dreams, alas! from which I have been rudely awakened. I pictured you, as you might have become, after a time, by efforts properly directed, prosperous and distinguished. I saw you restored to your former position, and blessed with the hand and affections of a being in every respect worthy of you. And though I knew that long ere that fortunate period could arrive, I should be gone, I did not repine. Now, all those hopes are annihilated.

" Fain would I release you from your vow! It rests not with me to absolve you from it. But I can pity you—I can forgive you from my heart—I can pray for you,—and this I will do to the last! Farewell!

" CLARE."

This touching letter moved Gage profoundly, and he almost felt inclined to obey the admonition, and turn back at once. But he had not force enough to shake off his thraldom. His good genius had deserted him, and, arrived at the door of the Temptress, he went in.

XXXIV.

A NIGHT AT THE GROOM-PORTER'S.

MRS. JENYNS professed the greatest delight at seeing him. She was exquisitely attired, and never looked more attractive. Brice Bunbury, Jack Brassey, and Nat Mist had been invited to meet him; and however disposed Gage had been to resent their late conduct towards him, he could not hold out against their present demonstrations of regard, but shook hands heartily with all three.

"I must beg you to accept my apologies for what occurred at White's the other day, Monthermer," Brice said. "We all behaved very unhandsomely to you—but we are devilish sorry for it."

"Say no more, Brice," Gage replied. "I have no sort of quarrel with you; but I am deeply offended with Sir Randal."

"I shall not attempt to palliate his conduct," Brice replied, "for it was indefensible; but he owns himself completely in the wrong, and is anxious to atone for his folly. Whenever you meet him, he intends to apologise—and so does Mr. Freke. Ah! how delighted we all were to learn that old Fairlie had paid your debts. But why have you kept away from us ever since? We have looked in vain for you on the Mall, and at the coffee-houses."

The announcement of supper at this moment saved Gage from the necessity of reply. Mrs. Jenyns led the way to an adjoining room where a repast was served, of which Loriot himself might have been proud. Every dish was a delicacy. Delicious wines went round in flowing bumpers, and the spirits of the company rose as the goblets were drained. Mrs. Jenyns had no desire to check the hilarity of her guests, but she took care that Gage should not drink too much for her purpose. So while she allowed Brice Bunbury and the others to quaff as much champagne and burgundy as they chose, she wisely restricted him to claret.

A NIGHT AT THE GROOM-PORTER'S.

As may be supposed, with the business they had in hand, the party did not sit long after supper—not half so long as Brice would have desired—but adjourned to Spring Gardens.

Before starting, Mrs. Jenyns took Gage aside, and reiterating her advice to him to play with extreme caution, she gave him a pair of dice, telling him they were the luckiest she had ever used.

Arrived at the Groom-Porter's, they went up-stairs and entered the room where hazard was always played. The large round table was crowded; but, on seeing our hero, a gentleman hastily withdrew, and Gage took his place. Our hero's appearance caused significant glances to be exchanged between Beau Freke and Sir Randal, but they both courteously saluted him. When it came to his turn to play, Gage put down a hundred pounds, and took out the "lucky dice" given him by Mrs. Jenyns.

"Seven's the main," Sir Randal cried.

"A nick!" Gage exclaimed, and swept all the money, amounting to some hundreds, off the board.

"Did I not tell you you would win?" whispered Mrs. Jenyns, who stood behind him. "Go on! Stake all you have won. Good luck will attend you."

And so it proved. In less than an hour he was master of upwards of five thousand pounds. Feeling he was in a run of luck, he went on, constantly doubling his stakes; and neither Sir Randal nor Beau Freke seemed disposed to balk him. At first they had intended he should win a small amount — feeling certain they could get back their money whenever they pleased — but they were out in their calculations. The dice fell precisely as Gage would have had them fall, and as if a wizard had shaken the box. Vexed as well as surprised at Gage's uninterrupted run of luck, and determined to check it, Sir Randal put down a thousand pounds, and his example was followed by Beau Freke. Mrs. Jenyns slightly touched Gage's arm. He was trembling with excitement, but the pressure calmed him at once. Again he nicked the main, and swept all from the table. His adversaries stared at each other. They could not understand it, but felt piqued to proceed. Four thousand pounds were placed on the table, and changed hands in a twinkling. Double again—dice-boxes rattled, and Gage was a winner of 8000*l*. His exulting and defiant looks goaded his adversaries to continue their play. The stakes had now become serious, and all eyes were fixed on Gage as he shook the box. Loud were his shouts of triumph—deep the curses of his opponents. Would they have their revenge? Did they dare go on? They answered by doubling the stakes. It was an awful moment—and Gage grew pale and drops pearled upon his brow. But he rattled the box boldly, and cast the dice with decision. Huzza! 'twas a famous throw. But it was the last. His antagonists have had enough. They would play no more that night; and Gage rose a winner of nearly 35,000*l*.

He was well-nigh frenzied with delight—he laughed extravagantly, and shouted as if inebriated. Such exhibitions were too frequent in that place to attract much attention, and few noticed his frantic cries and gestures. His opponents bore their defeat better than might be expected—better, indeed, than they would have borne it, if they had not persuaded themselves they should soon triumph in their turn. They therefore shook hands cordially with the winner, and telling him he was bound to give them their revenge on another occasion, which he readily consented to, they took their departure with an air of apparent unconcern. During all this time, Mrs. Jenyns had kept careful watch over Gage's winnings, and in order that there might be no misunderstanding between them afterwards, she divided the amount into two heaps; and when Gage came back to the table she showed him what she had done, and appropriating her own share of the spoil, left the rest to him. He was quite satisfied, and proceeded to secure the rolls of bank-notes and the gold allotted to him. This done, and the "lucky dice" returned at her request to their owner, a coach was called, and Mrs. Jenyns, with a profusion of tender adieux to Gage, stepped into it and drove off.

Gage remained standing for a moment at the door of the gaming-house, indulging in the rapturous emotions occasioned by his success. People were going out and coming in, but he took no notice of them. At last, however, he remarked a tall personage at a short distance from him, who, so far as the individual could be distinguished, was apparently watching him. Our hero had too much money about him at the moment to run any needless risk, and he was about to move off, when the man in question strode quickly towards him, and as he drew near, Gage perceived by the light of the lamp hung above the portal that it was Arthur Poynings.

Gage would have gladly avoided the meeting, but escape was impossible. Arthur seized his arm and held him fast.

" You shall not stir till you have heard what I have to say to you," young Poynings cried. " You have for ever forfeited the character of a gentleman and a man of honour, and must henceforth associate only with gamesters and sharpers. You have been guilty of the basest ingratitude, and, oh! shame to a Monthermer! have broken your plighted word. You have made yourself the tool of one of the worst of her sex, and have consented to become a partner in her tricks and dishonest practices."

" How, sir?" Gage cried. " Do you dare to insinuate that I have played falsely ?"

" You may have been that infamous woman's dupe, but that you have used loaded dice I am certain," Arthur replied. " I was present when you entered the room. I made way for you at the table—though you did not notice me—and took up a position where I could observe your play. I was struck with Mrs. Jenyns's manner, and noted a peculiar look when you first threw the dice. As you went on and continued to win, my suspicions were confirmed, and I only wonder at the blindness of your opponents. No doubt they were deluded by the belief that they were playing with a man of honour—a man of honour, I mean, in their sense of the term, not mine."

" It is false!" Gage cried. " Such deception cannot have been practised upon me."

" Have you the dice with which you played ?" Arthur demanded.

" I have not—I gave them back to her—but I will not rest till I have satisfied my doubts. If you have made a false accusation, you shall answer for it with your life."

Arthur laughed disdainfully, and, releasing the hold he had hitherto maintained of the other's arm, exclaimed in accents of disdain, but with which some pity was mingled, " Act as you please—believe what you please—I care not. You are born to be duped, and will, therefore, believe that woman's assertions in spite of positive proof to the contrary. But you will find out the truth ere long—and to your cost. I shall never withdraw the charge I have brought against her—nor recal a single expression I have used towards yourself. You merit every epithet of scorn that can be heaped upon you. But think not I will give you satisfaction. I cross swords only with a gentleman, and you have forfeited all claim to the title." So saying, he turned on his heel and departed.

Not many minutes after this, Gage had made his way to Mrs. Jenyns's lodgings, and, without announcing himself, abruptly entered her room. She was in the act of counting her gains, and looked surprised at seeing Gage, but not in the slightest degree disconcerted.

"Where are the dice you lent me?" he cried. "Give them to me at once."

"What! are you about to play again?" she said. "Be content with what you have won already. Your luck may turn."

"Perhaps it may if I play fairly, but I had rather lose than win in any other way."

"I don't understand you. Has any one been taxing you with unfair play?"

"Yes; Arthur Poynings was present while I played, and he declares the dice were loaded. Let me have them instantly."

"Here they are," Mrs. Jenyns replied, searching amidst a heap of gold, and producing a pair of dice. "Examine them, and judge for yourself."

Gage took the dice and broke them in pieces on the hearth. The cubes were of solid ivory.

"Are you satisfied now?" Mrs. Jenyns cried. "I wish you had had more confidence in me and less in Arthur, for in breaking those dice you have destroyed your own luck."

"It matters not," Gage rejoined; "a load has been taken from my breast by finding I have not been guilty—however unintentionally—of foul play, and I am equally glad to feel assured that Arthur's suspicions of you were without warrant."

"I am greatly obliged to you and to Mr. Arthur Poynings for your good opinion of me," Mrs. Jenyns rejoined.

"Forgive me, Peg, for doing you this great injustice. But Arthur's taunts and reproaches stung me to the quick, and his malicious charge against you seemed to have a certain consistency which I could not disprove, otherwise than as I have done."

"You will bring him to account for his slanderous insolence?" Mrs. Jenyns cried.

"I cannot obtain satisfaction from him, for he refuses to meet me. But I must and will set myself right. I have a strange scheme in view which I trust to carry out. You shall hear what it is to-morrow."

" Why not tell me now?"

"No; it would be useless to mention the project till I am certain of being able to realise it. But I think it will surprise you."

" Very likely. I hope you have given up your intention of repaying Fairlie?"

" I am more than ever resolved upon it. Indeed, that is an essential part of my design, as you will find when I disclose it to you."

" You are not about to leave me so soon?"

"I am a poor companion at this moment, or I would stay. Arthur's bitter reproaches rankle in my breast—and do what I will, I cannot help thinking of Clare. Her image constantly rises before me. Good night!"

And raising her hand to his lips, he departed.

XXXV.

A SINGULAR REQUEST.

EARLY next morning Gage sought Fairlie, and on seeing him the steward immediately demanded whether he meant to go abroad.

"No," Gage replied. "I shall remain. You must know that I went to the Groom-Porter's last night, Fairlie."

The steward instantly flew into a towering passion. "So you have been at the gaming-table, have you?" he cried. "And you have the effrontery to confess it—to boast of it? I told my daughter you would break your vow. I told her it was madness to pay your debts. And I was right."

"How much have you paid for me, Fairlie?" Gage remarked, taking a seat, which the steward did not condescend to offer him.

"How much!" Fairlie rejoined, with increasing fury. "Several thousands—but it was done to oblige my daughter. I am sorry now that I yielded to her importunities, and threw away the money so foolishly."

"But the amount!—let me know the precise amount?"

"I can't see why you require the information; but I have paid exactly 13,000_l._"

"And all my creditors are satisfied?"

"All of them. Nibbs alone was five thousand. The rest amounted to 8000_l._—a large sum—a fortune, in fact. But Clare would have it so."

"You never yet were a loser by me, Fairlie—and you shall not be a loser now," Gage rejoined, taking out a thick rouleau of bank-notes.

"Why, zounds! you won't repay me—you can't mean it?" Fairlie stammered, in the utmost surprise.

" These notes are yours when I have my creditors' receipts."

" Here they are,—every one of them," Fairlie answered. " How came you by such a windfall ? But I needn't ask, since you tell me you have been at the Groom-Porter's—ha! ha! You must have had rare luck, sir, to win so large a sum?"

" Do not concern yourself about the matter, Fairlie. We are now quits.'

" Entirely so, sir," the steward replied, obsequiously. " But I don't know whether I ought to take this money. Clare will never forgive me when she hears of it."

" She will never hear of it from me—so rest easy on that score. Hark'ee, Fairlie, I have a request to make of you."

" I am sure, sir, I shall only be too happy to grant it, if in my power," the steward replied.

" Perhaps you may not be so ready to do so when you hear what it is. I have a strong desire to pass a week in Monthermer Castle."

" Nothing easier, sir. I shall be delighted to see you there."

" But I do not wish to go there as guest—but as lord and master."

" I fear *that* is impossible," Fairlie replied, with a bland smile. " I am excessively sorry—but——"

" I knew you would object. But hear me out. All I desire is to resume for a short time the part I once played there. I will give it up at the end of a week."

" Well—well,—if that be all, I am willing to humour you.'

" But, more than this, I desire to give a grand entertainment to my friends—a princely revel, in short."

" But not at my expense, sir—not at my expense!"

" Certainly not. I have three thousand pounds left, and this I will devote to the entertainment."

" A wonderful notion, sir,—quite worthy of you. But you are quite sure you have no secret design in it?"

" My design is simply to give a last entertainment by which I may be remembered. When it is over, be assured I will not trouble you further."

" I am quite satisfied. You shall have such a revel as never before was given in the Castle, or elsewhere in the county. I know your sumptuous tastes, sir, and will provide accordingly. You shall feast like Belshazzar. But I must make one stipulation."

" Name it."

" Till midnight you shall be lord of the house. After that hour I shall assume the title."

" Agreed !"

" What day do you appoint for the entertainment?"

" To-morrow week."

" Ere then you may play again, sir, and your good luck may desert you. To prevent accidents, you had better pay beforehand."

Gage laughed, and handed him three bank-notes of a thousand each. " There, now you are quite safe," he said.

" Rely upon it, I will do you justice," Fairlie said. " Montheriner Castle is yours for a week, and if I come there during the time it will only be to superintend the preparations for the grand entertainment. Invite as many guests as you please. Live as you have ever been accustomed to live, in riot and profusion. Stint nothing. Carriages, horses, servants, plate, wine —I place all at your disposal till to-morrow week."

" In that week I will live a year!" Gage cried; " and when it is past—— But, no matter!—I will not think of the future. Present enjoyment is what I covet. I should like to set out for the Castle at once."

" The travelling-carriage shall be ready for you in an hour, sir, with four horses," Fairlie replied. " Bellairs and Chassemouche shall go with you, and I will send down the rest of the household in the course of the day. If you will favour me with a list of such persons as you desire to ask, I will send out the invitations without delay. You may safely confide all arrangements to me. I will give the necessary orders at once."

And as he rang the bell for the purpose, Gage left him, and repairing to his own chamber, sat down to write a couple of letters.

All was in readiness at the time appointed. Gage started on the journey in his own superb travelling-carriage, dashing out of town as fast as four horses could carry him; and such was the expedition he used, that, ere evening, he had reached the borders of the wide domains he had once called his own. The road led him within a short distance of the Beacon Hill, and he could not resist the impulse that prompted him to survey the familiar scene. Accordingly, he ordered the postilions to halt, and, descending, left the servants with the carriage, and mounted the hill alone. It was a beautiful evening, and the view from the summit had never looked more enchanting. All was unchanged since he had last beheld it. There were the richly cultivated lands, spreading out in every direction — the farms and the humble homesteads, surrounded with haystacks—the woods with their colonies of rooks. The reapers had been busy during the day garnering their golden produce ; but many of the fields were still studded with sheaves of corn. The contem. plation of this peaceful and beautiful scene seemed calculated to soothe a troubled breast. But it did not soothe Gage. On the contrary, it aroused thoughts of singular bitterness. For a moment the veil seemed rent from his eyes, and he viewed his conduct in its proper light. He regarded himself as a madman. To throw away such a property !—how could he have done it ? Was the mischief irreparable ? Was it all gone ? Yes! all! all!

Hitherto his gaze had avoided the Castle. He now looked towards it. Ay, there it was, towering proudly over its clump of trees—a magnificent object. Gone from him for ever! The thought was madness, and so intolerable did he find it, that, uttering curses upon his folly, he turned away and rushed down the hill.

Arrived at the foot of the eminence he found himself face to face with a man, whom he had not previously observed, but who had been watching him.

" Why, Mark Rougham, is that you?" he exclaimed.

" Ay, it be me sure enough, your honour," Mark replied ; " and it be a strange chance that ha' brought me here this fine e'en to meet your honour."

" Are you still one of my tenants—I mean a tenant to Mr. Fairlie?" Gage inquired.

" No, no; I be bailiff to Sir Hugh Poynings, at Reedham," Mark replied, " and a very good situation I have of it; quite comfortable for myself and my family. I have no wish to be a tenant to Muster Fairlie, though I can't help sometimes regretting Cowbridge Farm. Indeed it were merely to indulge myself with a look at the old place that brought me here now. Excuse my freedom in putting a plain question to you, sir? I ask it fro' t' strong interest I feel in you. I heered say you'd lost a mint o' money at play."

" It's true, Mark," Gage replied. " I have lost, as you say, a mint of money—more than I shall ever get back, I fear."

" That's a pity—a great pity," Mark groaned. " But that's not precisely the question I meant to ask, neither. Yo may ha' lost a great deal, and yet not a' your fortin. I trust it be not so bad as that?"

" Believe the worst, Mark. I won't deceive you."

" And it's true, then," Rougham cried, despairingly; " this noble estate—the finest i' a' Suffolk—it be a' gone—a' gambled away!" And covering his face with his hand, he wept aloud.

At last, Mark shook off his emotion, and said, " I never thought to hear this from your father's son, sir. He died i' my arms near this very spot, and this may gi' me a right to ask you, in his honoured name, what you mean to do?"

" I cannot tell you now, but you shall know hereafter, Mark Meet me at daybreak to-morrow week, on this spot, and you shall learn my final resolution."

" Here, did you say, sir? Do you mean that I am to meet you here?"

" As I have just said—on this day week, at daybreak."

" A strange place of meeting—and a strange hour," Mark observed.

" The meeting may be stranger," Gage said, gloomily.

" I hope it may lead to good," Mark said. " You know the prophecy relating to your family?"

" I have heard something about it," Gage replied. "What is it?"

" The rhymes run thus, if I can bring 'em to mind," Mark replied:

> " Hard by the hill whereon the Beacon stands,
> One proud Monthermer shall lose house and lands ;
> On the same spot—if but the way be plain—
> Another of the line shall both regain."

" A strange prediction, truly," Gage said, musingly. " ' *If but the way be plain*'—what can that mean ? No use inquiring now. —Fail not to meet me, Mark."

" On Friday, at daybreak, if breath be in my body, you may count on seeing me," Rougham replied.

" And whatever breath be in mine, or not, you will find me there," Gage rejoined. " And now farewell, Mark." And without another word, he hurried to the carriage, leaving Rougham to ponder over his parting words.

XXXVI.

A SLEEPLESS NIGHT.

GAGE'S reappearance at Monthermer Castle created an extraordinary sensation amongst the neighbouring gentry, and indeed throughout the whole county. No one expected to find him there again,—at all events, not in the quality of lord of the mansion, and such he was still, to all appearances. Tidings of his utter ruin had of course been received. Such news flies quickly. Moreover, it was rumoured that the whole of his estates had been seized by Fairlie; and though this report wanted confirmation, it obtained general credence, being quite consistent with the steward's known character for rapacity.

Precisely at this juncture, when everybody supposed him shut up in the Fleet, or some other debtors' prison, Gage suddenly returned, having travelled from town (it was said) in his usual magnificent style, and accompanied by his usual attendants. Nor did he appear to meditate any change in his extravagant mode of living; his first business on his arrival being to issue invitations to all his acquaintance, announcing his intention of keeping open house for a week—the festivities to be concluded by a grand entertainment, to which the honour of their company was requested.

The recipients of these invitations were naturally filled with astonishment. Not being in the secret of Gage's arrangement with Fairlie, they knew not what to make of it. One said to another, "Have you heard that Monthermer is come back to the Castle, and has begun again at his old rattling pace?" And the other replied that he *had* heard it, but could scarcely believe it, so he meant to ride over on the morrow and satisfy himself. Whereupon they both agreed to accept Gage's invitation.

Their example was generally followed. Many went from curiosity—many more because they felt certain of getting surpassingly good dinners—and some few because they liked Gage personally, and were really glad to welcome him home again. So great was the influx of guests, that on the third day every room in the immense mansion was occupied, except such as had been set apart for visitors expected from town. Those who looked for good cheer were not disappointed. Heretofore, the lord of the Castle had been renowned for profuse hospitality; but his present banquets surpassed all previously given, both in excellence and splendour. Nothing was wanting that the greatest epicure could desire; while the hardest-drinking foxhunter got enough—and something more than enough—burgundy and claret.

As may be supposed, the best of Gage's neighbours held aloof, and would take no part in his festivities, but the boon companions who did rally round him persuaded him he was better without such high and mighty folks. Good fellowship and good wine would be thrown away upon them. He himself was worth the whole set put together. He was the best and most hospitable fellow in the world, and deserved a dozen fortunes. Let the reader picture to himself a score of old topers (some of them six-bottle men), a like number of gay and dissolute youths, former associates of our hero, together with a sprinkling of the miscellaneous class of gentry who throng a hunting-field, and he will have some idea of the class of company now assembled at the Castle. From morn to night, and from night to morn, it was one continued round of revelry and enjoyment.

On the fourth day the party was increased by the arrival of Sir Randal de Meschines, Mr. Freke, Lord Melton, Brice Bunbury, Nat Mist, and Jack Brassey, with their attendants; and later on the same day came Mrs. Jenyns. The last visitor was a surprise to Gage—he had not expected her.

"You won't find me in the way," she said to him, perceiving his embarrassment as he endeavoured to give her a smiling welcome; "and I beg you not to stand on any ceremony with me, but to put me just where you please. Fairlie told me there would be no room for me, and that you didn't want me; but I knew better, so here I am. But, bless me, how ill you appear! What's the matter? I declare you look ten years older than when I saw you last."

This was said in jest, but it was not far wide of the truth. Gage had, indeed, entirely lost his youthful expression of countenance, and looked frightfully worn and haggard. Since his return to the Castle he had known little rest. The large bed-chamber which he occupied had formerly been used by his father, and he fancied he heard strange sounds within it. On the night preceding Mrs. Jenyns's arrival he had been more than usually restless. After tossing to and fro for hours upon his pillow, in the vain attempt to court sleep, he arose, and, full of superstitious terror, hastily attired himself, and stepped forth into the long gallery, lined with full-length portraits of his ancestors.

Pictures no longer, but fearful spectres.

The moon shed its pale radiance through the opposite windows, and, thus illuminated, the figures of the old Monthermers started from their frames like ghosts. The first phantom that Gage encountered was Radulphus, a mail-clad baron of the time of Edward I., and founder of the line. To this awful shade succeeded Sir Lionel, who had been knighted by Edward III.—then Kenric, the wise, Randal, the proud, Redwald, the gigantic—with many more: Oswald, who flourished in the reign of Edward IV.; Egbert, a galliard page in the days of Henry VIII., a crafty statesman in the time of Elizabeth; Sigebert, knighted by James I.; Arthur, the cavalier; Vernon, Gage's grandsire; and lastly, Warwick, his father.

Close beside the shadowy form of Warwick floated the semblance of a young and beautiful woman. Her regards were fixed tenderly and sorrowfully upon her erring son—so tenderly that his heart was melted. Agonising thoughts racked him at that moment, and he bitterly reproached himself. He had never known the caresses of a mother, had never received counsel from her lips—but would it have profited him if he had? Could a mother have rescued him from destruction? No—no. He deserved to perish. He had forfeited all claim to compassion.

Overwhelmed by dark and despairing thoughts, he glanced along the line of phantoms, and meeting their regards with looks stern as their own, gave utterance to a terrible resolution he had formed. But the spectres frowned, and seemed to mutter that even in the tomb he should have no place beside them.

Suddenly he was roused from the state of stupefaction into which he had been thrown, by the sound of laughter and revelry arising

from below. A large party of his guests were passing the night
in carousing. In their society he might find forgetfulness, and
without waiting a moment he hurried down to them. But, on
gaining the room where the party was assembled, he was completely
disgusted by the scene presented to his view. Prostrate forms were
lying across the room—some so overcome with wine and punch as
to be unable to rise—some fast asleep—their attire disordered, and
their perukes scattered about. But some half-dozen were still able
to maintain their seats at the table, and these valiant topers hailed
Gage with tipsy shouts, and called upon him to join them; but
unable to conquer his repugnance, he hastily retreated, and rousing
up a groom, proceeded to the stable, and bidding the man saddle
his favourite hunter, Hotspur, he rode forth into the park. The
groom thought he must have taken leave of his senses.

He dashed off at a gallop, and plunged into the most secluded
part of the park—but black care was on his track. A troop of phantom horsemen overtook him—and rode by his side. In vain he urged
Hotspur to his utmost speed—still the ghostly company kept up
with him. He knew them all—Redwald the gigantic, Kenric with
his towering brow, Randal with his lofty port, Arthur with his
flowing locks;—and his father—yes, his father headed the troop.
Go where he would, they went with him. If he swept along a
glade at full speed, the spectral horsemen were beside him—if he
drew the rein on an eminence, they paused likewise. He pressed
his hand before his eyes, but, on removing it, they were still there.
"What would ye with me?" he exclaimed. "Why do you follow
me thus?" The figures made no reply, but pointed to the Castle.
"I know what you mean," he continued. "You upbraid me with
having lost it. But be at peace. Ere many days my faults shall be
expiated."

As he uttered the exclamation the phantoms melted away into the
mist, and he rode back slowly and without further disquietude to
the Castle.

As the groom took his horse to the stable, he wondered what
the young squire had been at. Hotspur hadn't a dry hair upon
him, and looked as if he had been drenched wi' water from head
to heel.

The occurrences of this night had so changed Gage's appearance
as to warrant Mrs. Jenyns's observation that he looked full ten
years older.

XXXVII.

SHOWING HOW GAGE WAS AGAIN PREVAILED UPON TO PLAY, AND WHAT SUCCESS ATTENDED HIM.

SIR RANDAL and Beau Freke had come down to Monthermer Castle in the hope of winning back their money, but in this expectation it seemed likely they would be disappointed. Play—and pretty deep play, too—had been going on every night, but Gage took no part in it. The fact was, he had no funds, and was therefore compelled to be a mere spectator. It was an additional mortification to him to be reminded by his newly-arrived guests of his promise to give them revenge. He made the best excuses he could, but he felt they looked upon him as a shuffler—of all characters the one he most despised—and he writhed under the fancied imputation.

"This used not to be the case when we were here last, Monthermer," Sir Randal said. "Then you could not resist a game at piquet or gleek, and were my constant antagonist at hazard. Why not sit down with us now? What say you to a game at two-handed putt?—or, if you prefer it, lanterloo?—I am for anything—tick-tack—in-and-in—passage—or what you will. Only sit down."

"Excuse me, Sir Randal, I don't play to-night."

"Why, 'sdeath! man, have you made a second vow against cards and dice? If so, I counsel you to break it like the first. I would fain lose a few more thousands to you."

"And so would I," Beau Freke added. "We will absolve you from any new vow you may have made, Monthermer. And no doubt you will have as good luck as you had a short time ago at the Groom-Porter's."

Just then, Lord Melton, who was engaged with a party at five-

Q

cards, called out: " I'll bet a hundred pounds, Monthermer, that I win all the cards."

Gage felt desperately inclined to rejoin, "Done !" but he restrained himself, and merely said, " I don't bet now."

" Why, what the deuce prevents you?" his lordship cried. " See !" he added, displaying his cards, "if you had taken me, you would have won."

Not liking to be further troubled, Gage soon afterwards quitted the card-room, and did not return to it that night.

On the following evening, however, Mrs. Jenyns managed to lure him to the hazard-table. He had been excusing himself as before, when she took him aside, and urged him to try his luck once more.

" I must have money to play with, Peg," he said, with a forced laugh.

" Why, so you shall," she replied. " Take my pocket-book. It is full of bank-notes. I want you to play for me, and don't be afraid to stake highly. We will divide the winnings as before."

" Have you lucky dice with you ?" Gage rejoined, glancing at her significantly.

" You broke those I most relied on," she replied ; " but I have another pair, and you may try them, if you like."

" Let me have them," Gage rejoined. " To what extent must I go ?"

" That pocket-book contains almost all you won for me at the Groom-Porter's—about 17,000*l.* I am willing to risk it all."

" You had better not trust me."

" Pooh ! I haven't the slightest uneasiness," she rejoined, slipping a pair of dice into his hands. " I know you will win. Come along !" And leading him towards the table, she called out, " Gentlemen, I am happy to inform you that I have induced Mr. Monthermer to play."

The announcement was received with acclamations, and a place was instantly made for Gage at the table. Both Sir Randal and Beau Freke asked how much he meant to stake. A thousand pounds was the reply. The dice rattled, and Gage lost. Mrs. Jenyns, who stood at his elbow, looked surprised, but whispered him to double his stakes. He did so, and lost again. The actress bit her lips with vexation, but signed to him to go on. He obeyed, but without better luck. The stake was now eight thousand pounds, and he paused before laying down the money, but Mrs. Jenyns would have no cessation. The run of luck was still against him. The eight thousand pounds was swept off by his opponents. Altogether he had lost fifteen thousand pounds—within two thousand of the contents of the pocket-book.

"Stake what is left," Mrs. Jenyns whispered; "and play with care," she added, significantly. Gage strove to comply with her injunctions—but he was beaten, and the pocket-book was empty! His adversaries urged him to go on, but he shook his head, and left the table.

"I am sorry to have played so badly," he remarked to Mrs. Jenyns, who had followed him hastily. "But I might perhaps have done better if I had used the dice you gave me."

"What! didn't you use them?" she cried, with an explosion of rage. "This accounts for it! Fool that I was to trust you! You have ruined me."

"But, Peg——"

"Don't talk to me. I am out of all patience. Give me the dice, and let me try. But no—no—I cannot play. All my money is gone. Have you none to lend me? A hundred pounds will do."

"I have not the hundredth part of that amount left," he answered.

Mrs. Jenyns looked as if she could annihilate him—but her anger seemed suddenly to abate.

"Something must be done to repair this error," she said, in a tone of forced calmness. "We must confer together to-morrow about Fairlie."

"About Fairlie!" Gage exclaimed. "What about him?"

"Not so loud," she rejoined; "the servants are all his spies, and some of them may overhear you. I fancied that man was listening," pointing to Pudsey, who was standing at a little distance from them. "To-morrow I will open my design to you. You owe me reparation for the mischief you have just done me—and I will show you how to make ample amends. But let us separate. I am quite sure that man is listening. Meet me to-morrow morning early—in the library."

And she left the room, while Gage walked back to the hazard-table, and watched the play.

"I did right not to use her dice," he thought. "Better lose, than win unfairly."

XXXVIII.

AN INTERVIEW IN THE IVY TOWER.

THE last day but one of his term had now arrived, and in a few more hours Gage must for ever cast aside his borrowed honours, and cease to be lord of Monthermer.

Another day, and all would be over! Well, what matter! Had he not exhausted all the enjoyments of life? had he not feasted and caroused to satiety? had he not drained the cup of pleasure to the dregs?—He could now throw it aside without regret.

Without regret, perhaps,—but not without compunction—not without remorse. He dared not review his frenzied career—he dared not reflect upon the innumerable follies he had committed—such acts would not bear reflection—but he vainly sought to stifle the cries of conscience within his breast. These cries would be heard even in the midst of riotous indulgence; they chilled his blood, and banished sleep from his couch; they drove him at times almost to the verge of madness.

But there would soon be an end, and till then he would know no restraint—no pause. If his career had been brief and brilliant as that of a meteor—its close should be like the meteor's sudden extinction.

Such thoughts agitated him as on the morning of the sixth day after his return he crossed the broad velvet lawns of the garden, and mounted the stone steps of the terrace leading to the ruins of the ancient Castle. He was unaccompanied, for not one of his numerous guests was yet astir. The hour was too early for them after their prolonged debauches overnight, and many of them would not rise before noon, and would then require fresh stimulants to set them going for the day. But as their host

could not sleep, he quitted his couch betimes, and sought to coo'
his throbbing brow and fevered limbs in the fresh morning air.
Besides, he had another motive for his early walk. On retiring
to his chamber on the previous night he had found on his toilet-
table a note, in a female hand, with which he thought he was
familiar, though he could not assign a name to the writer. The
note bore no signature, and contained only a few words, begging
him to come next morning to the Ivy Tower, where a friend
desired to see him. Strictest secrecy was enjoined. Time was
when such a billet would have piqued his curiosity, and flattered
his vanity with the idea of a conquest, but no such idle feelings
now excited him. Still he resolved to go; and it was to keep the
appointment that he now shaped his course towards the ruins of
the old Castle.

He had not proceeded far along the terrace, when, raising his
eyes, which, owing to his melancholy musing, had been hitherto
fixed on the ground, he perceived a man advancing to meet him,
and at once recognising Mark Rougham, halted till the latter came
up, thinking him very much in the way at the moment, and considering how to get rid of him.

"Good day to your honour," Mark cried, taking off his hat as
he drew near—"you be well met. I were comin' down to the Hall
to try and get a word wi' you. But my errand's done, since you
be on the way to the Ivy Tower."

"Ah! you know I am going there!—Perhaps you are aware that
I got a note last night?"

"Aware of it! why, I brought it myself, sir—and got one o' th'
women servants to place it i' your bed-chamber, where you would
be sure to find it. You can guess who it be from, I suppose?
Lord bless her! I couldn't ha' believed in such goodness and devotion, unless I'd seen it. My heart has been like to burst wi' what
I ha' witnessed since yesterday—so much consideration for others,
so little care for self. Sure I am, if there be any one able to
save a sinful soul fro' destruction, it be she. There ben't such
another on earth."

"Such another as whom, Mark?"

"Why, whom else can I mean but Miss Fairlie! Such words
as I've used couldn't be true of any other of her sex—not that I
mean to say aught against 'em—but she be a paragon."

" You lead me to suppose she is here, Mark—but that is impossible, unless her health has greatly improved."

" She may be a trifle better than she has been," Mark replied, " but her life still hangs by a thread, which may be snapped at any minute. Howsomever, in spite of illness and fatigue, she *is* here ; and a wonderful thing it be that she can have gone through so long a journey; but her brave and good heart supported her—and no doubt Heaven leant her aid."

" What has brought her here?" Gage cried.

" Can your honour ask that question? She be come to see you —to speak wi' you—to try and move your heart ; and I hope, by Heaven's grace, she may succeed in doing so. You wrote to her, sir, didn't you, afore you left Lunnon?"

" I sent her a few hasty lines, telling her I was going down to Monthermer Castle for a week. I scarcely knew what I wrote, I was so hurried."

" Whatever you did write, sir, your letter caused her to follow you. In spite of all remonstrances, she set off on the same day as yourself, with my daughter Lettice, and travelled by slow stages to Bury St. Edmund's. There she took rest ; but, while doing so, she sent on a messenger to Muster Gosnold, the head gardener, to prepare the rooms in the Ivy Tower for her reception."

" I remember hearing she had taken a fancy to the old tower, and had had it furnished," Gage remarked.

" Ay, that was after Muster Arthur Poynings had the ill-luck to get wounded, and were removed there," Mark continued. " A sad affair that, sir, and might have turned out worse than it did. I thought the young gentleman would have died, and I'm pretty sure he would have done but for Miss Fairlie's care. She watched by him the whole night, tendin' him like a sister, and never left him till he was removed on a litter to Reedham. From that time forward she took a liking to the old tower. But, as I was sayin', while she rested at Bury, a messenger was sent over to Muster Gosnold to get the rooms ready for her—and at the same time Lettice despatched a man to Reedham to let me know they were comin'. As luck would have it, Sir Hugh and the family had just returned fro' Lunnon, so I could not help mentioning the circumstance to Muster Arthur,—and, as a matter of course, he tells Miss Lucy—and what does she do, but decide at once to come here and nurse her friend. A good deal was said against it, as your honour may suppose, by Muster Arthur and my lady, but the long and the short of the matter is, she comes."

"What! is Miss Poynings here, too?" Gage exclaimed, in amazement.

"Ay, in good truth is she, sir," Mark replied. "She and her brother joined Miss Fairlie at the cross-roads, half way betwixt this and Reedham, and Muster Arthur brought 'em here last night, and saw 'em comfortably settled afore he left—and that's all about it—no, not quite all, for Miss Lucy wrote the note to you, which I myself conveyed, as I've already told you. And now, sir, shall I conduct you to her?"

Gage remained for a moment irresolute, and then, as if nerving himself for the interview, he said, "Lead on, Mark."

Not a word more passed between them.

On reaching the tower, Mark went in, while Gage waited without till he received a summons to enter, and then following his conductor up a short spiral staircase, was admitted into a lofty circular chamber, which had been fitted up with considerable taste, and with every needful attention to comfort. The furniture was cumbrous and old-fashioned, but in harmony with the room. A copper lamp hung from the groined roof, and a dim mirror, in an ebony frame, was placed over the ancient chimney-piece. The stone walls were covered with old tapestry, and the deep embrasures shrouded by thick curtains. A wood fire was burning cheerily on the hearth, and its blaze illuminated the room. On a sofa near the fireplace, and covered by shawls, reclined Clare. In close attendance upon her were Lucy Poynings and Lettice Rougham. Mark did not enter with Gage, but having ushered him to the door, shut it, and remained outside.

For a few moments there was a profound silence, broken only by half-stifled sobs proceeding from Lettice. At length, a low voice was heard to say, "Draw near, I beg of you." And Gage approached the sofa on which the sufferer rested.

"Sit down beside me for a moment," Clare continued, in her soft feeble accents, "and let me explain the cause of my presence here. I had thought never to see you again, but compassion has overcome all other feelings, and I have resolved to persevere to the last. Therefore have I come. I will not reproach you with having broken your promise to me. For that I freely forgive you, and pray Heaven to forgive you likewise.

She then paused for a few moments, after which she resumed in a firmer tone:

"And now let me ask you a question—and I entreat you to a_ wer it sincerely. Have you repaid my father the money he advanced for your debts? Nay, do not hesitate—I must know the truth—I have a right to know it."

"Since you press me thus, I am compelled to admit that I have repaid him," he rejoined. "By doing so, I hoped, in some degree, to atone for my shameful conduct to you."

"If you had listened to me, this new distress might have been spared me," Clare exclaimed, in a tone of anguish. And she sank back for a few moments on the sofa, while Lucy flew forward to support her. "Oh, it is hard to bear," she exclaimed, after a while—"but it must be righted, if possible. Now tell me, Gage —and tell me truly—for what purpose have you come here?"

"To be lord of Monthermer for a week," he replied.

"But how came my father to consent to your return?"

"Oh! I found means of persuading him—to be plain, I made it worth his while to let me have the place for a few days. My term ends to-morrow at midnight."

"And then what do you propose to do?" Clare continued.

Gage made no answer.

After a brief, painful pause, he arose and said abruptly, "It is useless to prolong this interview. It can lead to nothing. I am past redemption. Do not concern yourself further about me, Clare."

"Stay!" she cried, detaining him. "You must not go thus. You have formed some terrible resolution. I read it in your glances. Do not add guilt to folly. Do not destroy your eternal weal. Oh, listen to me, Gage—listen to me!"

"It is too late—my resolution is taken!" he exclaimed, with a look and tone bordering upon frenzy.

"Oh! say not so. You may yet be spared for many years of happiness. Join your prayers to mine, Lucy—speak to him— speak!"

Lucy tried to obey her, but her voice was choked by emotion.

"All your prayers are in vain," Gage cried. "Nothing can turn me from my purpose. Farewell, Clare—farewell, Lucy. Think the best you can of me!"

And breaking from them he rushed out of the chamber.

"Oh! what will become of him!" Lucy exclaimed, falling on her knees beside Clare.

" A last effort must be made to save him," Clare murmured-- "a last effort."

XXXIX.

HOW MR. PUDSEY ENTERTAINED HIS FRIENDS.

WHILE the numerous guests made merry in the halls of Monthermer Castle, and the roofs resounded with their boisterous
revelry, similar bacchanalian orgies were held below-stairs. The
crowd of lacqueys, grooms, and other serving-men assembled in
the mansion feasted and caroused as lustily as their masters.
Riot and excess indeed prevailed throughout the house, and the
main study of its inmates, whatever their degree, seemed to be
how to gratify their appetites to the fullest extent. No one
attempted to check this unbounded waste, for Fairlie had not
made his appearance, and Gage gave himself no concern about it.
Provided his wants and those of his friends were supplied, the
servants might do just as they pleased, and we may be quite sure
they availed themselves of the license.

A more deplorable spectacle cannot be imagined than this noble
and once well-ordered mansion now presented. Heretofore, in
Warwick de Monthermer's time, true hospitality was ever exercised within it, and the vast establishment was admirably conducted. Liberal without profusion; generous without ostentation;
keeping an excellent and even sumptuous table; having the best
wine in his cellar, and never stinting it; frank in manner, courteous,
and excessively good-natured, yet always preserving his dignity
and self-respect;—the old squire was the very model of a
country gentleman. In his days, the Castle was constantly full of
company, yet disorder or excess were never known within it.
How different now. The guests took their tone from the host,
and gave way to unbridled indulgences, and, as a matter of
course, the servants, being under no restraint, followed the ex-

ample of their superiors. No one knew how soon Gage's career was to terminate, but everybody felt that such frantic extravagances could not last long, and they therefore resolved to make the most of their time.

Below stairs reigned a perfect saturnalia. The servants'-hall was in a continual scene of uproar. Tables were laid within it throughout the day, and the remains of the dainties served up at every repast to Monthermer and his guests reappeared there—with a good many other choice dishes besides. Neither was there any want of good liquor to wash down the savoury viands. Mr. Pudsey had unlimited control of the cellar, and no one could complain of niggardliness on his part in dispensing its stores. On the contrary, if he had been host instead of butler, he could not have behaved more handsomely. A great bon vivant, fond of society, and loving a cheerful glass, the Amphitryon of the pantry presided at the general dinners, placing his friend, Mr. Trickett, on his right hand, and Mr. Tibbits on the left, and taking care they were well served. He sat with them afterwards as long as he could, and when his duties called him away, left them with a good supply of burgundy and claret.

In the evening, when the toils of the day were over, a select party assembled by invitation in the butler's private room, where a nice hot supper awaited them, succeeded by a capital bowl of punch.

Here a little quiet play went on, as in the card-room above-stairs. Mr. Pudsey, we regret to say, had not profited by his experience, but lost a good deal of money—a good deal for him, at all events—as in former days,—at gleek and piquet, to those two rooks in livery, Tibbits and Trickett. Nor was he the only loser on these occasions. Bellairs and Chassemouche were equally unlucky; and so, for the matter of that, were some half-dozen other flats who sat down with these unconscionable sharpers. Strange to say, it never occurred to any of these usually suspicious gentry that they were cheated. But there is an infatuation about gaming which seems to dull the perceptions of its votaries. Be this as it may, two nights sufficed to Messieurs Trickett and Tibbits to ease the incautious butler of a half-year's gains. On the third night he was obliged to borrow money to go on ; and being stripped of this likewise, he might have felt considerable uneasiness, if he had not entertained the notion that he could raise fresh supplies, in a certain quarter, without difficulty. This persuasion buoyed him up ; but still feeling a little "down in the mouth," as he expressed it, he brewed a strong bowl of punch, and a few tumblers of the genial beverage soon produced the desired effect. Under its balmy influence the butler not only forgot his cares, but became less cautious than usual, and talked more freely than he ought to have done.

A second bowl of punch had been discussed, and a third placed upon the table, when Pudsey, who had become a little elevated, remarked, as he filled the glasses of his friends,

"Well, gentlemen, we've had a mighty pleasant time of it, you'll allow. It's a thousand pities such enjoyment can't last for ever. We've only two more days left."

"Only two more days, Mr. Pudsey !" Mr. Trickett observed. "What d'ye mean, sir ?"

"I mean what I say," the butler rejoined, with a knowing wink, and emptying his glass before he went on. "We shall shut up shop the night after to-morrow."

"Egad! I'm deuced sorry to hear it," Trickett said. "I've contrived to amuse myself tolerably well since I've been down here. Your master, I suppose, returns to town ?"

"Mr. Monthermer is not my master," Pudsey replied; "though, for the matter of that, I've no objection to his service, but I only enact the part of butler on the present occasion by desire of my real employer. I really don't know what the young gentleman will do, when Mr. Fairlie comes into possession—but I fancy he must turn out altogether."

"That's a pity," Mr. Trickett remarked. "You won't gain by the change, Mr. Pudsey. Things will be differently ordered under Fairlie's governance, or I'm greatly mistaken. He'll keep a tight hand over you all. You won't have the keys of the cellar then, I fear."

"I'faith, you're right, Trickett," the butler rejoined. "We shan't know the flavour of burgundy and claret when old Fairlie rules the roast; and as to a quiet supper with one's friends, and a bowl of punch afterwards, such things won't be possible—so we must make the most of time present."

"I don't think I shall remain in the situation," Bellairs observed—he was nearly as far gone as the butler. "It won't suit me at all. I can't make up my mind to serve a low fellow like Fairlie."

"A vile roturier!" Chassemouche exclaimed. "I, who have been accustomed to the best société, and have dressed de perukes of gentlemen only—morbleu! I cannot stoop to such canaille."

"He is not fit to be governor here!" Tibbits cried. "I should like to see him kicked out of the Castle."

"Ma foi! so should I!' Chassemouche exclaimed. "I should like to see him chassé par la belle porte—I would lend a foot to de task myself—ha! ha!"

"Replenish the glasses, Pudsey," Bellairs cried, "and let us drink 'Confusion to him!' "

"Vid all my heart," the French valet responded—"rasades, messieurs!"

The butler made no objection, and the rebellious toast was drunk amid general laughter.

What puzzles me," Tibbits observed, "is to think how Fairlie can have contrived to get the Monthermer property entirely into his own hands. You know all about it, I dare say, Pudsey, and can tell us if you think proper?"

"I know a good deal, certainly," the butler replied—"more than I care to mention. But I may say one thing, gentlemen—and you may believe me or not, as you please — that it depends upon me whether Fairlie retains possession of this noble property."

"You don't say so!" Trickett cried, pricking up his ears; while all the other listeners uttered similar exclamations of astonishment. "What! you have got him in your power, eh, Pudsey?"

"No, I don't exactly mean to insinuate that," the butler rejoined, fearing he had gone too far; "I mean, that Fairlie and I shall understand each other, when we come to talk matters over."

"I dare say you will," Trickett replied. "Well, I give you one piece of advice, old boy. If you make a bargain with him, don't let him off too easily."

"Trust me for that," Pudsey replied, laying his finger on his copper-coloured proboscis.

"You are not the only person whose secrecy must be bought,

Pudsey,' Bellairs interposed. "I know as much as you, and shall require as good pay for my silence."

"Parbleu, messieurs, you tink no one have ears as long as your own," Chassemouche cried. "I would have you to know dat mine are mush longer, and dat my mouth must be shut in de same vay as yours—ha! ha!"

"Well, I hope you'll make Fairlie smart properly amongst you," Trickett remarked, with a laugh. "I suspect he'll have some other accounts to settle before he's allowed to take quiet possession. My master, Sir Randal, may give him a little trouble; and I'm pretty sure Mrs. Jenyns has not come down for nothing."

As this was said, Bellairs looked hard at the speaker, but he made no observation.

"I think I could give a guess at the game she means to play," Trickett pursued.

"Ah, indeed!" Bellairs cried; "what may it be?"

"That's my secret. You shall have it for what it's worth, but I must make something by it. By-the-by, Mr. Pudsey, when does Fairlie come down?"

"I can't say, I'm sure," Pudsey replied, evasively.

"I'd bet a trifle he's here already," Tibbits remarked. "I saw somebody very like him cross the back yard this evening."

"Oh! quite impossible; you must have been mistaken," the butler exclaimed.

"Perhaps I might be—still I'm willing to bet upon it."

"Pooh! pooh! I shan't bet upon such a matter."

Bellairs and Chassemouche exchanged significant glances.

"Well, if he should be here, I hope he has overheard all we have been saying of him," Trickett observed, with a laugh. "You wouldn't stand very high in his favour, Pudsey?"

"Come, let's change the subject, gentlemen," the butler rejoined, uneasily; "we've had quite enough of it. A glass of punch all round!"

After this, the conversation flagged. Pudsey looked sullen and sleepy, and Bellairs and Chassemouche were not much more lively, so as soon as the bowl of punch was finished, the party broke up.

XL.

IN WHICH PUDSEY MAKES A MODEST PROPOSITION TO MR. FAIRLIE.

MR. PUDSEY awoke next morning with a racking headache, which he naturally enough attributed to the punch, and his uncomfortable sensations were not diminished by the conviction that he had tattled very foolishly overnight. That rascal Trickett, he was aware, was quite capable of doing him a mischief, and might report what he had said to Mr. Fairlie himself; and so, indeed, might Bellairs or Chassemouche, or any other of the party, for not one of them was to be trusted.

Our butler felt so ill that he would fain have gone to bed again, but he had a great deal to do that day, and must set about it forthwith, so, swallowing his customary morning draught of spiced ale, which somewhat restored him, he left his room, in order to take a survey of the house, and see how far it could be put to rights after the riotous proceedings that had taken place within it on the preceding day.

In the dining-room, whither he repaired first, everything remained in the same state in which it had been left. The atmosphere reeked with the smell of tobacco, and the table was covered with bottles and glasses—many of them broken—and flooded with wine and punch. In the midst of the shivered glasses stood the fragments of a magnificent china bowl. Underneath the sideboard was a vast collection of empty flasks—attesting the prowess of the tipplers, though some of them had been so overcome that they could not even reel off to bed, but were still lying prostrate on the floor, sleeping off the effects of their debauchery.

Picking his way over these inert bodies, Mr. Pudsey went towards the windows, to throw them open, and while thus em-

ployed he perceived Gage returning from the garden near the
ruins of the old Castle, and wondered what could have taken him
out so early. He kept an eye on him for a few minutes until he drew
near the house, and the butler then fancied he had discovered the
young gentleman's motive for early rising, as Mrs. Jenyns came
forth from a glass-door communicating with the library, and hastened
to meet him. But it was evident from Gage's manner that he was
annoyed at the rencounter. Mis Jenyns seemed from her gestures
to propose a walk in the gardens, and pointed to the terrace Monthermer had just left, but he shook his head, and it was only after
some persuasion that she induced him to enter the library with her.

"She is about to disclose the scheme to him, which she hinted
at last night in the card-room," Pudsey thought. "An inkling of
it might give me an additional hold upon Fairlie. Perhaps I
could get near the glass-door without being perceived."

Upon this he scrambled out of the window, and crept along the
side of the house till he came within a few paces of the entrance to
the library.

"Confound her!" he muttered. "She's too cunning by half.
The door is shut, and I can hear nothing. Let us see what can be
done on the other side."

So he went back, and, re-entering the dining-room, made his
way as quickly as he could to the ordinary approach to the
library, but unluckily it was closed. What was to be done?
He determined to go in—suddenly—when perhaps he might catch
a word that would enlighten him as to the lady's project.

The plan was no sooner thought of than executed. Throwing
open the door, he bounced into the room, but was greatly disappointed to find Mrs. Jenyns seated at a table, writing, while
Gage was pacing to and fro. As the butler entered, Monthermer
stopped, and, angrily regarding him, demanded his business.
Pudsey stammered an excuse, and hastily retreated; taking care,
however, as he went out, to leave the door ajar. But here again
his design was frustrated, for in another moment the door was shut,
and fastened inside.

Foiled in his plans, he went his way, and proceeded, with slow
steps and with a recurrence of the uncomfortable feelings he had
experienced on awaking, towards a room situated at the end of the
long gallery.

Tapping against the door, a voice, with the tones of which he was only too familiar, bade him come in ; and obeying the summons—not without considerable trepidation—he entered and found Mr. Fairlie, seated in an arm-chair, enveloped in a loose brocade dressing-gown, and under the hands of Chassemouche, who was arranging his peruke, and retailing all his (Mr. Pudsey's) indiscreet remarks of the night before. So, at least, the butler judged from the angry looks which Fairlie cast upon him. Nor was he left long in doubt on the point. Dismissing Chassemouche, who grinned maliciously at Pudsey as he retired, the steward thus spoke him :

" So, you have been chattering, eh, you drunken fool! boasting of your power over me, and what you can do. It depends upon you whether I am to continue master of Monthermer Castle, does it ?" And he burst into a disdainful laugh.

" Since Chassemouche has betrayed me, it would be idle to equivocate," Pudsey rejoined. " I was a great fool to talk as I did in such company. I ought to have known better. But the wine was in, and the wit out—and that's the truth, sir."

" A poor excuse, Pudsey. A drunkard is not to be trusted—you are unfit for my service."

" I deserve to be reprimanded, I own, sir; but I won't commit such an indiscretion again, you may depend upon it. As to disturbing you in the comfortable possession of this fine place, I wouldn't do it, sir——"

" Couldn't do it, Pudsey—couldn't do it, you had better say."

" Well, sir, for the matter of that, I entertain a different opinion," the butler rejoined, with a smile, for the other's taunts and sharpness of manner had roused him. " My testimony, I fancy, would be useful to Mr. Monthermer if he should take it into his head to contest your title, and I think I could put him in the way of finding some other important witnesses."

" Hum! you think so, eh, Pudsey ?"

" I'm pretty sure of it. I know exactly how the accounts have been kept, with fictitious entries, and so forth—how advances have been made to Mr. Monthermer out of his own money—how he has been induced to sign bonds and mortgages under false representations, and without even receiving the promised loans. Knowing all this, I might disclose it, if I thought proper."

" Of course you might make such scandalous assertions, Pudsey; but no one would believe you."

" Yes, sir, Mr. Monthermer would believe me, and that's enough for my purpose. You must not forget that he is in actual possession of the Castle, and unless he voluntarily surrenders it, you will fail altogether. You will fail, I repeat, because he will demand the production of the accounts—and you dare not exhibit them."

"But he *will* surrender the Castle—he has pledged himself to do so."

"He will NOT—if he learns how he has been dealt with."

Fairlie looked down in confusion, while the butler eyed him triumphantly.

"I have him now," he thought, "and I won t quit my hold till I've made all sure."

Suddenly, Fairlie started to his feet, and, grasping the butler's arm, exclaimed,

"What do you expect, Pudsey? Tell me—in a word!"

"In a word, then," the rapacious rascal rejoined, "a large sum down—and a pension for life!"

"A pension for life! You are mad to make such a demand."

"No, sir, I am not mad. On the contrary, I am sure I take a very rational view of the subject. I don't mean to let this opportunity slip. The matter must be decided within twenty-four hours. Either Mr. Monthermer maintains his own, and ejects you, or you become undisputed master here."

"I must have time to reflect upon your startling proposition, Pudsey. It has taken me quite by surprise."

"Oh! I have no desire to hurry you, but you must make up your mind in the course of the day. I won't be put off with fair promises. I must have a large sum down, as I've said—and good security for the pension."

"You shall be satisfied—quite satisfied, Pudsey, if I assent to the proposal."

"Oh! you are sure to assent. I consider the bargain already concluded. You'll never risk the loss of so rich a prize, just when you've got it in your grasp—besides the disgrace which is ture to fall upon you."

"No more of this, Pudsey," Fairlie said, collecting all his energies. "You presume too much on your fancied power. Bridle your tongue or go about your business, and do your worst."

"I beg pardon, sir. I've no desire to offend you,—not the slightest. You will think over what I've said, and give me an answer. If I don't hear from you before the evening, I shall go to Mr. Monthermer, and then of course any arrangement between us will be out of the question."

"Very well," Fairlie replied, pointing to the door.

"One thing more, sir. Before I take my departure, I must put you upon your guard against Mrs. Jenyns."

"Another serpent in my path. What of her?"

"Why, sir, I chanced to overhear a few words that passed between her and Mr. Monthermer last night, and I am certain she has some dangerous design on foot—dangerous to you, I mean. She lost a large sum at hazard—or rather Mr. Monthermer lost it, for he played for her—and she is desperate."

"And she must be bought, too, I suppose," Fairlie cried, with a bitter laugh. "'Sdeath! man, my property will never bear all these demands upon it."

"Don't misunderstand me, sir. I have nothing to do with Mrs. Jenyns. Be assured, I will never take a woman into my confidence."

"So far you are right. Well, I am glad you have warned me. Though this meddlesome jade can do little mischief, it may be prudent to nip her project in the bud. Send one of the women servants to her room, and say I would speak to her as early as may be convenient."

"She is already astir, sir; and I am almost apprehensive she may be beforehand with you, for she is closeted with Mr. Monthermer in the library at this moment."

"Zounds! this looks like mischief. I must find out what she is about to propose to him. In the library, you say, Pudsey?"

"Yes, sir—they're there, but the door's locked."

"No matter. They will find it difficult to keep their secrets from me. Walls have ears, Pudsey—walls have ears. Don't let the servants enter the drawing-room for a short time, d'ye hear? By-and-by we will have some further talk together. But I must dispose of this matter at once."

So saying, he hastily threw off his dressing-gown, and, with the butler's aid, putting on a coat, flew towards the drawing-room, while Pudsey followed him at a more leisurely pace, and stationed himself at the door of that apartment.

XLI.

ON entering the drawing-room, Fairlie proceeded to unlock the door of a small cupboard near the fireplace, and stepping into the recess, cautiously unbolted a second door, and passed through it.

He was now actually in the library, but concealed from view by a thin board, the front of which formed part of a bookcase, and being covered with the backs of ponderous-looking tomes, artfully contrived to represent ranges of folios, could scarcely be distinguished from the ordinary shelves.

A crack in the board enabled him to command the room, and allowed the conversation that took place within it to reach him. The two persons he expected to find were there, and at no great distance from him. Mrs. Jenyns was talking earnestly, while Gage listened to her with his arms folded upon his breast.

The very first words the listener heard alarmed him. He could not distinctly catch all Mrs. Jenyns said, for she spoke with great vehemence and rapidity—but he lost not a syllable of the close of her discourse.

"Now observe what I say," she concluded, in a deliberate and impressive tone. "As the sum of Fairlie's iniquitous practices towards you, I charge him with suppressing your father's last will, and substituting one of earlier date."

Fairlie breathed hard, and watched with deepest anxiety the effect of this disclosure upon Gage. It was something of a relief to him to perceive that the young man's countenance wore an expression of incredulity, though not unmingled with astonishment.

"Why do you bring such a serious charge against him—a charge which you cannot possibly substantiate?" Gage exclaimed, after a brief pause.

"But I can substantiate it. The rightful will is still in existence."

"Hell's curses upon her!" the listener exclaimed to himself. "She must have discovered the document when she peeped into my chest. Fool that I was not to destroy it!"

"But what motive can Fairlie have had for such a wicked act?" Gage cried. "There was no important bequest to himself in the will that he acted upon. My father, to be sure, left him a thousand pounds; but that was in consideration of his trouble in discharging the offices of executor and guardian."

"You have hit upon the motive," Mrs. Jenyns rejoined, "as I will proceed to show. Your father died from a fall while hunting, on the 10th of February, 1728."

"You are correct as to the date of the sad event," Gage remarked, with a sigh.

"Now mind," Mrs. Jenyns pursued, "on the 9th of February in that year, the very day before the unexpected catastrophe, your father made his last will, and constituted Sir Hugh Poynings, of Reedham, his sole executor, and your guardian."

"Sir Hugh Poynings—my guardian!" Gage exclaimed.

"Fairlie's name was never mentioned. Do you not now discern his motive for keeping back a document that divested him of all control over you? With Sir Hugh Poynings as your guardian, he, Fairlie, would never have had an opportunity of putting into practice his nefarious designs against you. Judging from what has since come to light, there can be no doubt that your father had made some discoveries respecting his steward, that caused him to appoint another executor and guardian in his place—and, probably, if he had lived a few days longer, Fairlie would have been dismissed altogether."

"And you have seen this will?"

"I have—but hear me out. Fairlie is in the house. He arrived here secretly last night. When you see him, let fall no hint of the knowledge you have acquired of his criminality, but summon Sir Hugh Poynings to the Castle to-morrow."

"Sir Hugh is not likely to come—and if he should, he will attach no credit to your unsupported statements. He cannot have a very high opinion of you, for I need scarcely remind you of the charge that his son, Arthur, brought against you, when I last played at the Groom-Porter's."

"That charge was a foul calumny—but let it pass now. Send for Sir Hugh—summon him in such urgent terms that he cannot refuse compliance. Let him bring his son with him, if he will —I care not. I will make good my words."

There was a brief pause, during which the steward felt as if stretched upon the rack. At length the silence was broken by Gage.

"All this may be as you assert, and I will not dispute it," he said, gravely; "but I will not consent to act thus against Fairlie unless the will can be produced."

"It shall be produced."

"In what way? If Fairlie has it, he is not likely to give it up."

"It is no longer in his possession."

The steward started, and could scarcely repress an exclamation.

"You shall have the will at the right moment, that I promise you," Mrs. Jenyns continued.

"But how have you obtained it? I must be satisfied on that score."

"You shall be satisfied," she replied. "Listen to me. When I made the discovery in question which is likely to lead to such important results, and overthrow Fairlie at the very moment he is about to clutch the prize for which he has so long been striving, I considered by what means I could obtain possession of the evidence against him, and at last I resolved to employ one of the servants whom I have long had in my pay."

"She means that double-dyed scoundrel, Pudsey," Fairlie muttered to himself. "Yet, no—if it were Pudsey, he would not have put me on my guard against her. I have it—'tis Bellairs. But the will is safe—quite safe—she cannot produce it."

"Go on," Gage said, perceiving that Mrs. Jenyns hesitated.

"You may not, perhaps, approve of the means taken, but in cases of this kind any stratagem is fair. Fairlie was watched by the spy I placed over him, and it was ascertained that he had taken the document in question from out of the large chest in which it had hitherto been deposited, and placed it with other papers of perhaps scarcely less importance, as tending to prove his dishonesty to you, in a small coffer. Now mark me! that coffer is in my custody, and shall be forthcoming to-morrow. Do you now feel satisfied?"

Gage made no reply, and she went on.

"All things have worked well for the project. You are here in possession of the Castle and the estates, and instead of surrendering them to Fairlie, you shall cast him forth with blasted character, never more to molest you."

To her astonishment, Gage seemed but slightly moved.

"You do not believe what I tell you," she cried, with manifest vexation : "but do not let your doubts of me ruin the scheme ; do not neglect to summon Sir Hugh Poynings—do not let to-morrow pass, or you will for ever regret your indifference."

But Gage preserved his apathetic demeanour. It seemed as if nothing would rouse him. Mrs. Jenyns lost all patience, and beat the ground with her tiny foot.

"You reject my proposal?" she cried, at length.

"I hesitate to accept it, because to engage in such a struggle will renew all my anxieties; and I am so weary of life, that I care little for the result, whatever it may be."

"What! has it come to this? Is the proud Gage de Monthermer grown so pusillanimous that he will tamely resign his estates to a sordid knave, when he may keep them? You will make me despise you. Rouse yourself, and act like a man."

"Well, the effort shall be made, but I looked to pass the few hours left me in repose. And now, Peg, what reward do you expect for the important service you propose to render me—for I presume you are not entirely disinterested?"

"Not entirely so. I like this mansion so much that I would willingly remain here."

"Nothing more easy, if I am once more master."

"Ay, but I must be mistress!" she exclaimed, haughtily, and regarding her superb figure, as reflected in a mirror on the opposite side of the room.

"I do not understand you."

"Yet, methinks, I speak intelligibly enough," she rejoined, with a smile. "In return for the precious document I shall produce, you must give me an equal title with yourself to the estates it will confer upon you."

" You cannot mean I should wed you ?" Gage exclaimed.

" On no other terms shall you have my aid. If you are to be lord of Monthermer Castle again, I must be lawful lady. I bring you an excellent dowry; better than the highest born dame in the county could offer you. Not another word now. Reflect on my proposal, and let me have your decision. But I will sooner consign that will to the flames, than alter my conditions. So decide as you think proper. Adieu !"

With this she quitted the room, leaving Gage almost in a state of stupefaction, while Fairlie at the same moment stole out of his hiding-place.

XLII.

FAIRLIE'S FIRST MOVE—AND HOW IT PROSPERED.

FAIRLIE was a man of great nerve. He did not underrate the danger by which he was menaced, but confronted it boldly, and thus regarded, its appalling proportions seemed to diminish, and he became, to a certain extent, reassured.

How was it, it may be asked, that he had not long ago destroyed the evidence of his criminality? Why did he preserve a document, the production of which must infallibly cause his ruin? The answer is, that certain scruples of conscience had restrained him; for after all, conscience will exert an influence even over the most stubborn nature, and hardened as he was, Fairlie was not entirely dead to her stings. Moreover, he was bound by a solemn promise not to destroy it; and though ordinarily, promises, however solemnly uttered, weighed little with him, in this instance his word had been religiously kept.

How he came to make such a promise we shall now relate.

On the very day of the death of his patron, while searching amongst poor Sir Warwick's papers, he had discovered this second will; and instantly perceiving the damage it would occasion to his interests if brought forward, he was about to commit it to the flames, when an unseen witness of his proceedings arrested his hand, and by prayers and entreaties prevailed upon him to forego the criminal design. He consented; but not until he had extorted from the person who had interrupted him a vow of secrecy, and he thereupon gave his own solemn assurance that the will should not be destroyed.

But the present circumstances made him view his conduct in a totally different light, and he could not now sufficiently reprobate his folly in observing a promise, the fulfilment of which had placed him in such fearful jeopardy. But regrets were idle. The past could not be recalled. The mischief must be repaired, cost what it might.

So he sat down for a short time to deliberate.

His plan of action formed, he arose and proceeded to the library, with the intention of directing his first movement against Gage. He did not despair of counteracting Mrs. Jenyns's scheme, and entirely effacing the ill impression she had striven to produce against him in the young man's mind.

He found Gage extended at full length upon a couch, on which he had sunk soon after the actress's departure. Fairlie coughed slightly to announce his presence, but it was not for some moments that Monthermer could be brought to notice him. Roused at length, the young man arose, evidently much annoyed at the intrusion. He constrained himself, however, to behave civilly to the steward, who, on his part, assumed a most conciliatory manner, and seemed earnestly desirous to please.

After a little preliminary conversation, chiefly conducted by himself, for Gage's share in it was slight enough, Fairlie signified that the motive of his visit was to ascertain from Mr. Monthermer that everything had gone on satisfactorily since his arrival at the Castle—to learn whether he had any further commands—and lastly, and principally, to consult with him about the grand fête to be given on the morrow.

Finding he had at length succeeded in awakening his hearer's attention, the steward went on:

" You may like to know what preparations I have made for the fête, sir ; but, before specifying them, let me say that I have spared neither expense nor pains to please you. If the entertainment is not perfect, it will not be my fault. I have stinted nothing, as you will find. Aware, from former experience, of he magnificence of your ideas, I have endeavoured, on this occasion, to realise them, and I flatter myself with success. But you shall judge, sir—you shall judge."

Hereupon he rubbed his hands complacently, and paused to give greater effect to the announcement.

" First, then, you will have a charming concert,—such a concert as has never been heard out of the walls of the Italian Opera House. I have engaged the best singers at that house. The divine Farinelli will sing for you—yes, sir, Farinelli. He, who has refused the most tempting offers from half the nobility to visit their country-seats, has consented to come down here."

"You amaze me!" Gage exclaimed, scarcely able to believe what he heard. "Farinelli here! Why it will be the talk of the town."

"Nothing else was talked of when I left. The report soon got abroad. At first, some folks affected to doubt it, but as Farinelli himself didn't contradict the rumour, of course it was universally believed. Farinelli cost me dear—very dear—in this way: he wouldn't come without Cuzzoni, and Cuzzoni wouldn't come without Senesino, so I had to engage all three."

"All three!" Gage exclaimed, with a burst of enthusiasm. "Why, we might perform Handel's Ptolemeo, if we had but musicians to accompany the singers!"

"You may play any opera you please, sir, as far as musicians are concerned, for I have engaged the whole orchestra."

The measure of Gage's astonishment was now full.

"Zounds! Fairlie," he exclaimed, "your conceptions far exceed mine. What other marvels have you in store? But I am insatiate. You have done?"

"No, sir, I have not half done," the steward replied, with a bland smile. "It delights me to find I am likely to satisfy you. You shall have a ballet as well as an opera."

"A ballet, Fairlie! Bravissimo! That will be enchanting—delicious! But who have you got?—surely not Colombe? She is not to be enticed."

"You think so, sir?" the steward cried, with a cunning look, and tapping the other's knee. "Like the rest of her sex, Mademoiselle Colombe is to be prevailed upon if the proper argument be used, and I have not neglected to employ it. A diamond collar proved irresistible. The dazzling Colombe comes, and not alone. Lisette—the charming Lisette—accompanies her—and Flore, and Léontine, and half a dozen other bewitching creatures."

"Colombe and Lisette—Flore and Léontine!" Gage exclaimed, clapping his hands in ecstasy. "Egad, Fairlie, you have done wonders. You must have spent a mint of money?"

"Don't mention it, sir. I haven't given money a thought, I assure you. Are you content with me, sir?"

"Content! I should be an ingrate if 1 were otherwise. You are the best fellow breathing, Fairlie."

"Delighted to hear you say so, sir," the steward rejoined, with a bend of acknowledgment. "My arrangements, I trust, are complete. Opera singers, musicians, ballet-dancers, all will leave town to-day in conveyances provided for them by myself, and will rest to-night at the Angel, at Bury St. Edmund's, where rooms have been engaged for the entire party. To-morrow, they come on here. Ah! sir," he added, in rather a sentimental tone, "once upon a time you used to be passionately enamoured of Colombe. But Mrs. Jenyns cut her out."

"Very true, Fairlie. But I don't know that I gained by the exchange."

"Poor Mrs. Jenyns!" Fairlie ejaculated. "She'll be driven to desperation when her rival appears on the scene. She heard I had engaged Colombe before she left town, and was so infuriated that she vowed the ballet never should take place. She will try to do me an ill turn I make no doubt, but I laugh at her malice."

The steward narrowly watched the effect of this speech, and saw that it had produced the effect he desired.

"I am glad you mentioned this to me, Fairlie," Gage said. "It explains the motive of some misrepresentations concerning you, which Mrs. Jenyns has thought proper to make to me."

"I shall not be surprised at any calumnies she may utter against me," the steward replied, "because I know the extent of her malice. Luckily the weapons she employs, in your case, at least, seem likely to miss their mark. I am sorry she is here; not that personally I have the slightest apprehension of her, but because I am sure she will make some disturbance in order to mar your fête."

"She shan't do that, Fairlie. If she becomes troublesome, you shall give her a hint that we can dispense with her company. But don't let us think more about her."

"Right, sir—right. Let us quit her and her paltry squabbles and jealousies, and turn to the fête, which, I confess, is uppermost in my thoughts. Opera and ballet over, supper will follow, of course; and this shall be a supper worthy of the occasion—a princely banquet, comprising every imaginable luxury and delicacy—wines—fruits—flowers—all of the choicest and best.

The table shall groan with silver plate, and sparkle with crystal glass. To ensure superlative excellence in the repast I have hired two French cooks, and the ices and patisserie will be prepared by the renowned Zucchero Pistacchi. The rooms will be decorated by artists from town, and I need scarcely add, will be most brilliantly illuminated. Now you have my programme, sir."

"And a wonderful programme it is. You have treated me nobly, Fairlie, and have far surpassed my expectations."

"It has ever been my wish to please you," the steward said. "Ah! sir," he added, pretending to heave a sigh, "I don't like to talk of the past, but this seems a fitting opportunity to revert to it for a moment. I know I ought to have thwarted your inclinations rather than indulge them, but I could not help it. It is easy for Mrs. Jenyns, or for anybody like her, to misrepresent my motives, but I can safely assert that I have ever acted for the best. You would have your own way, and I didn't like to trouble you with lectures which I felt would be unavailing. I answered your demands for money as long as any funds remained, and then of necessity I was compelled to stop. My conduct on some occasions may appear harsh, but reflection will tell you that I only obeyed the dictates of prudence."

If Gage was not entirely convinced by this harangue, he at all events listened quietly to it, and, when the steward had done, answered thus:

"You ought, perhaps, to have drawn the rein tighter, Fairlie; but, on my soul, I don't know that it would have had any effect. I fancy I should have got the money—if not from you, from some one else."

"Exactly what I felt, sir!" Fairlie exclaimed. "I reasoned in this way:—if I positively refuse to supply my thoughtless ward, he will get amongst those usurious rascals, the Jews, who will fleece him without mercy."

"So you resolved to play the Jew yourself, Fairlie, and get cent. per cent. for your advances," Gage cried, with a laugh. "Quite right! I don't blame you. Every man should do the best he can to improve his fortunes, and my extravagances have been the source of your prosperity. Nay, nay, don't shake your head. It is the fact." And he added, with a sudden change of manner, "Are you not master here—and am I not ruined?"

Fairlie did not relish the proposition, but he was obliged to notice it.

"I lament, indeed, sir," he said, shaking his head gravely, "that it should have come to such a pass with you ; and heartily wish the consummation could have been averted."

"But it could not, Fairlie,—it could not," Gage exclaimed. "I see the error of my ways as plainly as you, or any other man can see them. I know I have been duped, cheated, robbed— not by you, Fairlie, not by you—by others. I perceived all this at the time, but I voluntarily shut my eyes to it. I went on, determined to enjoy myself. It was my ambition to be the wildest rake about town—the greatest spendthrift of the day."

"No one can deny that you have fully achieved your object," the steward observed.

"Not yet, Fairlie," Gage replied, pausing and regarding him fixedly. "I have to put the finishing stroke to a career of folly."

"What d'ye mean, sir ? Do nothing rashly, I implore of you. Let me counsel you to go abroad for some years. I will provide you the means of doing so."

"Give yourself no further concern about me, Fairlie. After to-morrow I shall not trouble my friends."

"You alarm me, sir. Pray be more explicit."

"What more would you have, Fairlie ? Enough for you to know that I shall never cross your path again. Present enjoyment has been my aim. To purchase it, I have sacrificed the future, and must pay the penalty. I have no right to complain. I have had my day—it has been brief, but resplendent. Darkness is at hand. Men shall think of my meteor-like career, and its termination, with wonder. Never stare at me so, Fairlie. I talk strangely, but I am neither drunk nor mad. You will understand the meaning of my words hereafter. And now leave me. A moody fit, to which I have latterly been subject, is coming over me, and while it lasts, I am best alone. Leave me, I beg of you."

Thus exhorted, the steward was obliged to withdraw, but as he loitered on the way, he heard the unhappy young man fling himself upon the couch, and groan aloud.

" If he blows out his brains, it will be a good riddance," Fairlie muttered, with a grim smile, while closing the door.

XLIII.

FAIRLIE did not halt in his operations. His next business was to ascertain where Mrs. Jenyns was lodged. On consulting Pudsey, he learnt that she occupied a large room, with an ante-chamber or writing-cabinet attached to it, in the south gallery, and known as the Danaë Chamber, from the circumstance of the ceiling being adorned by a fresco painting by Verrio of the mercenary daughter of Acrisius subdued by the shower of gold. Accordingly, he repaired to the south gallery at once, and, on reaching the chamber in question, caused himself to be announced by the butler, who withdrew as soon as he had discharged his office.

Mrs. Jenyns was alone in the writing-cabinet, and her reception of the unexpected visitant was by no means encouraging. She arose as he entered, and remained standing during the whole of the interview.

In nowise rebuffed by the haughtiness of her deportment, Fairlie made a profound obeisance, and then advancing towards her, said in his blandest tones, and with a studied smile,

"I am come to bid you welcome to Monthermer Castle, madam. I trust you like the house, and sincerely assure you it will delight me if you can be induced to prolong your stay within it."

"I am infinitely obliged by your politeness," she replied, in a freezing tone; "but I have no present intention of leaving. I came here on Mr. Monthermer's invitation, and as long as my company is agreeable to him I shall remain."

Fairlie made another low bow, and smiled like a person who desires graciously to correct an error.

"Mr. Monthermer, it seems, has neglected to apprise you,

madam, that he ceases to be master here to-morrow night?" he said.

Mrs. Jenyns smiled in her turn, but very differently from the steward. There was a considerable spice of malice in her looks and voice as she rejoined very pointedly,

"Mr. Monthermer was certainly under the impression you mention when he came down here, but he has since been undeceived ; and I rather fancy you will find, when it comes to the point, that he has no intention of tamely surrendering his property. If any one ceases to be master here to-morrow, I suspect it will be yourself, Mr. Fairlie."

Another obeisance from the steward, and another smile almost as much fraught with malice as the actress's.

"Your words sound like a threat, madam?" he quietly remarked.

Mrs. Jenyns instantly accepted the challenge, and stamped her little foot. This time she gave full vent to her feelings of scorn and defiance.

"My words *are* meant to threaten, sir," she cried. "It is time you learnt that Mr. Monthermer understands his position fully, and possesses the means of setting himself right."

Fairlie managed to continue calm, though his patience was sorely tried.

"All this may be true, madam," he said, "and I will not for the moment dispute it—but it goes for nothing. Whatever means Mr. Monthermer may possess of 'setting himself right,' as you term it, he will never employ them—never!"

"And why not, sir—why not?" the actress cried, regarding him furiously, and again stamping her foot.

"Because he lacks energy for the struggle, madam," Fairlie replied.

"Don't reckon upon his weakness of character. I will supply him with resolution."

"Your efforts will be thrown away, madam. You have to do with one who never yet faced a real difficulty. He will succumb and disappoint you. I have no fears of him, as why should I have?"

"If you have no apprehension of him, you may at least recognise in me an antagonist to be dreaded."

"I should indeed tremble, if I could for a moment regard you

in the light of an enemy, madam," Fairlie rejoined, in a cajoling
tone. "But I can do no such thing. I am sure we shall speedily
come to an amicable understanding, as it is our interest to be
friends. For my own part," he added, in the softest accents he
could assume, and with what he intended for an impassioned look,
"I may say that I am influenced by a tenderer feeling than that of
friendship."

"A truce to this adulatory stuff, Mr. Fairlie. It has no effect
on me, and is out of season."

"Pardon me, madam, if the somewhat abrupt expression of my
admiration has offended you; but let me show you why at least we
should be friends—if we cannot be bound together by stronger
ties."

"If I am to tolerate your company longer, Mr. Fairlie, I must
insist upon a cessation of this annoyance."

"As you please, madam. But before dismissing me, you will
do well to look at both sides of the question. You have made a
certain proposal to Mr. Monthermer, with which he has acquainted
me."

This was a blow which Mrs. Jenyns could not parry—neither
could she conceal her uneasiness.

"How!—has he had the imprudence to repeat my conversation
with him?" she cried. "But no, you only say this to try me."

"I will state what I have heard, madam," he rejoined, "and
you will then judge whether I am correctly informed or not.
You are to produce a certain document—a will, supposed to be
made by the late Warwick Monthermer, and how obtained by you
I will not pause to particularise—you are to produce this will
against me, blast my character, and reinstate Gage in his forfeited
possessions. In requital of this important service, you demand to
be made mistress—lawful mistress—of Monthermer Castle. You
see, madam, I am tolerably well informed."

There was a brief pause, during which it was evident that the
superior craft of the steward was fast gaining the ascendancy.

"This man is right," Mrs. Jenyns mentally ejaculated. "Gage
will never prevail in an encounter with him."

Fairlie watched her narrowly, and read what was passing in her
mind. He saw the advantage he had gained, and determined to
improve it.

8

"I have nothing to say against your project, madam," he observed. "It is well conceived. But it will fail."

"That remains to be seen!" Mrs. Jenyns cried, recovering her spirit. "If Gage is but true to himself, he will triumph."

"When was he ever true to himself, madam?" Fairlie rejoined, with a sneer. "But the scheme will fail in this way. You have overreached yourself by your demands. Gage will not consent to the terms. Even in the dire extremity to which he is reduced, he shrinks from forming, what he considers, so degrading an alliance."

Fairlie was not prepared for the burst of indignation with which this speech was received. Mrs. Jenyns regarded him with ineffable scorn, and her eyes flashed fire.

"And you have the effrontery to repeat this to me, sir?" she cried, with a menacing gesture. "Even if Gage rejects my offer, I will produce that damning evidence against you, and drive you forth."

But Fairlie stood unmoved.

"No, madam, you will not," he rejoined, firmly.

"How will you prevent me?"

"By making you mistress of this mansion," he replied, suddenly resuming his adulatory tone and studied smile. "Gage cannot do this—I can—and will."

He awaited her answer, which did not come for some moments, still regarding her, all the time, with a crafty smile. At length she burst into a laugh.

"Upon my word, Fairlie," she cried, after a brief indulgence of her exhilaration, "it would be a thousand pities if we did not come together. We should be so nicely matched."

"I think so too, madam," he answered. "We are agreed, then —eh?—you take my offer?"

And he raised her hand to his lips with an air of devoted gallantry.

"Hum! I don't know," she hesitated.

"Nay, madam, let me have an answer of some sort. I am a plain man of business, and even in an affair of this kind, like to come to the point without delay. Give me that will, and in return you shall receive my written promise of marriage."

"No, no,—not so fast, Mr. Fairlie.   Flattered as I am by your proposal, I cannot assent to it immediately."

"You are trifling with me, madam !" he cried, becoming suddenly grave.

"I am bound to await Gage's decision," she rejoined.   "Till he is disposed of, I cannot entertain another proposition.   If he rejects my offer, I am yours."

"He has retired from the field, I tell you," Fairlie exclaimed, impatiently.

"I must be quite sure of that.   To place the matter beyond a doubt, I will write to him, and by his answer I shall be guided Nay, it is useless to urge me further.   I am inflexible.   And mind ! if our union is to take place, it must be to-morrow."

"So soon !" Fairlie exclaimed.

"To-morrow sees me mistress of Monthermer Castle—either as your wife, or Gage's," she rejoined.

And with a graceful curtsey, she glided into the adjoining apartment, and closed the door after her.

XLIV.

IN WHICH FAIRLIE MAKES ANOTHER FALSE MOVE.

THE steward was caught in his own trap. He thought to outwit Mrs. Jenyns, and was himself outwitted. He made sure she would give up the will in exchange for his written promise of marriage— a promise, which, it may be whispered, he never intended to fulfil, —but he found she was not to be duped by so shallow a device, and had too little reliance in his honesty.

For a few minutes he lingered within the writing-chamber, casting his eyes eagerly round it, to see if by any accident the coffer containing the precious document, which he was so anxious to secure, had been left there. He could discern nothing of it. But there was a large trunk in one corner of the room, and what so probable as that the box should be inside it! No chance must be thrown away. Fairlie stepped quickly towards the trunk, and finding it unlocked, opened it without hesitation.

It was full of female wearing apparel—rich silk dresses—under garments of less costly material—masquerade habiliments—high-heeled satin shoes—silken hose — ribands—lace—a mask with a lace curtain—fans—pots of fard, rouge, and pomatum—boxes of trinkets and jewellery—and many other things — all of which Fairlie pulled out and tossed upon the floor—but no coffer!

Not a vestige of it, or of the will.

Just as he had satisfied himself that his search was fruitless, and was preparing to put back, as expeditiously as he could, the various articles scattered about, he was startled by the appearance of Mrs. Jenyns and her maid.

Fairlie sprang up, looking as red as a turkey-cock, and, stammering an excuse, he would have beaten a hasty retreat, but Mrs. Jenyns stopped him.

"I will not affect ignorance of your intentions," she said; "I know perfectly well what you have been looking for, but you must think me careless indeed if you suppose I should leave an important document in an open trunk. But pray continue your search, sir," she added, pointing towards the room she had just left—"go in— you are quite welcome."

"Am I to take you at your word, madam?" Fairlie demanded, eagerly. "Do you really grant me permission to enter your room?"

"Most certainly," she rejoined. "Davies shall assist you in the investigation."

Fairlie did not hesitate a moment, but stepped into the adjoining apartment, followed by Davies,—a smart, olive-complexioned damsel, with a trim little figure, and a pair of quick black eyes, full of mirth and mischief. The lively soubrette glanced at her mistress, as much as to say she would punish him for his impertinent curiosity.

"Would you like to look into this, sir?" she cried, opening the door of a cupboard; "or into this, sir?" proceeding to another; "or into these drawers?" hurrying him to the wardrobe; "or under the bed, sir?" pulling him in that direction, and raising the valance. "Do look under the bed,—or over it—there, I'll draw aside the drapery—nothing at all you see, sir, but the crimson-satin coverlet and the laced pillow. Mount this chair, sir, and then, perhaps, you'll be able to examine the tester. Well, if you can't reach it standing on tiptoe, I don't think I or my mistress could. Ha! ha! ha!"

"What's in that portmanteau?" Fairlie cried, jumping down in a passion. "Open it quickly."

"Oh yes, sir, with pleasure. There, you see it's empty. Nay, don't go, sir, till you've examined the toilet-table. I don't think there can be anything behind those muslin folds," she added, raising the gauzy cover; "but we'll see—no,—nor behind the looking-glass, though it's large enough to serve for a screen; nor under the curtains—look, sir, look!—nor in this jewel-case," opening an écrin on the table, "except a pearl necklace and a wreath; nor in this dressing-case," opening a silver casket full of scent-bottles; "arquebusade and eau-de-luce, at your service, sir," she added, holding a couple of small flacons to his nose.

"To the devil with your scents and essences, you impudent hussy!" Fairlie cried. "Can you find me a small coffer?"

"A coffer! let me see, sir—is it covered with red leather?"

'Yes, yes. Find it for me."

"Well, if you'd told me what you wanted at first, you might have spared yourself all this trouble. A red-leather coffer, you say—with silver hinges, and a silver plate atop?"

"Yes, yes, have you such a one? Produce it."

"Sorry I can't, sir. It's not here!"

"Where is it, then?"

"Out of your reach, Mr. Fairlie," the actress rejoined, entering the room. "But, depend upon it, it will be produced at the proper moment. Did you think you were likely to make discoveries by searching a lady's room? Many a jealous husband has acted in the same way, and has only made himself supremely ridiculous."

"You are right, madam, I ought to feel ashamed of my conduct," Fairlie rejoined, now fully conscious of his embarrassing position, and trying to put the best face he could upon it.

"Yes, there's no denying it, you do look mighty foolish," Davies cried, with a provoking laugh. "Even the lightly-clad lady on the ceiling—Madam Danny—blushes for you—and I'm sure I do."

"Peace, Davies," Mrs. Jenyns interposed, signing to the attendant to leave the room. "Since you have satisfied yourself by this scrutiny, Mr. Fairlie, you can have no object in remaining here, and I will not seek to detain you longer. You must now be convinced that any stratagem you may devise will be ineffectual against me. My precautions are too well taken."

"So I find, madam," Fairlie rejoined, "and I must compliment you upon the acuteness you have displayed, even though I, myself, am a sufferer by it. Let me hope that what has just occurred will not interrupt the good understanding at which we had previously arrived. I am now, more than ever, anxious that we should be friends."

"I have already given you my answer—and to that I adhere. If circumstances should compel me to act against you, I shall regret the necessity, but——"

"We won't anticipate such an event," Fairlie interrupted. "I am well assured what will be Gage's decision."

" In that case, you have nothing to apprehend. And, as you seem so confident of a favourable result—favourable, I say, for I must own I rather incline towards your offer, though I consider myself bound to give Gage the refusal—I will tell you what I should wish to be done."

" Whatever you desire, madam, shall be performed—if within the limits of possibility."

" I will not tax your devotion by too difficult an achievement," she rejoined, with a smile. " Let a handsome collation be prepared at three o'clock in the dining-room, and invite some twenty or thirty of the guests, staying in the house, to partake of it. Sir Randal, Mr. Freke, and the others of that party, must of course be included."

" Naturally, madam. The collation shall be ready at the hour you mention, and the company bidden to it."

" You yourself must preside at the repast—and assign me a place on your right."

" Pardon me, madam, but you are aware that, for a few hours longer, I have abandoned my rights and privileges in this house to Mr. Monthermer. He may consider my assumption of the principal place as an infringement of our agreement."

" You must assume it, nevertheless. At the close of the repast, you shall announce your approaching marriage to the company, and present your intended bride to them."

Fairlie breathed hard, and seemed half suffocated in the attempt to reply.

" Ah! you hesitate !" she cried. " It will not, then, be too late to produce the will."

" I need no threat to make me act as you desire, madam," he rejoined. " The announcement shall be made."

" After that you cannot retreat."

" And then, since your object will be assured,—then, madam, you will give me the document ?"

" On our return from the altar—not before."

" But you will, at least, satisfy me that you possess it ?"

" Oh! rest easy on that score, sir, you shall be fully satisfied."

" Before I take my departure, let me implore of you, madam, not to keep me longer than can be helped in suspense ?"

" Well, I will be compassionate. In consideration of your uneasiness—impatience, I ought to term it—I will write to Gage at once. If his reply be in the negative—or if he fails to reply within two hours, I decide in your favour."

"In two hours, then, I shall know my fate?"

"You will. And now send Bellairs to me—I can trust him."

"I am aware of it, madam. I kiss your hand." And raising her fingers ceremoniously to his lips, he withdrew.

As soon as he was gone, Mrs. Jenyns marched to the toilet-table to survey her beautiful features, now irradiated with triumph, in the glass. Satisfied with what she beheld, she turned round, and an expression of scorn curled her lips.

"Fool!" she exclaimed, "did he think he had a child to deal with? Did he imagine I should trust such a precious document as that out of my own custody? I have it safe enough," she added, pressing her swelling bosom. "My heart beats against it with pride, in the full assurance that I shall speedily attain my object, and become mistress of Monthermer Castle."

XLV.

HOW GAGE'S EYES WERE AT LAST OPENED.

OF late, as we have mentioned, Gage had been gradually sinking into a state of lethargy and gloom, from which nothing but
some strong stimulant, such as had just been administered by
Fairlie, could rouse him—and this but temporarily. While
listening to the steward's glowing description of the approaching
fête, his breast had kindled for the moment with something of its
former fire ; but the excitement speedily died away, and left him
gloomier and more depressed than before. A miserable state of
mind—resembling the reaction from a powerful dose of opium.
Inertness and despondency prevented him from discerning the right
way out of his difficulties, and though he endured all the agonies
of remorse, he could not bring himself to a sense of repentance.
If any better promptings arose within his breast, he checked them
by the despairing ejaculation, " It is too late ! " Life seemed a
blank. The past was irretrievable—the future without hope.

But it must not be supposed that Clare's last warning words
were wholly without effect upon the unhappy young man. They
constantly rang in his ears ; while her looks—her earnestly-
imploring looks—ever haunted him. But an insurmountable bar-
rier seemed placed between him and all prospect of future happiness.
His energies were gone. Why continue a struggle in which he
was sure to be worsted ? Better end it at once.

So he yielded to the dark suggestions of despair, and shut his
heart to the gentle pleadings of hope.

He had not entirely shaken off his moody fit, and was still alone
in the library, stretched upon a couch, when Bellairs made his
appearance. The valet brought him a letter, intimating that it

was from Mrs. Jenyns. Without changing his position, Gage desired him to put it down.

"Pardon me, sir," the valet observed, " Mrs. Jenyns requested me to bring an answer. She will blame me if I return without one."

"You are in her confidence, I presume, Bellairs?" Gage demanded.

The valet smiled, and nodded an affirmative.

" Will not a verbal response, conveyed by such a trusty emissary, suffice?"

" I will charge myself with any response you choose to send, sir —verbal or otherwise," Bellairs replied. " But I venture to think, that your wisest course will be to write."

"You are an impertinent puppy," Gage cried, springing to his feet. " Well, since you insist upon it, I *will* write an answer. But I must first read the letter, though I can pretty well guess its contents."

So saying, he broke the seal of the missive, and ran his eye over the few lines it contained.

" As I supposed," he exclaimed. " She requires my immediate decision. But why so pressing ?"

" Does not the note explain, sir ?" the valet inquired.

" If it did, rascal, should I ask the question? Perhaps you can inform me?"

" I am not at liberty to speak, but you may be quite sure, sir, Mrs. Jenyns has a reason—a strong reason—for her urgency. On this account I recommend you to close with her offer."

"'Sdeath ! have you the presumption to offer me advice, sirrah? The whole thing is a trick. Mr. Fairlie has explained it to me."

" Why, sir, Mr. Fairlie——"

" Peace ! I won't hear a word against him !"

" Oh, very well, sir," the valet cried, in a huff. " I shall say no more. But you'll find it out in time."

" Don't interrupt me," Gage cried, sitting down at the table.

And snatching up a pen, he wrote as follows:

" You have often found me an easy dupe, madam, but this time you will fail in your design. Believing as I do that the story you have told me of the discovery of the will is pure invention, you cannot be surprised that I decline to bring a false charge against an honourable man. But were it otherwise—were your statement as well founded as I have reason to suppose it incorrect —I should equally reject your proposition. My fallen fortunes shall never be repaired by unworthy means; nor will I sully the name I bear by a degrading union. You have my answer."

Having signed this letter, and sealed it, he handed it to Bellairs.

"You reject the offer, I presume, sir?" the valet remarked.

"Peremptorily," Gage replied.

"Sorry to hear it, sir. You are playing into your adversary's hands. Mrs. Jenyns will now go over to Mr. Fairlie."

"If she does, she will meet worse reception from him than from me."

"No, sir," Bellairs replied, with a cunning smile. "He will agree to her terms."

"Why, zounds! rascal," Gage cried, in the utmost astonishment, "you don't mean to insinuate that Fairlie will marry her?"

"If I take back this letter the affair is settled. Mrs. Jenyns means to be mistress of the Castle, and, possessing the power of achieving her object, makes you the first offer. You hesitate, and Mr. Fairlie steps in. He sees the necessity of decision, and accepts her conditions at once. But Mrs. Jenyns will not throw you over without a word, and, before concluding the arrangement, requires your answer. You send it—and the door is closed!"

"You are lying, rascal," Gage cried, in angry astonishment. "I cannot credit such dissimulation—such perfidy!"

"You won't be kept long in doubt about the matter, sir, I can promise you. But it is not too late to frustrate Mr. Fairlie's designs. Write another letter to Mrs. Jenyns—or rather go to her at once. Agree to everything she may propose, and the game is yours. Surely you won't hesitate now? This is no time for silly scruples."

"I have no hesitation, Bellairs," Gage rejoined, in a tone of decision, for which the valet was wholly unprepared. "I might possibly triumph over Fairlie by the course you propose, but I will never engage in such a disgraceful conflict. Hear my determination, and repeat it if you will, word for word, to her who sent you. Not to win back all I have lost—not to avenge myself on

Fairlie for his deceptions and treachery—would I wed Mrs. Jenyns !
Take back my answer, without another word."

Struck dumb with astonishment, the valet bowed, and withdrew

The intelligence he had just received operated like a galvanic
shock upon Monthermer, and at once roused him from his lethargy.
After pacing to and fro for some time—now swayed by one
furious impulse, now by another,—he quitted the library, and proceeded towards his own room, astounding every person he encountered by his fierce looks and agitated demeanour. No one ventured to address him, except Mr. Pudsey, who threw himself in
his way, and got pushed aside, and consigned to the Prince of
Darkness for his pains.

On reaching his own chamber, Gage spent some minutes in
sombre reflection. He then took a brace of pistols from a case,
loaded them, and ascertained that they were perfectly ready for
use. This done, he attired himself in a riding-dress, fastened
on his sword, thrust the pistols into his girdle, and arming himself with a heavy hunting-whip, sallied forth. At the door he
once more encountered the officious Pudsey, who probably was
employed to watch his proceedings, and who now—to disarm
suspicion, no doubt—appeared with a silver chocolate jug and its
accompaniments on a tray. These Gage upset in his hasty exit,
and without bestowing a word or a look upon the discomfited
butler, strode down the long gallery with a firm step and haughty
port, glancing inquiringly at the portraits of his ancestors as he
passed on. The entrance-hall was thronged by a large party of
his dissolute guests, who were jesting and talking loudly, but
they were all so struck by his altered manner and deportment,
that they involuntarily ceased laughing, and stared at him in surprise. Coldly saluting them, he went on without a word.

In the court leading to the stables, which he next traversed,
a knot of young men were assembled, the most conspicuous among
the group being Sir Randal and Beau Freke. These personages
were all listening with evident amusement to some piquant piece of
information, which Brice Bunbury was detailing with great
unction, and Gage fancied that he himself formed the theme of
discourse, and became confirmed in the notion by Brice making a
gesture of silence to the others as he approached. It was with no
friendly feelings that Gage drew near the group. Since the

revolution which had just taken place in his sentiments and character, he regarded the persons composing it as amongst his worst enemies, and he had no desire to conceal his opinions. Eyeing the assemblage with a fierce and menacing look, he seemed as if singling out some one on whom to discharge his wrath. The bolt fell upon Brice's head.

"Out of my way, sir!" Monthermer cried, pushing him fiercely aside as he stepped forward to salute him.

The others looked amazed at the occurrence, and Brice, thinking himself sure of support, cried out, "Am I to understand that the affront you have put upon me was intentional, Monthermer?"

"Understand it as you please, and take that in addition to clear your comprehension," Gage exclaimed, bringing the horsewhip heavily upon his shoulders, and causing him to beat a hasty retreat, yelling with pain. It was impossible to avoid laughing at his ridiculous grimaces and outcries, and, meeting with no sympathy from his friends, Brice cried, "Is this all the return I get for the amusement I have just afforded you?" Whereupon, the laughter was redoubled.

This incident served to allay the wrath of the two principal personages in the assemblage, who had been highly offended by Gage's deportment towards them, and Sir Randal, with more good-nature than might have been expected from him, observed, "If what we have just heard from Brice respecting Mrs. Jenyns and Fairlie be true, it is natural you should be out of temper, Monthermer. So I am content to excuse your rudeness."

"I have no wish to quarrel with you, Gage," Beau Freke subjoined. "When your anger has passed by, you will, I am sure, be ready to apologise."

"Never!" Monthermer replied. "I will never apologise, either to you or to Sir Randal."

And with a scornful and defiant look he turned on his heel and departed.

"I never saw Monthermer exhibit so much spirit before," Sir Randal remarked, as soon as Gage was gone. "On my soul, he bore himself so proudly that I could not help admiring him."

"I don't admire him at all," Brice observed, still rubbing his shoulders. "You may do as you please, gentlemen, but I don't intend to put up with the insult he has offered me."

"Bravo, Brice!" Sir Randal ejaculated. "What will you do? —horsewhip him in return, eh?"

"Wait till he comes back, and you shall see," the other rejoined.

Meantime, Gage had arrived at the stables, and mounting Hotspur, he galloped off into the park. The groom was still wondering at the young Squire's strange, stern looks, when Mr. Pudsey hurriedly entered the stables.

"You must see where Mr. Monthermer goes to, Nat Clancy, and what he does!" he cried. "Mount one of the horses, and be off at once."

"Why, I do fancy fro' his looks, that he be goin' to make away wi' hisself," Nat replied.

"If he should make any such attempt, it's not your business to interfere, Nat—mind that. Things have gone so badly with him that he'll be well out of the way. But don't lose another moment. Be off with you!"

Thus exhorted, Nat took the first horse he came near out of the stall, sprang on his back, and rode off in the direction Monthermer had taken.

Gage could now give utterance to the emotions pent up within his breast. In-doors he had felt half stifled. The veil seemed rent from his eyes, and he saw clearly how he had been duped by Fairlie. He laughed savagely as he meditated revenge—a revenge commensurate with his wrongs. This accomplished, he had done with a world which he had ever found full of perfidy and the basest ingratitude. His pride was now fully awakened, and his former weakness seemed inexplicable to him. Ere long, he came to the edge of a large sheet of water, and, dismounting, tied his horse to a tree, and sat down at the foot of an oak growing near the bank of the miniature lake. The prospect was enchanting, but in his present perturbed state of mind, he was utterly insensible to the beauties of nature. The picturesque and sylvan scene surrounding him—the mossy bank, sloping down gently to the water's edge—the shining lake, reflecting the adjacent groves—to none of these did he pay attention. If he looked at the lake at all, it was with the frenzied wish that its waters were flowing above his head. How long he remained absorbed in this painful reverie he himself could hardly tell, but he was aroused by the neighing of his steed, and starting to his feet at the sound, he perceived that

Hotspur's attention had been attracted to another horseman, who was rapidly approaching, and who, as he drew near, displayed the features of Arthur Poynings. In another instant, Arthur was off his horse, and marching towards Gage. Even that brief interval allowed him time to note the remarkable change that had taken place in Monthermer, and he could not but feel impressed by the haughtiness with which the latter regarded him. As he drew near, Gage waved him off with a menacing look.

"Pass on your way, Arthur Poynings," he cried, "and trouble me not. I warn you that I am dangerous, and if you utter aught offensive to me, I will not answer for the consequences. I would not have your blood upon my head—but I am in no humour to brook provocation. Be warned, therefore, and pass on."

"Gage," replied Arthur, looking at him fixedly, "I have sad news for you, but ere I disclose it, let all unkindness between us be at an end. Your hand."

But Monthermer evinced no disposition to accept this offer. He shook his head, and in a stern voice, slightly touched with melancholy, said, "Arthur Poynings, we never can be friends again. You have dishonoured me without giving me the means of reparation. Begone! I say. I am a broken and desperate man, maddened by the sense of wrong, and if you tarry near me I may do you a mischief."

"Gage, I will not leave you——"

"You will not," Monthermer furiously interrupted, "then stand on your defence, for, by Heaven! one of us shall not quit this spot alive."

"Strike, if you will," Arthur rejoined, firmly. "Nothing shall induce me to fight with you."

"You hold me unworthy of your sword?"

"Not so—I do not deem you so now, whatever I may have done heretofore. Put up your sword, and let us talk calmly—rationally."

"Rationally!" Gage echoed, with a bitter laugh. "Have I not told you I am driven to the very verge of frenzy by the wrongs and injuries I have endured, and you bid me talk calmly—rationally! As well preach patience to the winds."

"At least, tell me what has happened?"

"Why, I have made a discovery which I ought to have made long ago, since it has been apparent to every one except myself.

I have detected Fairlie's perfidy and knavery—I know how my credulity has been imposed upon—how I have been plundered by him and others—how I have been cozened and cajoled."

"Your eyes are opened, then?"

"Fully. But not till too late. I have lost all—all, Arthur. My father's estates are gone from me—my father's house is gone from me—its master will be a villain—its mistress, Margaret Jenyns."

"You speak in riddles. What has Mrs. Jenyns to do with the Castle?"

"She will rule it—as Fairlie's wife."

"You must be in error now. Even *he* would recoil from such a union."

"Mrs. Jenyns has him in her power, and he has no alternative but compliance. He will marry her, I tell you—that is, if his course of villany be not cut off beforehand—as it may be. But enough of this. You said just now you have sad news for me. Fear not to tell it. I am proof against all further calamity."

"Be not too sure of that," Arthur replied. And he added, in a tone of profound grief, "Clare is dead!"

The shock caused by this intelligence was terrible. Gage uttered a piercing cry, and put his hand to his heart, as if a sword had passed through it.

"Dead!—Clare dead!" he exclaimed, in thrilling accents. "I thought my heart was steeled, but you have found a way to move it. "Oh! this is sad news indeed! But it is well she is gone. At least, she has died in ignorance of her father's dishonour."

"She died, praying for him and you," Arthur rejoined. "Calm yourself, if possible, and listen to me. I have much to say concerning her."

"Not now—not now," Gage cried, with a look of unutterable anguish. "My cup of affliction is full to overflowing. Farewell, Arthur—farewell, for ever! The race of Monthermer will be soon extinct!"

And motioning off young Poynings with an imperious gesture, he hurried to his horse, sprang into the saddle, and dashed off at a furious pace.

"I must not lose sight of him," Arthur said, mounting his own steed, and following in the direction the other had taken.

XLVI.

THE PROPHECY FULFILLED.

IT behoved Arthur to follow quickly, if he would prevent the
impending catastrophe. He endeavoured not to lose sight of Gage,
but this was all that could be accomplished, for the unhappy young
man had started off at such a terrific pace that to overtake him appeared out of the question. Already he was far away from Arthur,
whose shouts to him to stop he utterly disregarded, and being much
better mounted than his pursuer, the distance between them, in spite
of all the latter's whipping and spurring, was speedily increased.
They had proceeded in this manner for about a mile, dashing straight
across the park, and leaving the Castle on the left, when another person joined in the pursuit. This was Mark Rougham. He was on
horseback; mounted on one of Sir Hugh Poynings's hunters—a remarkably powerful animal, almost equal in speed to Hotspur; and
hearing Arthur's outcries, and seeing Gage tearing away at such a
break-neck pace, he essayed to stop him. Mark, it subsequently appeared, had been scouring the park in every direction in search of
Monthermer, whom he desired to see, when he thus unexpectedly
chanced upon him. His aim being to check Gage's progress, he
made a desperate but ineffectual attempt to accomplish the object.
Waiting till the furious horseman drew near, he dashed at him,
hoping to catch his bridle. The manœuvre was well enough executed, but it failed. Hotspur's impetus was so tremendous that he
upset both Mark and his horse, and left them rolling on the ground.
This occurrence did not cause the frantic young man to relax his
speed for a moment. He seemed altogether unconscious of it, and
went on furiously as ever. By the time Arthur came up, Mark
and his steed had both regained their legs; and though the former

T

was somewhat shaken by the fall, he was quickly in the saddle again, and joining in the pursuit.

"I know whither he is bound," Mark cried, as he rode by Arthur's side—"it is for the Beacon Hill. I'm sure of it, for he bade me meet him there a day or so hence at early dawn. I now understand for what purpose—it was to find his lifeless corpse. But distraction, it seems, has made him resolve to anticipate his fatal purpose."

"After him,—quick!" Arthur exclaimed. "You are better mounted than I am, and may succeed in saving him."

"I'll do my best," Mark rejoined, "but I doubt if I shall be able to catch him. Heaven grant he mayn't break his neck on the road! It seems like enough, from the mad way in which he rides."

Mark now urged his horse to its utmost speed, but though he left Arthur behind, it soon became clear that unless some accident occurred he had no chance whatever of coming up with Gage. However, he held on, vociferating lustily, till he grew hoarse with the exertion.

And now Gage had reached the boundaries of the park. Hotspur cleared the lofty palings at a bound, and jumped with equal ease over the fence on the opposite side of the lane skirting the park. The infuriated rider next shaped his course over the fields—never swerving to the right or left—never debarred by any apparent obstacle—but going straight on in the direction Mark had declared he would take. Many desperate leaps, from which, under other circumstances, he would have shrunk aghast, were now taken by the distracted horseman. He seemed to court peril—at all events, he did not shun it. That he escaped without injury was marvellous; and Mark, who witnessed his astonishing performances, could sometimes scarcely draw breath from terror. At last, he viewed these feats with less apprehension, for he became convinced that it was not Gage's destiny to break his neck. The stiffest hedge—the broadest dyke stayed him not. On—on he went. The pursuers now lost ground. Mark declined the worst risks so freely encountered by the foremost horseman; and if Arthur did not exhibit equal prudence, his steed had not Hotspur's untiring vigour, and began to flag. Nevertheless, both he and Mark held on. At last the open country was gained, and Gage could be perceived by his pursuers nearly a mile ahead, stretching out at the same pace as ever towards the Beacon Hill, which now rose majestically before them. They were once more together, for Mark had drawn in the rein to allow Arthur to join him, and they proceeded side by side. As the ground was perfectly clear in that part except an occasional tree, or small shed, Gage was not lost to view for a moment. They saw him reach the foot of the hill, and in a few minutes afterwards beheld him on its summit. Here he paused; but he did not dismount; and the figures of horse and rider relieved against the clear sky seemed dilated to gigantic proportions.

"He is takin' a last look at his forfeited estates," Mark exclaimed. "I am certain of it from his gestures. I make no doubt his eyes are strained towards the Castle, for his face is turned in that direction, as you may easily discern, sir."

"I have no doubt you are right, Mark," Arthur rejoined. "Would we were near him now! I tremble at the thoughts of what may next ensue."

"In my opinion, he doesn't mean to do the deed there, sir," Mark said. "When he has ta'en leave of a' he held dear on earth, he'll come down the hill, or I'm much mistaken, and go to the place where his father perished—for there, it's my belief, he designs to end his days. I come to this conclusion fro' what he let fall when I last met him—nearly a week ago—on that spot."

Arthur was forcibly struck by the remark, and acknowledged its justice.

"We will proceed thither at once, Mark," he cried. "If your notion be correct, and I think it will prove so, we may yet be enabled to save him."

"Heaven grant we may be enabled to do so!" Mark exclaimed. "But let us tie our horses to this tree, and conceal ourselves near the spot. If he should perceive us, he will never approach it."

Arthur signified his approval of the plan, and their horses were secured in the manner proposed. A small brook flowed through the valley, and they proceeded rapidly along its edge till they came to a pollard willow. Here it was, as we have stated in a former chapter, that the accident happened that had deprived Squire Warwick of life. A grey stone marked the precise spot. The banks of the stream were somewhat steep here, and fringed with a little brushwood, enabling them easily to conceal themselves behind it, and yet be close at hand, in case Gage came thither.

Here we will leave them, and scale the hill. As Mark surmised, Gage had gone to take a last look at his forfeited possessions. With what a pang did he survey the expansive prospect—noting all its beauties, and lingering upon them as if loth to quit the view. The last object he regarded was the Castle, and having gazed upon it till his eyes grew dim, he turned to descend the hill. He had done with this world as he deemed, and endeavoured to address himself to the contemplation of the next. The effort was vain. His brain was too bewildered to present any other than frightful images. His heart was full of darkness, despair, and doubt. He hoped to obtain repose, and tried to pray for it, but no prayer would rise to his lips.

But he shrank not from his fell purpose. Before he reached the foot of the hill a terrible calmness had succeeded to his previous distraction. He dismounted, flung his arms around Hotspur's neck, laid his head for a moment upon the animal's shoulder, as if parting with a dear friend, and left him. The horse followed him for a few paces, and then, at a gesture from his master, stood still, and uttered a plaintive, whinnying noise. A few steps more brought Gage to the grey stone. Arrived at his destination, he took out his pistols, examined them for an instant, and then kneeling down, laid the weapons on the ground close beside him. Up to this moment he had been unable to pray, but now suddenly, and as if some benign influence had interposed to save him from guilt, words of supplication rose spontaneously to his lips. He did not pray in vain. A gracious dew seemed to descend upon him and soften his heart. His father's image seemed to arise before him, enjoining him to abandon his unholy purpose; and when it was gone, Clare's image succeeded, and with gentlest looks implored him to renounce it. He stretched out his hands, and cried out with a loud voice, unconscious that his exclamations were heard. "Yes, I will live!—live a new life!—and strive to expiate past faults. This I swear before Heaven!"

As the vow was uttered, he sprang to his feet, and beheld Arthur Poynings and Mark Roughani standing beside him. They had cautiously approached, ready to lay hands upon him in case of need, but happily their interposition was not required.

"I have heard your vow, Monthermer," Arthur cried, "and I rejoice that it has been uttered. From this moment, rest assured, you will date a new and happier career."

"It may be so," Gage rejoined. "Indeed, I feel it will be so!"

"The prophecy! the prophecy!" Mark exclaimed. "It will be fulfilled to the letter. Bethink you how it runs—

> Hard by the hill whereon the Beacon stands
> One proud Monthermer shall lose house and lands.

That alludes to your father clearly enough, for here he lost all his possessions. But what comes next?—

> On the same spot—if but the way be plain—
> Another of the line shall both regain.

That must refer to your honour. You have now chosen the right way, and are certain to regain your own."

"Yes, yes, your trials are over, Gage," Arthur said, encouragingly, "and better days are in store for you. You must come with me to Reedham, where my father will rejoice to see you. I have much to say to you—much to explain. To-morrow we will go to the Castle, and take decisive steps against Fairlie."

"Why tarry till to-morrow?" Gage exclaimed. "Let us go thither at once."

"I am bound by a solemn promise to poor Clare to wait till to-morrow at noon," Arthur cried. "Then I will act as you please."

"In that case I must go alone," Gage rejoined. "I will not rest till I have taxed him with his ingratitude and villany."

"Your honour shall not go unattended on that errand!" Mark cried. "I am with you!"

"I will go too," Arthur said, "but I cannot adduce the proofs I possess of Fairlie's delinquency until the time I have stated."

"To horse, then, at once!" Gage cried. And snatching up his pistols, and thrusting them into his belt, he called to Hotspur, who had never stirred from the spot where he had been left. The faithful steed instantly trotted towards him, and Gage sprang on his back. The others went in search of their horses, and as soon as they had mounted, all three rode off towards the Castle.

XLVII.

THE LAST EFFORT.

FROM the hiding-place with which the reader is already acquainted, Fairlie had witnessed the delivery of Mrs. Jenyns's note,
and had overheard all that subsequently passed between Bellairs
and Monthermer; so that he was immediately acquainted with
the determination of the latter. From the same spot he had
also watched Gage's fierce and perturbed deportment when left
alone, and comprehended the violence of the storm raging in
his breast.   Once he saw him stand still, with features white and
distorted with passion, but on which a formidable energy was
now imprinted, and heard him mutter his own name, coupled
with a threat that made the blood grow chill in his veins, and the
flesh creep on his bones.   Though by no means destitute of courage,
Fairlie had a due regard to self-preservation, and did not think it
necessary to expose himself to the first ebullition of the young man's
wrath.   Accordingly, on quitting his place of concealment, instead
of repairing to his own chamber, where it was likely Gage might
seek him, he took refuge in Pudsey's private room; and in this
secure asylum he remained till informed by the butler that Monthermer had ridden forth into the park, in such a distracted state
of mind as rendered it highly probable he would lay violent hands
upon himself.   Gage had been cautiously followed, Pudsey went
on to say, by Nat Clancy, and had been seen by Nat to tie his
horse to a tree near the lake.

"And it is to be hoped he will drown himself," the butler continued, "for otherwise we shall find him confoundedly in the way.
But to turn to another matter for a moment, sir.   I was about to
ask you whether, under present circumstances, it will be necessary
to go on with the preparations for the fête to-morrow ?"

"Certainly not, Pudsey. An entire stop must be put to them. Never was such a gull as Monthermer. He will swallow anything. I told him I had engaged Farinelli, Cuzzoni, Senesino, and a whole host of opera dancers and musicians for the fête, and he was fool enough to believe me—ha! ha! But, as I was saying, all orders relative to the entertainment must be countermanded, and back-word sent to everybody invited. And hark ye, Pudsey, take care that a handsome collation is prepared in the dining-room at three o'clock to-day."

"I have already given orders about it," the butler replied. "You may confide the arrangement entirely to me. Covers for thirty guests, eh, sir?"

"For thirty—not more, Pudsey. I don't desire to have so many, but Mrs. Jenyns insists upon it, and her whims must be complied with. I shall be glad when the affair is over. Between ourselves, Pudsey, this marriage is a great annoyance to me. But it must be endured."

"Well, sir, I suppose it must,' the butler replied, shrugging his shoulders.

"Ah! if you will only bring me word that Clancy has been right in his anticipations, and that this hairbrained young man lies a fathom deep in the lake, I shall get my head out of this cursed noose, into which I am compelled to slip it."

"Better the noose matrimonial than the other, which is your due," the butler thought; but he kept the remark to himself, and merely observed, "You shall have instant intelligence if anything happens."

The coast being now clear, Fairlie proceeded to his own room where he found a note from Mrs. Jenyns lying on the table, but as he knew what it contained, and loathed the sight of it, he tore it in pieces, and trampled on the fragments. This did not prevent him, however—though he abominated the task—from writing a brief, cautiously-worded reply, in which he professed unbounded delight at the decision she had arrived at, adding that all should be ready at the hour appointed. Never, perhaps, was an assertion in such a case wider of the truth. The more he reflected upon it, the greater became his aversion to the alliance he was about to form. But there was no escape from it, unless he could, by some device, obtain possession of the will; or Gage

released him from further apprehension on this score. The latter
contingency seemed the more probable—but time wore on, and
still no tidings came of him. At last, suspense became quite
intolerable, and Clancy was despatched to the lake, and on his
return brought word that both horse and rider had disappeared.
Fairlie was now thrown into a greater uncertainty than ever;
but the hour of meeting his proposed bride was at hand, and he
must prepare for it. Chassemouche, therefore, was summoned, and
he had to undergo the annoyance of the Frenchman's chatter as
his peruke was arranged, and his toilet carefully completed—some
extra attention to it appearing necessary on the present occasion.
The perruquier was just about to depart, when he suddenly recollected that he had a letter for Monsieur. It had been given him by
one of the women, who had charged him to deliver it to Monsieur
instantly—but his memory was so treacherous. Diving into his
capacious apron-pocket as he spoke, he placed the letter in Fairlie's
hands, bowed, and departed. Fairlie looked at it in dismay. It
seemed the harbinger of ill tidings, and he scarcely dared to open it.
When, at last, he mustered courage to do so, and had glanced at
its contents, his eyes grew misty, and he staggered as if stricken a
heavy blow.

"What! is she here?" he groaned. "I wanted only this to
complete my perplexity. And to be made aware of her proximity
at a critical juncture like the present—when I have need of all my
firmness. But I have yet, perhaps, to learn the worst. Let me
see." And clearing his vision, he was at length able to read as
follows:

"I am here, father, in the Ivy Tower. I have come to perform
an act of justice—and to die. I shall never leave the chamber I
now occupy, except for the grave.

"I promised to keep your secret, and I have faithfully observed
my promise—though in so doing I have made myself an accessory
to your crime. That secret has been fatal to me. It has embittered
all my joys, blighted my youth, consumed me like a hidden fire,
and shortened my days. But I deserve my punishment, and must
not repine.

"I have seen how unjustly you have acted towards Gage—how
you have encouraged his weaknesses and follies for your own ends

—how you have placed temptation in his path—how you have kept away his true friends, and surrounded him by vicious associates, who were your accomplices in his undoing—thus justifying by your conduct the fears entertained of you by your patron when he altered his will, and declined to commit his son to your charge.

"I have loved Gage—loved him with an intensity of affection which could not, I think, have been surpassed. I love him still, with equal faith and fervour, now that my heart has nearly ceased to beat. I would have sacrificed my life for him. Judge, then, of my feelings, when I saw him driven headlong to ruin—and by *you!*—by you, father, who ought to have made every effort to arrest his downward progress. I once, as you know, indulged the dream that I might be united to him, and I fancied that in this way the wrong done by you and by myself would have been set right. Unhappy delusion! Perhaps, but for the false step I took, this great happiness might have been accorded me. But it was denied. I have sinned, and must bow my head in resignation. Yet has the weight of my affliction been too heavy for me. For truly it is written—'a wounded spirit who can bear?'

"I have made many efforts—all fruitless, as you know—to move your heart, father. This is my last appeal. May it not be made in vain!

"You will remember, on the unfortunate day when I stayed your hand from the commission of crime, when you enforced silence upon me—and I gave a promise—a rash promise, of which I did not foresee the fatal consequences—I told you that an hour might arrive when I should consider myself absolved from my oath. That hour would be the latest of my existence. It has arrived, father. The expiring taper merely flickers in the socket, and ere this reaches you I shall be no more.

"But my secret will survive!—yes, it will survive, and rise up in judgment against you, if you continue obdurate, and refuse tardy justice to Gage.

"Now mark me, father. I speak as one from the grave, and nothing can be urged in reply. I have made a full confession in writing of your criminality, and my own participation in it; and this confession I have signed and had attested, though the witnesses, while recognising it as a dying declaration, are, as yet, unaware of its nature. The packet containing this document will be confided to a faithful friend, who has watched by me in my time of trial and suffering, and who will receive my latest breath. It will be brought forward if its production be necessary to the ends of justice.

"I may be adding to my iniquity by consenting that this fatal secret should be buried in the grave with me, but I trust I shall be pardoned for the motive, which is commiseration for you. I cannot injure you, to whom I am bound by the ties of nature and affection, and I would hide your shame, if possible, from the gaze of the world—not proclaim it. Would that my tears could have washed out the stain!—would that my prayers could have moved your heart! May they move you now, and cause you to act uprightly! Then, father, there will be no accusation against you from your child.

"I have seen Gage this morning; and, in our brief and painful interview, I learnt, to my infinite distress, that you had received back the money which, at my instance, you advanced in payment of his debts. You have thus defeated my plans for his advantage, and acted in direct opposition to my wishes. Furthermore, you assented to a scheme so insanely extravagant, that you ought to have checked it rather than have promoted it: a scheme which could have but one result, and that you foresaw. By your sanction—yes, yours, father!—he was to have a week's command of his own house and his own houschold—a week's riot — and then the finishing-stroke was to be given to his prodigal career. You knew how it would end. You knew you were luring him to self-destruction,—that he had no hopes, no prospects, no plans beyond the brief term you allotted him—that his next step must be into the dark, dread abyss of despair—and yet you eagerly closed with his offer.

"I have seen him, I say, and have learnt the terrible truth from his own lips. He does not disguise it; but if he had sought to do so his looks would have betrayed him. If he executes his desperate purpose—and he *will* execute it if not prevented—his death will lie at your door.

"But this must not be. He must be saved; and I must, perforce, exercise the means I possess for ensuring his preservation.

Gage's life and your condemnation have been weighed in the balance, and the former has prevailed. It could not be otherwise. Filial duty shrinks before the decrees of inexorable justice. Gage must be saved, I repeat. To accomplish his preservation he must be lifted from his present state of despair. He must be extricated from the toils in which he is involved. His fortune must be restored to him—his whole fortune—nothing less. This must be your business, father. It is a hard task; but you have done wrong—grievous wrong—and are bound to make complete atonement.

"And observe!—there must be no delay. You must set about the work at once, and without hesitation. To-morrow must not pass by without seeing my injunctions strictly fulfilled. Gage must be reinstated in his possessions. The mode of doing so I leave to you; but I allow no choice between this course, and disgrace. At noon to-morrow, measures will be taken against you—measures you will find it impossible to resist, and which will cover you with shame and confusion. It is my prayer and hope that such a calamity may be averted.

"Alas! alas! that secret has killed me, father. It has preyed upon me incessantly, gnawing into my very heart, like a relentless worm. But it is quiet now, and I hope to depart in peace.

"'In peace'—O, may you comprehend the full meaning of that blessed word, father. May you be warned in time! Reflect that you may be summoned suddenly to your account—in the midst of your prosperity, and while planning schemes for the future—but with no preparation for eternity. In the hour of death prophetic powers are sometimes granted, and I have fearful forebodings. O, be warned, father!

"Ever since that unhappy day, when you bound me with those guilty fetters, our affectionate relations have been disturbed, and latterly I have incurred your displeasure for various causes, but chiefly because I felt compelled to refuse obedience to some of your mandates. In bidding you an everlasting farewell, I implore your forgiveness for any want of filial duty I may have exhibited, and, above all, for a step which may seem incompatible with the affection I profess and feel for you. Forgive me, father, as fully and as freely as I forgive you the grief and anxieties you have

caused me. We shall meet no more on earth, but I trust we
may meet hereafter. Farewell, for ever!

"Your unhappy and ill-fated daughter,

"CLARE."

Cold damps gathered on Fairlie's brow as he read this letter.
More than once he was obliged to pause, for the characters faded
from his view. When he came to the end, an icy chillness fell
upon him, and he shook as if seized by an ague-fit. He felt that
a power not to be resisted was at work to baffle his designs. She
was gone—his child!—the only object he loved on earth—and all
his toil was thrown away. Often before, apprehensions caused by
her evidently declining health had crossed him, but he had forcibly
dismissed them—hoping against hope. The frightful reality came
upon him with a suddenness that increased the severity of the shock.
He would have given all his ill-gotten gains at that moment to
recal her to life. Clare had been more than a daughter to him—
she had been a monitress—a guardian angel—if he had but listened
to her counsels.

But what was to be done? Must he obey the mandates of her
letter? Must he make reparation? Must he surrender all to
Gage, and cover himself with infamy? Impossible! Yet if he
refused, steps to enforce justice would infallibly be taken against
him on the morrow. No matter!—he would brave them. And
then, again, the fiend he served whispered in his breast that when
the morrow arrived Gage would have ceased to be an obstacle in
his path. Yes! yes!—he was determined to go on. As to the marriage with Mrs. Jenyns, it was a make-believe—a mockery—and
should never take place. Let him but once have possession of the
will, and he would face any charge that could be brought against
him.

While such rollections were passing through his mind, and he
was striving to reassure himself, Pudsey hastily entered, to inform
him that the guests were assembled in the dining-room. Mrs.
Jenyns was there too, and some surprise was manifested at his,
Mr. Fairlie's, absence. It was expedient, therefore, that he should
come down at once. The words were scarcely out of the butler's
mouth, when he was struck by Fairlie's haggard looks, and think-

ing he must be ill, he went up to him, and anxiously inquired what was the matter.

"I have had bad news," Fairlie replied, in a feeble tone. "I have just learnt that my daughter is dead."

"Bless me!" the butler ejaculated, "that is bad news, indeed! —most unfortunate that it should arrive at such a moment. I must make your excuses to the party down stairs, I suppose?"

"No; I will go through with the affair in the best way I can," Fairlie replied. "Give me a glass of water." And after swallowing a few drops, he added, "I am better now. Lend me your arm, Pudsey. I will go down at once."

"I admire your resolution, sir," Pudsey remarked, as he supported the tottering steward; "you have need of firm nerves."

"Ay, in truth have I, Pudsey," the other replied; "but I won't flinch. Come what will, I am prepared."

"And our arrangement, sir—pardon me for alluding to it at this moment—money down, and a pension—that is quite understood?"

"Quite."

XLVIII.

THE DENUNCIATION.

BEFORE they reached the dining-room, Fairlie had recovered his usual firm step and erect deportment, and though traces of the fearful struggle he had recently undergone were discernible in his countenance, these might be attributed to passing indisposition. As the butler had stated, the guests were all assembled, and Fairlie's appearance, which had been impatiently awaited, was hailed with satisfaction. Mrs. Jenyns was attired with extreme elegance, and looked so exceedingly captivating that Fairlie might have been almost excused if he had been really enthralled by her fascinations. So far, however, from this being the case, he regarded her with an aversion which he found it difficult to conceal. Essaying to look enchanted, though he only imperfectly succeeded, he excused himself in the best way he could for being behind time, and his apologies being gracefully accepted by the actress, he led her towards the table, and placing her on his right hand, prayed the rest of the guests to be seated. Beau Freke sat next to Mrs. Jenyns, and Sir Randal, on the steward's invitation, took a chair on his left. The repast was admirable in all respects, and the guests did justice to it—with the exception of Fairlie himself, who ate nothing. But if he could not eat—and he felt, indeed, as if the slightest morsel of bread would choke him—he drank several glasses of wine—and as he was habitually temperate, the effect of this unwonted excess was speedily manifest in his excited demeanour and speech. But his exhilaration was wild, and his laughter strange and dissonant, his jests odd and out of season, and his very compliments sarcastic.

Independently of any other circumstance, the sight of him in his new position was matter of amusement and curiosity to the guests, but they all admitted that he discharged his functions as host very creditably. The repast was unnecessarily prolonged—for there was a superabundance of good things—and when it was brought to a close, Sir Randal rose to propose a toast—the health of the new lord of the Castle. It was of course received with vociferous acclamations, in the midst of which Fairlie got up to make his acknowledgments. In the best terms he could command, he expressed his high satisfaction at seeing so many distinguished guests around him, thanked them for the honour they did him, and added, that his appearance in the character of host was somewhat premature, as he had consented to relinquish his rights to Mr. Monthermer for a week—one day of which period was yet unexpired—but he had not foreseen what might happen in the interim, and circumstances had compelled him to abridge the term. They would understand why he had been obliged to rob Mr. Monthermer of his last day, and would hold him excused for acting with apparent want of courtesy to his young friend, when he presented to them a lady, who very shortly—within a few hours, indeed—would be his bride. This announcement was received with loud shouts, and as Fairlie took the actress's hand to raise her, the plaudits were redoubled, and continued for some minutes. Mrs. Jenyns's breast swelled with triumph, and never in the proudest moments of her mimic career, when she had received the rapturous homage of a crowded house, had she felt so much elated. As to Fairlie, he too exulted, and for the moment forgot his troubles and perils. This was the first time he had been recognised as lord of the Castle. It was a moment to which he had long looked forward; and though it brought him not the transports he had anticipated, and was marred by the presence of Mrs. Jenyns, still it was a moment of triumph, and he listened with greedy satisfaction to the compliments and congratulations poured in his ear. After the outburst of enthusiasm had somewhat subsided, he again addressed the company.

"You came here, gentlemen," he said, "as Mr. Monthermer's guests. Henceforth, you are mine. To-morrow was to have been the extent of your stay at the Castle, but I hope you will remain with me another week, during which these festivities shall be continued."

Another round of applause.

" To-morrow it will be my turn to receive you, gentlemen," Mrs. Jenyns said; " and I promise you good entertainment."

" What! is the wedding to take place so soon?" Beau Freke cried. " I'faith, I'm heartily glad of it. You are a fortunate man, Fairlie, and quite right not to postpone your happiness."

" Mr. Fairlie had his own reasons for expediting the marriage," Mrs. Jenyns observed, significantly, " and recognising the force of them, I assented. Was it not so?" she added, appealing to him.

Fairlie merely nodded in reply.

" Well, I must say that Monthermer, by his strange conduct, has deprived himself of all sympathy," Brice Bunbury remarked; " I noticed a change in his manner yesterday, but to-day he seems to have taken leave of his senses altogether. I should not be surprised if he put an end to himself—and perhaps the best thing he could do."

This unfeeling remark was received as a lively sally, and was especially agreeable to Fairlie.

" Poor Gage! I am very sorry for him," Fairlie observed; " but really there is nothing to be done. As my ward, I found him utterly unmanageable; and since he got out of my control, you know what his career has been."

" Well, at all events, Fairlie, you have profited by his folly," Beau Freke observed. " If he had been more careful, you would not be now sitting in his chair."

" Certainly not," Fairlie replied, wincing at the remark. " His improvidence has been a source of gain to me, most unquestionably —but better I should profit than a stranger."

" Far better!" Brice Bunbury cried. " For my part I am delighted to find that eminent deserts like yours have been adequately rewarded. But now that you have assumed the rule and governance of the Castle, Fairlie, allow me to offer one suggestion. Have that portrait removed."

And as he spoke he pointed to a full-length portrait of Warwick de Monthermer suspended over the chimney-piece.

" The old squire," Brice continued, " doesn't seem to look upon any of us with a very friendly eye, and he evidently regards you as an intruder."

Fairlie endeavoured to laugh at this speech, but he succeeded indifferently. Hitherto he had avoided looking at the portrait, but now, in spite of himself, his gaze was drawn towards it, and he became deadly pale.

"You are right, Mr. Bunbury," he exclaimed. "That picture is out of place. The dynasty is changed. No Monthermer governs here now, nor shall ever govern here again."

"Ay, ay," Brice shouted, laughing uproariously. "The Monthermers are gone—never to return. Live Fairlie! Live Fairlie!"

"Fairlie for ever!" echoed the other guests.

"A bumper to Fairlie, and his lovely bride that is to be," Sir Randal exclaimed.

And the toast was drunk with fresh enthusiasm.

"I will mark my assumption of rule of the Castle by the removal of that obnoxious picture," Fairlie cried, unable to brook the annoyance of its gaze. "Take it down!"

"Yes, down with it!" Brice Bunbury echoed. "Down with the Monthermers! We have had enough of them. The dynasty has changed—ha! ha!"

"Do you not hear, rascals?" Fairlie cried to the servants. "Take down that picture, I say?"

Three or four of them flew to obey the mandate, when at this moment an interruption occurred. Pudsey, who had been absent from the room, suddenly entered, and with alarm very visibly painted on his countenance, approached Fairlie and whispered in his ear, "He is come back, sir."

"He! whom do you mean? Mr. Monthermer?"

"Yes, sir—he's coming straight to this room. Be on your guard, sir. He means mischief—I'm sure of it, from his looks."

"Don't let him in, Pudsey," Fairlie rejoined, in alarm. "Shut the door—bolt it—some violence will be done."

But ere the order could be obeyed, the door was thrown open, and Monthermer stood before him. His countenance was ashy pale, his looks stern and menacing, and his deportment singularly majestic. All rose at his entrance, and every eye was fixed inquiringly upon him and his companions—for he was not unattended. Behind him stood Arthur Poynings, looking almost as fierce and formidable as Monthermer himself, and close by Arthur loomed the stalwart figure of Mark Rougham.

Alarmed as she was, and uncertain as to what might ensue, Mrs. Jenyns could not help being greatly struck by Gage's appearance, and thought she had never seen him look so strikingly handsome before.

Monthermer was about to address Fairlie, when perceiving that the servants were about to remove his father's portrait, he cried, in accents that enforced obedience to the command,

"Let no one dare to disturb that picture."

"But I *will* have it taken down—I am master here," Fairlie exclaimed, trembling partly with rage, partly with apprehension.

"Master!" Gage cried. "Do you venture to style yourself master of this house in my hearing? Do you dare to usurp my place? Quit that chair instantly, villain, or, by Heaven, this moment is your last!"

And, as he spoke, he drew a pistol and levelled it at Fairlie's head.

Fairlie looked round, hoping some one would interfere, but as no one stirred, he hastily quitted the chair, and got behind the actress, placing her between him and the deadly weapon.

With a look of profound contempt, Monthermer replaced the pistol in his belt.

"Why do you shrink back thus?' Mrs. Jenyns cried to Fairlie. "Confront him! I have no fear of him—why should you be afraid?"

And she pushed him forward.

"I am glad you have put up your pistol, sir," Fairlie said, abjectly, and cowering like a beaten hound before the other. "If you have anything to say to me, I shall be happy to hear you—not now—but at a more convenient opportunity."

"The present opportunity will serve for all I have to say to you," Monthermer rejoined, with ineffable scorn; "and let those who hear me mark my words, though your character is sufficiently well known to most of them. I denounce you as a knave and villain. Not only have you been guilty of foul ingratitude to your benefactor, my father, who raised you from the menial position to which you originally belonged, and took you into his confidence—a confidence which you shamefully betrayed—but you have committed a fraudulent act in suppressing his last will, and substituting one of earlier date, which answered your purposes better, inasmuch as, by constituting you my guardian, it placed me in your power."

THE DENUNCIATION.

" It is false !" Fairlie cried, roused by these charges—" I deny it."

" You usurped this trust, I say," Gage continued, "and you put in execution a scheme you had contrived to possess yourself of my property. And you succeeded. But think not you will be suffered to enjoy your spoils. They will be wrested from you."

" These charges are unfounded. I deny them all, and defy you to bring proofs of your slanderous accusations. Where is the will you talk of?—where the evidence of my dishonest dealing ?"

" Where is it ?" Gage repeated. " Ask Mrs. Jenyns. Ask your intended bride. She can produce the will, if she likes. She first offered it to me, upon terms which I refused, but which you accepted."

" You have no warrant for what you assert?" the actress cried.

" No warrant, say you, madam?" Gage rejoined. " I have your own letter, written this morning, making me the offer. If I had been as unscrupulous and debased as Fairlie, you would not now stand by his side. But the wiles and artifices you have so often successfully practised upon me failed you at last."

" I am glad I have come in for a share of the attack," Mrs. Jenyns cried, " for I can defend myself. I can be at no loss to divine whence these calumnies have originated, when I see before me Mr. Arthur Poynings. It is not the first time he has dared to slander me behind my back. If I had been a man, I would have brought him to account; as it is, I can only tell him that he has been guilty of deliberate falsehood."

" And if Mr. Arthur Poynings utters any more calumnies against you, madam," Sir Randal remarked, " leave your redress to me."

" A sharper is a fitting defender of a lady who is in the habit of playing with loaded dice," Arthur rejoined; " and I have no doubt Sir Randal de Meschines, amongst his other accomplishments, can play the part of bully. But I have other uses for my sword. I only fight with gentlemen."

And wholly disregarding the furious looks and gestures of the incensed baronet, he turned to Fairlie, and said, " Since you refuse to listen to Mr. Monthermer, I give you notice that measures will be taken against you to-morrow, which will compel the surrender of your wrongfully-acquired possessions. Other proof of your delinquency exists, besides the will unlawfully detained by Mrs. Jenyns, and will be produced against you !"

"Ah! what means he?" Mrs. Jenyns mentally ejaculated. "Can other proof really exist?"

"Why not bring it forward now?" Fairlie demanded.

"Because I have promised one who is no more to give you that time of grace," Arthur answered. "You will understand what I mean!"

Mrs. Jenyns looked inquisitively at Fairlie, and was not without misgivings on noticing his troubled looks.

"You have asked for evidence of your dishonest dealings," Gage said to Fairlie. "I can bring fifty witnesses against you. All the household can testify to your knavery. But I will point out one who can fully expose you."

"Who is it? Let me see him?" Fairlie cried.

"He stands beside you," Gage replied, pointing to Pudsey.

"I, sir?" the butler stammered, utterly confounded. "I know nothing against Mr. Fairlie—nothing whatever. I believe him to be one of the most upright men breathing."

"Do you hear that, sir?" Fairlie cried, eagerly. "Your own witness turns against you."

"He will be glad to purchase his own safety by speaking the truth," Gage rejoined. "But if he hesitates, others will be brought forward."

"I defy you and all your witnesses!" Fairlie cried. "My actions will bear the strictest scrutiny. So far from shrinking from investigation, I court it."

At this juncture, Beau Freke stepped forward.

"An end must be put to this scene," he said. "A worthy man like Mr. Fairlie ought not to be questioned thus. You have always hitherto placed the greatest confidence in him, Monthermer—why accuse him now?"

Gage did not deign to answer the question, but looked sternly at the speaker. In no wise abashed, however, Beau Freke proceeded:

"Is there no way of arranging the matter, Monthermer? If you consider yourself aggrieved, I am sure Mr. Fairlie will listen to reason. But do not use intemperate language—do not bring charges which cannot be sustained. Withdraw the accusation you have brought against him, and perhaps a compromise may be effected."

Fairlie eagerly grasped at the chance offered him—hoping that his powers of cajolery, which had been so often successful before, might yet avail him.

"You judge me rightly, Mr. Freke," he said. "I bear Mr. Monthermer no animosity, and am willing to overlook the insults he has heaped upon me. I have always felt the greatest regard for him—always desired to serve him. If he will adopt a different tone, the dispute may possibly be accommodated."

"You cannot say more," Beau Freke remarked. "Allow me to act as mediator, Monthermer?"

"I decline your services, sir," Gage rejoined, scornfully. "Look to yourself—you will have enough to do to clear your own character. You are implicated in Fairlie's nefarious transactions."

"'Sdeath, sir!" Beau Freke cried, furiously. "Do you dare to asperse me?"

"An accusation is not a calumny," Gage rejoined, gravely. "What I assert I will substantiate. I charge you and your confederate, Sir Randal, with combining together to plunder me at play—with cheating me—ay, *cheating*, sir, I will not mince the word—out of large sums, and sharing the profits with Fairlie, who was a partner in the infamous plot."

"A lie!—a monstrous lie!" Beau Freke, ejaculated. "I will compel you to retract it at the point of the sword."

"Let him rave on—let him discharge his venom," Sir Randal said. "We have both an account to settle with him."

"True," Gage rejoined; "and you shall both pay me—but not in the way you suppose. I shall fight with other weapons than the sword. You are the principal cheats—but there are others who have defrauded me in a less degree."

"You do not point at me, I hope, sir?" Brice Bunbury said, advancing a step or two forward.

"You are beneath my notice," Gage cried; "a pander—a parasite—a hanger-on—a poor gaming-house rook—the tool and instrument of others; the cheats I aim at are of higher mark—and one of them has dishonoured a noble name."

"Your allusion to me is not to be mistaken, sir," Lord Melton exclaimed. "Dare you insinuate that I have cheated you?"

"You cheated in the horses you sold me; you cheated me again at Newmarket, and in every other transaction I have had with

you," Gage rejoined. "But you are one and all a pack of rapacious knaves and cozeners, of harpies and blood-suckers."

"Shall we stand quietly by, and hear ourselves abused thus ?"
Brice Bunbury cried, turning to the other guests behind him.

"No—no !" several voices responded.

"As long as he confined himself to Fairlie, it was all very
well," shouted a half-drunken squire; "but when he attacks us,
and calls us harpies and blood-suckers, we'll let him know who and
what we are. Harpies and blood-suckers ! nothing but blood can
wash out such opprobrious epithets."

"Do your worst," Gage rejoined, maintaining his firm attitude,
while Arthur and Mark Rougham drew nearer to support him, "I
shall not budge an inch !"

"Hold ! hold !" Mrs. Jenyns interposed. "Let me say a word
to Mr. Monthermer. Perhaps I may be able to quell this tumult."

"What d'ye mean, madam? Would you betray me?" Fairlie
whispered.

But utterly heedless of him, Mrs. Jenyns advanced towards
Gage, and said, in a low tone, "Are you still willing to come to
terms with me? I can make you master here with a word."

"I am master here, madam, without your aid," he replied,
repulsing her from him. "I have done with you for ever !"

"You have failed with him, you see," Fairlie cried, grasping
her arm fiercely. "Mr. Monthermer," he continued, "you will
consult your own safety by instant departure—not merely from
this room, but from the house. If you tarry here longer, I will not
answer for the consequences."

"He shall not depart in this way. His insolence must not go
unpunished," Beau Freke cried. And a roar of voices seconded
the cry.

"Upon him ! down with him !" they exclaimed.

"Back !" Gage cried. "I have done. I have denounced you
as a villain, Fairlie, and unmasked your confederates. I go. But
I shall return to-morrow as master of this house, and drive you and
this vile crew from it."

And as the words were uttered, he stepped backwards towards
the door, keeping his eye fixed on those who were most eager to
assail him. His departure was facilitated by Mark Rougham, who
took his place as he retreated ; allowing Arthur to go out at the
same time.

"Knock down that fellow," Fairlie cried, pointing to Mark, who still maintained his stand at the door.

But Mark was not to be disposed of so easily. He kept his assailants at bay for some moments with a knotty blackthorn stick, which he had picked up in his passage through the hall, and when at length he was overpowered by numbers and forced to give way, Gage and Arthur had disappeared.

By this time the whole household was alarmed, and came pouring into the entrance-hall, together with several other guests, who had not been bidden to the collation. It was speedily ascertained that Gage and Arthur had gone out at the back of the house, and taken the direction of the stables.

"Why have you not stopped them?" Fairlie demanded of the domestics, who could only reply that they had no authority to do so—and it seemed from their manner that they had no great inclination, either. Accompanied by a dozen of the most exasperated of the guests, Fairlie then set off towards the stables, breathing vengeance. But they were disappointed of their prey, and only arrived in time to see the two young men mount their steeds and gallop off.

The only capture made was poor Mark Rougham. On his return from the stables, Fairlie ordered him to be conveyed to the strong-room, and locked up within it, till further orders.

As may be supposed, these occurrences threw the house into the greatest confusion, and occasioned a vast deal of talk amongst both guests and servants. Amongst the latter, with two or three exceptions, the feeling was strongly in favour of Gage. All the company who had partaken of the collation, so strangely interrupted, returned to the dining-room, and sat down to a fresh supply of claret, brought by Pudsey, but Mrs. Jenyns withdrew to her own room, on the plea that her nerves had been a good deal shaken, and as soon as he had seen the wine placed on the table, Fairlie also retired, begging Sir Randal to do the honours for him. As soon as he was gone, his affairs began to be freely discussed, and it soon became evident that the majority thought rather badly of his case, and were of opinion that Gage, since he was determined manfully to oppose him, would have the best of it. Several of the party seemed so certain of this result, that they announced their intention of leaving the Castle that night—unluckily, as regarded the execution of their design, they drank so much that they could not even leave the room. Brice Bunbury stuck to the wine as usual, but Sir Randal and Beau Freke were not amongst the late sitters. Indeed, they only remained long enough to ascertain the sentiments of the party, and having satisfied themselves on this score, they left with Lord Melton.

As the trio stood together in the entrance-hall, Lord Melton said to the others,

"Well, gentlemen, what are your plans? I have no special fancy for witnessing the scene to-morrow, and shall be off at once."

"Your lordship is quite right to beat a retreat if you deem it the more prudent course," Sir Randal replied, " but, for my part, I have no sort of apprehension, and shall remain."

"And I shall stay, too," Beau Freke said. "Fairlie is not beaten yet, and I don't think he will be, so I mean to stand by him. Besides, our departure might be attributed to cowardice, and as neither of us have incurred such an imputation as yet, we won't run the risk now."

After an exchange of adieux they separated, Sir Randal and Beau Freke slowly ascending the great staircase, while Lord Melton summoned his servant, and ordered him to prepare his carriage without delay.

XLIX.

NIGHT AT THE CASTLE.

ON that evening a snug party was assembled in the butler's private room, consisting of those whom Pudsey generally delighted to honour. After supper, and a single bowl of punch, during the consumption of which they discussed the events of the day, and speculated as to the probable occurrences of the morrow, a table was formed at the request of Messrs. Trickett and Tibbits, and our card-loving butler sat down with them to piquet, hoping to repair his losses on previous nights. But he was somewhat dis-appointed in his expectations. The run of luck was constantly against him, and he found himself no match for his clever opponents. Long ago they had stripped him of all his money—but what matter? His debts of honour could be booked, his opponents said—they would trust him to any amount. And besides, he would probably win back all he had lost before they separated. No such thing, however. He became seized, as Gage had often been in days happily gone by, with the delirium of gambling, and went on doubling his stakes, in the hope of retrieving himself—but it is needless to say, the hope was vain. The two rooks were determined to fleece him—for it might possibly, they argued, be their last opportunity of doing so. Bellairs and Chassemouche were also losers—but not to an equal extent with Pudsey. The first-named valet bore his ill-luck with great equanimity; but the Frenchman, on being informed that he had lost a hundred pounds, threw himself into a transport of rage, plucked off his wig, trampled it under foot, and committed a hundred other extravagances, which, however, only excited the merriment of the beholders. So in-fatuated was Pudsey that he would have continued to play all night; and no doubt his antagonists, who had it all their own way,

would have been well pleased to humour him, but Bellairs broke
up the party by announcing his intention of retiring to roost.

"It's just twelve o'clock," he said, "and we shall have a busy
day to-morrow. I feel confoundedly sleepy."

"Twelve o'clock!" Pudsey exclaimed. "Oddsbodikins! you
don't say so? I didn't think it had struck ten."

"Because you are such a gambler dat you take no account of
time," Chassemouche remarked. "Ma foi! it would have been
better for you if you had left off an hour ago."

"Hold your tongue, sir," the butler rejoined, sulkily. "If the
cards have been against me, I know how to bear my losses like a
gentleman."

"To keep all clear, before we separate," Tibbits observed,
taking out his tablets, "I will make a note of the results of
the night's play. It stands thus: Mr. Pudsey has been unlucky,
certainly—but we shall always be ready to give him his revenge—
and we have to put him down at 600*l.*, or with the sum lost the
night before, and still unpaid, 750*l.* We shall let you off more
easily, Mr. Bellairs, and debit you with 200*l.* As to you, Mounseer
Shassy, your loss is a mere trifle—only 100*l.*"

"Diantre! you call a hundred pounds a mere trifle!" Chassemouche exclaimed. "It may be so to you, who can win nearly a
thousand at a sitting; but to me the loss is ruin. Parbleu! it's
more than a year's wages."

"Poh, poh! it's a mere trifle, I repeat," Tibbits rejoined.
"You must learn to bear a reverse tranquilly. Take pattern by
Mr. Pudsey, who has lost just seven times as much as you, and
yet never utters a murmur."

"Mais, mille diables! Mr. Pudsey has a privy purse to dip
into, which I have not. My cash-box is empty."

"Pshaw! you will find some expedient to fill it," Tibbits returned. "A clever fellow like you, Mounseer Shassy, who knows
how to take advantage of an opportunity, is never long without
funds. We are not uneasy about you, are we, Trickett?"

"Not in the least," his confederate replied, with affected bon-
homie. Trickett then turned to the butler, and said: "You will
excuse my mentioning it, Mr. Pudsey, but as our stay here is
rather uncertain—and as we none of us know exactly how things
may turn out to-morrow—perhaps, under these circumstances, you
will make it convenient to pay us the 750*l.* in the morning."

"You are rather sharp upon me, methinks, gentlemen," the butler rejoined. "However, you shan't go away empty-handed. I will either pay you or give you my note for the amount."

"We should vastly prefer cash, Mr. Pudsey, if all the same to you," Tibbits remarked. "We want the money—don't we, Trickett?" winking at the other.

"We have the greatest need of it," Trickett replied.

"Have no fear," Pudsey observed. "Between ourselves, I have concluded my arrangement with Fairlie."

"Bravo!" Trickett exclaimed. "But I hope you made him come down. Nothing like time present in affairs of this sort."

"I'm quite aware of it," Pudsey rejoined, uneasily. "And I mean to make him book up to-morrow morning"

"You will need to do so, since you have to book up yourself, you know," Tibbits remarked, drily. "I thought you had been a man of more prudence, Pudsey. Hush-money should be paid on the nail. That's the rule. Things have taken a strange turn here to-day, and may take a still stranger turn to-morrow. Fairlie mayn't be able to pay you—or he mayn't think it worth while to bribe you—there's no saying."

"You alarm me," Pudsey ejaculated. "Do you apprehend, then, that the chances are in Mr. Monthermer's favour?"

"No, I don't say that, exactly. But suppose it should go against Fairlie—where are you?"

"Ay, truly—where should I be?" Pudsey said. "In that view of the case, I'd better side with Mr. Monthermer."

"Side with whomsoever will pay best, Pudsey; that's my maxim," Trickett remarked.

"And a deuced good maxim it is," the butler responded. "I'll see Fairlie before I go to bed."

"Why, it's half-past twelve," Trickett observed, looking at his watch. "You won't venture to disturb him at so late an hour?"

"Won't I!" the butler exclaimed. "He *must* see me. I'm a privileged person—you understand, eh?" And he laughed at his own pleasantry.

"Oh yes, I understand," Trickett replied. "See him, by all means—if you can. You'll then ascertain how the wind blows, and can trim your sails accordingly."

"I know which way to trim mine," Bellairs said. "I shall go over to my old master—that's the best card to play now."

"I'm with you," Chassemouche cried. "I'm a partisan of Monthermer."

"Aha! traitors in the camp, I perceive," Trickett remarked. "But don't be in too great a hurry to turn your coats, gentlemen. Monthermer has right on his side, but he's not yet sure of the day —though story-books will tell you that right always wins. And now, good night, gentlemen—light slumbers and pleasant dreams attend you! You won't forget the hundred to-morrow, Shassy?"

"Peste! you destroy my chance of repose by mentioning it," the Frenchman rejoined. "Pleasant dreams, i'faith! I shall have a grand cauchemar."

Hereupon the company separated, and Pudsey was left alone.

After a few minutes' consideration, he determined to act up to his boast. Though it was late, Fairlie might not, perhaps, have retired to rest, as he frequently sat up after midnight—and even if he had retired, he would make bold to rouse him. Accordingly, he set out, and mounting the back staircase, soon reached the great gallery upon which it opened, through a small private door, scarcely to be distinguished from the adjoining oak panels. All was profoundly quiet, and the butler made little noise as he moved along with stealthy steps. Arrived at the door of Fairlie's chamber, he put his ear to the keyhole to listen, and not distinguishing any sound, tapped softly. No answer. He tapped again, rather more forcibly. Still, no answer; and then partly opening the door, he peeped in. The chamber was vacant, and glancing towards the bed, he perceived it was unoccupied. Perhaps Fairlie might be in the dressing-room?—but no, the door communicating between the two rooms was open, and the smaller chamber was empty. Where could he be gone? For a moment, the idea flashed across the butler that the person he sought had fled; but he instantly dismissed the supposition. Fairlie's absence, however, was strange and unaccountable. Should he await his return? But if he did, might not Fairlie be indignant at his intrusion, and refuse to hear what he had to say. He would run this hazard. So he entered the dressing-room. On casting his eyes around, he perceived that the table was covered with bundles of old bills, and after examining some of them, he found they consisted of accounts relating to Gage—accounts which, it instantly flashed upon him, would furnish most important evidence of the steward's nefarious transactions. But there was still further evidence in Fairlie's private ledger, which he discovered in removing the bills. How this book—and how these bills came to be left so insecurely, he could not comprehend. But they seemed destined to fall into his hands, and to offer him the certainty of enriching himself. He did not hesitate a moment. He put such of the bundles as he judged most important under his arm, and had just taken up the ledger, when the door opened, and Fairlie came in.

A spectre could not have scared the rascally butler more than the figure he now beheld, and he instantly let fall the things he had appropriated. Apart from his alarm at being detected in his knavery, Fairlie's ghastly looks were calculated to appal him. The steward seemed more dead than alive—haggard, hollow-eyed, broken down—Pudsey had not thought so great a change possible in so short a time. But little space was allowed the butler for reflection, for on seeing him Fairlie seemed suddenly endowed with preternatural vigour. Uttering a sharp, angry cry—almost a scream —he sprang like a wild cat upon Pudsey, and seizing him by the throat, clutched him with such force, that he forced him upon his knees.

"Would you rob me, villain?" he shrieked. "Give up all you have taken, instantly, or I will strangle you."

Pudsey's throat was so tightly compressed that he was utterly unable to speak. All he could do was to point to the ledger and bundles upon the floor, intimating that he had abandoned his spoil. Fairlie at length relinquished his grasp, and bade him begone.

Pudsey tottered towards the door, and when he reached it he stopped, and fixing a malicious and vindictive look upon Fairlie, cried, " You have half killed me. But you will repent your violence to-morrow!"

"To-morrow!" Fairlie echoed, glancing at him disdainfully. " Who knows what may happen to-morrow?"

"Ay, who knows?" Pudsey echoed. "But I know who will be master here, and who will have the property, unless my mouth be stopped—and only a thousand pounds can stop it. I must have that sum in the morning, and I *will* have it—or——"

"Begone!" Fairlie rejoined, imperiously. "Do not come hither again on any pretence whatever till noon to-morrow. I have much to do, and shall want repose."

"And if I consent to hold my tongue I shall be requited, eh ?
—I shall have my reward ?"

"You shall have it in full," Fairlie rejoined, with a stern significance not altogether to the butler's liking; but there was something in the other's manner that awed him, and he now yielded
to the imperious gesture that enjoined him to depart. On emerging into the great gallery he lingered for a short time, and would
have tarried longer, but he fancied he perceived through the gloom
a huge and mysterious-looking figure advance towards him, and
seized with superstitious terror, he hurried to the back staircase,
descended it with quick footsteps, and made the best of his way to
his own room.

The huge, mysterious figure was no other than honest Mark
Rougham. But in order to explain how he chanced to be there,
we must go back to an earlier period of the night.

On leaving his guests, Fairlie had proceeded to his own room,
where he sat down and pondered over the events of the day. He
had matter enough, as we know, for serious reflection. The magnificent pile he had reared with so much care wanted stability,
and seemed tumbling about his ears. The riches he had accumu-
lated vanished at his touch. Fortune had played him false, and
had beguiled him with a semblance of success, only to make his
fall the greater. No sooner had he proclaimed himself master of
Monthermer Castle and its domains than his title was contested,
and he was compelled—ignominiously compelled—to abandon his
seat. .And what would be the result of the measures taken against
him on the morrow? Could he stand his ground? In his first
sanguine view of the situation he thought so; but reflection shook
his confidence, and he grew more and more disheartened. He
was surrounded by a set of greedy hirelings, who would not
scruple to betray him. Then again the unexpected resolution
which Gage had displayed, coupled with the justice of his cause,
these struck terror into his soul, and forced upon him the conviction that he should be worsted. And what if his delinquencies
should be proved--and he should be cast forth with shame? He
trembled at the thought, and hid his face in his hands.

He was roused by hearing some one sobbing near him, and
raising his eyes, he beheld Lettice Rougham. The poor girl
looked the very picture of distress, and was so profoundly afflicted

that it was some minutes before she could command her utterance. At last, she spoke in a voice almost broken by emotion:

" The letter you have received, sir, would prepare you for the sad tidings I have to communicate; for, according to my poor lady's desire, it was not to be delivered until after her death. Oh, sir, hers was a peaceful end—a joyful end!—and it is happy for her that she is removed from a life of trouble, and gone to a better world. She fully forgave you, sir, and prayed for you in terms that must have softened your heart if you had heard her. It was her wish that you should see her when all was over. And I'm sure it will do you good to behold her angelic features. Will you come with me ?"

" Not now—not now. I am not equal to it," Fairlie groaned. " Later on, perhaps,—later on."

" As you will, sir," Lettice replied; " but, oh! do not fail to come; and at any hour, for we shall watch by her throughout the night."

" Who is with her ?" Fairlie inquired.

" Miss Poynings," Lettice replied. " My poor lady died in her arms."

Fairlie turned away his head, and Lettice departed.

For some time, Fairlie was utterly crushed. At last he shook off his emotion, and arose with a fierce and defiant countenance. He would never yield, be the consequences of resistance what they might! He defied them all—Gage, Arthur, Sir Hugh— all! He strode to and fro within the room, becoming each minute more and more excited. The blood mounted to his brain, and almost obscured his reason. He uttered wild and impious ejaculations, accompanied by strange, discordant laughter. Suddenly he staggered, as if a crushing blow had been dealt him—uttered a single cry—and putting his hands out to save himself—fell prostrate on the floor.

No one came to his aid, for no one knew what had befallen him, and it was long before he recovered. With great difficulty he regained his feet, for his limbs at first refused their office, and for some time continued benumbed and stiff. After a while, he managed to crawl towards a glass, and he could not repress a cry on perceiving the fearful change that had taken place in his aspect. He then bethought him of the warning he had re-.

ceived from his daughter, and how prophetically she had spoken, when she said that he might be summoned suddenly to his account, and no preparation made. Perhaps he had been spared for a short space at her intercession, in order to enable him to make this preparation, and it behoved him not to neglect the opportunity. Certainly, it was a wonder he had not died. Another such shock would infallibly kill him; and the final blow he felt equally sure would not long be delayed. A total revulsion had now taken place in his feelings, and he was just as eager to repair the wrongs he had committed, as he had lately been to uphold them. If Gage had been present, he would have confessed all to him, and implored his pardon. At all events, he could make ample reparation on the morrow. But what if another and severer attack should occur in the interim, and deprive him of his faculties, or perhaps of life itself? No, justice must be done, and without delay.

With this design, he unlocked a chest, and took from it certain bundles of bills of which he knew the importance, together with his private ledger, placing them on the table to be ready for delivery to Gage—or where they might be found by him in case his own dreadful presentiments should be verified.

He next wrote a letter, wherein he confessed all the wrongs he had done; and intimating that he desired to make the best atonement in his power, surrendered the whole of the Monthermer property to Gage. This document signed, he enclosed it in a sheet of paper, sealed the packet, and directed it to Gage. A great weight seemed taken from his breast, and death, whose near approach he had hitherto viewed with indescribable alarm, had now lost much of its terror. But he had another document to prepare—his will—and he set about it at once. It was brief, and speedily completed. But it must be executed in the presence of witnesses, and in order to find these he must go below. Accordingly, he placed both the documents he had prepared in his breast, and went forth. As he proceeded along the grand gallery, he perceived two female figures approaching him, one of whom bore a light, and instantly recognised in them Mrs. Jenyns and her attendant, Davies. He would have avoided them, if possible. but on seeing him the actress quickened her steps, and was almost instantly close beside him.

"I was coming to you, Mr. Fairlie," she cried. "I have something of importance to say to you."

"Another time, madam," he rejoined, coldly. "I have business on hand now."

"Ah! but another time won't do," she cried. "I must have an answer at once."

"An answer to what question?" he returned.

"Stand aside, Davies." And as the attendant retired, Mrs. Jenyns added, "Circumstances may prevent our marriage to-morrow. Are you willing to buy this precious document from me to-night?"

"Squire Warwick's will!" Fairlie exclaimed, starting. And then crushing the thought which the temptress had roused, he added, "No, madam. It is useless to me now. I care not for it."

"Ah!" she exclaimed, "you have formed some new plans, and fancy yourself secure. You think to juggle and cheat me, as you have juggled and cheated Gage, but you will find yourself mistaken. If I had married you, I would have made you the scoff of the county."

"It is well that I have escaped your snares, then."

"You have escaped this fate, but you have not escaped me, and you shall not do so. If I can have nothing else, I will have revenge. This is no idle menace, as you will find. Reflect upon it—sleep upon it, if you can. To-morrow morning I shall require an answer." And she hurried off with her attendant, while Fairlie slowly followed, and descended the great staircase.

On reaching the entrance-hall, he found some of the guests assembled there, with bed-candles in hand, talking together before they retired to rest, and he begged three of them to do him the favour to accompany him to the library, and witness the execution of his will. They laughed at the request, but readily complied, and the will was duly signed and attested.

Fairlie thanked them for the service, bade them good night, and the three gentlemen went away, wondering why he should be so urgent about his will, though they admitted to each other that there might be some necessity for the step, since he looked exceedingly ill.

Fairlie's next business was to liberate Mark Rougham. Procuring a key from a man-servant named Blackford, who slept on the ground-

floor, and whose chamber he visited for the purpose, he unlocked
the door of the strong-room, and discovered Mark reclining against
the wall, in a corner, fast asleep. Fairlie envied him the sound-
ness of his slumbers, but he interrupted them, shaking him with
some force, and at last succeeded in awakening him. Mark rubbed
his eyes, and seemed not a little surprised when he found who
had disturbed him, but his wonder increased when he heard what
Fairlie had to say to him, and fancied he must still be dreaming.
However, he became convinced at last that he was wide awake,
and, springing to his feet, declared he was ready to do whatever he
was directed.

"I am glad you have made up your mind to act rightly, sir,
and make amends," he said; "it will be a comfort to you on your
death-bed. Now gi' me your orders, and I'll obey 'em."

"First of all you must have something to eat," Fairlie said,
"for you will have to stand guard at my bedroom door during the
whole of the night, and will need support."

"Well, I shan't object to a mouthful of meat and a glass of ale,
seein' as how I've had no supper," Mark rejoined; "but I want no
more sleep, for I've had plenty of that to last me till to-morrow
night."

Fairlie then led him to the servants'-hall, in the midst of which
stood a long table, covered with the remains of a plentiful supper.
The room was quite deserted—all the servants having long since
retired to rest. Mark did not require pressing to commence an
attack upon a cold round of beef, and Fairlie, having filled a large
jug of ale from a cask which stood in an adjoining cupboard, set
it before him, and telling him when he had concluded his meal to
come up to the long gallery, he left him.

Fairlie then went back to Blackford's chamber, and told him that
he must rise at early dawn, and unfurl the great banner emblazoned
with the Monthermer arms from the flagstaff.

"Why, that banner hasn't been displayed since the young squire
—I beg your pardon for naming him—came of age," Blackford
replied. "It will bring all the tenantry to the Castle. They'll
look upon it as a signal."

"Never heed that," Fairlie rejoined. "Do as I bid you."

"Rest easy, sir; I won't fail. I'll call Tom Loes at peep of day.
He knows where the banner is kept—and we'll hoist it."

Fairlie then withdrew, and returned to his own room. On entering it, he discovered the butler, as we have already related.

Fairlie had not sought his chamber to rest within it. More remained to be done, and he now only awaited the appearance of Mark Rougham to set forth on a sad errand. While hardened in guilt, and impenitent, he had not dared to look upon the inanimate features of his daughter. He had sent away Lettice without even promising to fulfil her dying mistress's wish. Now he felt that it was a sacred and solemn duty to fulfil it.

Presently, he heard Mark's footsteps in the gallery, and came out to him. Bidding him station himself at the door, and not allow any one to enter his room during his absence, he again descended to the lower part of the house, quitted it by the glass door opening from the library upon the lawn, and shaped his course towards the Ivy Tower.

I.

HE stood before the tower. A feeble light glimmered from a narrow loophole. The light was burning in *her* room. He passed through the arched entrance, ascended the spiral staircase, and paused to draw breath. Another step would place him in the presence of the dead. But his approach had been heard; the door was opened by Lettice Rougham, and he rushed into the room.

He saw only one object—a marble figure stretched upon the couch—and, uttering a cry of anguish and despair, he sprang towards it, flung himself upon his knees, and taking her hand, pressed his lips to the clay-cold fingers—passionately imploring forgiveness.

After a while he became calmer. He arose, and with bowed head regarded his child. Yes, there she lay—she who had once honoured him—had loved him always, and whose latest breath had exhaled in prayer for him. There she lay!—placidly beautiful —an angelic smile on her lips—her dark hair unloosed, and wandering over her neck and bosom, and contrasting with the marble whiteness of her skin.

There she lay!—his only child—his only relative—the pride of his heart—cut off in the morning of life, in her bloom and beauty —destroyed by him—by her father! For had not she herself told him that the dread secret he had imposed upon her had killed her? *His* crime had weighed her down, and brought her to that bed of death! Madness was in the thought.

But, look again!—ay, he *must* look again, for he could not withdraw his gaze. The sight fascinated him. There she lay!—the virtuous, the irreproachable daughter of a wretched, guilty sire, whose greatest misfortune had been that she was *his* child—whose only fault was that she had obeyed *his* sinful injunctions! Yes, there she lay!—gone!—lost to him for ever!

Forgiveness! oh, forgiveness!

Again he knelt down by the couch, and clasped the icy hand. His groans and remorseful ejaculations made those who listened shake with terror.

But his grief was too violent to last long. Quitting his kneeling posture he looked round, and for the first time became aware that Lettice had a female companion. He could scarcely distinguish her, for she had withdrawn to the further corner of the room; but he knew who it must be. Who but Lucy Poynings could be there at such an hour—at such a season?

Slowly approaching Lucy, he said, in a voice of profound emotion, which was not without effect upon the hearer, notwithstanding the repugnance she felt towards him,

"I thank you, Miss Poynings, from the bottom of my heart, for the devoted attention you have shown to my lost child. You have been more than a sister to her, and have supplied that affection which she had a right to expect from me—but which (alas!) she never experienced. You knew her well, and appreciated her noble qualities. Though unworthy of it, I was not ignorant of the inestimable value of the treasure entrusted to my charge—but I blindly cast it away in the search after earthly dross. But having witnessed my anguish, you will understand the depth of my remorse."

Here he paused for a moment, and then continued with a solemnity so profoundly impressive, as to leave no doubt of his sincerity.

"Hear me, both of you," he cried, "and mark well my words! I ask no pity from you, for I deserve none; but do not turn away till you have heard me out. I am a wretched, miserable man, condemned of Heaven and my fellows. I have been guilty of the basest and blackest ingratitude to my benefactor, and have committed many offences, but that which lies heaviest on my soul is my daughter's death. I have raised no hand against her, but I feel, not the less, that I have brought her to an untimely grave. Can guilt be greater than mine? Can I hope for pardon?"

"Yes, if you make atonement for the wrongs you have committed, pardon will not be denied you," Lucy rejoined. "It was your daughter's last hope that you might be brought to a state of penitence."

"I am penitent—truly penitent," Fairlie cried, "and I will make all the atonement in my power. Herein," he continued, taking the sealed packet from his breast, "I have confessed the wrongs I have done to Gage Monthermer, and have given back all the property I have unjustly acquired from him. So far I have obeyed my daughter's dying injunctions. The packet will be found by Gage to-morrow. But this is not all; and I again pray of you to attend to me, for what I have next to say concerns you both."

"Concerns us!" Lucy exclaimed, in surprise. "In what way?"

"You shall hear. I have other property, which I may rightfully call my own, inasmuch as it was gained by honest means before the death of my benefactor, Warwick Monthermer. This property is not inconsiderable, and would have contented me, had my wishes been moderate. But let that pass. I am alone in the world—without relative or friend. My daughter has been taken from me. But I desire to fulfil her wishes, and to make such disposition of my property as may be in entire accordance with them. I shall therefore leave it to those who loved her, whom she loved, and who merited her love. I address myself first to you, Lucy Poynings, as her best and dearest friend. Nay, hear me out. It is not my voice, but the voice of my poor child, that now addresses you. I have left the whole of this property to you—subject to certain charges, which I will specify anon. Take it as a gift from Clare. Happily, you do not need wealth; but it will constitute a marriage portion, and if hereafter—when his reformation has been proved—you should (fortunately for him) bestow your hand upon Gage, the bequest will have accomplished its object."

"Oh, sir! speak not thus!" Lucy exclaimed.

"Such I know was my daughter's wish," Fairlie pursued. "And now as to the charges I mentioned. They are but two in number. The first is a marriage portion to this maiden—my daughter's attached and faithful attendant, Lettice Rougham. The few hundreds left her will but inadequately repay her services. The remaining bequest is of a sum of money sufficient to purchase

Cowbridge Farm, of which I unjustly dispossessed Lettice's father, Mark Rougham, and which I now leave to that worthy man. Except these charges," he added to Lucy, " all the rest is yours."

" I will not question what you have thought fit to do, because this is not a fitting moment for such discussion," Lucy rejoined; " but you speak of your will as if it were to take effect immediately. You may live for years."

" Lucy Poynings," Fairlie said, with increased solemnity, " many hours will not elapse ere I shall join my daughter. I have received a warning not to be mistaken. The sun will not arise and find me among the living. But Heaven be praised! I have made my preparations. I have done what lies in me to expiate my offences."

He then moved slowly towards the bed, and looking down tenderly upon his child, said, in a low tone, " Art thou content with me, my daughter? Have I obeyed thy wishes in all things? Speak to me! oh, speak to me!" he ejaculated, yielding to the passionate impulse, and clasping the inanimate form in his arms.

" I answer for her," Lucy said. " She *is* content with you. Regard well her features—and see if they smile not approval."

" They do—they do," Fairlie rejoined. " They speak forgiveness. Leave me alone with her for a short space, I implore of you. I would pray by her side."

Thus exhorted, Lucy and her companion withdrew, and proceeded to an upper chamber in the tower. Both were moved to tears, and Lettice sobbed audibly.

When they were gone, Fairlie knelt by the bedside, and prayed fervently. While thus engaged, he fell into a sort of trance, during which he imagined that his daughter appeared to him, with looks of celestial beauty, and a smile beaming of Paradise, telling him he was forgiven. He was still in this state of ecstasy when Lucy and her companion came down again. On hearing them enter the chamber he arose.

" I have seen her!" he cried. " She has promised me pardon."

Lucy said nothing in contradiction, for she feared his reason was disturbed.

" And now I have done," he continued. " I commit her dear remains to your charge. You will see the last rites performed. I shall return to my own room, which I shall never quit again till I am taken from it. She has assured me I shall speedily join her. And now mark my last words. The documents I have mentioned —the confession and the will—will be found near me, when Gage comes to-morrow morning to the Castle. Farewell!"

And once more bending down before his daughter, and pressing his lips to her hand, he quitted the chamber.

Strength seemed to have been granted him for the effort he had made—and for this effort only—for it was with the utmost difficulty he regained the Castle, and on reaching the foot of the great staircase he fell with a groan. Luckily, Mark Rougham heard him, from the long gallery where he was stationed, and hastily descending, carried him up the staircase. By his own desire Mark helped him to his dressing-room, where he sank quite exhausted into a chair.

"You will be better for some restorative," Mark said, greatly alarmed at his appearance, for he really believed him to be dying

"No—no—I want nothing. Leave me," Fairlie said, feebly.

"But I can't find i' my heart to leave you i' this state," Mark rejoined.

"Go, I beg of you—nay, I insist," Fairlie said. "Keep watch as I have directed in the gallery, and do not let any one enter my room till Mr Monthermer's arrival to-morrow. He will find all ready for him."

"He won't find you alive, I'm thinkin'," Mark muttered, as he reluctantly withdrew.

Left alone, Fairlie mustered all his remaining strength for a final effort. He locked the doors of his bed-chamber and dressing-room —took out the two packets he had prepared—laid them on the table, and extinguished the light.

Darkness and the voice of prayer. Presently the voice was hushed, and there was a deep sigh. Then profound silence reigned amidst the gloom.

LI

MORN AT THE CASTLE.

THE long, dread night is past, and morn is come. The new-risen sun shines brightly upon the lordly groves near the Castle, and disperses the white mists hanging over the marshy grounds in the valleys In the park the deer come tripping forth from their coverts in the fern-brakes, and their slim figures and branching horns can be distinctly discerned as they cross the lengthening glades. All nature is speedily aroused by the kindling beams of the beneficent luminary.

But not alone does sunshine glitter upon grove and landscape ; it gilds the proud vanes on the Castle, glitters on its many windows and clothes the magnificent fabric with splendour. The grand old pile puts on its most imposing aspect. But as yet there is little stir within. The God of Day peers in at the upper windows, and espies drowsy menials slumbering off nocturnal potations. He tries to look in at windows lower down, but thick curtains impede his gaze. If he could pierce through these, he would behold the gambler dreaming that his luck has deserted him—the epicure groaning from a surfeit—the bacchanalian fevered by excess of wine—the actress terrified by fancies that her beauty and fascinations have fled. These persons are safe from the sun's scrutiny. But into one room he looks steadily, and with an inquisitive eye. What sees he there ? A kneeling figure—kneeling, but in a strange posture, with hands extended, and head dropped upon the chair. He pours his radiance upon it. But it moves not. It feels no revivificating heat. The eyes will never again open to the light of day. So the sunbeams fly from it and settle upon the table—lighting up two sealed packets—and an extinguished taper—the emblem of the motionless figure at the chair.

But not alone does the sunlight glorify and gladden the Castle —it gleams on all around it—on the smooth velvet lawns, where gardeners are already at work with scythe and roller, pursuing their task gleefully—on the parterres—on the stately terraces, where other gardeners may be seen wending to their work—on the orchards—the stables, and outbuildings—on the grey walls of the ancient Castle—and on the Ivy Tower.

Why does the sunlight settle on that narrow loophole? Would it look into another chamber of death? Would it know what is passing there? A slanting beam shoots in through the narrow aperture and falls upon a marble countenance, giving the white transparent skin an indescribable beauty, and encircling the head and its crown of dark hair with a nimbus of glory like a saint. Two persons are beside that bed. One, overcome by fatigue, is wrapped in slumber. The other watches with admiration the magical effect of the sunbeams on the features of the dead. Never has she seen aught so seraphic in expression—so effluent of beatitude, as that countenance. As she gazes, a conviction crosses the watcher that the spirit of her departed friend is hovering near her, whispering that she is about to wing her flight to Heaven. All she has stayed for on earth is accomplished. Even as the thought crosses the beholder, the stream of sunlight has left the face—the effulgence vanishes from brow and hair—and the marble features resume their rigidity. Filled with unspeakable joy, the watcher kneels by the couch and prays.

Meanwhile, the sun shines brightly on the Castle and its broad domains; and many of the tenantry who look towards it are struck with surprise as they see, floating from the tall flagstaff on the roof, a banner displaying the arms of Monthermer. The sight diffuses universal joy throughout the whole of Monthermer's domains, for all who behold it look upon it as a harbinger of the young squire's restoration. He has come to his own again. He has defeated the unjust steward. None have any love for Fairlie, and therefore all rejoice in his downfal. With all his faults, Gage is a favourite with the tenantry. They like him for his father's sake, whose memory is universally revered; and though not insensible to his errors, they regard them with a lenient eye. He has had bad counsellors; and his guardian, who should have screened him from it, has thrown temptation in his path. Thus they reason, and, from a variety of causes, are overjoyed that a Monthermer will still rule over them. To this joy, their own escape from Fairlie naturally contributes. They all know what they had to expect from that hard, griping man.

Rumours have spread abroad—with the unaccountable rapidity with which rumour always travels, as if wafted through the air—of the disturbance that took place at the Castle on the previous day; and it is said that on the day, which has just commenced, Gage, who has gone over to Reedham with young Arthur Poynings, is to return to the house of his ancestors, and drive the intruder from it. Their best wishes are with him; and when they behold this banner—a flag first used by Squire Warwick on the occasion of his son's birth, when it gave the signal to all beholders that he kept open house—floating from the summit of the Castle, they make sure that their hopes will be realised. Fairlie, they imagine, would never willingly permit the flag to be unfurled. Little do they think that it was he who commanded its display. However, they regard its appearance as a favourable omen, and one and all accept it as a signal to flock to the Castle.

Thus the farmers, for miles and miles around, leave their work and return to their homes, to tell their wives that the old flag is floating from the Castle, and that they must go thither to see what it means. So they don their best attire, and prepare to set forth. Mounted on rough steeds—all stout Suffolk punches—they take their way through the lanes leading to the Castle, their numbers gradually increasing, until they form a troop of nigh two hundred horsemen—a formidable band—and many of them declare that if the young squire wants a hand to set him in his place again, he will easily find it. The elders amongst them talk much of Squire Warwick, and of the loss they sustained in his sudden death. Ah! if he had but been spared, some of these greybeards say, his son would have been a different person. A father would have watched over him in his youth, and not encouraged him in his follies like Muster Fairlie. All these seniors express a hope that at last the young squire has sown his wild oats, in which case nothing more ought to be said against him. But young and old confidently predict that Fairlie will be defeated, and the county rid of him. They little think that the object of their detestation is incapable of doing them further harm, or they might be more charitable in their remarks. As it is, there is not a word of ill spoken by any one against his daughter—who is equally beyond applause or censure. On the contrary, every tongue wags in her praise.

Chatting in this way, they enter the park, and ride slowly along the broad and extensive avenue leading towards the Castle, from the windows of which their approach is viewed with astonishment. Arrived within a bowshot of the mansion, they come to a halt, and after a little consultation with their leader—an old farmer named Wingfield—they dismount, and lead their horses to the side of the road, while one or two of their number are despatched to the house to ascertain how matters stand.

Within the Castle all is confusion and insubordination. A downright rebellion seems to have broken out amongst the household, and it is difficult—if not impossible—to get an order obeyed. Pudsey, who has latterly acted as a sort of major-domo to Fairlie, and exercised supreme command over the servants, has lost all authority.

The butler has had a quarrel and a fight. After a loud and angry altercation with Messrs. Trickett and Tibbits, who having called upon him to pay the money he had lost to them, and not being able to obtain it, had termed him a miserable shuffler and a cheat, besides applying other opprobrious epithets to him, he had given them both the lie, and defied them to fistic combat. Tibbits accepted the challenge; and at the same moment another fight was got up between Trickett and Chassemouche —the Frenchman having resented the application made to him for his debt of honour. Chassemouche would fain have had recourse to the sword, as the only proper and gentlemanlike weapon wherewith to settle a quarrel, but this being refused, he was compelled to box. Needless to say that a few well-delivered hits put him *hors de combat*. But he was speedily and completely avenged a few minutes later, when a set-to took place between Bellairs and the victor. In this encounter Trickett got the worst of it, and was very severely handled by his antagonist, for, fine gentleman as he was, Bellairs exhibited remarkable proficiency in pugilistic science. Tibbits was equally well punished by the butler, who knocked out two of his teeth and cut open his mouth, after a dozen well-contested rounds. Pudsey's own countenance bore pretty strong evidences of the fray, his huge copper-coloured nose being darkened to an inky dye, and swollen to twice its usual dimensions; but this he did not mind at the moment. These conflicts took place at an early hour, in the back yard near the stables. After the fight, the butler withdrew to his own room to repair his damaged features as well as he could; and from this moment, as we have stated, his authority ended. When he came forth again, with a piece of brown paper, steeped in brandy, fixed to his swollen proboscis, all the servants laughed at him, but none of them would do his bidding.

Never was such downright rebellion. The cook and her assistants refused to prepare breakfast for the guests up-stairs, and the other servants said they wouldn't wait upon them. They might shift for themselves for what they cared. As to Mrs. Jenyns, the women declared they were not going to wait upon the like of her! They wouldn't even let that forward hussy, Mrs. Davies, who made so free with the men, enter the servants'-hall. In vain Mr. Pudsey warned them that if they continued this disobedient conduct Mr. Fairlie would infallibly discharge them all. They didn't acknowledge Mr. Fairlie as master. And if Mr. Fairlie *was* master—as the butler pretended—why didn't he show himself—why did he keep his room, and order himself not to be disturbed before noon? Pudsey couldn't exactly answer this question. He owned he thought it rather odd and injudicious, but Mr. Fairlie no doubt had his reasons for what he did. This solution satisfied nobody. They had seen Mark Rougham stationed at Mr. Fairlie's door, and Mark had told them that Mr. Fairlie was not to be disturbed, on any account, till Mr. Monthermer's arrival. What did that mean? The butler couldn't say. Why had Blackford and Loes unfurled the great banner? Mr. Pudsey couldn't answer that question. But he would have the banner pulled down. A dozen eager tongues, however, told him that this would not be permitted. In short, it became manifest to Pudsey that Fairlie's control over the house had altogether ceased, and that he, as his delegate, could no longer act. He therefore withdrew, since his orders were only treated with disrespect and derision. Not knowing exactly what to do, and beginning to feel considerable uneasiness as to the result of the day, he proceeded to the great gallery with the fixed determination of having an interview with

Fairlie. But Mark Rougham was still there, and would not suffer him to approach; and as Mark was now supported by Blackford and Loes, Mr. Pudsey found himself in a minority, and was compelled to retire.

By this time, some of the guests who had passed the night at the Castle began to make their appearance, and all of them expressed their dissatisfaction at the way in which they had been treated. Loudly and repeatedly as they had rung their bells, no one had come near them. Where were the valets?—where was the perruquier? Not a coat was brushed, not a wig dressed, not a shoe cleaned. Never was such shameful neglect. And where were they to breakfast? Not in the dining-room, that was impossible! The table was covered with bottles and glasses, with a great punch-bowl in the centre, and the room reeked of tobacco.

The slumbering sots who had made their couch upon the floor were awakened by the entrance of the others, rubbed their eyes, and asked for their morning draught, but no one would bring them a tankard of ale. The guests then betook themselves to the library, but in this quarter they experienced similar disappointment. No preparations were made for breakfast. The bell was pulled violently—no one answered. What the deuce could it mean? They swore and stormed to no purpose. At last some of them went forth and shouted lustily for Pudsey; and thus invoked, the butler at last deigned to make his appearance, and expressed his regrets—but really the house was in such confusion, the servants were so unmanageable, he feared there was very little chance of breakfast.

No chance of breakfast! Zounds! They would see about that. So a large party, headed by Brice Bunbury, marched to the servants'-hall, and by their clamorous demands and incursions upon the larder, increased the confusion already reigning in that quarter.

Sir Randal and Beau Freke fared no better than the others. Luckily, as it happened, neither of them were very early risers, and never thought of getting up until called by their valets, so they did not undergo the annoyances that the rest experienced. But when Mr. Trickett made his appearance in his master's room, he apologised for not bringing his chocolate, and declared that neither he nor Tibbits could obtain anything.

"Never was a house in such a state, sir!" Trickett said. "The servants are all at loggerheads, and will do nothing."

"And you seem to have been helping them, rascal," Sir Randal cried, noticing the patches on the valet's countenance. "You have been fighting."

"I was compelled to strike a blow or two in self-defence, Sir Randal," Trickett replied ; "but if I may presume to advise, sir, I would recommend your departure before Mr. Monthermer's arrival. From what I can gather, the day will certainly go against Mr. Fairlie."

"Poh! nonsense," Sir Randal rejoined. "Give me my dressing-gown. No chocolate, you say. 'Sdeath! I must complain of this neglect. Fairlie must rate his servants."

"Rate 'em, sir! Mr. Fairlie daren't show his face. He has locked himself up in his room, and won't see anybody. As to the servants, they have revolted—forsworn their allegiance—gone over to the opposite faction."

"How d'ye mean, sirrah?"

"They refuse to serve Mr. Fairlie any longer, and intend to go over in a body to Mr. Monthermer. Our position at this moment is the reverse of agreeable, sir. We can get nothing, sir—abso lutely nothing—except cuffs and kicks."

"As soon as I am dressed I will see Fairlie," Sir Randal said.

"No use, sir—time thrown away. He won't be disturbed, and has placed people at his door to prevent intrusion. That great, hulking, chairman-like animal, Mark Rougham, has stood on guard there all night, they tell me—though how he came to have the post assigned him I can't think, as he is one of Mr. Monthermer's staunchest adherents. Pray allow me to order horses to be put to the travelling-carriage, sir. If we stay, I don't know what may happen from this mutinous household when the young squire ar· rives."

"Perhaps it may be as well to have the carriage ready," Sir Randal said, after a moment's reflection. "Assist me to dress, and then go and give the requisite orders about it."

Pretty much the same scene was enacted in Beau Freke's chamber, Mr. Tibbits complaining just as bitterly as Trickett of the servants' conduct, and expressing an equal desire to be off. Mr. Freke, however, said he should be entirely guided in this respect by Sir Randal, and depart or stay, as his friend elected.

As to Mrs. Jenyns, her morning dreams were broken by Mrs.

Davies, who stood by her couch with a look of dismay, and described the turmoil going on down stairs, and how grossly she had herself been insulted.

"I told 'em, mem, you would send every one of 'em about their business; but they only laughed at me, and went on worse than afore. I couldn't get any chocklit for you, mem,—and if it hadn't been for the perliteness of Mr. Bellairs, I shouldn't have got a mossel of breakfast myself."

"What is Mr. Fairlie about, Davies, that he allows such a disturbance to take place?"

"Goodness knows what he's about, mem,—but he's locked up in his room, and will see no one."

"He will see *me*," Mrs. Jenyns rejoined. "I must make all haste I can with my toilet. I will wear my white negligée."

When fully attired, Mrs. Jenyns went towards Fairlie's room, and as she entered the long gallery she perceived Mark Roughain and the two servants standing before the door. Blackford advanced to meet her, and told her that if she was coming to Mr. Fairlie she might spare herself the trouble, as he could not be seen at present.

"Not be seen?" Mrs. Jenyns echoed, struck by the man's manner. "Is he a prisoner?"

Blackford made no reply, but bowed, and stepped back to his companions.

Mrs. Jenyns felt a presentiment that something strange had happened, but it seemed useless to go on, so she retired with Davies. Shortly afterwards, as she stood at the head of the staircase, debating within herself what it would be best to do, she was joined by Randal and Beau Freke, with whom she had some talk, in the course of which they told her that, like herself, they had been unable to see Fairlie—and they all agreed that his conduct, to say the least of it, was inexplicable and mysterious. Mrs. Jenyns learnt from the gentlemen that they had made preparations for immediate departure, and, by their advice, she sent Davies to have her own carriage got ready. The party then descended to the entrance-hall, where they met Brice Bunbury, who told them how badly he had been used in regard to breakfast. "However, by foraging about in the larder, I managed to pick up something," he said. "Between ourselves," he added, "I suspect it's all up with Fairlie."

It was at this juncture that the troop of farmers halted, as we have described, at the end of the avenue; and the party, wondering what they were come about, went forth in front of the house to look at them, and having satisfied their curiosity, were about to return, when they were arrested by hearing loud and repeated huzzas from the troop, and it was then perceived that another cavalcade was coming along the avenue. The shouts of the farmers left no doubt that the young squire was now at hand; and the party, having no especial desire to greet him on his arrival, withdrew into the house.

Concluding Chapter.

HOW THE YOUNG SQUIRE CAME TO HIS OWN AGAIN.

The cavalcade approached; headed by Monthermer and Arthur
Poynings. Close behind them rode five or six gentlemen of the
county, who had been hastily summoned for the purpose, and
then came Sir Hugh's carriage, in which sat the old baronet himself, his chaplain, Parson Chedworth, and Mr. Clavering and Mr.
Houghton, both of them magistrates and neighbours. After the
carriage rode a posse of constables. Thus attended, Gage approached the house of his ancestors. His features were extremely pale, as might naturally be expected from the anxiety
he had recently undergone, but his deportment and manner were
firm and determined in the highest degree, and it was evident to
all who beheld him that he had become an altered man. On seeing
the troop of tenantry collected at the end of the avenue he
quickened his pace, and rode towards them alone. Arthur holding
back for the moment.

"Welcome! my good friends, welcome!" Gage cried, removing
his hat as he drew near the farmers. "I am right glad to see you
here to-day. But how have you been summoned?"

"We all saw that flag, your honour," Farmer Netherfield replied, "and took it as a signal to repair to the Castle."

"I beheld it myself—miles off," Gage rejoined. "I know not
by what friendly hand it has been unfurled, but the signal was well
given, since it has brought you hither. Supported by you, I
fear nothing—and you may unhesitatingly support me, for my
cause is just."

A deafening shout followed this brief address, and Gage, escorted
by the whole of this immense retinue, rode slowly along the broad

gravel walk towards the principal entrance of the mansion.   His approach had been watched by the inmates of the Castle, and instead of any opposition being offered to his entrance, the doors were thrown wide open, while a crowd of servants rushed forth to bid him welcome.   There was a contest amongst them as to who should aid him to alight.   At a sign from Gage, the band of tenantry moved on to a little distance, where they got off their horses, and a certain number of them proceeded with the animals to the stables, while the others came back to the house.   Meanwhile, Arthur Poynings and those with him had likewise dismounted, and were received by Gage, who stood on the threshold.   They passed on, and Sir Hugh Poynings, the chaplain, and the magistrates next alighted. and entered the hall, where Gage awaited them.   The constables stationed themselves at the door, and then Gage, turning to Sir Hugh and the magistrates, said:

"Gentlemen, I hereby take possession of my house and the domains belonging to it, of which I have been wrongfully deprived by Mr. Fairlie, and I call upon you to aid me, in case of need, in maintaining possession."

"You shall have such assistance as the law can afford you in establishing your rights," Sir Hugh said; "but, as far as I can discern, you are not likely to meet with much opposition.   Where is Mr. Fairlie?   I expected to see him come forward to contest your claim."

Scarcely was the question asked, than Mark Rougham (who on hearing the noise occasioned by the arrival of Gage and his retinue had hastily descended the great staircase) broke through the ranks of the servants, and approaching Monthermer, whispered a few words in his ear.   Their import must have been strange and startling, to judge from their effect upon the hearer.   He gazed inquiringly at the speaker, whose grave looks confirmed his relation.

"If this be so, it entirely alters the complexion of affairs," Gage muttered.   "I must pray you, Sir Hugh—and you, gentlemen (to the magistrates), and you, Arthur—with the officers, to accompany me to Fairlie's rooms.   Your presence will be needed."

Attended by the persons he had indicated, he ascended the staircase, and proceeded along the gallery.   He looked so grave and pre-occupied, that Sir Hugh forbore to question him.   Arthur also was silent, for a suspicion of the truth had flashed upon him. They soon reached their destination. Mark Rougham, who had preceded them, was standing at the door of the dressing-room. The other servants were gone.

Gage rapped against the door, but no answer was returned.

"I did not expect it," he said, in answer to Sir Hugh's inquiring glances. "The door must be burst open."

"Stay! let me try," Mr. Clavering interposed, "before you have recourse to violence. Mr. Fairlie! Mr. Fairlie!" he exclaimed, knocking sharply against the door.

"Muster Fairlie cannot answer," Mark Rougham said.

And hurling his huge frame against the door, it burst open.

Then it became apparent to all why no answer had been returned to their summons. They entered reverently, for the presence of death always inspires respect. Awe was impressed on every countenance, but Gage was far more profoundly moved than the others.

Casting his eyes round the chamber, Mr. Clavering at once perceived the two packets on the table, and ascertaining how they were addressed, called Monthermer's attention to them. One of the packets bore the inscription—"To be opened first;" and complying with the direction, Gage broke the seals, and withdrew for a few minutes to the window, to read the letter enclosed. After perusing it, he turned to the others and said, "The unhappy man has made full atonement for the wrongs he has done. Feeling the near approach of death, he has herein confessed all his offences, and surrendered the whole of the Monthermer property to me. He also states that the will under which he wrongfully acted was not my father's last will, but the true will is still in existence, and in the possession of Mrs. Jenyns, by whom it is unlawfully detained. He ends by imploring my forgiveness.

"And he has it," Gage continued, advancing towards the body and standing beside it; "Heaven is my witness, most unhappy man, that I fully and freely forgive thee!"

Deep silence prevailed for a moment, and the chaplain then advanced towards Gage, and said:

"You have done well, sir. He deserves your forgiveness, for he has made reparation. A lesson may be learnt from the end of this misguided man. Possessed of many qualities calculated to advance him in the world—great intelligence, acuteness, industry, perseverance—he lacked one quality, the want of which rendered all others void—Integrity. Hence his talents were ill-directed, and led him into oblique paths. Excessive cupidity was his bane. Determined to grow rich—no matter by what means—he yielded to temptation, and fell. Had he but been honest, he might be now alive and respected. And how many anxieties—how many afflictions would have been spared him! Vainly did he endeavour to build himself up a mansion with his ill-gotten gains! The baseless fabric at once crumbled to dust. But he is gone. And let us look upon him with an eye of compassion. Let us hope that he may obtain remission of his sins. Are we not told, that ' When the wicked man turneth away from his wickedness, and doeth that which is lawful and right, he shall save his soul alive ?' He has done justice at the last, and would appear to have sincerely repented. He has died in the act of supplication. May his prayer be heard! May Heaven have mercy on his soul!"

"Amen!" Gage fervently ejaculated. And the exclamation was repeated with equal fervour by all the bystanders.

"And now I can commit poor Clare's confession to the flames," Arthur Poynings observed to Gage. "It is well that its production has been unnecessary."

"Here is another packet which you have not yet examined, Mr. Monthermer," Mr. Clavering observed.

The latter took it, broke open the seals, and, after casting his eye over the document it contained, said, with evident emotion,

"It is his last will, and concerns you, Sir Hugh."

"How so?" the old baronet rejoined. By the aid of his spectacles he managed to decipher the will. "Why, so it does concern me—that is, it concerns my daughter, to whom—for there must be no secret in it—he has bequeathed all the property rightfully belonging to him, and which he himself estimates at about 10,000*l*—subject, however, to two deductions—namely, to a sum sufficient to purchase Cowbridge Farm (if Mr. Gage Monthermer be willing to sell it) for Mark Rougham (hold your tongue, Mark! —hold your tongue, sir! and let me finish), and another sum of 500*l.* to be bestowed as a wedding portion upon Lettice, daughter of the said Mark Rougham."

"Has he done all this, Sir Hugh?—has he, indeed?" Mark cried.

"Why, haven't I just read the will, fellow?"

"Cowbridge Farm mine! the object of all my wishes," Mark exclaimed.

"Ay, it is freely yours, Mark," Gage cried. "I bestow it upon you."

"Stop! stop!" Sir Hugh interposed. "Give him the farm, if you please, Gage; but it must be valued, and the price agreed upon added to Lettice's wedding portion. That's the proper way to settle matters. Egad! this is the strangest will that ever came under my inspection. Have you read it through, Gage?"

"I have, Sir Hugh," the young man replied. "He states that his desire is to carry out his daughter's wishes; and I know that it was poor Clare's wish that the event therein mentioned should take place."

"Well, there shall be no obstacle to its fulfilment on my part provided——"

"Enough, Sir Hugh; I understand," Gage interrupted, gravely. "When I have proved myself worthy of an alliance with your daughter I shall not fail to seek it."

"I have no fears of you now—none whatever," the old baronet rejoined. "After the conversation we had together last night, coupled with what Arthur has told me of you, I entertain no doubt of your thorough reformation. I stand in the light of a father to you, and look upon you as a prodigal son—and a sad prodigal you have been, it must be owned—but let that pass. If, after due probation on your part, Lucy receives an offer of your hand, and is disposed to accept you, I shall raise no objection. But let us change the subject. We have plenty of other matter before us."

"I presume there can be no doubt that Fairlie's death arose from natural causes?" Mr. Clavering remarked.

"He expressly mentions in the preliminary part of the confession which I hold in my hand," Montherner replied, "that he had been attacked by a fit of extraordinary severity, and that having little hope of living till the morning, he employed the interval allowed him between the attack and its expected recurrence in preparation for eternity."

"Enough, sir," the magistrate replied.

All papers lying about were then placed in the chest, which was locked and sealed up by the magistrates. This done, the whole party quitted the room, leaving the constables at the door, with strict injunctions to allow no one to enter without authority.

As they descended the staircase, Gage observed to Sir Hugh, "I have now a disagreeable duty to perform. The house must be cleared of all the harpies of whatever degree that have so long infested it."

"You are right," Sir Hugh returned. "A grand clearance must be made. But I should think most of them will have spared you the trouble, and have taken themselves off already."

The old baronet's surmise proved correct. As they reached the entrance-hall, several of Gage's late dissolute associates were seen hastily traversing it—evidently beating a retreat—and so precipitate were their movements, that Sir Hugh could not refrain from laughing at them. But his mirth was speedily checked, as he observed four persons issue from a room on the ground-floor. They were in travelling attire, and were attended by a couple of valets and a lady's maid. It is needless to say who they were. Simultaneously with their appearance in the entrance-hall, two travelling chariots drove up to the open door. Sir Randal's carriage being first, he walked slowly towards it, accompanied by Beau Freke. They both looked disdainfully at Gage and his companions, and raised their hats as they passed. Close behind them walked Brice Bunbury, looking rather crest-fallen. When Sir Randal had passed Gage a few paces, he paused for a moment, and surveyed the young man scornfully. Monthermer might have yielded to the provocation if Arthur had not restrained him. As it was, he dismissed the insolent baronet with a gesture of contempt.

While these persons were getting into their carriage, Mrs. Jenyns came on with Davies. The actress had not abated a jot of her spirit, and looked beautiful as ever. At a sign from Gage, Mr. Clavering stepped forward.

"I am sorry you cannot be permitted to depart, madam," he said. "You are charged with having in your possession, and unlawfully detaining, the last will of Warwick de Monthermer, Esq., late owner of this mansion, and unless you deliver it up, I and my brother magistrate shall be compelled to order your arrest."

"I have no intention of depriving Mr. Monthermer of his father's will, sir," Mrs. Jenyns replied. "It is here." And taking it from her bosom she gracefully presented it to Gage. "That ought to have been worth something to me, but since Mr. Fairlie is no more, it is valueless as waste paper." And then she added, smiling maliciously at Gage, "You are in luck just now. I wish you joy of your fortune. But how long will it last?—I give you a year."

"Your jests are out of season, madam," Sir Hugh observed. "Mr. Monthermer means to lead a new life. He has reformed."

"His reformation is of too recent date to offer much security for its continuance," Mrs. Jenyns replied, "and for my part I have little faith in it. Gage reform! You must be credulous indeed, Sir Hugh, if you believe in such an impossibility!"

"But I do, madam," the old baronet cried, angrily. "He is setting about it in the right way, clearing his house of such pestilent vermin as have just gone out, and such worthless baggages as you."

"Much obliged to you for the compliment, Sir Hugh," she replied. "I suppose you think he will make an excellent son-in-law, but if you give him your daughter, I suspect you will find out your mistake. Better wait a few months, I think, sir. Adieu!"

With this she was about to move on, when her progress was arrested by an extraordinary noise outside the door. Yells, groans, and menaces were heard, followed by the crash of broken glass. Sir Randal and his friends, it turned out, had scarcely got into the carriage, when the farmers, who were collected in front of the house, having been made acquainted with their character by the servants, commenced a sudden and furious assault upon them. Three or four stout varlets seized the horses' heads, and though the postilion used his whip vigorously, they kept their hold. Others rushed to the carriage-door, shivered the glass in the window, which had been hastily pulled up, and forcibly dragged out the persons inside, pulling off their perukes, tearing their finery, and belabouring them without mercy. The two valets were treated in the same way; and Joyce Wilford—Lettice's suitor—who owed Messrs. Trickett and Tibbits a grudge for their foppish assiduities to his intended, did not neglect this opportunity of revenging himself. All the while the crowd were shouting, and loading their victims with every ignominious epithet, of which gamblers, sharpers, and scoundrels were the mildest terms. "We'll teach you to come to the Castle again," the aggressors roared; "let's take 'em a' three to th' horse-pond, and souse 'em in 't within an inch of their lives."

And the threat would undoubtedly have been executed if Gage had not rushed forth, and with difficulty effected their liberation.

"Leave 'em to us, sir," the rustics cried. "We know how to deal wi' 'em. Don't concern yourself about 'em."

"But I *must* concern myself about them, my good friends,' Gage replied. "I command you to release them instantly."

The injunction was reluctantly obeyed. Brice Bunbury, with his frightened looks and torn apparel, looked a most deplorable object. Beau Freke had received some severe contusions; but Sir Randal was the worst off, for his arm was broken. Gage proffered assistance, but the baronet haughtily refused it, and eycing his aggressors fiercely, he got into the carriage, which was then allowed to drive off.

"Yo'n gi'en that proud chap summat to remember yo' by, lads," Farmer Netherfield remarked, with a grin; "and yo'n spoiled a' their finery."

"Those two impudent puppies won't forget me in a hurry, I'm thinking," Joyce Wilford chuckled. "I've given both a smartish taste o' my cudgel, to teach em what to expect if they make love to another man's sweetheart. Ho! ho!"

Mrs. Jenyns had witnessed this scene with much alarm.

"Am I to be exposed to like outrage?" she cried.

"No, madam," Arthur Poynings rejoined; "I will answer for it these worthy fellows will never injure a woman. They have too much respect for the sex, however unworthily it may be represented in your instance."

Mrs. Jenyns did not think fit to make any rejoinder, and only partially reassured, she tripped off to her carriage with Davies, and ensconced herself as quickly as she could inside it. As Arthur Poynings had promised, she received no molestation; but as she looked out, she beheld nothing but scowling and indignant looks fixed upon her, while hisses and hooting could not be entirely repressed. However, the postilion bore her rapidly out of the reach of these unpleasant sounds. This was her last appearance at Montheriner Castle

" Well, at length you have got rid of them all," Sir Hugh cried

" Of all, except certain rascally hirelings," Gage replied.

" Pudsey, Bellairs, and the French hairdresser, have already de-camped, with some others," Blackford observed.

" In that case, the house is completely cleared," Gage said.

Then, going to the door, he called out in a loud voice, " Come in, my friends—come in! I am once more master of Monthermer Castle."

Thus invited, the whole of the tenantry rushed in, and the area of the entrance-hall was scarcely large enough to contain them. The young squire stood at the foot of the grand staircase to give them welcome. Then arose such a shout as had never been heard before within that mansion. A hundred hands were stretched out eagerly to Gage, who heartily grasped all that came within reach. Blessings were showered upon his head by all the old men, and every good wish was lavished upon him by the young. It was impossible not to be affected by such strong demon-strations of attachment, and Gage was greatly moved. In a voice of profound emotion, he cried, " If anything were wanting to complete my cure, my good friends, your kindness would effect it. But, believe me, I am a changed man. I have seen the folly of my ways, and the rest of my life shall be modelled upon that of my father, whom you all loved and respected."

" A better model could not be selected," Sir Hugh cried.

" Impossible! impossible!" several voices responded. And the cheering was renewed even more enthusiastically than before.

" Now listen to me for a moment, my good friends," Sir Hugh said. " The young squire has told you that he means to model himself upon his father, and he could not do better. I am sure he will act up to his word, and in this persuasion, I tell him before you all—and you know I'm a man of my word—that if he comes to me a year hence and asks me for my daughter, he shall have her."

Gage warmly grasped the hand extended to him.

Sir Hugh's announcement was received with immense cheering, as well as a good deal of laughter. Some of the younger rustics thought a year's probation too long, and that the term ought to be abridged to a fourth of that period; but the seniors held that

Sir Hugh was quite right—not that they had any fears of the young squire—but it was prudent and proper.

Gage then once more addressed his tenantry, thanking them for their presence and support, and begging them to make themselves at home in the house. Everything that circumstances would admit should be done for their accommodation—but he could not precisely answer for the state of the larder. However, he could venture to promise that there was wine enough in the cellar to enable them to drink his health. He concluded his address by requesting a certain number of them to follow him to the servants'-hall, whither he proceeded, and where, by his directions, refreshments of all kinds were speedily served. A cask of strong ale was broached, and liberally distributed. Meanwhile, the dining-room had been hastily put to rights, and here a still larger party sat down, while the rest were elsewhere accommodated—so that all fared equally well. It is needless to say that the young squire's health was drunk, and in bumpers, as he himself had proposed.

Life is a mingled yarn of joy and woe, and we must interrupt these festivities for a moment to follow Gage and Arthur Poynings on a sad errand to the Ivy Tower. Neither of them went to the chamber of death, but they saw Lettice Rougham, who told them what had been done. Already Clare had been placed in her coffin, and Lucy Poynings having fully discharged all the offices of friendship, had gone home in a carriage which had been sent for her by Sir Hugh. Her strength was completely exhausted. We pass over the consultation that next took place between the two young men. But it was decided that the father and daughter should be interred in a village churchyard hard by—in a grave which had already one tenant—the mother of one and the wife of the other.

And now, ere parting with little Lettice Rougham, let us say that, some three months later, she made Joyce Wilford one of the happiest young fellows in Suffolk, and brought him a good wedding portion, too. But happy as Joyce was, he was not a whit happier than his father-in-law, Mark Rougham, who by this time had become owner of his long-coveted Cowbridge Farm.

When Gage and Arthur, after a while, returned to the mansion, with slow steps and saddened looks, the tenants were still making the roofs ring with their shouts of " Long life to the young Squire, and may every blessing attend him !"

A blessing *did* attend him. Poor Clare slept in her grave, but her wishes were fulfilled. In little more than a year afterwards, Lucy was united to Gage, and his good resolutions being strictly adhered to, and his character modelled, as he had promised it should be, on that of his father—a perfect English country gentleman —she found that there is some truth in the saying that "A REFORMED RAKE MAKES THE BEST HUSBAND."

THE END.